LOWBOY #22

Murder & Romance on 18 Wheels

by

John Aalborg

Bleep-Free Press.
http://bleepfreepress.com

FIRST PRINT EDITION

ISBN: 978-0-9849365-2-6

Cover illustration by Baugmo

*This is a work of fiction. Specifically, the story
and the characters in this book are fictional but the
author and publisher are not sure about the monkey.*

Author rating: All Ages
Publisher rating: PG-14.
Home Schooler: R (USA)

"Bull Schaffner" ™ *John Aalborg*
This character first appeared in the novel
"Harry & Ivory", and in the award winning short
story "Morton's Fork Crossing".

Acknowledgements:

Thanks to John Schaffner, Victor Chapin, and Barney Karpfinger — New York literary agents whose early encouragements went unheeded for so long. Too long.

Special thanks to Perry Gamsby, founder and CEO of StreetWise Publications AU, who recently stepped in with a much needed kick in the ass.

About the author:

Internationally published writer and trucking columnist John Aalborg has written a hard-boiled and often touching trucker / crime / adventure novel here, with both male and female points of view and involving serial characters from his radio plays.

There is a mysterious aspect to big trucks — *eighteen-wheelers which the average citizen can see but cannot see inside* — trucks so huge that only some men and women can master driving them. Trucks providing experiences often too harrowing or bizarre for most people to want to even try, with drivers out of the public eye when they dock, when they fuel, and when they lay over during the night — if they stop during the night at all.

Despite the foreboding most citizens feel when getting too close to semi trailer-trucks on the interstate, in *LOWBOY #22* a unique, risky, and beautiful young-love story emerges from within the crimes and adventures. A love story the reader will not forget.

CHAPTER 1
Atlanta GA

Grabbing the first payphone in sight, his cellphone dead, Bull Schaffner punched in the 800 number for the McKay terminal in Missouri while keeping an eye on the huge parking lot beyond the fuel islands. It was late afternoon and the truckstop was filling up fast, the parked rigs shimmering in the August heat and the asphalt rank with the sharp stink of evaporating urine. It had not rained in Atlanta for weeks but the dark thunderheads rolling in from west of the huge TA truckstop were no comfort to Bull. A storm breaking loose right now would be bad timing, well, maybe not so bad. The rain and the thunder could provide some cover....

He involuntarily jerked at a shadow moving up on his right but it was only the clatter of a UPS driver with an empty handcart heading for the restaurant kitchen.

"Come on, Kate, come on, pick up!"

A huge, orange Schneider rig turned out of the lot and roared by in low gears. Bull Schaffner, aka Perry Schaffner, (aka "Bullperry" by his aging parents), mashed the phone to his ear to press out the racket. He needed Kate, the McKay Trucking dispatcher and part-owner, but Bull scored her smart-ass, thirteen year-old brat instead. Little Harold.

"Harold, listen up. I found your missing truck!" Bull waited in vain for a reaction, then continued. "That missing driver of yours, whatsisname, Denver? I found his rig, his Pete, but..."

Kate's fatherless, two-hundred pound son let out a long, wet, trolling burp.

"Harold, this is serious shit! I found Denver's rig but it's hooked to the wrong load and the wrong trailer. Got that? The wrong load? Where's your mother?"

Another wet but less enthusiastic burp. "She's in the bunkhouse fucking Benny."

"Benny? Who's... Wait. Ring the phone over there."

But Kate had already picked up the extension. "I'm not fucking Benny, Harold! Damn!"

"Well, who then, Mama?"

"Benny. But I'm not fucking him."

"Well, maybe not this minute, not as-we-speak, but..."

"Hey! Can we get serious here? This is Bull Schaffner! I'm at the big TA in Atlanta. I found it. But he's hooked to the wrong trailer and the wrong load. A big Airstream trailer on a marine yacht-hauler. A lowboy. The Airstream has a tarp over it and the doors are locked. You only sent the tractor keys."

"Bull, I told you, he was pulling a flatbed, no, that's right, our new trailer, the lowboy!"

"Kate, this lowboy's got somebody else's name on it. Duplan Marine Transport or something. Detachable gooseneck. The Airstream was loaded from the front."

Little Harold burped again and Kate yelled at hIm to hang up his end.

"Bull, listen, you looked around? Our new lowboy trailer's gone?"

"Not at this truckstop. And another thing, the generator on the Airstream is running and there's a hole cut out of the tarp on top and one of the air conditioners is running. In other words, I need to know stuff. Like what if somebody's sleeping inside, or maybe Denver's sleeping inside, or..."

"What if he's not?!"

"Right. Then what? Unhook the tractor and haul ass? I don't have much time, Kate. I checked the fuel tanks–they're full and the engine's idling. Somebody's fixing to take off with it soon. You want me to drop the trailer since it's not yours, and take off with the tractor? Leave the trailer?"

"You sure you got the right unit?"

"Burgundy Peterbilt-377. Small crack in the right windshield like you said. McKay Trucking painted on the doors. Number twelve painted on the hood. That good enough?"

Kate did not answer immediately and Bull jumped at the sound of a sharp crack in the phone, lightening, and listened to her shuffling through some papers up there in Missouri before the thunder rolled in. "It's fixin' to dump here in a minute, Kate. I need to know what you want!"

Bull felt a cool burst of fresh air, and watched the loose paper and litter swirl up around the parking lot. A few drivers began heading out of the building toward their units, and Bull's focus softened for a moment as his eyes followed a young couple holding hands and running toward their rig in the front row, a flatbed hooked to an old, R-model Mack with a one-man slee-per.

"Okay, Bull, listen, Denver was supposed to load up two brand-new Massey Ferguson 4-wheel-drive farm tractors in Marietta, on our lowboy to Florida City. I checked after he disappeared and he made the pick-up but not the delivery. Those babies are fifty thousand dollars a pop!"

"Kate, you already told me that. I need to know what to do **now!** I can call the law, I can drop the trailer and get your tractor back, I can run off with the whole mess and ..."

"Don't call the law! Shit, they'll impound the rig. This is a small company. We can't afford lawyers and we need every unit we have on the road hauling booger! That was a new trailer, that missing lowboy, and all we got is liability insurance on it. And I got to hope the load is insured. Shit, Bull, take the whole hog. Then we'll have their load and their trailer to trade for ours."

"Their trailer? Who's 'their'?"

"Whoever's trailer!"

"Maybe it's legit. What's Denver like? You know him pretty good? You could FAX me a picture and I can look around for him."

"Legitimate? Bullshit. He went off the screen over a week ago, and his family is reporting him missing. Either he flew the coop, or he got hijacked, or he's ripping us off, or he's dead. He's an older dude. We almost didn't hire him. Carries a laptop and gets shitty because we still don't use email. Has some ex-wives and a bunch of kids he can't support.... In other words, picture you in twenty more years."

"Thanks, Kate."

"In other words, if he's not in the cab or in the load, haul ass. Don't be a pussy!"

"Bust the locks on the Airstream first and see what's inside?"

"No! Why is there a tarp on it? Why tarp a travel trailer? Well, what we don't know we can't be held accountable for, right?"

"You sure? You thought about this?"

"Hell no, you just called me! Go! Call me back when you can. And before you get back here to MO, okay?"

"What about a manifest? What if they ask for it at a scale or if I get nailed with a DOT inspection?"

Kate groaned. "How does the unit look?"

"Good! Even with all the miles it has on it...."

"No, no, Number-12 is the Pete we bought from Deke's widow. It sat for a couple years and now it's just broke in. Denver said he was fixin' to clock the first 100k before he dropped off the radar. That baby is mint! This is the one we promised you, if you can bring it in."

"Yeah, OK.... But mine was midnight black, with gold pinstripes and had my name in gold leaf on both sides of the hood and it didn't have a scratch on it before you guys wrecked it..."

"And ready for an in-frame overhaul and new brakes and..."

"...and had that AC I could regulate from the sleeper and..."

"Bull, Denver's unit you can reg the AC and start the engine from the sleeper, jeez! It has a separate AC for the sleeper! You got time to argue about this now?"

"Well, I got time if it's going to be my tractor!"

"How does the trailer look? Tread on the tires?"

"It looks new."

"Then go! Go hide it somewhere for tonight and get some sleep."

"Okay, but if I don't call back soon I'm leaving my rental car in front of the drivers' motel. I'm at the big TA in Atlanta. Not the Petro. The TA, got it? The car's on my credit card so I need you to call the rental office. Wait..." Bull tucked the phone under his chin and fished a card out of his shirt pocket, and gave her the number. "Tell them the keys will be at the motel desk. Tell them I got sick or something."

"Got it."

"I'm gone."

Bull looked up at the sky and muttered out loud as he headed for the car. "Dear MasterVisa, Sir!" Another week like this and he'd be maxed out on both of them, and max-out was death for a self-employed trucker. Especially one who was doing private investigation and property retrieval on the side.

There was only a spattering of raindrops, and the wind seemed to be flagging. He had not really expected to find the missing rig here and was glad he had looked around before checking into the motel. Now all he had to do was move his shit from the rental to the tractor, drop the car keys at the desk, and boogie. He drove down to the back row of the lot and parked in front of the big Peterbilt, in effect blocking it, then had to move the little economy rental out of the way so a Florida Tank Lines rig could back into the empty hole beside him. The tanker made it in there in one, quick shot, something that always made Bull a little envious. The driver was out and chattering away before Bull could finish snatching his stuff out of the car. A suitcase, his motel bag, his laptop-computer carry-on bag, his cooler, his cardboard snack box... He set them all down on the ground beside the Pete's passenger door.

"Looks like I got the last hole! This place always fills up quick before dark."

"Yeah, well, I'm fixin' to make another hole as soon as I get my gear squared away."

Shit!

I don't know if there's anybody in the sleeper!

Bull's heart was pounding now, and he wished the other driver would buzz off. But the guy just stood there, short and plump, gray hair, coke-bottle glasses and red suspenders and a CAT POWER cap, jeez.... Bull pounded on the sleeper with his fist and waited.

"The old lady got ya locked out?"

"Pound on that camper-trailer under the tarp for me, will you?" Bull had already knocked on it before calling Kate, after looking underneath to make sure it was chained down.

The other driver looked puzzled, then winked at Bull. He obliged with both fists and with almost enough force to dent the aluminum. "Who'd be in there with this tarp over the doors? How much they charge?"

"They're free. Two young ladies. Hot, built, and ready."

"Yeah, sure, in your dreams."

Bull dug into his Levi's pocket — past the .22 Beretta — for the two tractor keys McKay Trucking had FedEx'd him down to his home in Miami, when he had scored this job. He guessed at which one was the door key and it turned without a hitch. He could have picked the lock almost as easily. *Hundred-thousand-dollar truck, ten-dollar lock....* A second ignition key would be inside because the motor and AC were running.

A few, large, ice-cold raindrops splattered the shiny fender and Bull's clean-shaven face, and the top of his balding, crew-cut head.

"Climb in and I'll hand up your stuff."

Bull turned and the tanker driver already had the laptop bag in hand and was reaching down for the suitcase. Shit! Bull was tired and nervous and he would have liked a moment to look around, check out the cab — and scan the lot again for anybody headed directly for this particular truck — hell, he didn't even know what kind of gearbox he would be driving. But he recognized the fifteen speed immediately, a unit he was reasonably familiar with, and the cab was cleaner than most, the walk-in sleeper empty and the bunk made, and the AC set on LOW. There was a black-leather, laptop case — an airline carry-on not unlike his own — lying on the passenger seat. Bull flipped that onto the bunk and turned back to reach for the stuff the tanker driver was handing up.

"The chicks split, huh, McKay?"

"Maybe they're getting a shower over in the building. Primping, you know, getting ready for me." Bull reached for his computer bag first. His other gun, the 9MM CZ-P01, was in there with the laptop, plus his credit cards and logbook, his Florida and Alabama carry permits, his eye-drops and his deodorant. All the important stuff.

"Thanks."

"Hey, we ain't gettin' any younger."

"I'm not as old as you yet."

"You will 'fore you know it."

Bull pulled up the bulging B-4 suitcase next, glanced through the windshield again, and reached down with both hands for the box of truck snacks: little microwave buckets of corned beef hash, ravioli, scalloped potatoes with ham, Beenie-Weenies, Sweet Sue chicken & dumplings; jars of cashew nuts, and bags of York chocolate mint patties....

Still no real rain, and no sign of whoever had parked the McKay Peterbilt here. Bull didn't want to be rude to the driver who had just helped him but it was time to boogie.

Shit, the car! "Hey! Do us both a favor?"

"How much are the showers - still five bucks?"

"Free if you fuel here. Listen, it's fixin' to dump. How about you taking my rental car to the building and drop the keys at the desk? They're coming to get it."

"Yeah, sure, OK!"

"'Preciate it. Hey, when the girls get out of the shower they're yours. Tell them PBS said so. My handle.

Perry Bull Schaffner. Or Public Bull Station, take your pick."

"Okay, PBS! Happy trails!"

Bull reached over and snatched the passenger door shut.

Happy trails, Christ!

But he looks honest....

That was dumb. Letting him know who I am....

Bull could even hear him: "His handle's PBS, the guy who stole that rig!"

One more glance back into the sleeper to reassure himself that he was alone, and a mash-down on both door-lock buttons. Then a quick settle in behind the wheel and a fiddle with the height of the Ultra-Ride seat and the realization that the previous driver was the same, average-joe size. The idling engine sounded steady and smooth, the temp was at 180, both fuel gauges showed full, the brake-air gauges were at 120 where they belonged.... He would have to assume that all the lights worked.

The AC felt good through Bull's sweaty shirt, and he tested the wipers. Okay! Deciding to leave the seatbelt alone until he was in the clear, he dug into his laptop case for his glasses, which he needed for driving in poor light. He studied the fifteen-speed's gear lever for a moment, but when he released the parking brakes Bull was startled by the familiar, exploding hiss which would be heard all over the lot. He looked from the mirrors to the windshield and back to the mirrors, half expecting someone to come running up and shouting.

The storm broke with a flash of lightening and an instant crack of thunder, and in the ensuing downpour no one noticed McKay Trucking's unit No.12 ease out of the hole.

CHAPTER 2
Atlanta to LaGrange GA

Bull switched on the wipers as the big rig eased on down to the end of the back row, but he had to grope around on the unfamiliar dash for the defroster control. The windshield was fogging quickly but there was no roll of paper towels handy, something he would have had in his own tractor. At least the mirror heaters were working, and Bull could see that the red marker lights at the rear corners of the lowboy trailer were visible on both sides, good, because he wasn't sure of the trailer's length and it was time to swing around — no stopping now — and angle down alongside the rows of parked rigs, by-pass the fuel islands, and booger the hell out of there.

Two hours to sunset but the sky was nearly black. At least the rush hour should be nearly over.... The engine sounded like a big, mechanical Caterpillar, maybe a 4 1/4 like his own, but the Airstream chained to the lowboy trailer felt heavy. Bull made the next turn even more slowly and watched that the rear trailer lights, a dim, red dazzle in the rain spattered mirrors, would clear the nose of a big Freightliner festooned with extra, bright-amber lights. The oncoming truck was waiting for him to get out of the way.

The CB crackled. "Driver, looks like your tarp's ready to blow off."

"Yeah, well, I'll get out and fix it after this rain and wind stops...."

"I heard that I did!"

"I left a hole for your light-show in the back row."

"And now everybody knows it. Thanks."

"Fuck you, I'll pass you a note next time."

Bull smiled at himself, but just for a moment, before hitting the brakes. He hadn't swung wide enough to make the turn and the end of his trailer was about to cut into the other man's unit.

"Hold it, I'll back a little."

Bull grinned. "Sweet of you."

"Okay, you got it. Last row, huh?"

"Last row, middle, next to a tanker."

Bull made it around and then blocked another rig coming in so the Freightliner driver could make his move and nail down the hole. Past the empty guard shack, Bull headed out for Thurman, which looked like a deserted street in a war zone with a sudden burst of blinding light and thunder. The curb farther down the block was crumbled and Bull eased the rig off the street and over the sidewalk, hoping the lowboy would clear everything. Some minor scraping sounds and he was rolling over the mashed-down chainlink fencing of a trailer graveyard. Out of sight of the truckstop, the parking brakes hissed him to a stop. The rain continued to pelt down but Bull took his time getting out, unfamiliar with the steps down to the ground on this tractor. The rain was stinging but cool, and was splattering the glasses he had forgotten to remove. Once on the ground, Bull set to running through the downpour along one side of the lowboy and then the other, snapping off the loose bungee cords and collecting them all into a pile. The area smelled like dead fishing worms and to Bull's surprise, the puddled ground was crawling with them. Before he could rush to the back again to slide the tarp off the Airstream, the wind billowed up underneath it and Bull had to scramble for it, tripping hard on a section of the laid-down fence. His hands slid out from underneath him as he slammed facedown in the mud. "Shit!" His glasses frames were smashed and Bull was momentarily stunned. When he could get up on one knee he crammed the remains of his glasses into a shirt pocket and felt of his cheek. Just a little blood, not too bad, and he was back to his feet and pulling at the tarp. Another flash of light illuminated the specter of two black guys heading straight for him. The .22 Beretta was stuck too far down into his jeans to grab quickly and Bull tensed up into a half crouch, then relaxed as the two young men split to either side and began pulling and folding.

"Ten bucks apiece, Whitebread."

"I only got a twenty."

"We'll tear it in half."

"It's my supper money."

"Go hungry like we do. Twenty a piece, then."

The larger of the two said: "Any white girls in that camper?"

"Yeah, but they're real old. Wrinkly." *Why does everybody think pussy when they see an Airstream?* "They used to be beautiful, but that was before you were born."

Bull moved up beside the other man, after freeing up his pocket pistol when they weren't looking, and helped him pull the tarp away from a corner of the torn fencing. When it gave way, Bull's head banged into the man's wet, woolen watch-cap.

"Sorry. Didn't mean to smudge your cap."

"Get out of the way, man!"

"Yes sir."

In no time they had the tarp rolled into a neat bundle and shoved under the Airstream. One of them turned to him and Bull gave him a twenty, and shoved his hand back into his pocket.

"Got another one of those?"

"Blow your head off."

"Oh, man...."

"It's a cruel world."

The rain had thinned some and Bull, soaking the driver seat, eased the rig backwards onto Thurman, with considerably more scraping noises coming from under the lowboy. A lightening flash lit up the left turn he would need to make onto Highway-23 down at the end of the street.

Normally Bull would have stayed parked long enough to change out of his wet clothes, but the mysterious Airstream looked so loud and shiny in the middle of the trailer. So obvious....

Shit, I don't even have a towel.

How can they stand those wool caps in the summer?

Bull kept glancing into the mirrors, half expecting the owner of that beautiful RV to come running up — or the cops with the lights flashing — but all he could see back there was the two brothers, wobbling from side-to-side, seeming to be bumping into each other as they ambled away.

What's that stuff in their hands?
The bungee cords!
Bull groaned.
Can't stop now....
Fuck it....

Bull took his time before pulling out onto Macon, aka "The Macon Highway" — aka US-23 if you were a Yankee — and slowed again as he scrunched his eyes for the turn to 285, the Atlanta beltway. He really needed his glasses to drive in the dark, especially in the rain and traffic, and he passed by the north-bound ramp without thinking. So southbound it was. He could always go all the way around Atlanta or he could pick up I-75 north through downtown, usually a lot faster, or he could take I-85 south and head to Montgomery, and three hours after Monkeytown he could be snug in his old bed and in his old room at Mom and Dad's in the Florida panhandle. The opposite direction from the McKay Trucking terminal in Missouri, of course, but his mother would make breakfast and wake him up with a hot coffee. Bull was tired and he hadn't slept for two days. Besides, at his parent's place on a dead-end road deep in the woods near the Choctawhatchee River, only a dedicated chopper pilot would be able to see the stolen lowboy with a brand-new Airstream parked under the live oaks....

Plus Mom and Dad had been begging him to stop by and pick up his mail....

On 285, the northbound I-75 ramp hissed by in eighteen wheels of slung-off steam and rain. Bull was surrounded by big trucks now, all doing seventy or more, and he jockeyed for the right-hand turn-off and the left-hand angle for Montgomery and I-85. This part of Atlanta he knew well. Piece of cake. Multiple lanes of big rigs loaded for every place in the country, and mousey little four-wheelers whizzing their way home to the suburbs and bratty kids and TV. And overhead: huge, lumbering airliners, one right after another, sinking down for the airport with their landing lights ablaze....

All he needed now was a dry towel and a place to pull off to change. And to scrape the dead worms off his boots. Not here, though. Too much law. Well, would they want to stop and get out in the rain? Bull pulled off onto the emergency lane with the four-way flashers set, unlaced his boots, and moved between the seats to the back, switching on the sleeper lights. Twelve-volt fluorescents which did a hiss-and-flicker before slamming on full bright. He shoved the strange carry-on bag to the foot-end of the bunk — there would be time to pilfer around in that later — and plunked down onto the bed, bumping his already banged-up head.

Top bunk!

Bull's heart pounded up and his stomach muscles bunched. He rose slowly and turned. The bunk had a flat side to it that flipped up to keep anybody or anything from falling out, and Bull sucked in a deep breath before peering over it. Clothing. Folded but not very neatly, with a slight odor to it, of deodorant? Stuff the driver thought he could wear again before going to the laundromat? Some girlie magazines underneath. Hustlers and Club Internationals, no less. Oh Boy! And on top of everything a clear-plastic dry-cleaner bag with the tag still on it. Bull smiled, happy to have found the mint, open-beaver books full of pictures of girls holding up their young, firm tits with their hands, offering them to the camera.... He pulled the dry-cleaner bag out a little, feeling of the two hangers inside. Two small, white dresses, with blue ribbons, like little school-girl dresses. Ruffles and lace and pure, pressed white, with those puffy Filipino type short-sleeves. To the left of the bunk the closet was slam full, and Bull carefully hung the bag in the other closet where some jackets and a rain-coat were waiting. He ducked, and leaned over the bottom bunk to slide open the roll-up cabinets. The first one was a score: a wind-up alarm clock and a stack of towels.

God is good.

An angel bringing a cup of hot coffee would be even better....

Bull did not want to stop again until he was clear of the Atlanta area. He could pull off at Exit-2 at LaGrange, just before crossing into Alabama, and work the rig into the back row of the truckstop there — such a nice and plain-vanilla truckstop — and eat, then sack out in the sleeper, call Kate in the morning, well, no, let her wait, let her sweat a little.... Call Mom and Dad in the morning and let them know he was coming and that he'd need a straight shot under the oaks in back of their double-wide to park the rig for a day or two. And to-night he'd have a long rest in the sleeper, in the truck-stop parking lot.

An hour later he was washing up in LaGrange, and checking out his bruised face and the tiny cut above his cheek. Tired but dry and comfortable, he pulled himself onto a stool at the restaurant.

The driver next to him grunted. "Don't know as I'd leave that rig alone in the back row. Somebody's shot out the lights back there."

Bull sighed. "Hey, the lot was full. Besides, anybody touches my stuff I'll kill 'em."

That line should have finished it, but somebody else from one of the tables chimed in: "Can't miss that Airstream. How much? 'Bout a hundred grand brand-new?"

Bull looked up at the clock over the rectangular hole to the kitchen. A young guy with a round face, looked like a Cambodian, was doing dishes, and an old black lady was cooking. Her gray Afro was so huge her head looked like a shrunken mummy embedded in steel-wool. But the food smelled good from back in there, and if he could get into the bunk by 8:00 or so he could be out of here at the crack of dawn and still have breakfast and eight hours of sleep. He would even have time to catch up his log. He'd have to remember to look at the tractor and trailer number and stuff and log in the new rig and some other bullshit....

Bull said: "A hundred grand?"

"Well, yeah...."

"And you could see where I parked? I can't see my rig from here."

"We all saw where you headed, Honey." The waitress was young, with a happy face and plump legs shaped like inverted bowling pins. Bobby socks.... "All the lights from every rig parked out there was shining off you, well, like that Airstream was a shiny big mirror on wheels coming in here. Like a Christmas tree on wheels."

Anything wrong with the back row? I need to sleep after I eat."

"Nothin' wrong with our back row, Honey. Don't listen to them. The sheriff comes by here and cruises around every hour or so."

Bull ignored the snorts of derision from both sides. It had been a while since he'd had liver and onions, and mashed potatoes and gravy. He tucked the menu away beside the napkin dispenser, and ordered.

§

The rain diminished to a cool misting, and Bull had cranked the AC up before going into the restaurant so he could shut everything down before going to sleep. He would need to hear things back on the trailer behind his sleeper, although he knew from experience that he would be awakened more often than not by the feel of movement back there rather than noise. Something most drivers wondered about: how you could always feel somebody climbing up onto a trailer when you were in the sleeper, no matter how heavy the rig was....

Both trucks he had parked between were gone, and so were a few others in the back row — the drivers had probably just stopped to eat before moving on — and yes, the yard lights had been shot out. Big deal. Thieves and muggers rarely bothered a person carrying a gun. There was a confidence you gave off when you were carrying, and Bull would never understand how the anti-gun people could live with constant fear and impotence, unable to protect themselves or their family or their property. Yet he usually felt safe enough going up into Canada, where you had to leave your guns this side of the border. It was because nobody else was carrying up there, either, he figured.

What did Kate mean by saying he would end up just like her missing driver in twenty years. A bunch of ex-wives and kids he can't support....

Well what the hell did she know!

Those missing four-wheel drive farm tractors.... Fifty grand apiece? No insurance? No insurance on their new lowboy?

Unbelievable....

No insurance....

If I find their stuff they'll owe me for life!

The windows were all fogged over and it was cold inside the cab but Bull did not shut down the engine and AC right away. It was still August, and the sleeper would heat up soon enough. In the harsh fluorescent lamp, Bull eased back the covers of the previous driver's bunk and checked for hairs and fleas, and the pillowcases for lice and nits. There was that deodorant smell but everything looked clean enough and Bull didn't feel he had a choice. He was weary but this bed should be remade! With a sigh he set to it, pulling everything off and grabbing clean stuff from one of the cabinets. Ten minutes later Bull had the curtain drawn which separated the sleeper from the cab, and was sliding between crisp, clean sheets naked. "Bunk naked" he would say, making fun of other drivers when they confessed they couldn't do it: crawl into a sleeper bunk in a public area naked. The fact that nobody could look in didn't seem to help those dumb-ass wimps.

Pulling up to his toes Bull cracked the vent over the bunk at that end and then hunted for the light switches, and shut down the AC and the engine from the control panel at the head end.

silence....

Even the misting rain on the metal roof was deathly quiet. This was a part of trucking which Bull truly loved. That cavey feeling, same as when he was a little kid, burrowing under the covers, all enclosed and warm and safe. Bull felt for his pistols in the dark, the 9MM under the covers and the little Beretta under the pillows, and fell instantly to sleep.

About 3:00am he awoke to pee. If it had been his own truck he would be able to feel for the empty, brown-glass prune bottle he kept under the bunk, and stand up and do it right there without having to get out. Maybe the other guy.... Bull switched on the reading light and leaned over. A brown jar! Yup! But it was full. The man had failed to empty it in the morning. A real jerk. What a slob.

And if it had been his own rig he would have had a pair of zori handy — flip-flops — to wear outside for a piss on a tire or a dump in the bushes, but no.... Bull pulled on his jeans and boots, skipping the socks, and slipped outside. No rain now but no sky, either, no stars or moon. A truck had pulled alongside him while he slept, a J B Hunt, engine shut down but still warm, and Bull listened to its engine heat ticking away while he pissed. He heard the distant sound of a trash can way over at the restaurant, and a man and a woman laughing. Jiving. People who were at home here, on the job. People who would go home in the morning, take a shower in their own bathroom, eat in their own kitchen, crawl into their own bed....

Bull shook off the last drop and waited for a moment before climbing back in. Even in the dreariness of that overcast night, the Airstream's polished aluminum glowed as if it had its own energy. It gave Bull a shiver.

CHAPTER 3
Homer County Florida

Annie Schaffner, Bull's dope-smoking, acid-head mother, jumped when the phone rang. She had gotten high on some home-grown just fifteen minutes earlier, so after waiting for the answer machine to screen the call she grabbed for it.

"I'm here, Perry!"

"Mom, my name's Bull. For twenty years now."

"Bullperry, right...."

"I'm in LaGrange, Georgia. On my way home soon as I catch up my log and stuff. I should be there before noon. Burgundy red tractor and a lowboy with an RV on it, an Airstream. I'll need my parking spot under the oaks. Maybe you could clear all the shit out of the way so I have a straight shot in there."

"There's no shit in the way..."

"The boat, the canoe, the busted lawnmowers, that iron power-pyramid you were sitting under in the middle of the driveway last time I came home, the..."

"Oh, Perry, I gave that up months ago. Anyway, you ruined it with that big punching bag you hung in there."

"That was for kick-boxing practice, not punching."

"Well, Some raccoons or whatever tore it all up and ate the leather. Your father uses the frame now to hang this big gong he found at the flea market. You should hear it!"

"Okay, but where is it?"

It took a moment for Annie to think. "Your kick-boxing bag?"

"Your power-pyramid, Mom!"

"The driveway's clear, Bullperry. I'll go tell your dad, he'll be back soon. Oh, and you have a pile of mail."

"You told me about the mail last time I called. Bye, Mom."

"Oh, and Janey will be here."

Bull hesitated.

"Your sister."

"I know who Janey is, Mom. Bye!"

§

Annie waited for her husband down at the bottom of the hill where the farthest spigot from the well was located. The storm which had been predicted missed them, and it was necessary to carry water to the plants they were secretly growing on one of the neighboring properties. As the sun slowly cleared the trees at the eastern boundary of the meadow, she was resting her aging, lumpen body on a tree stump, smothering it with her brightly-patched jeans. In the middle of the clearing, the sun suddenly struck the heavy, two-foot diameter gong hanging from the power-pyramid frame, and the flash of blinding bronze forced her to look away just as Harry emerged from the woods. He was walking briskly with the water jug in his backpack empty.

Annie spoke up before he could shuck-off the pack. "Perry's coming. He'll be here before noon."

"Hey, great! One more load."

"No rest first?"

"No. How about something to eat before he gets here. I don't want to starve to death while everybody's talking, with Janey coming, too." Harry braced himself while Annie used the hose to fill up the four-gallon jug on his back. "Both dickweeds home at the same time!"

"You're getting too old for this, far-out husband. Oh, and Perry's driving a different rig, so don't shoot if you see it. Not the black one, not the Captain Midnight one, you know, the Darth Vader truck. This one's red, or burgundy, he said, with an RV on the trailer."

Both of them flinched at the sudden racket of a low-flying chopper which appeared out of nowhere, turning at the tree-line and heading back. They listened to it dive down over at the farm to the east of them — not the property where Harry was growing reefer.

"I hate it."

"I know...."

"It's not like we're growing it to sell...."

"I know. But we used to...."

"That was then, Annie. This is now!"

"I know.... Oh, I told Bullperry Janey would be here but I forgot to get him ready for, you know, her cosmetic surgery..."

"It's called a boob job."

"I'm going to tell him not to make fun of it, she's been having a such a hard time lately. And I think he hates your new greeting on the answer machine. He hung up the first time before I could pick up. That message you have on there, that "High-dee-high-dee-high-dee ho, we're not here!"

"Oh, Annie...."

"Well, I'm happy. Both children here at the same time!"

Harry made a face and jerked at the backpack, full and heavy now. Annie pulled his gray pony-tail out from underneath a strap and he looked back at her and winked, his beard bright and his tanned, bald pate gleaming with sunshine.

"God loves us, Annie."

CHAPTER 4
LaGrange GA

The evening before, Bull had awakened to movement on the lowboy trailer just before dawn. Even
though it didn't feel heavy enough to be teenagers or
thieves pilfering around the Airstream, the feel of
movement returned just as he decided he was too tired
to get up and go out to check. From the sleeper there
was no way to look back there without popping the escape door, so he pulled on his jeans and eased down
out of the cab barefoot, his second and last pair of
glasses in place, a Mag-Lite in a back pocket, and his
new 9MM CZ-P01 in hand. Nothing but silence and the
empty, warm night, a clearing sky, and stars up above
the shot-out parking-lot lights. Must have been raccoons — no, raccoons were too stealthy — maybe a
stray cat or two jumping down from the roof of the Airstream to the lowboy deck. He shined the flashlight
around and picked up a small pair of eyes under a trailer in the next row.

Bull's feet felt sticky with urine — you could smell
the ammonia of it — and he wished he had pulled on
his boots. Now he would have to hunt around in the
tractor for whatever the previous driver kept handy (he
hoped) for shit like this. The toolbox door, on the outside of the tractor, was unlocked and he fished out a
dirty rag from the pile of chains and binders and pad-

locks. After wiping the soles of his feet he rummaged around in the sleeper. A bottle of alcohol and a roll of paper towels would be nice.... His heart skipped a beat when he found the driver's wind-up alarm clock again. According to his wristwatch it was right on the money — and still ticking — and when he went to winding it up it didn't take but a few twists. Bull had to wonder just how close he had come to running into this guy, Denver, before confiscating his rig. And if they had collided back there in Atlanta maybe the whole thing would be straightened out now. But when he had called McKay Trucking, Kate told him to haul buggy — not to wait around — so, fuck it. But he needed to get this case solved and his ass back to Missouri so he could get all his stuff. And get paid....

He'd call from Mom and Dad's and ask Kate for an advance.

A half-hour later, in the gray dawn, Bull got dressed with the dry clothes from the day before, and cranked up the engine and the AC. He made up the bunk and sat on it, rummaging through his carry-on bag for a blank manifest. He would have to be careful — only one left — and use a pencil (and only one of those left, a stub). He was running out of everything. All but two of his credit cards were maxed out and the last one would be dead if he hadn't canceled his cell's direct billing. He would also need to remember to hook his laptop to somebody's printer and create more blank manifests, but change the line for weight to include an UNDER-MAXIMUM check-off box for loads he didn't have a clue. Like what was the weight of the Airstream? It didn't seem to have much wind-resistance but it sure pulled hard off the mark.... The Georgia scales just NE of La Grange had been closed when he passed by during the night — pure luck — and there were no more mandatory checkpoints between here and his parents' place in the Florida panhandle. But with no legal right to the trailer and the load, Bull wanted to have something on paper in case he got pulled over.

He dropped down to the crunchy, gravel-strewn asphalt, which had been so painful and sticky when he was barefoot, and was heading for breakfast at the truckstop restaurant when he heard a curse. The J.B. Hunt driver next-door was kicking away a small, white, bulldog puppy, a cute one with a black eye patch.

"Git away!"

Another, harder kick and the pup went flying with a startled yelp. Some kids off in the distance hollered something unintelligible, like they were calling for it, and Bull decided to lay into the driver. He was a young, clean-cut looking guy wearing a J.B. Hunt cap loaded with a collection of goofy hat-pins.

"Here, kick me, asshole. I'm your size."

"Fuck you!"

Without thinking, Bull twisted to the side and nailed the man with a high kick to the stomach, doubling him up and dropping him to his knees.

"What'd you tell that puppy-dog? Git? When you want somebody to go away you kick 'em and yell git?! Well, excuse me, I'm just learning. Did I do the kick part right?"

"Oh, man...."

Bull watched the guy turn a little and try to dig into a back pocket, then freeze when his eyes locked onto the steady, one-eyed, beady stare of Bull's little Beretta.

"Oh, man...."

"You got a Georgia carry permit?"

"Man...."

"Well, I see you got a big vocabulary." Bull was still trembling with the quick rage which could trigger him off at times, often to his regret, but his words were coming out just fine: "Understand this, Charlie Tuna. You're leaving now, you know, like git! Oh, and from now on you're going to be kind to animals. Next little critter you see I want you to give it a big hug. And a kiss on the lips. Food, water...."

"Yeah, well, fuck you!"

"In your dreams."

§

The storm had tracked NE instead of south, and the early morning sky was bright. Bull walked back across the emptied-out parking area from the restaurant, his gut full of eggs and toast and hot-buttered grits and black coffee. The J.B. Hunt truck was gone, and the polished aluminum of the Airstream hurt his eyes in the low sun's glare, an elongated shadow of the RV and the lowboy painting the ground beside it. Bull knew he was getting to love the tractor — he could hear it half-way across the lot — the idling engine with that sound of quality and authority. And with the weapons-grade air-conditioner Bull didn't care how hot it was going to get today. He pulled a small notebook from his shirt pocket and walked around the lowboy, jotting down the tag and trailer number, and checking his spelling of "DUPLAN MARINE TRANSPORT". He noted the Airstream number and the tractor tag and number, too — all necessary for the phony manifest and daily log he was about to fill in. As every truck driver knew, showing officials at checkpoints an up-to-date and neatly filled out log-book or manifest beat honesty and integrity every time.

Home sweet home!

Rounding the last bend in the dirt road, Bull smiled at the sight of the family dog, Cooter, wagging her tail tentatively at the sound of the big Pete but looking concerned about something unfamiliar. She had a pretty face and was a large animal, white with black, Holstein-like spots, but ever lean and hungry-looking, and pregnant with long, dangling tits. Her collar was fashioned from the end of an old lamp cord, the plug hanging down from the knot below her neck.

Bull rolled down the window and felt the summer heat tongue in.

"Cooter!"

The dog perked up, and gamboled along in front of the tractor the rest of the way in. The huge rig trolled right on by the double-wide, which was smothered with ivy and wisteria and scuppernong vines, and hissed to a shuddering stop under the row of live oaks in back. Bull eased himself down to the ground and gazed with some satisfaction at the shabby building he had grown up in. Under the aggressive foliage — except where it had been trimmed around the doors — it looked more like a buried, Mayan ruin than a large trailer.

Annie had heard the big truck coming and was running around inside the double-wide, the interior lights dimming as she switched on air-conditioners from end to end. She emerged from a door framed with ivy, and gave her son a hug while Cooter ignored both of them and sniffed around the Airstream.

"What happened to your face? You been in another fight?"

"No, Mom, I just slipped in the mud this time, and smashed my glasses...."

"Well, it's going to be good having both my children in the house together!"

Bull hugged Annie back and looked at her. The patched hippie jeans, the long, gray Indian braids one on each side of her gaunt, weathered, but pleasant face. The dumb, wampum headband....

"It's not a house, Mom, it's a fucking trailer!"

Annie laughed. They both laughed because it was something Bull used to yell frequently when he was a boy, when the trailer was relatively new.

Then Bull wiped the smile off his face and repeated something else from the old days. "Janey sucks, Mom."

§

"You would not believe, Dad. This is the first moment of peace I've had in a month. But I need to get off my ass in a minute...."

They were sitting on some aluminum folding chairs Harry had carried over to the shade near the lowboy trailer and the Airstream. There was a breeze under the oaks and Bull felt contented. He had already given his father a spotty rundown of what had happened since he saw them last, and what his present job was.

"I love you, Bullperry."

"Jeez, Dad, don't spoil it!" Bull paused. "I love you, too."

Harry was re-lighting a roach of marijuana and he handed it over.

"No, no, I won't be worth a shit after that. I've got to call the people who own the missing stuff, and I've got to see if I can get into the laptop computer this guy left in the tractor. And before I call I need to pick the lock on the Airstream, too. See what's inside."

"We could pry it open...."

"No, Dad, that Airstream is worth big bucks. The lock is a good one but I'm sure I can pick it."

The two of them were finishing off a six-pack when Annie came out with more — a cooler-bag full of Coronas — and she plunked down next to Harry. Bull popped the cap off one of the Mexican longnecks for his father, using the opener on his big key-ring.

"The beer most fine!"

"La cerveza mas fina!"

"Un dolor en cabeza."

Annie took a swallow of hers and a long hit from Harry's doobie. "I just talked to Janey. She'll be here in half an hour."

Bull looked up to Heaven and Harry smiled. "If you get high first you might find out you really like your sister, Bullperry." He burped and smiled. "Your mother tell you about the boob job yet?"

"I heard."

"Don't make fun of them, Perry."

"Mom, you called it them. Does that mean she had both done?"

"Bofe," Harry said. "There were these two colored girls..."

"Dad, I heard the bofe'us joke a hundred times."

"I didn't," Annie said.

"Yes you did, Mom."

"There were these two colored sisters, first time in the big city with their mother, who warned them not to go anywhere without her. Well, the two of them took off anyway and stopped in this photography studio and the guy has them sit down together on this red velvet bench and he says, 'Okay, smile. Good. Now hike the hem of your skirts up just a little, okay, good, now, just a little more....okay. Smile.' Then he goes behind the camera and he says, 'Now hold still while I focus.' And the two colored girls look at each other and they say, 'Bofe'us?'"

Bull pried the cap off his fourth beer and swallowed.

"You're right, Perry, I heard that one." Annie was lighting up another joint, and when she handed it to Bull he accepted.

"Okay, but just one hit. I got serious shit to handle here. Besides, I never know when I'm going to be popped with a piss test."

"Janey and you will get along just fine. You did last time!"

"What, five years ago? For five minutes?"

Harry smiled as he watched Bull suck down a second hit. "We save this stuff just for family, Bullperry. From last October. Pure bud stored at ground temp with all the air removed from the jar. No oxygen to fuck it up...."

"Shit, I have work to do, god.... Sure smells good!"

And so it went. When Janey finally pulled up in front of the double-wide in her new, refrigerator-white Saturn, and honked, nobody got up out of their chairs.

"She'll find us...."

"Perry, remember, don't laugh at her boob-job. It cost a lot of money and it's a good one. They're long and pointy, with nipples even."

"Jeez, Mom, spare me!"

"I don't want you to criticize. Six thousand bucks is high-dollar for a Mexican clinic. Your father shot at them with the BB-gun last week and made her cry, when she was in the outdoor shower, but the BB bounced off one and hit him in the face and just missed his eye."

"Dad...."

"Look out for yellow-jackets. There's a nest of them around here somewhere and they love this beer.... I got stung on the lips once, remember?"

"Dad, remember? I got stung twice on the lips once. Hurt? Swell up? Boy!"

"God loves us," Harry said.

Janey finally figured it out and came over with a folding chair, her kinky, dyed-red hair radiating about her heavily made-up, attractive face like an electrocuted lion. The remanufactured breasts swayed from side-to-side, half out of an off-the-shoulder peasant blouse. A short, flouncy, colorful skirt completed the presentation.

"Don't anybody get up."

"Ahhhh, my elder sister...." Bull leaned back in his chair. "I see you made it around Deadman's Curve, well, that's good 'cause they say life begins at forty."

Janey blew Bull a kiss. "I'm only thirty-five, Perry!"

"Most blondes turn gray when they get old. That your Romanian whore outfit?"

"Gypsy". After unfolding her chair next to Annie's, away from Bull, Janey suddenly snatched the roach from her mother's hand. "I didn't get any of this yet!"

"You weren't here!"

"I'd wear a longer skirt over that cellulite, shroom-head."

"Bull, Perry! I don't do mushrooms anymore."

"But you still fuck for money, right?"

"Fuck you!"

"In a heartbeat."

"You? Not for a hundred dollars. Not two-hundred."

Bull grinned. "You're still dumb as dirt, Janey."

Annie and Harry looked at each other, beaming with joy, their faces hurting from so much involuntary smiling due to the reefer high.

Suddenly everyone jumped as the auxiliary power generator on the Airstream roared to life without warning, followed by one of the air-conditioners on the roof.

"Holy shit!" Bull froze, half-way out of his chair.

Annie plunked back down. "It must be on a thermostat. It's warm now, even in the shade here."

Harry hadn't moved a muscle. "Pretty fancy rig. Maybe you can keep it!"

"Dad...."

Janey was on her feet. "An Airstream?"

"Duhhhh...."

"I love those!" She went over to it, stepped up onto the lowboy, and opened the door.

Bull kept on saying, "Oh, jeez. Now I'm too high to do anything. And all this beer.... Shit! Oh, jeez...."

"Woe, it's like brand new in here." Annie was all the way down at the bathroom end. "Look at these paneled cabinets!"

"Oh, well, wouldn't you know," Janey said. "Black people.... Black people own this."

"So?"

Harry and Bull moved up beside her. She was looking at the single Polaroid held to the refrigerator door with a magnet. The snapshot had that forlorn, lost-in-the-past look that Polaroids often exude. A photo of two black girls — not more than ten years old or so — smiling into the camera and holding up a small, white bulldog puppy with a black eye patch — the girls in crisp, white dresses. An elegant but very old, white lady was standing between them.

"Oh, jeez...."

"Not you, Bullperry. Prejudiced?"

"No, Dad, me? No! Oh, jeez god...."

CHAPTER 5
Homer County Florida

Annie returned from the overgrown double-wide and found the rest of them plunked back down in the lawn chairs around the Airstream. The breeze had died and the air was heavy and hot, even though the shade had begun to darken under the live oaks. Bull was hunched over the laptop he had found in the truck, facing away from the others to shade the screen.

"Iced coffee!"

Janey and Harry, fresh Coronas in hand, shook their heads.

"The house is nice and cool, we could all sit in there."

Bull straightened up. "Thanks, Mom. I don't know what to do.... I'm so high from drinking and smoking."

Janey laughed. "Bullperry, that's why we do it! To get high!"

"Yeah, but I'm on the job! Shit, you wouldn't know.... And besides, Mom, it's not a house, it's..."

Janey chimed in right along with him. "It's a fucking trailer!"

Bull raised a glass to his lips and drank it all down. "Cold coffee, thanks, Mom. I have to go inside.... I got to transfer the files from this laptop into mine so if it gets rough later, you know, the missing driver, Denver, if he reincarnates, he won't be able to tell I've been into his 'puter."

Janey got up and looked over Bull's shoulder. "Reincarnates?"

"That tit on my neck feels cold, Janey. They say that silicone doesn't transfer heat as good as...

Annie yelled. "Don't start, Bullperry!"

"I think it's just the opposite," Harry said. "It reacts to your normal tissues and creates heat. It can be fatal. You hear about that Baywatch actress that self-combusted? She tried to douse herself but didn't make it from the life-guard shack to the water in time. She's just a burny, black grease-spot on the beach now."

"Self-combust?" Janey leaned over farther so that Bull had a jug on each ear. "Look up that SER-KILL one."

"I did. The guy is writing a whole book on serial killers or something and it goes on forever. I'm looking for stuff, like, why he swapped trailers, or if he's working for somebody else besides Kate and Axel McKay, you know...."

"Duplan Marine Transport," Harry said. "Duplan. That's a Haitian name. When we were living in Miami..."

"I'm going to look them up after I copy this stuff, but, well, I don't want to tip them off, and I'm so fucked up right now...." Bull hooked his elbows between his legs and held his head with both hands. "I always wanted to haul boats. Go to exotic places.... Marina to marina.... Fuck rich girls.... Listen to rich people thank you for bringing their toys on time.... Mom, does the DSL-line work? I need to download a program."

"From the internet?" Janey said.

"From the Crystal Cathedral. Christ, Janey...."

"Perry, you called us this morning, remember?" Annie nudged Harry's chair with a foot. "Remember? High-dee-high-dee-high-dee ho, we're not here?"

"Mom, that doesn't mean the broadband is working. I can't think straight. And I gotta call Kate, too."

"Well, maybe you should give up this private trucker-eye stuff and haul boats like you always wanted," Annie said. She was staring at the lip of Harry's beer bottle. A yellow-jacket wasp was half-way down into it, getting a sip.

"Tell him, Mom, jeez...."

"Husband, there's a yellow-jacket on your beer."

But Harry was already raising the bottle to his lips, still staring at the lowboy trailer. He hesitated. "That trailer number, zero-zero-two-two, that's a Haitian thing. Papa Doc's limo used to be number twenty-two. And that bottle of Fruit Kola we found. You can't buy that here...."

"Dad, stop! Your beer!"

By the time Harry looked, the bee had flown off. "They save the bottles. The return on just one of them is more than a week's pay down there. The average income is about a hundred bucks a year in Haiti."

"Oh, nobody would believe that, Daddy."

"Daughter, your ass isn't worth ten cents down there."

"Daddy...."

"Unless you sell the title to the whole thing," Bull said. "Hey. Maybe those little girls in the Polaroid were kidnapped."

"Just what I was thinking.... But not if they were able to unlock the Airstream door to get out."

"And I know where they are.... Hiding out in the bushes near the truckstop in La Grange. With that bull-dog puppy."

"Somebody would have noticed them by now," Annie said.

"Yeah...."

"What about the law? Shouldn't somebody call them?"

"Janey, the law's too busy checking out topless clubs," Bull said.

"You mean, too busy looking for pot fields," Harry said.

"Setting up road blocks to see if you're wearing seatbelts."

Annie said: "Running down kids riding bicycles for not wearing helmets."

"Sorry I asked!" Janey said. "But I would call the law, you know, in this case."

Bull turned around suddenly but wasn't quick enough to bite one of Janey's new implants. "Janey. When you're driving along in that Barbie-and-Ken Saturn you just got, and you see a cop car all of a sudden, do you cringe? Be honest now. When you first see a cop, don't you get a little scare?"

"Well, yeah!"

"And you want to call one of them?!"

Janey finally sat back down, crossing her legs and dangling a cork-soled platform clog from a big toe.

"Besides, cops do it for free. I need the money." Bull closed the lid on the laptop. "And your toe-nail polish is chipped." He tried to get up but stumbled, and the laptop tumbled onto the grass. "Oh, jeez, I'm too fucked up to do anything!" He had just been consider-ing driving back to LaGrange and seeing if he could find the two little girls there. And their bulldog puppy. "Think maybe those kids are Haitian? Speak French?"

Harry nodded gravely. "I'll go with you."

"No you won't," Annie said. "One nigger in the middle of my marriage is enough."

"If you'd look at everything as life instead of mar-riage..."

"You still see Ivory, Dad?"

"Yes he does! Three, four times a week he's over there!"

Bull laughed. "You still do that, Dad?"

"Still!" Annie yelled.

"Life's a woodpile! She must be getting on by now, huh Dad? Getting near that big four-oh?"

"He loves her!"

"Dad loves you, too, Mom, come on!"

"I don't believe you guys!" Janey said.

§

"That was an omen, Bullperry," Harry said. "Me tell-ing that bofe'us joke and then we go in the trailer and there's a picture of two colored girls...."

"Shit, Dad, that's hippie talk. Every coincidence is an omen for you. Like you say, you did a couple LSD trips too many."

"I never learned anything doing acid that didn't prove out later."

"Yeah, right. Dad, listen, there's a Kodak program in this guy's laptop but no pictures. If we can find the digital camera in the Airstream.... I've already combed through the tractor and I could be downloading the stuff I need while you look for it?"

Harry grinned at his son, both of them still anchored to their lawn chairs. "Digital camera?"

"Doesn't use film. Jeez, Dad.... It puts the pictures in digital form so you can load them into your computer and see them on the monitor."

"Can you look at them while you're high? No, wait, can you look at them while you're drunk? I can look at regular pictures while I'm drunk. Without electricity, too."

"Yeah, but I can send a digital picture to somebody on the other side of the world in a minute, and no long distance charge."

"Take a picture of Janey's new tits and send it to the Dalai Lama in Tibet. Don't they drink a lot of milk over there?"

"Goat milk. And he doesn't live there anymore, Dad."

"Send it to his father, then."

Bull heaved himself up, managing to keep his balance this time, and headed toward "the house" with a laptop computer bag on each shoulder, his and the other driver's. He was sweating, not so much from the warm, sweet humidity but from the fear which building, the scariness of running out of time, the inability to function in a crisis he couldn't see or feel. And the darkness inside his parents' double-wide didn't help — the windows all overgrown with vines and stuff — but at least is was cool in here and didn't smell like Cooter and puppy shit like it had on his last visit.

But the desk in his room was full of stacks of un-opened mail. He moved everything off to the bed in the order in which he found it and in ten minutes had the other driver's laptop hooked to his own and was copy-ing the contents. Next, he hooked to the DSL modem and began downloading the program he needed. That would take a few minutes so he headed down to the kitchen for another coffee. He could check out the mail his mother had been bitching about some other time.

He found Janey — so foxy looking — not like the sister he grew up with — about to pick up the kitchen phone.

"Janey, touch that phone and you're dead."

Janey hesitated, her hand still out.

"As soon as you're dead I'm calling the guy who paid for your new Saturn and tell him he can fuck you for free now. For a limited time only. While you're still warm and pliable."

"Okay! OKAY!"

Forgetting the coffee but remembering the Schaff-ner pantheon of telephones, most of them old Christ-mas presents, Bull started down the length of the double-wide. He pulled out phone jacks as he went along so that the modem connection in his room would be undisturbed. The one under the dry aquarium with the live tarantulas in it was the worst, and Bull had to get on his hands and knees to reach it.

The download was something Bull had just heard about, and he wasn't sure the program would work. Whoever designed it called it "CallerPD" and if you typed in your own area code and a false one of your choosing, it would override the original if you let your computer do the dialing. To test it, he called Kate first, in Missouri, using the 615 Nashville area code and the number of a Peterbilt dealer there. Kate believed in caller-ID and she used it to find out where her drivers were calling from — to see if they were lying. Bull was lying because he needed to keep some cards on the table. And maybe he could up the ante later, too, if everything turned up flowers....

When he finally got her, she sounded excited. "Oh, Bull! Denver called." There was a pause and the sound of slapping in the background. "Harold, get away!"

Bulled gulped down another slug of coffee, from one of his father's favorite cups, pastel purple with a faded picture of a beady-eyed Timothy Leary, grinning.... "Yeah, and..."

"He wants you to call him. No law. You call the law yet?"

"No.... Have you?"

"How can I, especially now!? What about the passengers? He wanted me to describe passengers! Then before I could say anything he hung up. What fucking passengers?!"

"Kate...." Bull hesitated. "You got a make on this phone?"

"Nashville? You're more than half-way here. Why?"

"I thought I had caller-ID disabled." Bull grinned but his head was pounding and he couldn't think of what to say next. "Kate...."

"He left a Miami number. But his caller-ID was blocked. Harold, get away! Bull, wait a minute...."

Another pause. "Bull?" It was Little Harold. "Mama's wrong. It wasn't Denver. And he didn't sound mad when I talked to him. I picked up when he called. He had sort of the same voice, but not quavery like Denver's, you know — not as old sounding — and he called me "Porky", and when I got hot about it he apologized and then, with a real straight voice, he calls me "Fatty"! Denver never called me that. It was always, like, "Pork Chop" or "Tiny" or stuff like that. It was me got his phone number. Mama was too busy telling him off. Mama grabbed the phone away from me and started yelling at him and he hung up."

"Ha! You did good, Little Harold."

"Before I hung up, I called him Dopey."

"Dopey, huh? Okay.... Listen up. I'm going to be pretending I'm up near you guys in Missouri and I've got the rig parked at Uncle Ralph's place, okay? Make sure your mother understands. You've just seen me at the terminal making phone calls, but the rig is at Uncle Ralph's. Only don't tell Dopey or anybody who Uncle Ralph is or where his place is. Specially his last name. Got that?"

"Okay. You're at Uncle Ralph's? Who's he?"

"Good dog."

Bull punched in the CallerPD number for the McKay Trucking terminal in Stony Hill, MO, then the Miami number Little Harold had given him. Busy. After checking that his phony CallerPD setting was saved, he found the number for Duplan Marine Transport on the internet yellow-pages, leaned back with his fingers locked behind his head, and let the computer do the dialing.

CHAPTER 6
Stony Hill Missouri

Little Harold, agile for his weight, bounded up the stairway to the loft above the office where his new room was, where his new multi-line desk-phone was so he could take company calls from his bed. Pretty good for going-on-fourteen, he thought, but then there were all these kids at school who had new smart-phones that did all kinds of stuff. He plunked down on the bed and looked at the posters on the opposite wall. Four-wheeler All Terrain Vehicles — ATVs — his favorite a bright-red 4-wheel drive Kawasaki Bayou-400. His birthday wish. Five-speed, go-anywhere, limited-slip drive, but fat chance of that happening now that the company lost a load and a trailer.

Harold looked up to Bull and was hoping that he would become a regular McKay driver. And if he could help Bull get everything back the Kawasaki was his. He was sure. Well, pretty sure. The Yamaha 4-wheel drive would do, too, and if there wasn't enough money he could settle for a used Kawasaki Lakota or Mojave, but that Kawasaki Bayou-400, mmm-mmmm, an engine-red male, almost brand-new at the dealer, $3,000 loaded. His fourteenth birthday was coming up at the end of summer, two days before school started, and two days was all he would need to practice on it.

Little Harold rolled to one side and looked out the little window by the bed, the other window filled with the groaning, 5,000 BTU air-conditioner, bought used and not sounding too good. If that broke down now, with him right under the hot roof, and no money, shit! He pictured picking up the new girl whose family had moved down the road last month, at the edge of town, near the quarters. Hot, hot, hot! Long, straight, black hair and such a beautiful tan, and she was going to be in his home room at school. He saw her from time to time in their front yard, and when he would ride by on his bicycle and wave she would wave right back. Such white teeth. And she had tits, too, which few of the other girls his age had. You could picture them under her T-shirt.

Just the sound of her name, *Juanita*....

Harold stared out the window onto the graveled truck yard below, a few empty trailers and Bull's wrecked but still shiny-black tractor which a new hire had rolled over on his first and last day. Harold was not really seeing anything down there but he could sense how hot it was outside in the middle of the afternoon; you could feel the heat from the window glass. He pictured Juanita and slid a hand under his shirt and bunched up the flesh around his left nipple. Harold had never felt of a girl but he knew that one day he would and that her tits would be wonderful. Juanita's tits. He would never get enough of them, the feeling and squeezing and kissing of them. Lying with her on a blanket, his favorite plaid one, under the willows off the trail along the creek behind the terminal, his faithful, red

Kawasaki Bayou-400 waiting patiently while Harold and Juanita explored each other....

The machine would have a cooler bungeed to a rack, and a holster for his .22-magnum High Standard "Double-Nine" revolver which Axel McKay, his uncle, had given him on his last birthday. It had been Axel's half-brother's pistol, "Uncle Ralph", who had so many guns in his collection he didn't care if he gave one up, especially now that he was into collecting military automatics, and anti-tank guns. One thing was for sure: Juanita would feel safe with him as her boyfriend, out in the woods by the creek, knowing he had his own gun.

And Juanita would never tell on him, that he carried it around....

Harold jumped at the sound of a wire slapping against the outside wall, a scrunch of gravel and something smacking the building again. Then, through the floor boards, the screen-door directly below him, the *clunk* as it invariably slammed anybody coming in through the front door, which was on a heavy closer of its own to keep the office cool. There was a car out in the lot now, but Harold had not seen it pull up or heard a door slam. A maroon Cadillac Sedan DeVille, clean and looking like new, was backed up to the front door and facing out, and an old lady in a straw hat and a Sunday dress was standing next to it.

His mother's voice and a man's, low at first. Then his mother saying, loudly: "Nobody. That's our store-room up there."

Little Harold's heart pounded up and he eased off the bed onto his hands and knees, hoping the springs

wouldn't creak. The floorboards were cool but sandy —
he had promised his mother he would sweep a week
ago — and he slid his knees and his black Reebok originals along without a sound as he reached for the .22
mag revolver stuck under the mattress on the other
side. His heart was pounding so fast it was making him
feel sick, but he held still and listened to the floor.
Worn, gray paint and junk in the cracks....

His mother's voice, quiet again. It was her *everything's-cool-and-normal* voice which, Harold was sure,
everyone could see right through. "I think he said he
was stopping at Uncle Ralph's."

The man's voice, so calm and low Harold could not
make it out.

"He lives way down on Highway E. I'd draw you a
map if I knew what your business is."

Harold pressed an ear closer to the dirty floor. *Why
did she tell him what highway?*

His mother again: "He doesn't have a phone. He's
old and deaf and near blind."

All lies....

The man remained calm and Harold could only hear
the words "...deep shit."

"Fuck you, then!" his mother said. "It's time to call
the law. You ready for that?!"

The hard slap cracked through the floor and Harold
rolled over to the phone. No dial tone. He scrambled for
the jack, which was always pulling out, but it was okay.
A look out the window and the man was already pulling
his mother toward the Cadillac, his elbow around her
neck and her feet dragging the ground. His shaved head

gleamed in the sun. Rolls of pasty-white fat bulged from the collar of his gray suit, his hulking body a fright beside the frail-looking old lady holding open the passenger-side door. Harold wheeled around toward the staircase, gun in hand, and missing a grab for the wooden railing he smashed right through it.

Harold's forehead had smacked on the stairwell cut-out on his fall down the steps but the sharp pain he felt was in his neck as he raced through the front door and slapped away the screen. The dirt and gravel stung as the Cadillac DeVille burned out of the yard to the highway, his mother's head visible through the back window, slumped to the side. The bright heat of the day was blinding as Harold squinted his eyes and watched the Caddy turn right and then make the crossing to Highway-E. He looked at his revolver and was surprised to find the hammer cocked.

§

By the time he was within a mile of Uncle Ralph's, which was normally only twenty minutes from the McKay Trucking terminal, the tears had dried on Little Harold's face. His body was jerking forward-and-back, forward-and-back, in a steady rhythm as if his body weight could help his mother's old Chevy Silverado pickup make it any farther with an empty fuel tank. Once again the engine sputtered to life and sped up from five mph to about thirty before it began conking out again. No houses in sight, but another pickup was gaining fast in the mirror and Harold frantically waved an arm at it through the open window. The young woman driving stared straight ahead as she went by, and a moment later the Chevy died for good. Harold was able to coast it almost all the way onto the shoulder.

During the scramble over the barbed-wire fence, the tears came back as Little Harold caught his new Levi's and pulled a six-inch rip through them at the groin. His mother had been planning to buy herself a pair when she brought these home for Harold instead. "Money is tight right now," was all she had said as she helped him remove all the labels without cutting any threads. Now, stickers and prickly blackberry bushes clawed at the torn jeans as Harold ran diagonally across the empty and abandoned fields to Uncle Ralph's. Through the trees of the windbreak up ahead he could see glimpses of the large outbuilding which stood away from the house and blocked the view of it. Harold headed for that, hoping no one could see him coming.

CHAPTER 7
Homer County Florida

Bull went back outside into the heat and sunlight, back to the cozy family scene at the lowboy and the Airstream under the oaks. Back to his beautiful Peterbilt tractor-to-be.

"I love you guys," he said, plunking down into his chair. "You, too, Janey. Sort of...."

"We love you, too, Bullperry!"

"Sort of!"

"Family...."

"Family!"

"You need more coffee," Annie said.

"Yeah, but I'm coming down fast. That reefer kicked ass but it can't hold it's liquor."

"That was Spring reefer," his father said. "Happy reefer. But it doesn't keep.... I thought I had the stuff from October before."

"Well, good. Anyway, I called Duplan Marine. They're right on the Miami River near Twenty-Seventh Avenue. Near where you used to work, right? Those Cubans?"

"Uhhhh.... Maybe, but there was no Duplan Marine there. Not that many Haitians in Miami then, either, before we moved up here...." Harry smiled and his bright-blue eyes looked off into the distance. "What'd they have to say?"

"Check this. They say they don't even have a trailer number 0022, or 22, and then they tell me all their trailers are in the yard right now. Well, I never told them I knew it wasn't in their yard, know what I mean? I didn't tell them anything. Just mentioned the trailer number. They're lying. Then they say I should come over and look if I don't believe them. I mean, what would that prove!? Duhhhh.... Oh, shit! I forgot to ask Kate for an advance."

Harry seemed unimpressed. "I couldn't find a digital camera, just the Polaroid."

"He didn't look more than a minute," Janey said. She got up and wavered for a moment before catching her balance. "Come on, Bullperry. Let's pilfer!"

The floor inside the Airstream vibrated with the sound of the generator, which was running again. Bull turned the thermostat up some and sucked in a deep breath. He thought he could smell Pine Sol, and fresh varnish. Everything was so neat and clean....

"This is what I found so far," Janey said. "These Polaroids were right on the table under the newspaper, only they all have the old lady in the middle, holding the puppy on a leash. The kids must've picked the one without the leash to put on the fridge door."

"Yesterday's Miami Herald...." Bull sat down in the dinette and squinted at the snapshots. The same two girls, same outfits, and that cute puppy. The white lady standing between them was tall and thin, dressed in what looked like a neatly pressed, linen dress. A spotless, Panama hat cocked slightly to one side above her pale and deeply wrinkled face. White shoes.... Classy for somebody so old.

Bull mumbled. "I wonder if she was with them when I..."

"Look what else I found. Wrapped in a coat, bottom drawer. This old album. Guess who's in it? Oh, all the old lady's other stuff and clothes are right up front in the closets and top drawers. Expensive-looking clothes. The girls' stuff is always behind everything. I noticed that!"

"God bless."

"One is missing." Janey, uncharacteristically up-beat, mashed him to the side as she slid onto the bench with the open album. "Look, these little corners holding the pictures in the front, these old ones, all black and white. And these old-timey deckle edges.... What's the matter? The missing photo's not in the drawer. I looked."

"I'm thinking about what I'm going to say to Dopey. The dude in Miami when I call.... Hey, she was a real beauty! God, look, there's a fucking mule behind her. Probably was born in that same shack. Her and the mule bofe."

"Not poor for long!" Janey touched the first photo on the third page with a vampire-red nail. The girl/lady must have been late teens then, but was now standing on a tiled floor between two columns entwined with flowering vines — elegant, calf-length dress — her hair wrapped in a snood. Janey and Bull pored over the pages, the later photos in color and all with opulent backgrounds, some of them of the lady with tall, grave and prominent-looking, dark-skinned men in double-breasted suits and broad-brimmed, light-colored fedoras. Different men, bad-ass looking men with mirrored sunglasses, and near the end of the album, the men not nearly as old as the lady.

"No children anywhere," Janey said. "Not one."

"Hmmmm...." Bull came within a hair of blurting Janey a compliment but caught it just in time.

§

"I figured it out," Janey said.

They were back in Bull's old room in the double-wide, Janey poking around the unopened mail on the bed while he scrolled through the contents of the missing driver's laptop computer.

"He's writing a novel about a serial killer."

"Little brother, what are you doing to these women?!"

"This is juicy stuff!" Bull looked up. "What women?"

"All these letters! And these dumb Soldier of Fortune magazines.... What about these poor postcards from Dianna? Huh? Apparently you haven't been home for awhile. And these powder blue envelopes with the perfume from 'Mrs. Perry Schaffner'. Where's Kendall? Postmarked Miami? Mrs? You and Dianna move down south? Mama says you're a bigamist. That true? Another thing, why do you keep your old room here? Mama and Daddy could use it for other stuff. I mean!"

"So I'm a polygamist, so what? It's a truck-driver thing. Can we get back to the program here?"

"And this court order from Milwaukee for child support?"

"Janey!"

"And this book on handgun silencers. So important you opened it but not the love letters?"

"The PO must've done that. They're always pilfering through my shit."

"Ho! And you say I'm bad?!"

"I never said you were bad. Just dumb."

"Yeah, well, I just figured out where your kidnapees are and how to get 'em back."

"Rave on."

"The kids are in that place you stopped overnight and the old lady is where you found the truck, in Atlanta? She was probably in the restaurant getting them something to eat and told the girls not to move until she got back. That sandwich in the fridge in the Airstream is old. And there's no lunch makings in the garbage thing. They've been eating out."

"You're forgetting the rig had a driver. It was running when I found it."

"You said not to worry about the driver."

"I changed my mind. He's a sicko."

"Well, but you're getting paid to swap the trailers, right?"

"Yeah, but finding the driver'll be the gravy."

"Bullperry. The gravy is getting paid and then taking time off. You're the dumb one. You always were. And I don't pay child support, I get child support."

"Yeah? Then where are the kids?"

"I made a deal. Like I said, you're the..."

"Yeah, yeah, I heard."

"So can I come along?"

"May I come along."

"May I, then?"

"Yes! Okay? Yes!"

Later, Bull dialed the Miami number again and was relieved when he didn't get an answer. He needed to line up a few more ducks and then nail this guy from the high ground. With luck the dude had a caller-ID recorder and would think the call came from the terminal in MO.

Next, he dialed McKay Trucking again but the lines were busy. Too bad. Kate would have asked him where the hell he was calling from and he had planned to say from the wine cellar at the Vatican. He would probably forget that cute line later, so he tried dialing one more time.

It was nearly twilight by the time they were set to go, Janey taking her time changing, then moving a considerable amount of gear from her Saturn to the big Pete, then making a series of "important" phone calls. The few Bull overheard dealt with breaking dates. When she was through with that, Bull ordered her to make-up the top bunk in the tractor.

"I thought we could cozy up together when we get to the truckstop. We used to sleep in the same bed when we were kids...."

"I sleep naked."

"Me, too!"

Annie yelled at Janey from the kitchen. "I heard that!" She was slapping together some smoked ham sandwiches for them to take along.

Janey yelled back. "it's different nowadays, Mama! There's AIDS now. You can't just fuck anybody like when you were young!"

§

"No vanity mirror on my side."

Janey looked out through the windshield with one hand on her head as Bull eased the rig over the railroad tracks.

"This tractor won't bounce as bad as the junk rigs you've been riding in." Bull flicked on the right turn-signals.

"It's been a long time, for me, riding in a big truck. I love this! Left on 90."

"No, right. I'm going to go west to 331 and take that to Montgomery. There's no quick way up to La Grange from here and I don't want to drive a lot of back-road shit when it gets dark. I need new glasses. Maybe I should've taken you up on going in your pussy new Saturn."

"Yeah, well we already went through all that. We have to take the Airstream back. And stay with their trailer."

"Lowboy."

"Bullperry, correct-oh. You be sure you mind the important stuff."

"While you were primping back home I tried to call the terminal again but the line was still busy. I wanted

Kate to fax us Denver's picture to LaGrange — the missing driver — and a rider pass for you."

Janey settled back after turning down the AC a little. "Rider pass?"

"Yeah, it's illegal to carry a passenger without one. And by the way, hands off the AC. The driver controls the radio and the temperature in this unit."

"Oh, bullshit. I went all the way to Oregon once with this guy and I didn't have a pass. He just picked me up and away we went! California first. The whole nine yards. Mountains, the desert.... Bumpier than this Petey-hood. It was a cabover."

"Shit, Janey, when was this?"

"Back when we were still living at home. I was going on sixteen. Remember when I disappeared for a month and Mama filed me a missing person? Then. My first eighteen wheeler."

"How often he hump you?"

"Oh, God, he was pulling over every hour at first. The sleeper was small and the ceiling upholstery was a light color and I was barefoot when he picked me up and my feet were dirty on the bottom and I made footprints on his ceiling. I thought he would get mad about it but he never saw it. Took him a couple weeks to get a load back this way but he was nice to me the whole trip. Seemed like a real happy person for a married guy."

"Right. Jeez, Janey, you never told us it was a truck driver."

"Yeah, well I didn't want to get him in trouble. I sure was a sleazebag back then!"

"I'm so glad you reformed. You never caught any-thing?"

"No! Never! I practice safe sex! I've only had three abortions in my whole life. Plus the two kids, of course."

"Which none of us have ever seen."

"And never will. Not so long as the checks keep coming."

"All heart, you are."

"Hey! What kind of mother would I be? Huh?!"

"You packing? I might need some backup later."

"Am I wearing my pants?"

"I wouldn't know."

"Thirty-eight Smith & Wesson Airweight."

"Bless your heart, Janey."

"Dad always asks, too. Remember when we were little, still in Miami, and the other kids were jealous be-cause we had our own guns already? And all Mom and Dad's hippie friends would put them down for it?"

"Yeah, all that flower-power...."

Bull felt the urge to tell Janey how good it felt to have her along but he could not remember ever paying his sister a compliment and he stifled it.

"If it works, don't fix it."

"What?"

"Just talking to myself. Another truck driver thing. How come you don't act fucked up right now."

"I didn't drink and smoke that much. You didn't, ei-ther, but you never could. You were always a wimp."

"A wimp...."

"Wimp."

"Yeah, well, that was a long time ago. I work out now, I don't get asthma attacks anymore, and I'm tough as nails."

"Yeah, right. Show me the money."

"Speaking of, do you think you can..."

"Stop! Stop right there! You still owe me over a thousand."

"A thousand even."

"That was then, when you said you'd pay me right back."

Bull had nothing to say to that. They slowed a little through the bleak nothingness of Ponce de Leon, and passed Sally's restaurant — two empty stick trucks and a smattering of pickups parked out front — before speeding up. In a half hour they were out of DeFuniak Springs and heading up 331 to Montgomery.

It was long dark by the time they reached Luverne, Alabama, and Bull slowed before coming up on the brightly lit Hardee's on the left.

"Truck parking behind this Hardee's."

"We can stop later."

"Well, don't holler for me to stop for a pee where there's no place to pull sixty-seventy feet of truck over."

"Mama and Daddy made us sandwiches."

"Coffee. We forgot to fill my thermos."

"You forgot to fill your thermos."

"Just like being married."

The big rig rumbled past the Hardee's, the shiny Airstream behind them reflecting all the colors of the rainbow. Janey gave a little wave to two, scruffy-looking, gray-haired bikers standing beside their Harleys parked on her side, then pulled up her shirt and flashed her tits. Loud whistles and yells....

"Jeez, Janey, you're thirty-five years old for Chris' sake."

"Yeah, but they were older."

"And?"

"Well? Think about it!"

"Oh, well. Yah, okay...."

"Be proud, Bull. They don't have shit, and you have me!"

The bikers didn't take long to mount up, and were rumbling alongside Bull as he made the last turn at the end of town. They both gave him a thumbs-up before passing, and Bull grinned.

"I'm so proud, Janey!"

"Quit it, Bull. Tell me this. What would you do if you were in a normal family? What would you do with a normal sister? Huh? You'd have to keep track of all her kids' birthdays!"

Bull could no longer hear the deep rumble of the Harleys and in another minute the diminishing taillights glimmered out of sight in the distance. The road was black, the sky dark, but the trailer tracked well and Bull had to ease the Pete back down from eighty — the big CAT engine turning only 1850 R.P.M. in top gear — not the first time he had caught himself speeding accidentally in this rig. He settled back in the seat and held her steady on course with one gentle hand.

"Pure pussy!" he yelled. "The rig, Janey. Not you."

CHAPTER 8
Stony Hill Missouri

Little Harold was still too far away to see if anyone was inside the maroon Cadillac Sedan DeVille parked in front of Uncle Ralph's house, but he thought he spotted the old lady's hat through the back window. Running out of breath now, he angled off to the right so that the single-story studio building up ahead would block any view of him as he climbed over the last fence. Half-way over, he lowered his pistol to the ground to free himself of the barbed wire, while his mind replayed the sound of his mother being knocked out and hauled away in the Cadillac.

I'll get him, Mama!

The door at the side of the studio was padlocked, and he stopped at the far wall, standing up against it and holding his breath to listen. Under the roof overhang, on both sides of him, tall grass grew up between piles of Honda SuperHawk motorcycle parts, Uncle Ralph's obsession before he caught military gun-fever. The motorcycle stuff, enough to build at least three of them, would normally have interested Little Harold but his mind was at sea now with the thought that everything was going to depend on him.

Unless Uncle Ralph could figure out what was coming.

Harold licked at the salty taste in the corners of his mouth. He was afraid his breathing was too noisy and he held his mouth wide open to keep quiet. There was no wind, the air-conditioner was not running, and the only sound was the motor in the Sedan DeVille idling on the other side of the building, and now, way off in the distance, the soft sonority of a truck rolling down the highway.

Harold had tried to give Uncle Ralph a puppy the year before, which would be a big dog by now and a big help. His mother had rejected the little, black Labrador, too, and who knows where it was now, probably starved to death and dead in a field somewhere, rotting fur stuck to a broken skeleton. Harold had found a dead dog like that once, and with that thought he sucked in a deep breath and eased around the corner of the building, his revolver in both hands.

The old lady was in the car, her head leaning back, the hat on the back ledge. Was she asleep? Harold moved in a crouch, up to but behind the car, ready to use it as a shield if the man spotted him and fired from the house. For a few seconds another part of him saw himself doing this, like on TV — saw that he had learned this from television — while he considered sneaking past the Caddy and getting the house between him and the old lady. Not that she could be much of anything if she woke up.

Tired of waiting behind the car and the sick-smelling exhaust, he pushed off into a semi, fat-boy run to the side of the house and didn't stop until he got to the back corner, turning then to check behind him. Just the end of the DeVille's trunk was visible now and he felt safe for the moment. He pressed against the rough, cool brick and caught his breath again.

Suddenly, from somewhere inside, Harold's mother screamed.

The adrenaline squirt stabbed him like a knife and his stomach bunched up.

Then, his mother's voice: "No, please, no!"

Harold lunged around the corner and through the back door, ducking through the kitchen behind the bar which separated it from the rest of the house — nobody in sight but the guy suddenly busted out of the guest bedroom in front, a thick, black moustache dangling from his shiny head. He was looking from side-to-side with an automatic in one big hand while Harold laid his revolver across the bar and pulled the trigger. Moustache spotted him just as Little Harold's hammer fell on an empty chamber. Harold frantically pulled again — another empty chamber. He dropped behind the bar as the man's first three rounds smashed through the cabinet underneath — BAM! BAM! BAM! — ear-splitting misses which stung him with shattered glass and spraying whiskey and splintered wood. Two more shots — BAM! BAM! — missing him again on the other side and blowing a cabinet door open. His ears ringing, Harold turned the gun toward himself to look down it, the remaining cylinders shining with little copper-jacketed missiles ready to launch, and he tensed for the lurch back up to fire over the bar.

"Halt!"

The voice behind him didn't wait and a deafening shot rang out not ten feet away, the blast stinging the back of his neck and the round zinging past his right ear.

"Drop it!"

Another stinging blast to the left of him and Harold froze, then dropped his High Standard Double-Nine. The small, old lady was over him in a heartbeat, and a thin, stockinged leg kicked his gun away. Harold stared down at moustache's shiny, wing-tip shoes which were now parked under his nose, the empty brass from the lady's gun rolling toward them on the Linoleum. The shells stopped at the growing puddle of booze running from the cabinet under the bar.

"That was close! Where'd he come from?"

"Shut up, fool. Turn around, kid!"

Harold turned, very slowly, and straightened up. The weapon in her tiny, blue-veined hand was a huge, government-model .45, the hammer of the automatic cocked and the gaping barrel looking him right in the eye. Harold's lips were quivering, and his nose wrinkled at the spilled whiskey and burned gunpowder.

Moustache lowered his voice. "You want to live, boy?"

"I – I want my mama."

"After you tell us where your driver is. Our trailer."

"After you turn Mama loose." Harold cringed at his own words and tensed up for the blow that never came.

"Look at me!" The old lady kept the cocked .45 aimed right at his eyes. He knew that Uncle Ralph had guns hidden all over the place. One in every room, he was always bragging. "Nobody's ever going to get the drop on me!" Behind him he could hear moustache's wheezy breathing.

"Turn around!"

Sounds of the old lady reloading behind him as Harold stared at two new guns aimed at his chest, shit, one of them was Uncle Ralph's pearl-handled 1935 "Navy Model" Beretta. Harold's shoulders slumped, then jerked back up when the old lady jammed the barrel of her pistol so hard into his lower back his knees buckled.

Kate was sitting on the edge of bed in the guest-room, a white, nylon rope cinched around her neck, the other end tied to a bedpost. The line was cinched so tight that Little Harold could hear her struggles for breath before he even saw her, when they were shoving him down the hall to the room. Her flushed face looked up when they pushed him in. Her hands were cuffed behind her and her eyes were bulging.

"Mama!"

"Boy, you better tell us. Your mother's suffocating to death, you know what I mean? She won't last much longer."

"Where is my trailer?" The old lady with a quavery but sharp, banjo voice and a strange accent.

Kate was nodding vigorously and looking right at him while Little Harold's mind raced for something to do, to say...

"It's not worth it, boy." Moustache, sounding so reasonable after trying to kill him in the kitchen.

Kate still nodding.

"You got ten seconds before your mother gets to watch you bleed to death."

Harold glanced out the gauze-curtained windows, thinking he saw Uncle Ralph's body lying in the yard. But it was just the old lady's crumpled suit-jacket lying out there in the grass in front of the Cadillac, like a sleeping dog....

"Five seconds. Where's your driver?"

"He's not here," Harold said. "He was pretending."

"Pretending?"

"He can fake the caller-ID on the telephone."

Kate was still nodding, and her bloodshot eyes remained fixed on her oversized son, her breath coming in screeching struggles as she tried to suck in more air.

"Last time it said he was calling from Nashville."

"Bullshit!"

"He might be still around Atlanta."

"Where does he live?"

"In Florida somewhere. In Miami. He has a house in Miami."

"Bullshit! Where in Florida?"

"His... His parents live next to the Chattahoochee, no, the Chatawatchie River, no, Choctaw, Choctawhatchee!"

Moustache turned to the old lady, so small yet tall, her steely eyes never blinking. "I'm getting the phone. If he moves, shoot 'im."

"You are the one who doesn't know what to do is the problem!" she screeched.

With her eyes and the barrel of her .45 never leaving Harold's face, she sidled up to the window and yanked the curtains off the rod with one jerk. Harold watched moustache lean into the DeVille and get a cell-phone out with his pistol in his other hand and Uncle Ralph's smaller, pearl-handled Beretta tossed to the ground. He turned toward their window and looked back at them as he speed-dialed a number — two punches on the keyboard — and brought the phone to an ear, his suit-coat open and a short, wide, emerald-green tie laid on top of a white shirt bulging over the belt.

His mouth and moustache moved, no smile — a pause — mouth moving again, his head turning from side-to-side suddenly, then back to their window, the other party doing most of the talking while moustache shifted his weight from one leg to the other, one finger pulling at the short tie in the bright heat, the old lady stone quiet and unwavering and Kate screeching for breath on the bed.

Harold saw it before he heard it, moustache's hips suddenly jerking to the right before his stomach ex-ploded into a bloom of red roses. **Ka - bam!** The win-dow rattled as the man went down five feet from the car in a splatter of meat. Harold ducked as the .45 went off over his head, the old lady heading for the door now as Uncle Ralph's second round smashed through the window and took a chunk out of the back wall where she had been standing. Harold grabbed for his folding knife, tearing at it to get the blade out, momentarily deaf as he slid it alongside his mother's neck and sliced through the rope.

"Mama, Mama, Mama..." He could hear himself through the fuzzy ringing in his head, his arms around her and his cheek against her heaving chest. "Mama, Mama."

CHAPTER 9
Road Block in Alabama

BULL SLAPPED Janey's hand away from the stereo above the dark windshield, above the CB radio which had been silent for the last ten minutes. "I like to listen to this engine."

"Bullperry...."

"This is going to be my new tractor. The best one I ever had." He looked back to the array of gauges, the dash-lights adjusted to his satisfaction and not a single bulb out. Air-pressure, water temp, oil pressure, oil temp, differential temp, gearbox temp, manifold pressure, cylinder-head temp...

"Why are we slowing down?"

"Lot of cops here through Auburn and Opelika...."

"I didn't see any."

"Believe me. And I don't want to get pulled over for something dumb and get caught with a phony trailer manifest."

They were on I-85 northeast out of Montgomery, heading to Georgia at 10:00PM, traffic picking up a little through the Auburn exits, 4-wheelers whipping past them like bees. Farther on, Bull and Janey were trolling past the Opelika exits at 60mph — which felt like 40 in the big Pete — when Janey's big handbag started beeping. She grabbed for it.

"My phone."

"Duh."

"Mama? Louder, Mama."

Bull pictured himself back in Stony Hill, MO, at the McKay terminal, getting all of his own stuff moved in, and installing his own cell phone setup with the killer, exterior antenna.

"Speak up, Mama, you're breaking up. Who's Kate?"

Bull glanced to the side and watched his sister glow briefly under the lights as they passed the last Opelika exit.

"Who's Uncle Ralph?" "Dead?" "He shot him?"

Bull reached for the phone but Janey slapped him away.

"You're breaking up Mama. Bullperry, pull over so I can get out."

"Stick the phone out the window." Bull pulled the air switch that operated the passenger side window.

"You're still breaking up, Mama. You didn't give her my cell phone number? Oka-a-a-ay.... Okay. She could hardly talk? Right. Okay. Thanks, Mama. I love you, Mama."

Warm, heavy, night air was mushing into the cab and Bull ran the window back up as soon as Janey could get her arm and head back in.

"My hair's a mess."

"What was that about?"

"This lady, Kate, called Mama. She and her son were kidnapped and the dude got some information out of them, apparently, before their uncle or some-body blew the guy away."

"Uncle Ralph shot him? Woe!"

"I mean! Anyway, this Kate person thinks the kidnapper got a phone call out before he died. He wants the Airstream, bad, and her son told him you were in Atlanta."

"Great.... Shit. Fuck!"

"What's wrong with that? We can meet whoever it is there. Beats looking for him!"

Bull thought about it.

"Well?"

Barely visible and far up ahead, Bull spotted blue and red flashing lights. "You're okay, Janey."

For a second he wondered why his dog, his radar detector, wasn't barking over the activity up there, then remembered he didn't have it with him. The feds had made bird-dogs illegal on big trucks, anyway, but fuck that.

"Yup, Janey. You're okay. For a chick."

The trucks and RV's ahead of them were ablaze with brake lights but it looked as though the roadblock coming up was letting passenger cars through. Bull slowed to a crawl to avoid the stops and starts, and so he could catch up his logbook.

"Uncle Ralph shot the guy who was going to kidnap Kate?"

"He shot him afterwards is what Mama said. They must want your trailer pretty bad."

"It's their trailer."

"Yeah, but they want to hold hostages for it?"

"And here we are coming up on a roadblock. Jeez. Sometimes they get out the portables in Alabama. Portable scales. Well, we're not overweight."

"Dogs. I can see dogs up there. It's dope dogs, Perry."

"You better not have any dope on you Janey. Do you?"

"Uhhhh, no!"

"Janey...."

"No, thank god. But only because I forgot it. In the Saturn."

"You're sure."

"Positive. I mean, negative, ha ha."

"Oh, man...."

"Yeah, I know what you're thinking."

"The Airstream."

"Yeah."

"No water in the tanks. The toilet wouldn't flush...."

"Yeah...."

"We're fucked, Janey."

"You're fucked, Bull. I'm just riding along here."

"You're my sister!"

"And they're never going to know!"

The line came to a halt, the action about seven or eight trucks and RV's up ahead, and Bull let the clutch out in neutral, rested the logbook against the wheel, and began scribbling. An out-of-date logbook was often an excuse cops used to search. Janey and Bull sat in silence for a moment before Bull remembered he had turned down the CB when Janey was on the phone, and as soon as he caught his log up, he switched it on.

The radio was alive.

"They oughta have to make an appointment, just like everybody else."

"They checkin' logs, driver?"

"Dope. They lookin' for dope."

"That leaves me in the clear!"

"Me, too."

"Are Marlboros still legal?"

"Regular or menthol?"

A lady's voice: "Fuck 'em! I thought we were in America!"

"You on the wrong planet, girl!"

"Line's movin'."

Bull shoved in a gear.

The lady's voice again: "Why are they waving that tanker through?"

"They're using a profile."

"They not stoppin' everbody. Just Mexicans. An' white boys wif' fine-looking bitches in the cab."

They're stopping just the niggers, boy."

"Bullshit, they wavin' me through right now. Sayonara, honky asshole!"

Bull moved up the line — only three trucks ahead now, with a couple RV's pulled over along the guardrail beyond that — the area at the side of the interstate bright with portable lights and generators. The dogs looked black, with square heads and tan markings. Two of them. Rottweilers? Bull turned to Janey. "Shit, they're waving out another one. Get in the back and pull the curtain. Like you're sleeping if they bust in here."

"Bullperry! This is America. I can sit right here!"

"Janey, they got a profile."

"Not with me in it!"

"Believe me. With you in it."

Two officers, no hats, dark flak jackets, signaled the truck ahead of them out of the line and back onto the highway. Bull nodded to them, smiled, gave a little wave, and began to pull out himself but both of them snapped their red-coned flashlights at the rear of the Mayflower household moving-van already parked at the guard rail along the emergency lane. Bull shrugged his shoulders and pulled up behind it, and jerked on the air-brakes.

"Shut her down! Shut her down!"

"Christ, Janey, I told you!" He switched off the engine and rolled down his window. The air outside here was not as warm as before but it was heavy with fumes and the noise of the portable generators.

"They didn't even see me. They already decided. Maybe they got an APB on us."

"No, no, this roadblock is a fishing expedition. Janey, I saw them look at you!"

"Bullperry, they spotted our goofy load."

The two cops moved down, frantically waving some of the trucks behind them out of the line and back into traffic.

Bull reached down and grabbed his 9MM. "I'm not going to jail. Not for a minute."

"Perry!"

"I heard what happens in there."

"Bullperry. We don't even know what they want. You heard? Didn't they lock you up last year when you killed that lady?"

"Shit, no, that was self-defense. Anyway, we all know what happens in jail and I'm not going."

"You'd die to stay out of jail?"

"Fucking A. I haven't been having that much fun, any-way."

"Getting fucked in the ass is not the end of the world!"

"You want to share what that feels like with me?"

Another ten minutes went by, and Janey persuaded Bull to put the automatic back under the seat. In the mirrors, Bull watched another truck get selected, a bull-hauler, and no sooner had it parked behind them they could smell it. One of the dog cops was called over to do a quick walk-around the cattle truck and wave it out of the holding line.

"That dog didn't alert on us when he went past."

"Bullperry, the handler has to let the dog know they're searching."

"Yeah? Well, leave it to you to know the important stuff in life. Once again."

A huge wrecker pulled off the interstate and parked ahead of the line, flashing lights blazing, followed by an Opelika police cruiser, and two county cars. The county-mounties had brought sandwiches, and a convention began, cops standing around in groups, so happy-looking — you could hear the laughter through the open windows — now an argument, one of the state troopers calling out two guys in D.E.A. flak jackets for letting their sandwich wrappers blow away in the breeze.

"That wrecker.... If a driver gets arrested they're not even going to let his company come get the rig," Bull said. "Fuckers. All these lights are making me sea-sick. Look, they're taking the cuffs off that driver up there so he can pick up their litter. Bunch of shit."

"I believe prisoners should work."

"Janey, what if it was you had dope on you? Does that make you a criminal?" Bull jerked lightly on the air-horn-pull and the horns blipped. All the cops turned to look.

"Bull, I thought you were afraid of going to jail!"

"Fuckers are taking a break and we need to keep moving. And I'm tired of looking at that yellow "Mayflower" on this trailer in our face. And don't you know that driver has an appointment to keep, too. This whole shit here sucks! Look at that old couple standing next to their RV."

Ten more minutes and some of the cops broke away, two of them, each with a Rottweiler, started on either side of the Mayflower truck. Before they could get to the van, the dogs were barking on each side of the dark-green cab.

"Oh, oh...." Janey switched on the dome light and got out her makeup kit and a small mirror.

"Janey, you're lighting yourself up!"

"They're not looking at us now. I've been waiting for this moment."

Bull watched as some flak jackets ran up to the K-9 cops at the Mayflower rig, their guns drawn.

"Out! Out! Hands over your heads! Hands up! Out! Out!"

"Black woman getting out my side," Janey said.

"Out! Out!"

"Some movers take their whole family along. To help load, pack..." Bull watched a thin, middle-aged black driver clamber down and get shoved to the ground, his legs kicked apart, another cop kneeling on his back and cuffing his hands together.

"They're cuffing the lady," Janey said. "Shit, there's kids getting out of the truck!"

The K-9 cop on her side, hatless, young, handsome, with a full head of neatly combed, blond hair, turned to look at Janey through the windshield. She lowered her mirror and smiled, and the cop opened his mouth and ran the tip of his tongue around it.

CHAPTER 10
Stony Hill Missouri

The first deputy to arrive at the scene was so worried about whether the high-powered rifle Uncle Ralph
had used was legal — Missouri having such a podge of
arcane gun laws — that Little Harold was able to sneak
into the ambulance with his mother when they hauled
her to the ER. The man did ask Kate some hasty questions while they were loading her but her throat was so
bruised she couldn't talk, and Uncle Ralph knew nothing
other than armed people had busted into his house and
were torturing his sister. Little Harold, who wasn't sure
how much he should say, was glad of his ambulance
rescue from the stage.

But they would be looking for him as soon as they
figured out he was the only witness who could tell them
anything. On the ride to the hospital, tight and secure in
there with the back doors closed and the paramedic
hovering over his mother, Harold decided he would
refuse to say anything to the cops without his mother
present. The two of them would be able to keep their
stories straight that way — his I.Q. didn't test high at
school for nothing — fuck 'em. All he had to do now
was keep anybody from finding out that the rolled-up,
paper grocery-bag at his feet had his .22-magnum High
Standard "Double-Nine" revolver concealed in it so he

could get it back home, and Moustache's blood-spattered cell-phone.

Uncle Ralph arrived at the hospital after dark, after the last cop had left the building and just as Kate was signing herself out AMA. On the walk back to the parking lot, Ralph's cigar stub did a dance around his lips as he talked non-stop. "I was out across the road when that new Caddy pulled in so I whipped out my old Alpine binoculars and saw it was a rental from St. Louis International, and..."

"You had your binoculars?" Little Harold said.

"Always, son. Anyway, that rental Caddy was the only thing I could tell those asshole cops, and then they asked me where it was like I should know where that old bat took it. They keep on hiring these kids out of the academy. I used to know every deputy around here, but now..."

"The cigar, Ralph," Kate said, as he herded her into the back of his ancient, camouflage, 1966 Land Rover.

"Jeez, it's not lit!"

"Mama, you can talk!"

"Shhhhh.... I didn't know what you were going to say in there. That's why I couldn't write, either, with that headache. The headache I've still got."

Uncle Ralph slammed the tinny-sounding door on them and got in behind the wheel. Although he was a little stockier than Axel, it was the longer hair and the moustache which set him apart as Kate and Axel's half-brother. But his rap was the same, and he seemed to be pissed but trying not to show it. "You guys ever consider just telling the police the truth?"

Kate's voice was gravelly but clear enough. "Didn't you just tell us they confiscated your rifle?"

"Yeah, but..."

"What kind was it, Uncle Ralph? The whole middle of that guy was all over the yard!"

".375 H & H mag elephant gun. Legal."

Kate laughed, then held her head from the pain. "Did you tell them about the machine guns you haven't had time to register yet?"

"No!"

"I still got my revolver, Uncle Ralph. Your old .22 mag Double-Nine." Harold smiled in the darkness, the paper bag on his lap, and listened to the starter rasping the Land Rover's trusty four-cylinder to life. He decided if the phone in there rang, he would answer it.

"Good thing these seats are metal," Kate said. "You didn't bring me any clean clothes."

"Nobody told me you pissed your pants." Uncle Ralph pulled out his old army Zippo but changed his mind about re-lighting the cigar.

"I pissed the bed in your guest-room, too."

They passed by Kate's abandoned, out-of-gas pickup, which Ralph said he'd stopped for on the way to the hospital, to push it farther off the road, and then he went on and on about how it was a good thing he had the good stuff, the illegal stuff, the machine guns and recoilless rifles, stashed at the McKay Trucking terminal now that the BATF was crawling all over his house.

"Can't we be honest with the police about those guns?" Kate said.

"Yeah, yeah, touché."

The Land Rover didn't go very fast but Uncle Ralph didn't like to use the brakes much, either, and Kate and Little Harold braced themselves for the anticipated, gravel-slinging turn into the McKay Trucking entrance at highway speed. But at the last minute he had to hit the brakes hard to miss the Cadillac Sedan DeVille chirping rubber on the way out, the old lady's stony face just above the steering wheel, her octagonal-lensed spectacles glinting back the glare from the Land Rover's Lucas headlights.

The office was a shambles, and both computer monitors were on.

"Dial 911," Ralph said.

"Phones are dead." Little Harold looked at his mother, and hoped that the stolen cell phone in the bag didn't ring just now.

"Not before you get your crazy gun collection out of here!"

"Oh. Yeah...."

Ralph picked up the nearest phone anyway, just to see. "Dial tone!"

"They cart off everything for an investigation nowadays, and I've got drivers on the road!"

"Yeah, right...."

Little Harold laughed. "They even have gun sniffing dogs!"

Okay, okay! I don't know anything about what's happening, anyway."

"No you don't, dear half-brother."

"We don't either, Mama!"

§

Little Harold was sitting on the edge of his bed and jotting down the three, speed-dial numbers he found on Moustache's phone. He had turned off the AC, and outside the window of his loft, bugs and moths were dinging into the metal shade on the yard-light over the front office door. The peaceful, summertime sound was suddenly broken by the loud, machine-gun rap of the Jake-brakes of a semi on the highway, slowing down for the entrance. Harold looked out and watched the lights of Axel's big, green Kenworth anteater swinging in. His uncle was pulling a load of steel pipe chained *and* strapped to the flatbed trailer, Axel's trademark security overkill. Harold slid the cell-phone under the bed before deciding what to do. Axel was good to him, like Ralph was, sometimes like a real father, but Harold knew better than to rush down as soon as he arrived without giving him a little breather. No telling how far he had come and how long he'd been behind the wheel without a break.

A long time, apparently, because through the floorboards Little Harold could hear the bitchy-whiny sound which Axel turned on whenever he was tired and pissed. And Harold's mother's voice just as plaintive as her brother's, mumbling at first, then both of them loud enough to hear.

"The load wasn't insured? Kate.... The whole rig? Just liability?"

"Well, you've been no help!"

"I'm out there driving all day and night and all week and all month! It's my company, too, and I could be sitting here on my ass in an air-conditioned office while you get out there and jam gears!"

Little Harold was on his hands and knees now, an ear to the floor, when Axel quieted down.

"What happened in here? What happened to your neck?"

His mother would never hold back any of the facts from Axel, and Harold listened to her tell her brother what had happened. She even admitted to taking out the first two rounds of his pistol one day, when Harold was away, to make it safer. A mistake, she knew now....

Harold decided to come down the stairs when the conversation switched to Bull Schaffner.

clump...clump...clump... Down the wooden stairs he had fallen on earlier. "I think Bull's okay!" Little Harold said.

Axel was wearing a white, McKay Trucking, uniform shirt — shirts he had to buy himself — and he went back to whining. "Yeah, well, I don't think we know enough about him. How do we know we're better off with him than with the cops? And we're supposed to give him title to the best tractor we've got when he's done? And if we owe him the tractor anyway, what's in it for him if he recovers Denver's load or not?"

"And our new lowboy," Harold chimed in.

Axel groaned.

"I've already warned him we might not be able to pay his fifteen percent..." Kate cleared her throat. "...and that the tractor he's driving would be part of the settlement if the company goes under."

"Like I said, Kate! What's in it for him? Jeez!"

"He loses his new tractor if we go bankrupt, right, but why would he turn over their Airstream and their lowboy until they hand over our stuff?!"

Axel groaned again. "For money! Kate, this guy Bull has you eating out of his hand. You've been swallowing too much of that driver you have a crush on, too. Benny. His dick is rotting your brain. I mean, apparently they want their shit back badly, right? So why can't we just swap rigs and be done with it? Can somebody explain that to me? Kate? Harold?"

The mother and son looked at each other.

Axel raised his voice another notch. "Well? You know? A swap? Huh? duhhh.... Nobody can explain that? What's been going on here? I can't expect some sense around here when I'm away? Unbelievable! Harold, fuel up my rig for me. I've got to catch a nap. My load's gotta be in Indianapolis in the morning." He looked at the two of them. "It's a **paying** load!"

As Harold bounced through the door to Axel's truck, he heard him say, in a lower voice, "I'm sorry you got hurt, Kate. Your neck going to be okay? Your throat? Hope so, for Benny's sake. Just kidding. I'm sorry..."

Harold wanted to get up into Axel's Kenworth and get going toward the fuel dock before the man changed his mind about his driving the big KW, especially in the dark with half the yard-lights burned out. Axel loved this tractor. He called it "Jezebel", and if he was in a good mood when he pulled in he could sometimes be heard singing a line from the old Frankie Laine song as he was getting down from the cab: "If ever the devil was born, without a pair of horns, it was you, Jeh-hez-uh-bell, it was you-u-u-u...."

CHAPTER 11
Opelika Alabama

The search of the Mayflower household moving truck ahead of them wasn't going well, even though the dope dogs had alerted on it. For a few minutes, all of the cops in view were concentrating on the thin, little black driver and the huge, well-fed black woman they had cuffed and made to sit on the ground, their children of all ages running around screaming. Comments and laughter accompanied the items flying out of the open cab doors — tacky stuff tossed out by the search party inside. Tightly taped, plump, fully-packed, disposable diapers were hitting the pavement with dull thuds. Giant brassieres and tent-sized panties floated down alongside flapping PLAYBOY and PLAYERS magazines, caught in mid-air by the officers standing around, and ZipLoc blivets of food leftovers which they dodged.

"Janey, go! Now, while they're busy. Get next to the old couple with that RV."

Janey didn't require much prompting and she was out in a heartbeat. Bull watched her stride over there, glowing and alive in the portable halogen lights — so sexy for thirty-five, he was reminded — and Bull marveled at the ease with which she struck up a conversation at the old couple's RV. He squinted his eyes and realized there was a large hose running from it.

They're pumping out their holding tank!

War on Drugs.... Fuck!
Janey looks so good for all those miles....

Show time. Bull tensed as the two K-9 cops and their dogs approached his Pete, splitting up to the sides. The dogs sniffed around the cab just under the windows, then were moved back past the sleeper to check out the lowboy and the Airstream. Nothing. Bull had forgotten to breathe and he opened his mouth to catch up. In the mirrors he saw the two cops linger near the Airstream door and discuss the problem. The problem being, Bull suspected, that his unit fit the profile but the dogs had not alerted.

He jumped at the sound of a police whistle. They were motioning for Janey to come back. Bull watched her cool expression, her finger pointing to herself, like, who, me? Her confident stride toward them, right up to the fucking dogs. Dangling her purse right in the nose of one of the Rottweilers. Was her .38 in there? Did she have a carry permit? Bull didn't know.

A loud knock on his door. "Out!"

Bull eased on down. He didn't have to pretend to look angry, but he tried to keep his mouth shut.

"What's in the Airstream?"

"The owner's clothes. Or his mother's clothes and stuff. Some spotted-owl sandwiches in the fridge...."

"Mind if we search your cab? Who's the lady?"

"Yes, I mind. And the lady is my sister."

"Sister, huh. Can you prove that?"

"You carry papers on your sister?"

"You wanna be a smartass I can send you up for a sex change."

"You can't do shit to me that won't end your fuck-ing career. The Airstream's been sold to a United States senator and you don't have probable cause. Think about it."

The man tried to remain unfazed but Bull had no-ticed the almost imperceptible twitch.

Shit, which senator? What name?

"Tell you what. You brush the excess hair off your dog, I'll get out, you let the dog poke around in here for a minute, and we're gone. I got a schedule to make and you don't have a fucking appointment.

"No, no, not so fast. We're going to have to pump out the holding tank in that RV you're hauling."

"Oh, get real! Listen. My sister has this Persian cat that's trained to use the commode. The tank's full of it. Think about it. Persian cat shit. Islamic cat shit."

"Step down please?"

The Mayflower situation got worse when the DEA and the local cops began arguing about it. But they al-lowed the children back inside finally, and uncuffed the wife and the driver. And as soon as there was room, they ordered Bull to pull the Airstream up far enough to reach the pumper hose. Janey hopped up into the cab with him.

"It's the tanks, Bullperry. Full of dope. Gotta be. There was really grody stuff coming out of that other camper. Looked like empty pill bottles floating around in the turds and tampon inserters...."

What are they doing? They straining it for God's sake?"

"This guy was just poking around in it with rubber gloves on. I can smell it in here!"

A loud whistle outside, and Bull set the brakes and shut her down again.

"Out! Out!"

"I don't believe this."

The cop who had run his tongue at Janey when they first arrived was all over her as she stepped down, and Bull hurried around to her side.

"Driver, will you pull out your holding tank hose, please?"

"No! I don't know anything about these things and it's not my fucking Airstream! It's just a load to me. You want to fuck with somebody else's property pull out the hose yourself. I don't even know where it is!"

"There had better be one." The cop wiggled his eyebrows at Janey and turned toward the camper and crouched down. "Good, it's on this side."

In another minute, after the hose was hooked to the septic pumper, the pump engine began to speed up and whine.

"It's empty!"

"The valves turned off?"

"Valve's on. It's empty!"

Janey whispered in Bull's ear. "We're dead. It's why the toilet wouldn't flush. There's no water in there, either. The tanks are full of dope."

"Dope, dope, I'm tired of it. What kind of dope? Marijuana? Cocaine? Heroin?"

Two of the officers went inside the Airstream and Bull tried to follow them but was strong-armed back out. The old guy walked up, leaving his wife at their trailer.

"It must be new," Bull said to him. That's why the tanks are empty."

"Or they're full of dope."

"Aw, come on!"

"It's not new," the old guy said. I'm going to guess this beauty's at least ten years old. Been rebuilt. See? This tag? Classic RV, Irvine California, see? When they're done with it, they're better than new. I'd rather have this than a new one. Probably has a new interior, too. Saw one at an RV park last month the guy said he put in 20 grand on the paneling alone. Imported from France. I wouldn't have these 12-ply tires, though. Too hard. These were made for moving big house-trailers, You can haul a five tons a piece on these! If it were me I'd put the tires that belong on it. Smoother ride." As the old guy rambled on, Bull noticed Janey stepping up into the Airstream and getting away with it.

§

"They're dumb," Bull said as he idled the big Pete out of the emergency lane and waited for traffic. The air-conditioning began to cool and he rolled up his window and used the air-switch on Janey's. "They didn't even look at my log, or my CDL or the manifest for the Airstream. Nothing!"

"They were thinking about me. Anyway, I don't guess your phony manifest is our problem." She waited for him to pull out and get up to speed.

"Duh. Problem?"

"I was waiting for you to get going. I know you only have one channel left. God, I hope I don't smell like shit and fuel all night. There wasn't any air back there."

"Problem?"

"Well, yeah, but.... Well, since there's no dope in the Airstream, and one person's already dead over this, then they think we've got the kids."

"Two little rich kids."

"I'm not so sure. They weren't being guarded very well...."

"And the more I think about it, we need to get a percentage. From either side. In other words, when we find 'em it's finders-keepers. For a while. At first. If we can get away with it. You know...."

Janey sighed, loud enough to be heard above the rumble of the big CAT four-and-a-quarter and the whine of the turbo as Bull speeded up.

"Janey, was that your everybody-else-is-so-dumb sigh?"

"You've got too much spit in your harmonica, Bull-perry."

"Thanks."

"How long before we get to LaGrange?"

"Before midnight."

"I was hoping to get there earlier."

"Those tits the kind when you lie on your back they still stick straight up?"

"Yup!"

"My favorite kind."

They crossed the Alabama-Georgia line in silence, and Bull reset the trip-odometer to zero for the fuel tax report. He half expected Janey to request a stop at the Georgia welcome center, for a restroom break, but she kept quiet. He figured she was thinking about his question. Her boob job. Well, let her think. No way was he going to fuck his own sister.

CHAPTER 12
Homer County Florida

After the woman hung up, Annie looked around in the dark to see where Harry was before deciding to shove the portable under a nearby pillow in one of the corners. The unit had a loud ring, which Bullperry had adjusted for them once, but that was then and it was loud again. The night was dark — no moonlight coming in — not that a full moon helped much with the bedroom windows overgrown with vines. Annie sighed, and picked out a spot to burrow back to sleep in, fishing in the dark for her favorite pillow. The bedroom was wall-to-wall mattresses on the floor — all the way to the door — covered with pretty blankets and stuffed animals and pillows of all sizes. Eccentric and Sixties-hippie looking, but clean. Most everyone outside the family, upon seeing the arrangement for the first time, claimed to wish they had the guts to do the same thing with their own bedroom at home. Yeah, sure.

Harry stirred from underneath a pile of covers near the air-conditioner. Quilts which, in the morning, would be bright heaps of color and flower-power, sprinkled with teddy-bears and other stuffed toys.

"Annie, you can't have a conversation like that and then hang up without telling me."

"Thought you were asleep. I think it was the wife from Miami."

"The wife?"

"Bullperry's wife. The old one, not Dianna. That's what she sounded like, anyway. Old. Foreign. It had to be the Miami one, yeah. Wanted to know where he is. Important. Death in the family."

"So it's important but she didn't say which wife? Leave a number?"

"Harry, they don't know there's others."

"We don't know that."

"We are guessing that, Harry!"

"I heard you say you didn't know where he is."

"Well, we don't! And tomorrow I'm opening up all that mail in his old room. It's been piling up and I keep on telling him to take care of it and now he's off again somewhere."

"To Atlanta."

"We don't know that for sure."

"With Janey, too. That's neat, after all these years. Perry and Janey doing something together. I don't know about opening his mail, though."

"He was warned. I'll tell him I couldn't hold it any longer. I'm a woman and I feel for these other women. I'm his mother. And I'll tell him — and this is the truth — his mail pile was giving off these vibrations. It had an aura."

"Oh, good one, Annie. He'll like that excuse the best."

CHAPTER 13
LaGrange Georgia

"The kids are probably gone by now," Janey said. "Either found by somebody, or reported by somebody, or they just walked in hungry somewhere, or..."

"Jeez, Janey, it's not a whole day yet. Seems longer, though, like two days." Bull was idling the big Peterbilt at the stop-sign on State Road 219, the turn signals blinking for the turn to the bridge over I-85 at Exit-2 at LaGrange.

"You could have made it between that pickup and this pokey garbage truck," Janey's eyes squinting at the garbage truck coming up, it's headlights on brights. "Okay, after the garbage truck."

"It's hard to get this rig turned and hauling booger, Janey, shit! And the lowboy doesn't have any ground clearance. If I don't dodge all the potholes it scrapes bottom."

"Yeah, yeah.... The guys I rode with never made a big deal about all this stuff."

"It's the smell of free pussy does that. Free tit, all hot and spitty. Besides, it's hard to talk and drive and get a blowjob at the same time. Shit, now there's a dumbass four-wheeler pulled up right behind us and if we roll back — how's it look now — I can't see over there with this road angled." Bull glanced into the mirrors again, for the first time a little irritated at seeing the same, goofy sight: the Airstream RV all shiny and reflecting lights and looking out of place chained to the lowboy.

"Go, go!"

Bull pulled out and made the swing, and in a few seconds they were across the interstate overpass and making the right turn into the truckstop.

"You remember where you parked last time? We just passed the entrance."

"Back row. Here and in Atlanta, actually, the back row. And we're going in the exit so I can back into a slot from the driver's side down there." Bull looked from side to side as the rig rolled past the garage bays at the end of the building. After spotting his previous parking place from the night before, he pulled into a front door slot in the second row. "Don't panic, dear sister, but I can back straight in from here. Easier. I remember that tree in the field behind. This is it."

"Not much going on here."

"Shit, it's near midnight!"

"Yeah, but..."

"Middle of the night."

"Okay, but where are the dope dealers and hookers and stuff?"

Bull groaned. "Janey, we're in the country!"

"Yeah, but people like to fuck and get high in the country, too!"

"They fuck their wives!"

"Oh. Yeah. Okay, but it sounds boring...."

"Yeah...." Bull backed the trailer at a creep, and looked to the sides to see how far back the other rigs were parked. Keep it lined up. Professional like.

"That why you have more than one wife? Not as boring?"

"Yeah. No! There's more to it than that. Well, that too, but.... Remind me in the morning to pull up to the gas pumps in front. Gas up the generator on the Air-stream." Bull, satisfied the rig was lined up properly, pulled on the air-brakes.

It was not as humid and warm as the night before, and only a few of the trucks in the lot had their engines and the air-conditioners running. And the rigs on either side of them both had windows rolled down and the sleeper vents cracked.

Bull clambered down to the ground and lowered his voice when Janey got out. "The way I see it, if kids that age hang around the restaurant all day, eventually somebody will mention it to a cop and we end up without 'em. If they've been hiding in these empty lots and stuff around here, they might've seen us pull in."

"Repeat." Janey also spoke in a hushed voice. "You repeat yourself, Bullperry. All the time." She wrinkled her nose. "Sure smells like piss around here."

The two of them jumped when the generator on the Airstream fired up.

"Shit, Perry! Can't we switch that thing off?"

"You said we should leave a light on in there while we sack out, and lights take battery power, and the kids are used to the air-conditioner being on, so...." Bull climbed back up into the cab and handed out the dresses he had found on the top bunk when he first found the McKay Trucking unit No.12. They were still in the dry-cleaner bag, which Janey had crammed into his closet when she moved into the other. "Stick these in the Airstream while you're at it. Might make 'em feel better if they see their own stuff."

"There's already some dresses like this in there.... Hey, we could run into the restaurant, too, and get some chow to leave out for them? You know, like we used to do when we were kids at Christmas, leave cookies out for the reindeer?"

Bull groaned, and looked up at the sky. The stars were out. "I've got it, Janey. Listen. We get some take-out food, break it up in small pieces, and leave a trail across the parking lot to the Airstream door. But get this. We save some for dribbling just inside the door, and leave a trail all the way to their bed."

Janey snatched the dry-cleaner bag out of his hand and stomped off toward the RV, turned around suddenly and came back to him. "I'd cuss you out right now, Bullperry, but we have to act cheerful." She lowered her voice to a whisper. "We have to act friendly and kind. Like a sweet couple, you know? Two people the kids wouldn't mind being with. Who knows, they might even be watching us this very minute." She leaned forward, puckered her lips, and pecked her brother on the cheek.

§

There were not many drivers in the restaurant, and just a few clean-up people. The way they all were talking it seemed everybody knew each other, too, including the waitress, an older woman this time with silver hair. And none of them gave Janey a second glance when she and Bull picked a table and sat down. Plus there was a young blonde floating around and talking to everybody, the heels of her cowboy boots clacking the floor when she walked, her brand-new jeans tucked into them, the big, silver belt-buckle gleaming, the red-plaid blouse poking out in front like she was wearing a bra forged from steel. So many truckstops seemed to have one of these polished-looking, cow-girl blondes, and despite his years on the road Bull could never quite figure out who and what they were — whether they were drivers or hookers or local chicks with nothing to do — all he knew was that it wasn't anything he ever wanted. Simply not his type. Too plastic, or too fresh-looking. Bright, blue eyes without a hint of bedroom in them. But what ticked Bull off most was the way all the other men in the room would be captivated by this face polished-like-an-apple, and the platinum-blond shit. He would never understand it.

The blonde caught his eye and gave him a wink and a little wave of the hand as she clicked on past to another table, behind them, where three drivers were sitting and drinking coffee.

"I saw that," Janey said.

Bull shrugged and shook his head. My sister Janey.... Older, yes. Sexier, yes. Sultry, fucky, sister Janey. Before he could stop himself, he leaned forward across the table and whispered: "I'd fuck you before her any day." His face flushed and he straightened up. "If you weren't my sister, that is."

"Oh? Thanks!"

"Forget it. Just a figure of speech. It's not going to happen."

"I don't see why not."

"I grew up with you for chrissake. We bonded when we were little or whatever happens there. I'm not interested. Even if I wanted to I wouldn't be able to get it up for you."

"Bull, Perry!"

"It...is...not...going...to...happen. Ever. When we get back to the rig, you're sleeping in the top bunk. And don't even think about climbing down after I'm asleep and sliding in."

"Okay!"

Heads turned. The blonde laughed her tinkly, Christian, Christmas tree ornament laugh.

"They heard what you said," Janey whispered.

"Fuck'em.

§

They were walking back to the rig with two take-out burgers, wrapped separately in white paper, for the little girls.

Janey said: "Whoever owns the lowboy or the Airstream could spot it here."

"We're still a ways from Atlanta."

"I got my Smith. In my purse...."

"I got my little .22 on me."

They had just rounded a tractor in the first row and didn't know a man was standing beside it, close enough to hear. He was shaking off the last drop, and when he heard them he tried to shove it back in and stick the other hand into a back pocket at the same time.

"For bad guys," Janey smiled.

The man looked blank, or shocked at this gun-toting doll who had appeared out of nowhere. But he kept a hand in his back pocket until they passed by.

The Airstream, so shiny even though the lot lights were not working, was reflecting reds and bright ambers from the clearance lights of trucks in the next row. Janey was first up to the door of the Airstream and she turned to Bull with a surprised look, her hand on the locked doorknob.

She whispered. "Bingo!"

"Already? Woe!"

Bull walked up and tapped lightly on the door. Nothing. Janey held up the white paper-wrapped burgers to the window in the door, at the small opening in the drapery, while Bull went to another window to see if he could angle a look in. He was sure he had left a light on at each end but the one at the rear was out now.

"They're scared, Janey. Tell you what. I'll get back to the cab and you see if you can talk them out, or get them to open the door for the food. Shit. We forgot to get drinks."

"There's water in the fridge. Okay, scoot, Bullperry."

Bull went back to the cab, the big Cat idling so faithfully, hell, it was his tractor now, he was sure. Piss on Dopey and Denver and all these other assholes, and as he climbed up in he looked back one more time. Janey — a walking fuck-movie — his sister — on her toes at another window, holding up the hot-off-the-grille hamburgers. He didn't wait, though, but he was picturing it. A slender, brown arm sticking out the cracked door, a little, brown hand grabbing the food.

He moved quickly between the seats and back into the sleeper compartment, pulling out his small medicine stash first and sucking down a shot of the Jack Daniel's whiskey he kept disguised in the hydrogen peroxide bottle — oh, so good — and then off with his shoes and socks, his jeans, his shirt. He wanted to be in and under the covers before Janey came back. Quickly tearing off a couple paper-towels, he doused some rubbing alcohol on them and sponged the sweat off his cock and balls, careful not to get any on the tip, which would burn like hell. Fuck! He forgot to brush his teeth. Well, this one time.... No, he would not be able to sleep without brushing his teeth. He grabbed a pair of shorts and his flip-flops and climbed down on the passenger side with the toothbrush in his mouth, eased open the tool-box door on that side where he had stored some bottled water from his parents' deep well, and went to it, spitting the foamy toothpaste onto the asphalt, hearing Janey's voice back at the Airstream, so gentle. A quick rinse and he was back inside. Just in time, too, under the covers as Janey opened the cab door on her side.

"That was almost too easy. But you're right. Scared as hell."

"What'd they say?"

"Nothing. I got an arm, a hand.... You wouldn't believe how quick a little brown hand can grab up two burger bags with one snatch."

"You saw both girls?"

"One right next to the other, just like in the pictures. Just for a second. Kind of cute. But they'd never
fit those two dresses from the cleaners."

"No? You sure?"

"Well.... I didn't look that good, but I'd say the
dresses were for girls a little taller and thinner."

Bull sighed.

"I know, baby brother." Janey sat down on the
edge of his bed, bending to keep her head from hitting
the bunk above.

"Off!" Bull said.

"I could make it all better...."

"Off!"

CHAPTER 14
LaGrange Georgla (continued)

Safely under the covers, Bull was on his side and facing the back of the sleeper while Janey undressed, with his bunk light turned off to make it easier to sneak a peek if he changed his mind.

"I wonder what the girls are thinking. All alone in there."

"They're scared, Perry. We need to do something about getting the water tank in that Airstream filled, too. No shower, whew, well, us, too. I don't know how you do it every night, Perry. You rent a shower at truckstops often? Maybe not this one, but.... It true what Mama says? You wash your balls and your dick every night and with alcohol? Even at home?"

"Yah, yeah...."

"Do you keep it shaved?"

"I quit doing that."

"But you feel everything more, right, when you slide it in, with it shaved all smooth."

"Janey! The stubble feels like broken glass. Can we change the subject?"

"Your wife tell you that? Ha ha. Okay, I'm ready to climb up. No peeking!"

"No peeking? That's a switch!"

"When I climb up. You know, that cellulite you mentioned back at Mom and Dad's, well.... But you can peek at this!"

Bull turned. Janey was leaning forward, her head under the top bunk and her new tits dangling right over him. Bull's mouth opened in amazement, and he wished he had left his reading light on. They were perfect, full and tight and pointy, with dark, protruding nipples. He avoided looking at her face, his sister's face, to avoid spoiling the rush.

"Nipples like..." Bull's voice choked off. "Like lug-nuts!"

"Best clinic in Mexico. Okay, turn around while I climb up."

But Bull did not turn away, and he watched Janey boost herself part-way up and then swing a knee up onto the top bunk. He couldn't see much but he said: "First white girl I ever saw with left-hand threads."

"What?" Janey disappeared into the top bed.

"Asian girls have left-hand threads. Did you get re-barreled in Mexico, too?"

"Bullperry! You like my Democratic bikini trim?"

"Democratic?"

"No more Bush."

silence....

"You didn't get it."

"I got the joke, jeez, it's a million years old. I'm just thinking...."

"Changing your mind?"

"No, no.... I'm thinking about the next step." Bull tried to picture the kids in the Airstream but all he could see was Janey's nipples.

Janey switched out the top bunk light. "Next step?"

"Yeah. We got the girls, and now it's time to call Dopey."

"Dopey...."

"That's what Little Harold calls him. The guy who called the terminal and pretended he was Denver."

"Denver...."

"The missing driver! Duh, Janey! Jeez...."

"You told me already, right? Okay. I even figured it out. You haven't been able to figure out anything yet! Okay. Dopey. The reason he called that kid, Little Harold? The reason he called him Fatty and stuff is because he beat it out of Denver that the kid is chubby, only Denver didn't give out his real pet names for Little Harold, see?"

"Beat it out of him?"

"It had to be that way. How did you get along without me all these years?"

"It's been a walking death, Janey. Anyway, as soon as it's light I gotta call this dude, and I need you to make sure the girls don't take off again."

"Yeah, well, the sooner we get to that Atlanta truckstop to meet this guy, the better. Get it over with."

"No! We can't go back where I took the rig. Hell, I was glad to get out of there the first time. Think about it. There's a confrontation. Maybe we flash guns. It's a crowded place and there's phones everywhere. Somebody calls the law. The other dude turns up with papers on the trailer and the Airstream, and we can't. I go to jail. An Atlanta jail. Uh-unh, Janey. We have to pick a better spot to meet. And bob-tail there after we hide the lowboy. And it's not just the Airstream and the girls we have to worry about, it's the missing McKay trailer."

"What does the load look like?"

"Well, their lowboy will look something like this one but with two, big four-wheel drive farm tractors on it, chained down one behind the other. They're probably painted red. Massey Fergusons. Made in England."

"Okay. I need to know what to look for, too. We'll be fine. We're a team, now."

"Exciting...."

"You'll be fine, you've been through worse. That woman you shot last year — she the only person you killed?"

"I'm not going to say!"

"You think I would tell anyone? Jeez...."

"It's not just that. Look at all the cops who are proud they never had to discharge their weapon. Professionals."

"Tell me about that woman. Did you have to? Harry said the newspaper pictures of her she's beautiful."

"Dad would. Yeah, she was something. In fact, no joke, as soon as I laid eyes on her it was love, Janey. Love at first sight, like a knife stuck in my chest, I mean! It almost got me killed. My prejudices, too, like here I am waiting for this hijacker to show up, assuming it was a man, in fact I could almost picture him from his MO, and this chick comes in wearing a slick, beige suit and carrying a briefcase — long, wavy-black hair, like an Italian — gold earrings, thick, bushy eyebrows and this straight nose and her eyes were like dark fire looking right at me and I'm standing there, duh, thinking, you know, I've finally met the woman of my dreams, and she lays the briefcase down on the table, pulls out an automatic with a silencer on it just like in the movies, and turns it on me! If I'd have waited one more split-second.... I mean, I emptied a whole clip into her I was so scared. One of my first rounds nicked her gun or I'd be dead because she got off two shots herself. Big fucking ten millimeter. Found out later she was Portuguese.

"I'm horny."

"Janey!"

"Mama says your wife in Miami is real old. What's her name?"

"Mrs. Perry Schaffner."

"Bullperry...."

"Her name's Connie."

"How old?"

"She's seventy something."

"And you're legally married?"

"Yeah."

"Why?!"

"It's what you would do."

"Which is?"

"Okay. She has this big house on two acres, right in the middle of Kendall, Miami suburb, I mean, gorgeous! Real tile roof and two stories with a basement — imagine a house with a basement in South Florida — and a guest-house, a big pool, and a four-car garage."

"And...."

"And it's all paid for."

"And...."

"Okay. When I get home, which isn't often enough except I was there last week, she treats me like a king. The maid does my clothes, we have a big dinner like in the wine commercials on TV, she has a lady chauffeur who is related to the maid who drives us to the theater or to the foreign film club, stuff like that, I mean! Plus, I'm in her will!"

"Wow, Perry! Can you park the truck there?"

"No, I have a place to park it in Miami and then I take a cab, or if she knows ahead of time, the driver picks me up."

"Yeah, but what if she lives forever?"

"That's okay!"

Bull felt movement, but it was Janey leaning over, hanging her head over the side and looking at him. "What about sex? I'll bet she wants to get laid the minute you get there."

"No, not really.... She usually asks if I want something to eat first."

"No fun, huh?"

"Ha! You wouldn't believe!"

"Try me."

"It's embarrassing."

"Go for it. I tell **you** everything."

Bull hesitated. It would be easy to pretend he wasn't enjoying this conversation, having Janey here, considering all of the hostility they had shared over the years, evident during every reunion at their parent's place. How many years exactly since they lived together as kids? His mind seemed to be blocking the math — the calculation refused — over fifteen years, anyway. Well, as Harry was always saying: "Be here now." Or: "Enjoy the movie before the lights come back on."

"Perry. The sex?"

"Okay. Usually just once a visit, on the first night, and that's okay, but it's not what you think. Sometimes when I'm on the road I think about it and I get hard."

"And? Jeez, Bullperry!"

"Okay, after dark, she has this room — originally the dining room — and there's this narrow, polished-oak table in the middle of it, and all these portable candles on iron stands you can move around, like in Dracula movies, I mean, that's what I see before she blindfolds me and straps me down on my back, and then she goes down on me while she's still standing next to the table with this music in the background, harps and shit but just perfect, the candle-light flickering through the blindfold, until I can't stand it anymore, and then she climbs up on top and I pull on her old tits with my teeth and stuff and I explode."

"Wow!"

"Tell anybody this and you're worm food."

"Hey, there's hope for me, if she's twice my age."

"If you say so."

"I met Dianna once."

"Yeah?"

"At Mom and Dad's. She's so sweet! Kinda young, too, I thought. She must've been jail-bait when you married her."

"Yeah."

"So when do you see her?"

"When I have a run through West Virginia."

"Which isn't often, the way she tells it. Why did you have to marry her? You don't have to marry any of them, do you? She says you're real possessive, too. That right? Ha!"

"Hey. She inherited forty acres in the mountains with a stream running though it, she's beautiful, she's mine, and nobody else is going to fuck her. Got it?"

"Okay!"

"And she loves me."

"Okay! What about the one in Wisconsin? Milwaukee. The one with the three kids."

"The last kid's not mine."

"Why should it be? You're never there! You ever think about the ones that are? Yours?"

Bull didn't answer. He was back to thinking about where to move the rig in the morning, and how to handle the phone call to Dopey.

"Perry! Your shaved dick. I was thinking..."

"Janey, jeez, forget about it."

"Remember when we were kids how Mama would leave books out, like, you know, by accident, hoping we'd look in them?"

"Huh? News to me."

"Oh, come on. Dad did it, too. Don't tell me you didn't know they did it on purpose. Okay, like that girlie magazine Harry had of only black girls and you would sneak it in bed and look at it?"

"Yeah, but he had that book hid."

"So you could find it. He was trying to explain to you about Ivory."

"Hmmmm...."

"Yeah. And that book about sex, from India? Mama's? That's how I lost my virginity."

"Johnny Smalls, that old fart."

"No, no, that was after, fucking for money he was the first."

"So who was first? A broom handle?"

"Close! Remember that story about this cult in India where these girls, on the first full moon after their twelfth birthday or something, they have to go out at midnight and get in line to sit on this short, iron spike on this altar in the garden, how shiny it looked in the moonlight, with this little curve to it, shiny metal showing through the blood running down?"

"Oh, yeah, I remember."

"Mama left that book out on purpose."

"Bullshit. She say so?"

"No, I just know!"

"Uh huh."

"See, you're the dumb one, Bullperry."

"Maybe."

"No offense."

"Yeah, sure, Janey.... I remember reading the book, though. I can still see that scene. That iron horn on the altar in the garden, in the moonlight, polished and smooth from all those centuries of use."

"Centuries?"

In the darkness of his bunk, Bull grinned.

CHAPTER 15
LaGrange Georgia (Morning)

Bull had trouble sleeping — usually not a problem when he was tucked away inside the coffin-like sleeper bunk with the comforting vibration of the faithful diesel idling. The trouble wasn't Janey, who was sawing logs above him — the trouble was knowing the two children were in the Airstream alone.

About 3:00 AM he felt movement back there again, and noticed Janey wasn't snoring.

"Janey, you awake?"

"Yeah. I felt it, too."

"I felt them go out a couple times, or get back in, while you were asleep. Snoring."

"I snore?"

"I thought about padlocking it from the outside, but..."

"They have to go out to pee. Somebody must've told them not to use the toilet, with no flush water, you know. The commode was clean when you picked up the trailer, right? They must be pretty good kids."

"They're good kids, and you snore."

"I thought of something else, Perry. That bulldog puppy was acquired recently. There's nothing for pets in the camper, no food, you know, no flea stuff or dog dishes...."

"Yeah? Well, if I can't go back to sleep I'm going to sneak out in a little while, early, and get over to the restaurant before it gets crowded, and make the call to Dopey. I gotta take my laptop in there and use the computer to dial. So if you see I'm gone, you know, see what you can do to reassure the girls."

"Yes, papa."

"Ask them what they want for breakfast."

"I can handle it, Perry. I'll pick up the restaurant check again, too. And get something for the dog. You're the one I'm worried about."

"I'm not going to take any shit off anybody."

"And I don't snore."

§

In the bleak, pre-dawn silence a nearby diesel cranked up, and at another part of the lot, airbrakes released and a stiff gearbox engaged. A few drivers heading out early, either to beat the Atlanta rush-hour or to get another day's driving in before hunting another place to park before dark. Bull hit the Jack Daniel's in the peroxide bottle again (for good luck with Dopey), slid into his well-worn jeans and the shirt from last night, pulled on clean socks and the black Reebok originals (the same kind Little Harold was proud to own), and eased on down from the cab with his laptop bag. He had seen that Janey was already out but was surprised at where he spotted her. She was barely visible, standing with the two girls — their white dresses glowing in the gray light — in the middle of the vacant field behind the parking lot, all three of them looking down at something.

§

Bull snuck off and rehearsed himself on the way to the restaurant. After ordering breakfast, he pushed the table phone up off its bracket and wired in his laptop. It took a couple minutes for him to program the dial-out sequence for this joint, and Bull hoped the kitchen was slow this morning. A young driver sitting not too far away, big cowboy hat and Fu Manchu moustache, was watching every move. Bull said: "This Eastern or Central time here?"

The driver either didn't know or didn't want to talk, and Dopey picked up on the second ring. He said: "Speak."

"My name's McKay. Who are you?"

"McKay, huh." There was a long pause "And?"

Bull was pissed, and not a little intimidated, this guy with the rough, whiskey-throat voice acting like he was doing people a favor by answering his phone.

"Ralph McKay. I'm the guy put your dummy out yesterday."

"Speak up, I've got important shit to handle here."

Bull raised his voice. "Your big guy. In MO. Fat. Moustache. Dead."

"Oh, I get it. You're afraid I'll miss the funeral. Well, the only one I've been to lately I had a reason. I knew the guy inside the box was still alive, okay? I don't know that inanimate biped you snuffed — I don't hire bottom feeders — and I don't know you. All I want is the Duplan lowboy and the Airstream."

"And the two girls."

"Grind those two Twinkie-brained pubescents up for dogfood."

Bull hesitated. He wasn't ready for someone this bad, with brains and a vocabulary. And if the girls were worthless...

But Dopey saved Bull the squeeze. "I didn't mean that about the kids." His voice had switched to gentler-kinder. "They're going to fuck the whole thing up if we are not careful. Getting on my nerves. Making me edgy and unpredictable. Keep that in mind."

"Fuck you. What do you mean: 'if **we** are not careful'?"

"Right. We. You want to go down with that jerk you shot? Or do life for kidnapping little girls? Or do you want to make some money. Your call. I got other shit on the grill here. Where are you? I have you down for La Grange, Georgia."

Bull's heart jumped. So much for CallerPD.... Maybe it was the restaurant phone set-up. The local dial-out.

Dopey continued. "That caller-ID from Missouri was bullshit? Uh-huh, had to be, well, you fucked up and I'm not sure I want to deal with a fuck-up. What'd you say your name was? You fly from St. Louis to La Grange?"

"We call you 'Dopey'."

"Sticks and stones. You ready to deal?"

"Did you beat it out of Denver, that our dispatcher kid was fat?"

"Denver?"

"Our driver."

"I bought him a six-pack, okay? Ready to trade?"

"Our lowboy and two Massey Ferguson 4-wheel drives."

"And the two girls."

"Right."

"Don't forget to feed 'em."

"Where?"

"Down here. Your load was headed for Florida City, right?"

"Uhhhh.... Yeah."

"Down here. You head on down, give me a call back when you're near..."

"Bullshit. How do I know you have our stuff. You drive our shit up here, park it at the Atlanta TA, no, I'll tell you later where to park it."

"I'm a broker, not a dumb-ass driver."

"I know where the girls are, you don't."

"Yeah, but I know who they are and you don't. You think this is some fucking game? You head on down, give me a call back when you're near enough to Miami to know your ETA. That'll give me time to get a tractor and a driver lined up. Then we swap, I check to see if the two pickaninnies are still breathing, we shake hands, I never see your redneck ass again."

"Pickaninnies? Fuck you, Dopey."

"Okay, I apologize. Little black females with potential. Come alone."

"Be there alone with ten grand. For my travel expenses."

"Ten grand?"

Bull waited for the man to finish, then heard the *click* — the hang-up. When Dopey had repeated "ten grand" Bull felt the immediate and distinct sensation he had surprised the man. Was it too much? Or worse?

Only ten grand?

§

The sun was a bright, fuzzy ball in the fog at the horizon. Half the trucks had departed while Bull was in the restaurant, and he found Janey cutting across the lot toward him. Janey, a glorious sight in the silvery haze. They met in the middle, where nobody could hear.

"Janey, we have to boogie. He knows where we are. And he's making out like he didn't hire that guy who kidnapped Kate." Bull explained the telephone conversation, and the meet down south.

"How do we know he has our trailer?"

"Same thing I told him."

"And?" Janey did not wait for an answer. "Jeez, Bullperry! We go all the way down there and we don't know shit what we're in for?"

"Yeah, but I know South Florida like the back of my hand."

"You got us a cemetery plot down there, too? Next time, I do the talking!"

"Woe! Get all hot about it, Janey, why don't you."

"Yeah, well I don't see how you get through life. Fspecially your jobs. Or why you do it."

"Luck and adventure. They go together, like Dad always says."

"Oh?"

"You know, he says if you don't lead an interesting enough life your angels switch to another channel?"

"I remember...."

"I believe it. It's why you are still alive. But if guardian angels had remotes and didn't have to get off the couch to change the channel, you'd be history, Janey. Where the girls?"

"They're hiding in the trailer. I told 'em I'd bring their breakfast back. The dog is dead. I'm looking to borrow a shovel. We're going to bury it after breakfast."

"And then we have to get back on the road. ASAP. Are they going to accept me? The girls?"

"Hey, they recognize you. When that guy was beating on their puppy they saw you beat his ass."

"Just one kick is all, doubled him over, knocked the wind out of him, put him down on the ground on his knees."

"They told me they saw it. I'm sorry I called you a wimp yesterday."

"Mmmm - hmmmm."

"You're still dumb, though. After you left him there, he got up and finished off their dog."

Later, Bull watched them eat, in the Airstream, Janey putting on her best mother-hen act, well, maybe it wasn't an act. It looked real, her continual fussing over them, fixing up the ribbons in their hair, frequently bending over and kissing the tops of their wooly little heads. A wonder, since she never talked about her own kids.

The girls were sitting at the dinette, their short legs dangling in white socks and patent-leather black pumps, with straps and silver buckles — so cute. They didn't talk much, and refused to give their names. A shake of the head and a hand over the mouth is what you got if you asked. They seemed to be close in age, but not twins.

"Remember when we were kids Janey, in Miami? That food-stamp family Mom and Dad were always talking about? The kids all the same age and the adults couldn't keep' em straight? Some of the kids were aunts and uncles to each other?"

Janey nodded, along with one of the girls.

"She your aunt?" Bull said.

A shake of the head but the other girl pointed a finger to herself.

"You're the aunt?"

A nod, and another mouthful of a bacon, egg, and cheese biscuit. Crumbs raining down on clean, white dresses. Janey leaned over for the umpteenth time to dab at them, their clothes, their mouths. Bull thought they were too old for that, but....

"Somebody told you not to tell your names?"

Nods. "Mama."

"You know where you live? What city? What town?"

"Mmmm - hmmmm."

"Where?"

Vigorous shaking of heads.

"Your puppy — can you tell me his name?"

Janey protested. "Bullperry...."

"Pele." "It's a girl. Pele."

Janey said, "Pele? That's a nice name."

"Janey, Pele's the fucking volcano goddess in Hawaii."

The girls' eyes brightened. "Mmmm - hmmmm."

"When we got her she throw up."

"On the kitchen floor."

"Twice."

"So Daddy call her 'Pele'."

The girls looked at each other. "**Your** Daddy call her 'Pele'." They looked at Bull. "Mama call her daddy 'That Foreigner'. An' she call'im 'The Alien.'"

The other girl said: "**Your** mama."

Janey and Bull looked at each other and smiled.

"They're Americans, Bullperry."

"Yeah...."

The whole deal was coming to a head, soon, and nothing turning up made sense. And he should've known the J. B. Hunt driver would take his frustration out on that puppy. It seemed no matter what he did good always turned out bad.

"You guys finish up. I'll go and see about borrowing a shovel."

"No, I'll go, Bullperry. Nobody's going to let a stranger who looks like you just go borrow their shovel."

CHAPTER 16
Homer County Florida

Annie awoke to pencils of light streaming through the breaks in the overgrowth outside the windows of their bedroom. She crawled for the door and got to her feet after crossing the last of the mattresses, then stumbled, ugly-naked, down the hall to the coffee maker in the kitchen. Harry would already be out there opening the chicken coop and changing feeders and waterers, no, by this time he'd be down one of his trails to the reefer patches. There were so many patches now because they had to be small — just a couple of plants in each to fool the air surveillance — so much more work than in the old days when they grew it in one place and simply moved the garden hose from row to row. Water from a gasoline-powered portable pump which they could leave right out there — just cover it up a little — during dry spells. Instead of carrying water every day, all they had to do was bring out a gallon of gas. The good old days.

They could just give up growing reefer. They were both old now, and got tired easily, but Social Security simply wasn't paying them enough to live comfortably. Without the cash crop there would be no more vacations out west in the Fall, or to The Keys, selling dope along the way. Three-hundred dollars an ounce for the good stuff, the buds, packed and sealed to dope-sniffing dog perfection.

Harry and Perry often talked about how they would never go to jail, or never be taken alive. Not for reefer. Not for a fucking plant. So they kept their guns clean and they'd practice together. About that shooting it out with cops bit, though, Annie wasn't so sure — about herself.

Harry would say: "If more pot-heads would stick up for their rights, like our soldiers do for other people in other countries by shooting people, the War on Dugs would be over."

She lingered with her coffee in the doorway of Perry's old room, the door partly open, the sign on it in two-inch letters:

The name is "BULL"

The stacks of his unopened mail beckoned to Annie, and she was just about to dig into them when she heard the chopper. That sound, or that of the spotter-plane that flew over sometimes, always gave her a stab of fear. Harry, too, said he always felt it. A stab in the heart that actually hurt. It was the possibility that one day they could be caught red-handed. Harry's admitting to experiencing this painful adrenaline-burst of fear is what kept Annie convinced he had every intention of shooting it out and going down, right here at home, before they could cart him off to a life of chains and courtrooms, and eventual death in prison.

With Annie, that decision would depend on her mood at the time, and she thought about it as she got dressed. Jeans on "over my blobby old ass" (Annie spoke to herself more and more as the years went by), "shirt on, fuck underwear, socks on..." As if she were giving orders. "Boots on. Pistol belt." No need to check if her piece was loaded. All of their guns were always loaded.

And then, on the way out the back door, Annie saw that Harry had left the pistol he usually took with him hanging on the nail. In a way, seeing that was not a relief.

He was nowhere in sight. The sun had not cleared the treetops yet, but bright shards of it found passages through the brush to flash Annie in the eyes when she looked East. She could hear the chopper off in the distance making a turn, a low bank, and heading back. But it was what she saw when she looked down their driveway that made her heart jump this time. The plain, light-blue car parked there, blocking it, nobody inside. Another stab in the chest.

Feds....

Annie pulled her shirt out of her jeans and let it flop over her pistol, holstered on her right side, and looked back toward the house. Just a flicker, but did something move there? Slink behind the shed? Cooter?

Annie pulled her .45 single-action revolver and walked briskly toward the shed — her thumb on the hammer ready to cock it and let loose — surprising herself with her determination.

Fuck these people, this is my place!

You honk when you pull into somebody's driveway, Mister!

Annie rounded the shed and stopped. On the other side of it was a woman talking into a cell-phone, no, it was a little radio, like a walkie-talkie. Like the VHF they used to have in their boat. She was small but tall for her size, and wearing a thin dress. Her back was to Annie and she was looking up, looking at the chopper which from the sound seemed to be coming straight for them although Annie couldn't see it yet for the trees. The woman's left shoulder seemed to sag from an obviously heavy handbag slung from a strap, and her hair was in a large, tight, silver-gray bun. Suddenly the chopper was over them bap bap bap bap but not as low as the spotter planes usually flew, much higher, actually, and the lady was clapping a hand over one ear with the radio up to the other. Annie stopped in her tracks and shoved her revolver back into the holster before the woman turned and saw her.

Old-timey glasses with silver arms — octagonal lenses — not even a flinch when she saw Annie standing just twelve feet away. Cold eyes through the lenses, then a smile. She dropped the little radio into her bag and did some shoving around in there without breaking eye-contact. Annie was looking her over, noting that she was not hurting for money. The dress, the shoes, the rings....

Perry's wife....

The old, rich one in Miami.

"I'm Perry's mother," Annie said. "Annie."

"Yes, well, I see I missed him! Perry?"

"Yeah, well we still call Bull that out of habit." Annie recognized the lady's foreign accent from the phone conversation the night before. The Miami wife. Annie said: "I noticed you use 'Bull' on your letters, the envelopes." And then Annie's mouth hung open for a moment when it dawned on her that Perry's wife had hired a chopper to look for him, him or the truck, probably thinking he's cheating on her, doesn't even know he's married to somebody else and has kids, good thing she didn't spot him with Janey — who would believe that Janey was his sister?!

But they couldn't just stand there. Annie wanted to invite her inside the house but she'd have to find an excuse to close Perry's door. All those other letters....

"You want to come in?"

And then if Harry suddenly came up she'd have to clue him in immediately so he wouldn't give anything away. Perry was probably in this woman's will.

"Yes, thank you."

Annie led her toward the back door, glad she had not had the time to get high this morning. What did Perry say her name was? Connie? Annie waited while the woman stopped on the way to look at the cedar, wood-fired hot tub Harry had made years before, and the string-bag hanging from a bungee cord in the middle so you could reach up and get stuff while you were in the water, like another hit on the water pipe.

"Water pipe," the lady said, smiling, so kindly now, nodding her head.

Annie wondered how much Perry had told her. And about his boyhood.

"Water pipe," the woman repeated, with her strange accent, and pointing to the cobweb infested mess in the string-bag. "The old days. Hash oil, grass five-cents a match-box, LSD."

They were still standing at the hot tub. Annie said, rather wistfully: "LSD twenty-five...."

"I can still get it, you know, yes."

"You can?"

"Yes. Pure LSD-25. Not that Ecstasy shit the kid's think is tripping. No, pure Sandoz. Out-of-you-body shit go back to The One, go direct to The Big Movie Screen, sit and watch movies with the Gautama."

Annie could hardly believe her ears. Exactly! And she stepped up and hugged this new find, Perry's wife, such a neat old lady! When the woman hugged back her arms seemed thin, but thin like steel rods, and that's when Annie felt the huge, weighty bulge in the woman's purse, a big gun, and the purse was half-unzipped, well, a shock but just for a second. After all, the woman had just bumped into her own gun, in the holster under her shirt.

"Come on in, sister. I mean, daughter! Oh!"

"I'm old enough to be your mother, you know."

They both laughed.

"Connie, then."

"Connie?"

"Well, I can't call you 'Mom'!"

CHAPTER 17
LaGrange Georgia to I-75 South

While they were trying to pull out of the LaGrange truckstop, Bull was muttering to himself and casting sideways glances at Janey, sitting there so fucking calm, so perfectly made-up, pursing her lips at the windshield all the time. It was taking forever to find a gap in traffic so he could make the right turn onto Hwy-29 to pick up 27 south to I-185 to Columbus — bunch of shit, these goofy roads here — how can a no-place backwoods country highway in Georgia have a morning rush-hour, anyway — must be food-stamp day at the HRS office — and he shifted into neutral while he was waiting and then ground a pound when the hole he was looking for came up suddenly when a string of three vehicles all turned off without signaling, dumbass Twinkie-heads! Dropouts!

A racial mix of kids at a mailbox down the highway, waiting for a yellow-jacket, a school bus. Janey waved but one of the kids spit. A boy. White. Wouldn't you know.... Big man, big man.

A half-hour later, when they were finally humming along nicely down I-185, Bull took it out on Janey.

"That ringtone you downloaded. Did you have to get one sounds like somebody sucking on the windshield?"

"Perry, I didn't download that. I recorded it!"

Bull shot a sideways glance at his sister. "You rec-orded kissing your toilet tank? You do that while I was busy helping the girls? Burying that dead little bulldog puppy? Well, that was time well spent!"

"Jeez, Perry! What's the matter? You so out of shape you got sweaty digging that hole?"

Bull diddled with the air-switch and ran the window up on Janey's side. He didn't want any more hot air in-side. Maybe he was a just little out of shape — just a little — it had been days since he last worked out — and right at this moment he felt strange and also weak — a feeling which came on often and without warning when he felt powerless and stressed out — and he was glad they were out on an open stretch of road so he could relax and get his shit back together. Do some deep breathing. Forget about Janey.

He said, "What were you doing back in the sleeper when we were done? Looked like you were rearranging all my stuff. Thought you wanted to be there when we put the dog in the hole."

Janey sounded uncommonly patient. "You didn't call me when it was time."

"Looks to me like you're moving in here perma-nent. And that new ringtone goes before you get off this trip. Before we get back to MO."

"Well maybe by that time I'll be glad to be the fuck out of here."

"You need to. You watch. It'll be just my luck I meet some real fox now, and the minute she sees you..."

"You're married!"

"Uh! Janey...."

silence....

Bull didn't feel well. Maybe he was going to be one of those rare cases where you get Alzheimer's early. The feeling he would get sometimes was just the way this old driver was telling him one day, the day the man's company asked him to consider retiring, after he was tentatively diagnosed with the 'heimers.

The first signs you get come and go. It's like you leave a loading dock or something and you get to the main gate and you can't remember which way to turn, where you are, where you're going, you can't remember your fucking name.... So you sit there and wait for all that shit to come back so you can get rolling, and when you do you still don't feel right. Something's missing. It's like something just ate a piece of your brain. You feel like you're watching a movie of yourself.

Bull broke the silence. "Janey, you really don't have anything better to do, do you?"

"What do you mean? Sure I do! But this is fun. I love it. Besides you need me on this one."

"Good. You can buy the next load of fuel. You got close to a thousand bucks left on your card?"

silence....

Bull couldn't shake the feeling. They were trailing behind an old Toyota pickup now, lacey rust spotting through white paint and a beat-up camper top on the back, a combination which spelled-out "loser" to Bull every time he saw one like that. It was double-lane interstate and there was no reason not to pass the pathetic vehicle — 45 mph — oh well.... Bull banged the side of his head with a fist to get his brain back on line.

"Perry, I don't get it. If you don't know what you're doing, why do you do it? Huh?!"

Bull smiled. A key. He was doing what he had been doing all his life. Muddling through but with a spark of genius. Yup.

Nobody else knows what they're doing, why should I?

"For the money and power, sister Janey."

"Power?"

"Yeah. When I get paid, I have power over women."

"That sucks."

"Hey, go to The Lord with your complaints. I didn't create any of it. Myself included."

silence....

Bull could feel it. Janey had actually heard what he had said and was digesting it. The cloud was lifting. A cup of coffee would be nice, too. And then the cell-phone rang. It was their mother. Annie. While Janey jabbered away, Bull pulled out his raggedy "Motor Carriers Road Atlas" and propped it on the steering wheel with one hand, trying to open it to the GEORGIA page, trying to look up their route and keep the rig from running all over the paint at the same time, the map all marked up from previous trips with notes he had written in where all the good truckstops and restaurants with truck-parking were. The big rig fell behind the old pickup a little more, 44 mph, 43 mph, ho-hum.... Then Bull put down the map and hammered down to pass, grabbing the CB mike as they went by.

"Sorry-ass welfare loser motherfucker." Bull hoped the CB antenna on the little pickup was for real.

silence....

"You don't know what, do you?"

Bull set his jaw and tossed on the left-turn signals to pass a Mayflower moving van. He wondered if it was the same one that had gotten into all the shit at the roadblock the night before — unlikely — and as they went by Bull saw that the tractor was a conventional. Black driver, though, and the two drivers waved to each other, the black guy leaning forward over the wheel.

"That driver was leering at me."

"Oh, jeez.... He had to lean over to see who I was. When you're being passed it's hard to see into the other cab..."

"Yeah, yeah...." Janey had the map out. "I have a plan. We stop in Valdosta. For the day. Head for South Florida in the morning. Early."

"For the day...."

"I at least have a plan, Bull. We stop in Valdosta. We call everybody — Mama, Dopey, Kate — we work out our strategy. We rent a motel with a pool and we get the girls' confidence. We eat lunch and dinner. We rent a movie. What was your plan?"

silence....

Janey said: "Is there a motel with truck parking?"

"Well, yeah, but... Yeah, there is!"

"You sure sound happy about it all of a sudden."

Bull did not answer. But he liked that Days Inn motel, and the truckstop next to it, and the restaurant, and the waitresses, and... "Exit-4," he said. "Exit -4!"

Janey glanced up from her map and looked at him. "You got laid there once, didn't you. Stop. No need to

explain. That's okay. I understand. Good boy, Perry.
Good boy."

CHAPTER 18
Valdosta Georgia

Bull hoped she would get over it soon — worse than being married — his sister pissed off, ignoring him, but smiling and doting on the girls as they traipsed by him, hauling some of their stuff from the truckstop parking lot over to the motel, the three of them laughing as they hopped over the concrete curb, then Janey turning back to Bull and hissing: "The damage is done, Perry!"

He was making his second trip from the tractor to the motel, carrying the laptop and his suitcase when they crossed paths again, in the motel driveway at the side, just as a city cop came roaring up and slamming his cruiser to a stop not five feet away, door half open, waving his arm through the open window for them to stop. A big black guy with a thick, shiny, sweaty neck, shaved head and no hat, name tag said BEAUFORT. One leg on the ground now, white sock in a shiny-black shoe on the hot pavement, the sun directly overhead. He appeared to be riffling through a stack of faxes with one arm still poking through the window, the hand making dangling, lazy circles at the four of them to indicate they were to come closer. The faxes he was flipping were stapled together at one corner and had pictures on them.

Bull's armpits began to damp but Janey didn't miss a beat and was in the cop's face in a heartbeat, the girls right with her, one on each side clinging to a hand, the kids not particularly worried. Routine stuff to them, was what they looked like, the little black girls still in their white dresses and black patent-leather pumps. Bull winced when Janey spoke up, his spectacular sister leaning into the open doorway, her flaming red hair falling forward into this huge, armed person's face.

"Missing children? I don't think so!"

The cop grunted, expressionless, and without looking up from the stack of papers, he said: "Two little sisters? With you? I don't think so!"

Bull could smell himself now, the fear.

The cop grunted: "There's a reward. Don't move." He flipped another page over and found it, Bull getting just a glimpse of what he was looking at, a photo of two black kids together. The cop looked down at the girls and said: "Oh."

"Oh?" Janey said. "Is that all?"

"Oh."

The cruiser lurched forward an inch as the cop shifted out of PARK with the brake on, and they all jumped back. When the door slammed shut Bull could feel the woof of cold air rush out, and he watched the cop make a U-turn in the lot while rolling up the window, the man's face a shiny-black stone looking straight ahead as he went by.

"Perry, that was a scare!"

"What did they look like? The kids on the bulletin."

"I couldn't see. Two girls. Not ours, obviously."

A meek sort of voice came back, trying to sound as-sertive. "What makes you think I'm on welfare!"

"Because you don't work, fuckhead. People who work go the fucking speed limit."

Janey laughed and bagged her phone. "That was Mama."

"And...."

"You won't believe this but your wife is looking for you. The Miami one."

"Yeah?"

"Guess where."

"Janey...."

"She's at Mama and Daddy's. Even-as-we-speak, as you like to say."

"Bullshit."

"No?"

"No. Never."

"She didn't want to talk to you, anyway." Janey thought about it. And Annie telling her how Bull's wife had hired a chopper to look for him. "You sure? She wouldn't do that?"

"Janey, Mom's having one of her smoke dreams."

§

At 9:30am they were barreling through Columbus, Bull feeling much better now and keeping the big rig in the middle lanes, keeping it moving. 70-mph plus to keep up with the traffic.

"Best truck I ever had, yup!"

"While you have it," Janey said. She had been nod-ding off but was wide awake now and sitting up straight since they hit the city, her feet off the dash and back into her clogs. "When you were burying the puppy, did you try to find out where they live?"

"The girls? Yeah, no luck."

"They clammed on me, too."

"Listen, we're going to hit Highway-280 in a minute and take that to Richmond and then to, no, wait." Bull had to think. "Dawson. Don't let me start daydreaming and turn with 280 at Richmond. We're going to Dawson. We turn there on 82 to Albany.... Pick up I-75 at Tifton. Anyway, nobody will be able to figure out what route we're taking. Maybe we should skip I-75 altogether and head into Florida on 19, no, wait, we need to head to Valdosta."

"Bull, I don't have the faintest idea what you're talking about. You navigate, and I'll do the thinking here about getting this case figured out."

"Case, huh, ha ha. That's a joke."

"Case. They've got my cell-phone number now, too, I bet. Let them call us."

"Fuck'em."

"I told Mama to give my number to that Kate person of yours, too, okay? And we need to make a pit stop soon. And check on the girls."

"They should be riding up here with us."

"If you knock 'em in the head first. I tried to tell them, and I even tried to carry one up here, shit Bull, she was hanging onto that Airstream trailer door like a monkey!"

"Like a monkey, huh?"

"Well, I meant...."

"We know what you meant."

§

They hit I-75 at lunch-hour, traffic piling up near Tifton before they could nail the southbound on-ramp, and Janey furious with Bull.

"We've been running four hours without a stop!"

"Not four hours yet. And all that fucking road construction...."

"Four hours, and what if the girls have to go? Obviously they've been told not to use the bathroom in there and..."

"Okay, okay!"

"So are we stopping?"

"We're just now getting on the interstate! Shit! Okay...."

Bull had to wet a tire himself, and as soon as the rig shuddered to a stop on the shoulder, half-way up the on-ramp, Bull jumped down to the ground. Little four-wheelers were whizzing around, the vehicles honking now as Janey made it to the side of the trailer and the Airstream, looking more like a twenty-five-year-old than thirty-five to the lunch-hour drivers flying by, Bull at the side of the tractor tandems letting an overdue piss fly between the tires and the right-hand fuel tank, the heat from the tractor and the hot pavement blasting his face.

It was a long piss, and when Bull zipped up and turned to look back to see why so many cars were honking — the Doppler effect trailing away kind of tinny and weird with the pansy-assed, PC, Politically Correct horns modern cars all seemed to have nowadays — he saw that Janey had led the two girls out onto the grass, the three of them squatting down, the girls looking like two, big, white flowers with their skirts spread around them and Janey like a drunk chick in a bar parking lot, jeans shoved down off her bare-ass and drilling a piss-hole into the dirt.

Bull smiled. It was scenes like this which made his truck-driving life so worthwhile.

Walking around to the front, around the grille of the big Peterbilt, the engine idling and water dripping from the drain-pipe under the air-conditioner, he stood there at the edge of the hot pavement, looking through the windshields of the cars as they whined past him, little gas pedals mashed to the floor because the drivers had slowed down to rubberneck Janey's bare ass but seeing the truck driver now — holy shit — Bull staring back at them and grinning.

Fuck'em....

§

Janey said: "We're hungry." They were rolling down I-75 south of Tifton.

"We? We're?"

"Me, the girls, and you."

"We can pull in at the truckstop in Valdosta."

"That's almost all the way to Florida, Bull. We are hungry now!"

"Half hour from here. Valdosta. Florida line's an hour."

"Bull, Perry!"

"I've been up and down here a hundred times, moon-ass. And we can be down to Miami before mid-night. If we don't stop and fart around all the time."

"Miami to do what?"

silence....

"You don't know what, do you?"

Bull set his jaw and tossed on the left-turn signals to pass a Mayflower moving van. He wondered if it was the same one that had gotten into all the shit at the roadblock the night before — unlikely — and as they went by Bull saw that the tractor was a conventional. Black driver, though, and the two drivers waved to each other, the black guy leaning forward over the wheel.

"That driver was leering at me."

"Oh, jeez.... He had to lean over to see who I was. When you're being passed it's hard to see into the other cab..."

"Yeah, yeah...." Janey had the map out. "I have a plan. We stop in Valdosta. For the day. Head for South Florida in the morning. Early."

"For the day...."

"I at least have a plan, Bull. We stop in Valdosta. We call everybody — Mama, Dopey, Kate — we work out our strategy. We rent a motel with a pool and we get the girls' confidence. We eat lunch and dinner. We rent a movie. What was your plan?"

silence....

Janey said: "Is there a motel with truck parking?"

"Well, yeah, but... Yeah, there is!"

"You sure sound happy about it all of a sudden."

Bull did not answer. But he liked that Days Inn motel, and the truckstop next to it, and the restaurant, and the waitresses, and... "Exit-4," he said. "Exit -4!"

Janey glanced up from her map and looked at him. "You got laid there once, didn't you. Stop. No need to

explain. That's okay. I understand. Good boy, Perry.
Good boy."

CHAPTER 18
Valdosta Georgia

Bull hoped she would get over it soon — worse than being married — his sister pissed off, ignoring him, but smiling and doting on the girls as they traipsed by him, hauling some of their stuff from the truckstop parking lot over to the motel, the three of them laughing as they hopped over the concrete curb, then Janey turning back to Bull and hissing: "The damage is done, Perry!"

He was making his second trip from the tractor to the motel, carrying the laptop and his suitcase when they crossed paths again, in the motel driveway at the side, just as a city cop came roaring up and slamming his cruiser to a stop not five feet away, door half open, waving his arm through the open window for them to stop. A big black guy with a thick, shiny, sweaty neck, shaved head and no hat, name tag said BEAUFORT. One leg on the ground now, white sock in a shiny-black shoe on the hot pavement, the sun directly overhead. He appeared to be riffling through a stack of faxes with one arm still poking through the window, the hand making dangling, lazy circles at the four of them to indicate they were to come closer. The faxes he was flipping were stapled together at one corner and had pictures on them.

Bull's armpits began to damp but Janey didn't miss a beat and was in the cop's face in a heartbeat, the girls right with her, one on each side clinging to a hand, the kids not particularly worried. Routine stuff to them, was what they looked like, the little black girls still in their white dresses and black patent-leather pumps. Bull winced when Janey spoke up, his spectacular sister leaning into the open doorway, her flaming red hair falling forward into this huge, armed person's face.

"Missing children? I don't think so!"

The cop grunted, expressionless, and without looking up from the stack of papers, he said: "Two little sisters? With you? I don't think so!"

Bull could smell himself now, the fear.

The cop grunted: "There's a reward. Don't move." He flipped another page over and found it, Bull getting just a glimpse of what he was looking at, a photo of two black kids together. The cop looked down at the girls and said: "Oh."

"Oh?" Janey said. "Is that all?"

"Oh."

The cruiser lurched forward an inch as the cop shifted out of PARK with the brake on, and they all jumped back. When the door slammed shut Bull could feel the woof of cold air rush out, and he watched the cop make a U-turn in the lot while rolling up the window, the man's face a shiny-black stone looking straight ahead as he went by.

"Perry, that was a scare!"

"What did they look like? The kids on the bulletin."

"I couldn't see. Two girls. Not ours, obviously."

"Yeah, and it's a good thing ours didn't start running or screaming when he pulled up, too. Fucking cops."

"Notice how I handled that? If we'd both looked like you did when he stopped, like you just shit your pants, he'd have asked what we were doing. We got two kids here won't even tell us their names!"

"Fuck'em. We got stuff to do."

"We're going to the restaurant first," Janey said. The girls looked up at Bull, two pairs of lost-and-starving-in-the-woods Bambi eyes. They were nodding their heads.

"Okay.... Bring me back something. I got to check out some stuff. I'll be in the room."

"And you could've told me from the beginning Denver lived in Valdosta. You let me believe we were stopping here because it was my idea, and all along you were going to stop here anyway!"

"You didn't ask." Bull was surprised to see Janey was close to tears, and he backed off. "I'm sorry, it's just that..."

"It's just that without me you'd be up shit creek without a paddle right now."

"Right. Bring me some food when you come back."

§

Bull was only one day behind on his email, and there were just a few routine messages, plus this:

From: Pierretta Z. <pierretz@sis.it>
Reply-To: pierretz@sis.it
To: bullperr@jbaal.com
Subject: Airstream

Dear Mr. Bull:
LMK ASAP if you get msg.
Do not deliver Airstream to Mr. Ahearn in Miami.
We can make deal NQA. I pay cash double his offer.
I am the lady in the pictures with the girls.
RSVP ASAP
s/ Pierretta Z.

Bull stared at the screen for five minutes before realizing he needed to make some phone calls before Janey got back with his food. He would call Kate first, get a description of the lady who had kidnapped her, then his mother — check that out and see if it was the same woman — but Denver, well, why tip him off? Maybe just call to see if anybody was at home and hang up.

After hitting the bathroom for a pee he plunked back down on the bed nearest the window. The laptop screen stared at him with that strange message as he reached for the phone.

When Janey and the girls finally got back with his take-out, Bull punched the old lady's message back up. "Janey, you gotta see this."

She looked over his shoulder. "No mention of the girls...."

Bull said: "Italian email address, that's a surprise. 'Course she relayed this message from somewhere else — somewhere near here, I'll bet. What'd you bring me to eat? Oh, Janey, I called Denver's house and some-body picked up the phone, sounded like a teenager, and I got Kate, too, and Mom, and they both described the old lady in those Polaroid's. But the email came from

Italy. Maybe not intentionally to kill the trail but that's her regular address when she's not in The States? Harold, Kate, and Mama all say she sounds foreign but perfect English. Hey, check this out, Janey. Mom likes her!"

"You call Dopey?"

"No, it's not time yet. Little Harold is going to call him first, anyway. I discussed it with him when I called Kate. Oh, and my email address is in my computer file at McKay. That's how the old lady got it."

Janey was still looking over Bull's shoulder at the message. "Bullperr? You use the forbidden name 'Perry' in your email alias? ha ha." She snapped a finger at the back of his head. "Little Harold? That kid?! You're afraid to call Dopey yourself?"

"No-o-o-o-o, Janey. I want to check out Denver's place first."

"When?"

"Now. Soon as I eat. Take a cab. And when Little Harold calls Dopey he's going to make out like he needs to know where I am, like I'm his step-father or something, you know, and he misses me."

Janey groaned. "How old is he?"

"Thirteen. But he's a star. Going on fourteen. Harold is a little genius, well, a big genius. He's a tad overweight."

"This is such bullshit!"

"Keep in mind I have solved all my cases to date. All of them."

"With help from kids?"

"Even with help from red-headed, silicone-enhanced, deadbeat mothers."

"Well, if you ever do call Dopey, maybe one day, all by yourself, smartass, use my cell-phone. That'll blow the caller-ID. What do we do with the girls?"

"What do **you** do with the girls, shit, you're their mother now. You stay here with 'em. Stick 'em in the pool. Cool 'em off!"

"Fuck you, Perry!"

"You've been saying that since I was eleven years old, Janey."

"Well, you better hurry. I'm not getting any younger!"

§

The cab driver looked and sounded like an Indian, a from-India Indian, and Bull prided himself, like his father did, in his ability to distinguish races and nationalities by looks and accents and mannerisms,

"No, no! Pakistan! No India. Nuke India!"

"Umm.... Which are more beautiful? Indian or Pakistani women?"

"Pakistan woman very beautiful."

"How can you tell?"

"I know everywhere here Valdosta. You want tour? Cheaper than bus. Private tour?"

"I'm in a hurry. I need to go to this address." Bull, on the front seat, showed him the slip of paper he had written it on. "Now."

"Oh, I know place. Crestwood not far. Crestwood. Old house build in nineteen and fifteen. Valdosta very historic." The man seemed about thirty with a sing-song voice. "Very old, prosper city. Second city in world with Coca Cola bottle factory. Very special cotton grow here, Sea Island cotton, very rich. In 1915 Val d'Aosta was richest people in USA. Per Capital."

"Yeah, well, looks like Hooverville to me. This neighborhood, anyway...."

"In 1917 Europe have World War One. In 1917 Valdosta have Boll Weevil. No more Sea Island cotton."

They had turned off of Highway-84 and Bull had no idea where they were going. He wished he had checked a city map first. The neighborhood they had just entered looked ratty, 50's era, with chain-link fences and swing-sets in bare-scrabble yards, and those little plastic pools from Wal-Mart. Small, red-brick, matchbox houses with worn-out, dusty roofs shimmering in the heat. Harry used to say, when Bull and Janey were kids: "Red brick is the construction material of choice for rebels who dropped out of school and never got past the story of the 'Three Little Pigs'."

The car slowed to a stop.

"Here?" Bull looked for a number on the house.

"No, no. Over street."

Bull hunkered down in his seat to look across the street. Red brick. Swing set missing the seats. Plastic pool. The place had it all, but the chain-link fence was a cut above with an extra, large, double gate at one end. Bull could see the ruts in the grass behind the gate — from the sidewalk all the way back alongside the house — a parking spot long enough for an eighteen-wheeler. Denver's house.

Bull looked at the driver and noticed for the first time there was no meter. "This a real cab?"

"No, this is my cab."

"You could park under that shade tree. Make a U-turn. Wait for me there."

"Shade tree?"

"Oak tree."

"Oh, yes, live oak, yes."

On the other side of the front yard was a smaller gate, unlocked, and Bull stepped through that, looking from side to side for dogs. Before he got to the front door, he shouted: "Anybody home?" There were two, dead bicycles up on the front porch, and a charcoal grill which looked like it had been used recently — a smell of burned fuel and rubber — a can of starter fluid lying behind it on its side. He pounded on the front door. Bells, chimes, a siren, more bells.... *Somebody inside playing some kind of video game?* A girl came to the door, opened it right up, and beyond her Bull could see a woman with her back to him hunched over a joystick on the coffee table, the TV flashing colors and sounds, some kind of pinball game. To her left, hanging onto the back of the couch, was a big monkey, leaning forward toward the TV and watching every move. The animal took only one quick look at Bull before going back to watching the game. The TV suddenly said "Sorry!" — the digital voice not the least bit sorry — followed by the sound of a deflating balloon and a descending siren.

The woman said: "Shit!"

The monkey was the size of a cocker spaniel, and he was wearing a diaper. A nice sky-blue one, hole in it for the tail. "A monkey!" Bull said, sounding pleased with the discovery, trying to break the ice.

The girl said: "He likes to watch. He likes "Wheel of Fortune", too, stuff like that, but we have only one TV and when Mama has to play her game we can't watch TV. And the cable company shut us off, anyway. His name's Clive. I'm warning you, though — he hates nature shows." The girl shook her mane of limp, damp-blond hair, grimaced a half smile through too much makeup, and looked Bull up and down with half-open bedroom eyes. It was her best, early teens, woman-of-the-world look. She turned and motioned for Bull to follow her in. Short denim skirt and chunky-little meatball ass.

Bull stopped in the middle of the room, seeing there was a teenage-or-so boy asleep in another couch, hat over his head and an empty bag of potato chips on the floor at his side — could be either his or the monkey's — and Bull waited for the girl to announce his presence or something but she kept on going — past her mother still hunched over the TV and batting away at the keyboard beside the joystick — on into the kitchen.

"Ma'am?" Bull said.

"You have to wait!"

"Okay...." This time the monkey turned and eyed up Bull a little longer, baring his teeth and his pink gums, bubble-gum pink with black spots on them like watermelon seeds. He smelled like a moldy toilet-tank cover and his canine teeth looked sharp and germy.

The TV suddenly let out a blast of happy-sounding gongs and whistles. "Bingo!" the woman yelled. She jumped up and stepped over a cable running along the floor from the computer to the corner of the living-room where an old Coca-Cola vending machine had started to grind and clunk. A half-pint bottle of Jack Daniel's whiskey slammed down into the tray at the bottom, bounced, and plunked down to the floor. The woman had it snatched up before Bull could blink.

"He refills these when he's home," she said, sucking off the top third and screwing the cap back on. "He doesn't trust me to ration myself."

"He?"

"My husband, Denver."

The boy on the couch spoke, without moving or removing his cap. "If she's too fucked up to win a game, she's too fucked to drink more's the idea."

"You could help her," Bull said.

"Oh-ho! Yeah, right. When Dad gives orders, they're orders."

"My name's Marlene," the lady said, a smile on her thin, haunted face — but beautiful at one time, Bull thought — and she took another hit.

Without thinking, Bull said: "Well then couldn't he just order you not to drink so much?"

"Alcohol's a disease. Not the same thing. You must be Bull. You better be Bull."

"Bull Schaffner." They shook hands, so strange, Clive staring at Bull full-time now and baring his teeth and holding his tail in one hand. A thick, triangular wad of hair grew straight out his forehead and Bull thought he looked like a little Serbian, all that hair on top and peaked to a point between the eyebrows like Dracula. The long canines looked like they could suck blood, too.

"He told you about me? I never met him."

"Yeah, but he figured the company would send you, you know. Or send somebody."

"Will he be home soon?"

"Couple days maybe."

"You sure?"

"Listen, I've been married to him since the mountains were formed. Anyways he told me not to tell you anything. I'd offer you a drink but as you can see.... Hey, I could show you how to play the game. Score me another bottle and you get half. Deal?"

"Mom, the computer won't reset for an hour...."

"You could run me to the liquor store?"

"Sure, if you want."

In vino veritas....

They don't have a car.... Or Denver has it.

"I want. You can try to ply me. That right? Ply? Remember, though, not all drunks are dumb."

"They told me you filed a missing person report on Denver."

"Take me to the store first? Got enough for a quart? The old man takes all my money, too, so I can't buy more."

"Mom...." The boy on the couch was still under his hat. "He doesn't take your money. It's Dad's money!"

Marlene went on: "That was a mistake, the missing person thing. I thought he was cheating on me so I figured, well, put the heat on 'im 'til he gets his act together, you know?"

"He's not missing then...."

"I don't think so...."

Bull was afraid to blow this opportunity by offering to rush right out with Marlene, and he looked around the room, wondering whether the couch with the monkey, who had hopped down onto the arm-rest on the far side without taking his eyes off him, was safe. Or if it had fleas.... He couldn't stand there in the middle of the room forever, well why not, and besides, the pictures on the wall behind the couch, family stuff, were dreary but informative, and now Bull knew what Denver looked like. Thin and old, but wiry looking, smiling through a large, white, handlebar moustache. Full head of silver hair swept straight back. Another fucking Serbian.

Never could trust a man with a full head of hair....

Bull was thinking of what to say next, needing to gain some confidence here, some degree of comfort. He thought of: "Where do you get diapers with a hole for the tail?" Bull shifted his weight from one leg to the other.

"In the kitchen," the girl hollered from back there.

Bull looked in. There was a huge butcher-block with a stack of disposable diapers at one end, which the girl was unwrapping and spreading out. "I'll show you," she said. "Dad made this cutter out of a piece of pipe, sharpened on one end, but you have to hit it hard." She flattened out a diaper on the board, positioned the cutter about a third of the way up in the middle, and without taking her eyes off it she reached for a large mallet and raised it over her head. WHACK! The girl turned and smiled at Bull and poked the little round diaper plug out of the cutter with a long, red fingernail.

Bull said: "Excellent!"

The kitchen smelled like monkey-shit but the girl had a sweeter smell to her, like baby shampoo and sour milk, and her nails were not chipped like Janey's always were. The girl's fingernails were perfect.

"What's your name?"

"Lolita."

Bull blinked. "Yeah sure...."

"Really!"

"Uh-huh."

"It was both their idea. Ask them."

"Ever read the book?"

"No-o-o-o-o.... But I heard about it. I don't read much."

CHAPTER 19
Pussy

After his shower, Harry wandered gone-ass naked into the living-room of his vine-covered, moldering double-wide, grabbed for the remote, and plunked down onto a pile of huge pillows in front of the TV. It was 4:50pm-CT and The PBS News Hour was coming up. He wished he could get the BBC news via satellite but that was still on the wish list. The corporate propaganda on the local channels he refused to watch.

He was aiming the remote between his feet and was about to fire when Annie walked in. Dressed.

"Harry..."

"No cable, no satellite.... Anything good for supper?"

"Harry! Bullperry called while you were gone. Early this afternoon. Said the lady I thought was his Miami wife might be a killer. Good thing she left, huh?"

"His Miami wife's a killer? She must be, for her age."

Annie explained. She knew she had less than ten minutes before the sacred news came on and she took five. Harry was not impressed.

"Perry's always got some weird shit going. Janey, too. I couldn't live like them."

"You used to."

"That was then."

"It's then for them now."

"I didn't get high yet," Harry explained. He raised the remote. "Real life coming up. The news."

"This is real life. Here. Us. And Bullperry and Janey."

"Fifty wars going on — on our planet — this planet — at any given time," Harry's grip tightened on the remote, his thumb feeling of the "POWER" button, grazing over it, tentatively depressing it a little. "People getting blown away all over the place, civil wars, rebel soldiers betting on pregnant women whether the kid is male or female, then slitting her belly open to see. Sometimes more than fifty wars going on, sometimes seventy. Pure pussy! Better than watching sitcoms, that's for sure."

"I'll bring you a doobie."

"I'd appreciate that, wonderful wife." Harry leaned back into the pillows, his knobby, old knees sticking up from the plushness like bleached and scarred cypress stumps. He aimed the remote between them, and fired.

§

Back in his room at the McKay Trucking terminal in Stony Hill Missouri, Little Harold was ready for 5:00pm, too, when Kate would leave the office to make supper and it was his turn to man the phones. With only five drivers and rigs moving right now, and all of them called in and accounted for, he could take a chance and get online. He was supposed to be checking out the Mozilla email program for his mother to learn but he had more important things to do right now, like check Dopey's connections in Miami before calling him, stuff like Duplan Marine — they pronounced it Doo-plan, he had already learned — and check out the Duplan Waterfront Mission he had found, and the Duplan Seaman's Union — all those duplicate phone numbers — and if that went well, check out the HotnWetHispana web-site, get a better idea what Juanita looked like naked, so fine-looking this morning when he rode past her yard on his bicycle. He'd seen what a few blond girls looked like, just lucky glances, looking down their blouses — nipples didn't look much different from his own — but Juanita, oh, you could tell, there was serious stuff wanting to bust out of that T-shirt.

So pretty, her white teeth, that thick mouth and lipstick so red, smiling and waving at him. Him!

Little Harold tried to suppress the sudden erection growing in his jeans — like not thinking about Juanita would help — no luck. He would need to get serious tonight, not much time left with Axel threatening to call the law about the missing rig situation if Kate didn't, which would cut Bull out of the picture. But if he could find out stuff that would help Bull, real stuff, Bull would be saying later: "Yeah, if it wasn't for Little Harold here..." Then he could have that Kawasaki 4-wheeler, take Juanita to school on it, and to the creek after school. Be all alone with her under the willows....

Kate was calling up the stairs to his loft. "I'm leaving now. Don't tie up both phone lines! Oh, I installed that porn-guard program, what's it called, Net Nanny? So don't get any ideas...."

"Mama!"

"Just kidding!"

"I'm learning the computer for you, Mama! I got serious shit to do, anyway. I'm helping Bull. I'm gonna get a cut."

"Says who? Bull? Just remember, a cut of nothing is nothing!"

The screen door slapped behind her and Little Harold was down the stairs before the automatic closer could get the main door. He had downloaded and installed the latest version of FireFox the night before and he was ready this time, his search notes in hand, the hard-on for Juanita swelling again and asserting its authority.

He started with Google.

Search Results for <muchachas hot>

"Latin Ecstasy Hot Latinas Hot Hardcore!"

"Hundreds of Free Hot Hardcore Latina Pics These Hot Chicas and Sexy Muchachas, Latin Celebs, Latina Pornstars!!!"

"...young sex - porn whoppers - nude teens, lesbians, schoolgirls, lolitas, slutty frijoles, tight virgins ..."

"... Juanita's Spicy Sisters: we just love hot spicy cum! Lesbianas jovenes ... apenas amamos picante caliente cum!"

Little Harold stopped.

Juanita?

Well, that's a common name....

He clicked back to one of the previous sites and scrolled through some free photos, stopping at a dark girl with long, sleek, black hair. Hair like Juanita's. She was smiling and looking right at him while she sucked on a finger, and a firm, pointy tit was poking out from each side of her raised forearm, so fine!

Harold was sure that Juanita would never do that, though. Pose nude for pictures. Pose in front of the camera for other men, for money.

CHAPTER 20
Carrollton Georgia

Denver loved it, Abner's small, backyard enclosure
— an oasis of peace and beauty — the protective maze
of high, stuccoed walls with the razor-wire on top of
them overgrown with wisteria, grapes, ivy, and bou-
gainvillea. The small, heated bathing pool adjoining the
hot-tub, the 4-foot wide teak decks which led here and
there to the dressing cabana, the strawberry patch, the
tile-inlaid stone table and benches, the pole-bean
patch, the tomato patch, and the pink commode atop a
stepped pyramid.... Where else could be found so much
wonderful shit assembled and landscaped into one,
small, ghetto backyard?

The two, naked girls — so pretty kneeling there at
the tiled sides — were dipping their little buckets into
the bathing pool and pouring the water over Denver's
head, laughing with their strange, deaf-mute giggles.
The hair on their heads cropped close, their pubes just
showing the first signs of darkening, their little breasts
yearning.... Denver pulled one wooly head down and
kissed the girl on the lips, then turned to the other, with
a lingering brush of his palm over her protruding nipples. A passing whiff of chlorine and his feet touching
the gritty bottom at the poured-concrete corner.

"You quit doin' that 'fore you can' stop," Priscilla said, waddling her overweight, middle-age carcass out from the back door of the house.

"I know it."

"Abner's home."

"He comin' out or should I get out?"

"He comin'."

Denver grabbed for one of the girls, lifted her up over his head, and straddled her on his shoulders, a slender, black leg on each side of his tanned, white-haired chest, her toes tweaking the water. "I can feel your bare pussy nibbling on the back my neck," he said. "Ohhhhhhh!"

Other than their strange, girlish giggles, neither of them reacted.

Denver lifted her off his shoulders, turned her around, and gave her knotty belly-button a lick, raised her up some and got his tongue in there between her legs.

Abner stopped at the side of the tiny pool, loosening his tie, drops of water shining on his black shoes. "Deafer than termites, ain't they?"

"Abner, if I had me an extra quarter-million I'd keep 'em myself and to hell with Julius Duplan. Short of that, why don't I just keep 'em anyway."

"Yeah, and wear a Goodyear necklace for the rest of your life. Take about thirty minutes, I hear, the rest of your life."

"Huh?"

"After they mash the tire down over your head they pour just enough gasoline in it to roast your face off but not enough to kill you right away. Tie you to a telephone pole so you don't fall down. By the time the fire eats through the ropes and you fall, well, your head look like a chunk of roasted goat. Before the ants come.

"Goat...."

"Goats is big in Haiti."

Abner shucked off his suit jacket, carefully draped it over a lawn chair, and picked up a thin, green garden hose. He adjusted the nozzle to a fine spray and began to water the orchids cascading out of some hanging pots. "Got to bring these babies in every night, or Priscilla does when I'm not here, or she s'pose to when I'm not here.... So what's the problem?"

"I just called home. Guess what, the truck company, uh, McKay, has this private dick on my ass and the motherfucker stopped at my house. Went inside my house, took my wife to the liquor store and got her drunk and then leaves her with a fucking half-gallon of Jack. I got her on a rationing system but no, this fool has to come inside my house, override my rules, eyeball Lolita my daughter... He's dead, he's a dead mother fucker, Abner, dead. Dead, dead, dead!"

"Did she talk?"

"She don't know nothing. Well, yeah, she told him I came back to get my car after the asshole hijacked my unit in Atlanta."

Abner paused to wait for the noise of a passing truck to rumble by on the road out in front. Two trucks. The house was on a highway feeder near the end of the black neighborhood, near South Wire, the copper wire and recycling plant. After the trucks passed, all Denver could hear was the spray from Abner's garden hose and the *thump-thump-thump* of somebody dribbling a basketball in a driveway a few houses down, Abner long ago having bought up the houses on either side of him, renting them cheap to old people, couples with no kids and loud music. A plug of diesel fume briefly penetrated the fragrance of Abner's garden, then the passing scent of budding reefer from some distant marijuana patch.... So quiet back here, Denver with both girls in the water with him now. So pretty.

"You know what this P.I. look like?"

"No, but I got a good description of him when the company wrecked his tractor. His name's Bull. He's not a real pee-eye, neither, he's a fucking truck driver like me. In fact Kate told me we got four things in common, him and me, except I'm a lot older. Four things in common, she said. We're both truck-drivers, we both clocked too many miles, we both clocked too many beers, and we both never get enough pussy."

"Yeah, well, ain't that everybody?"

"No."

"I mean, the pussy."

"Hell no. I'm tellin' ya, Abner, people are always bitchin' about trucks and truck drivers and what a menace and all that but guess what. Ninety-nine percent of them got families they love and they're lonely on the road and they burn up half their pay on long-distance calling the old lady, and as horny and lonely they get they still brag on how they never cheated, I'm tellin' ya. Oh, these girls here got me so hard my nuts are achin'."

"Leave 'em alone then!"

"I can't."

"They make me horny, too, and I been gone all day an' they better still be cherry or we both be wearin' that necklace."

"They're so young, look, they blush when you finger 'em, blush pink right through those pretty black cheeks, look, now they're both blushin'. You sure they're deaf?"

"Deaf as dirt. You watch your hands, Bro, they need to stay cherry!"

"Yeah, yeah...."

"I'm gonna check soon as I change clothes."

"Check?"

"Yeah. Quit with 'em now, you're gonna go over the line here. We'll go down to Salmie's and pick up some hoes in a minute. Quit!"

"Okay! Shit...." Denver gave each girl a shove up out of the pool, his hands lingering down their legs as they got out. More of their deaf-mute giggling. Teeth flashing smiles at him, eyes bright.

"I'm gonna check 'em."

"I wouldn't know how to do that."

"Uh! You so old an' you don't know what a cherry look like? You never fuck a cherry? Uh! That must be a white thing." Abner laughed. Priscilla came back out and picked up Abner's jacket and Denver sank back into the pool with his big, white-meat hard-on.

"She's my slave," Abner said, giving Priscilla a slap on the ass when she went by. "After she marry me she got old and fat, and now she can't go back to the whore-house, no, she ain't got no place to go, now, she's my slave!"

Priscilla laughed on her way back to the house but Denver didn't think it was all that sincere. He lowered his voice. "She was a...? No, never mind."

"A hoe? Yup. Prettiest one in the state of Georgia. At one time. I was a fool for her then. I'm a fool for her now!"

"Yeah, but...."

"A regular wife, you think she'd put up with this shit?"

"Well, now that you mention it. Was she a junkie?"

"I never told you? uh! Well, one day I couldn't stand it, everybody fucking the object of my dreams, and I kidnapped her and chained her to the bed in the first house I ever bought, when I first got involved with real estate, and I cold-turkeyed her off all that shit, and then I moved her to that garage I used to have, the warehouse one I showed you a couple years ago, re-member? Had her locked up in there for three months until she was eatin' out of my hand. That's right, bro. Pure eatin' out of my hand. But she didn't know just how serious I was 'til these two guys busted in one night, and when I just happen' to drop by they'd already found her and they was standin' there gawking at her — I had her chained to the wall — and I killed bofe 'em before they could get their pants back up — with a crowbar — right in front of her — and after that I set her loose and she helped me get rid of 'em, that same night, and after that she love me as much as I love her. Forever and ever. You know forever and ever?"

"Yeah...."

"Don't sound like it."

Abner moved on down the walkway with his garden hose and Denver saw that he could get out of the pool now — he had pictured the crowbar and Abner and the blood splattering in that warehouse — he'd heard stories about how bad Abner could get but never before from the man himself — and Denver toweled off and wrapped the towel around his waist and went through the back door to the kitchen. The girls were in there with Priscilla, dressed already, in matching mint-green shorts and halter-tops, so pretty.

Denver said: "They're twins for sure, ain't they. They got that same Ethiopian nose, too, so fine."

"That Julius Duplan's fancy wife, that nose," Priscilla said. "She got her tubes tied after she had the twins. Permanent. Before they knew they was tards. Now she can't have no more."

"You know them?"

"Shit, no. Abner does." Priscilla looked down at Denver's towel, then up to his white-haired, wrinkled but tan chest, and shook her head. "I read the National Enquirer when they was kidnapped. After the Marines lef' and Duplan had to split."

"They're not retarded, are they? They're just deaf and dumb, right? I mean, if they had a chance to go to one of those special schools? Not tards?"

"Oh, they smart all right, I'm learnin' that real fast."

"So, what about, well, let's say after Julius Duplan gets them back and they can go to a special school and they learn how to write, hell, even talk — don't matter if it's in French or whatever language — and they get to tell him how we played around with them..."

"You think he's gonna get 'em back?"

"Uhhhh...."

"Well, nevermin' that, I want mine back, tha's for sure. Money runnin' out on these two, anyhow. She only pay me for one week."

"Well, I guess I need to be taking them with me then."

"No you don't. They not movin' till I get my own chirren back. And I know what's going to happen if that don't happen soon, too. Soon as Christmas they're gonna forget about keepin' they mouths shut and they gonna start talkin'. They probably talkin' they sweet asses off now!"

"Are yours twins, too? I didn't think they looked it."

"Twins, no. Same age, yes. The smiley one, Chessie, she's Mama's, and Tammy's mine."

"Mama's?"

"My mother. Chessie's my step-sister. But they was both born on the same day though. Twelve hours apart. Same hospital, same doctor.... Mama and me had a room together for a day. Now they send you home right after."

"Same father?"

Priscilla gave Denver a swat with her dishtowel. "Mama died last year and she never did tell who. Abner's Tammy's father, and he don' act like it but he's gettin' worried, too. 'Bout bofe 'em. Get some clothes on, honky!"

"Tammy does favor Abner...."

The girls eyes went wide with the second towel swat.

"Deaf as dirt, huh? I love 'em. I want to marry 'em. Bofe 'em."

"Fool! Not so loud!" Priscilla laughed.

§

Denver hadn't told them that the old lady, Pierretta, was staying at the hotel nearby and he felt guilty when Abner turned off Route 166 and drove right on by it. Salmie's Bar was not five minutes away.

"Lot a nice girls here before the factories let out," Abner said. He looked much too big, even for the big Lincoln Town Car, but the AC felt good and Denver was ready.

Abner turned half his body toward Denver and said: "An' after this you need to get down to business. Hard business. Hardball."

"Yeah, yeah, I know it."

"One of them is mine you know, and we raised up both of them."

"Yeah, yeah...."

"We treat 'em both just the same."

"Bofe 'em."

"I'm serious!"

Denver wiped the smile off his face. "I'm sorry, Abner. I know you love them. I understand."

"You ain't never loved nobody in your life."

"You don't know me that good, Ab."

"First thing, we need to get the old lady out of the loop. Second, we need to know where Ahearn's got the McKay lowboy hid. That means you're going to go there. Soon as we're done here."

"Miami?!"

"The Magic City."

"I don't think so. I'm going home! You go to Miami. Think about it. Take the old lady with you!"

They were crunching into the gravel lot in front of Salmie's where three young hookers were hanging out under the entrance canopy and Denver said: "Oh, my...."

"Second we need to... What?"

"The old lady's not five minutes back there at the motel."

"Yeah? I was supposed to know this?"

"The one on the left, the sequin shorts. Mine."

Abner hit the brakes harder than he needed to and Denver lurched forward in the seat, no belt. "We need to swap the McKay load for the Airstream and get my girls back."

"And the Airstream is where?"

"Your man Bull has it, just like you figured."

"How you know?"

"I have a telephone. Don't you have a telephone? Apparently your Bull don't know how to use a phone, neither, and believe me, if I could drive a tractor-trailer you all'd be in a different movie."

"Hey, don't get hostile on me, bro. And he's not my Bull! Aw, shit, they're all going inside. Look. Two things. There's more money in this if we play it right. Two. No way is Ahearn going to turn the McKay load loose so I can swap with Bull."

"That what he said? He wouldn't say that."

"Dumbass is never there when I call."

"He's bad but he ain't dumb. He just doin' his job."

"Shit, what job is that?! He's a fancy dresser packs a gun and sits on the wharf all day watching babes on yacht decks tan their hides."

"He just a broker. He got a family, big house, teen-age kids, all that...."

"Broker my ass."

"He's a broker. He pays taxes. He's on the books mos' the time. He tells me all that personal shit."

"I'm not impressed. Let's go take..."

"They's white people likes to deal with black people better than fuckin' with another snaky whitey."

"Let's go take the girls to a motel room, do them right. I don't want a blowjob in the car."

"Motel room takes too long. I called McKay, too. Something you could've done, made some excuse, some story, you know? If this dumb nigger can think up cool stuff why can't you? They don't know where he is and they wanted to know who I was so I told 'em I'm holding you and their load hostage 'til we get the Airstream and the two kidnapped girls back — and when I reminded them that kidnapping is a federal offense this kid gets on the line and he says: okay, that's a deal, but keep Denver, he says. Grind him up for dog chow."

Abner backed the big car a little, then pulled around to the rear. Ten minutes later he was on the passenger seat with the door half open and the girl he had picked out was on her knees in the gravel. Denver was sprawled out across the back seat with sunlight flashing all over the parking lot, reflecting off a tight pair of sequined shorts sticking out the door, bottom up.

Denver said to her: "Do you think I taste like dog food?"

"No, Baby, you taze like a man. You taze jus' fine."

CHAPTER 21
A Valdosta Georgia Motel

Bull had staked out his claim to the bed closest to the motel-room door — that being a man's responsibility, he thought — which left the other bed for Janey and the two girls and what would Janey say about that? He lay on his back, hands behind his head, trying to concentrate on what they had learned so far — not one of the pieces fitting together — and lapsed into a fantasy regarding giving in to Janey's demand she sleep in his bed. Just as he was floating the various possibilities of how she would try to seduce him the three of them returned, and as the light streamed past them through the open door the blood rushed back up to his head.

"Where do you go all the time? You don't have to walk them like dogs."

"They can't keep on wearing the same clothes. Well, guess what? None of the stuff in the Airstream is theirs. Doesn't fit."

The girls, still in their fluffy, white dresses, stood side-by-side next to him as Bull sat up. They were looking him in the eye and nodding in unison, sucking on red lollipops.

"We need to buy them some stuff."

"Janey.... With what money, huh? Listen, I was scrolling through some text on Denver's laptop while you were gone. Sister, you would not believe this guy.

He's worse than Dad. He's a fucking pervert pedophile, and into colored chicks up to his pits..."

"Colored? Bullperry, you are one backward, short-haired jerk.

"Colored."

"And Dad's not a pervert, he's just a normal man with normal male fantasies. Duh. Men. Duh."

"Heard ya the first time."

"Well, if you and this Denver were females you'd be working together on this by now. Duh. You know, like, teamwork?"

"Duh is a girl word."

"For men."

"So we'd be working together, huh? In which case, how would I make any money?"

"You split it! Anyway, when do you ever make any money? Well, if what I'm thinking is correct, we won't have to worry about money anymore. I figured it all out."

"I hope so, 'cause if Marlene gets in touch with Denver he could be here anytime."

"You told her where we were?"

"No, but how big is Valdosta, I mean, how many truckstops? If it were me, I'd look here first."

"He'll spot the Airstream first, which means you're sleeping in the rig tonight."

"Oh. Yeah...."

"Yeah, what?! You can still use the bathroom here, the shower...."

The remnants of the fantasy with Janey in the mo-tel-room bed vaporized along with the tingle he had gotten when Janey first announced she had figured everything out. He never wanted to sleep with her anyway. Never. That was always her idea. Her trip. With his sister? No, never....

Even if she pretended she was somebody else....

No, even if he pretended he was somebody else.

Which would work better?

Actually, either one. Hey, both!

No. Never....

§

That evening, Bull made more than a few trips between the rig and the motel-room. The old "Blues Brothers" classic was on a cable channel, and it would have been fun to watch that with Janey and the kids, but "business before pleasure", and it wasn't until Bull crawled under the covers in the sleeper that he realized the Airstream was still unlocked. Well, let Denver try to get in here!

Wiggling around in the sleeper bunk with just a sheet over him and the AC and the engine shut down so he could hear, Bull checked to be sure both the .22 and the 9MM were handy but out of sight. Then, in the snug darkness, he played back the incest fantasy again. Janey was now a distant cousin who had spent part of her childhood with him and his family after her parents died in a plane crash, and he was a truck driver just passing through and Janey was only asking twenty dollars.

But Bull didn't fall asleep until a new fantasy took over. In this movie, the Portuguese woman who had tried to kill him didn't have a gun, she had a proposition. It was hard at first to imagine her still alive with

the vivid memory of how her wounds had looked, especially the round that smashed into her face and
punched a chunk out of the back of her skull, squirting
arterial blood and brains all over the floor. From her
attaché case, the case which she had opened on the
table to grab her weapon, Bull had snatched out some
of her papers before the cops arrived. The picture in her
American passport was what he was seeing in his mind
now, so pretty and vulnerable looking in that straight-
ahead, official photo, the place-of-birth line simply stat-
ing: Portugal. That same, almost innocent look as she
stared at the camera for her New York CDL, her commercial driver's license....

If it had gone the other way I'd be dead now.

She'd be able to live a long life like that old lady,
Pierretta Z.

He pictured a life with the gun-toting mink he had
killed, the two of them as master criminals, with Pierretta Z as her grandmother, and the three of them always coming home to their castle in Sicily or wherever,
burying their ill-gotten booty in the family cemetery,
no, not Sicily, maybe Morocco somewhere....

The knock on the sleeper was gentle, a female
knock. Bull glanced at his watch but it was too dark to
read it. And it was hot. Well, he could always crank the
engine and the AC. His heart pounded up when the
knock came again, so meek, and Bull was totally awake
now but he feigned sleepiness as he carefully popped
the sleeper escape-door a crack and peered out and
down. A waft of heavy, summer evening air tongued in,
and looking up at him was this little blond, young-

looking thing in the shadows, jail-bait young, and familiar. Bull spoke before he realized what was happening.

"Lolita?"

"Yeah."

That was it, one word. Just standing there, looking
up at him.

Bull ran a couple possibilities on his movie screen
but Denver popped into every scene, with a gun. "Yeah
what?"

"Can I come in?"

"It's '*May* I come in'. Uhhhh...."

"Me and Clive?"

The fucking monkey. "Where is he?"

"He's, um, he's taking a dump under the truck."

Bull saw the empty leash in her left hand. "Jeez....
Where's Denver? Your father."

"In the motel."

Bull noted the raggedy condition of her blouse. Barefoot. Torn, short skirt. "What number?"

"The room? I don't know. The one with the hostages."

"The what? Wait. He's in there now? How'd you
find which..."

"Daddy says y'all think he's dumb."

"Yeah, well, I never said that. Go around to the
other side, I'll unlock the door. Clive stays outside. No.
Wait! Stay put. I have to get dressed. Stay right there!"
Bull waved the 9MM where she could see it. "Try to run
off and I'll drop you and the fucking monkey."

The girl flinched, and Bull said, "I'm sorry. But,
well..."

"I thought you liked me."

"I do! But, well, uhhh..."

"You don't have to get dressed just for me."

"Yeah I do."

"Wait!"

Bull hesitated.

"I can tell you stuff if you'll take me along."

Bull slapped the sleeper exit-hatch shut, wrapped himself in the sheet, and stretched an arm toward the passenger-side door to pull up the lock button, then retreated back into the sleeper when she clambered up in. No leash.

"I hooked Clive to the tow-hook, so don't drive off."

"Lock the door behind you. How'd you get so ripped up? You okay? Hey, don't come back here, wait till I get dressed, stop, leave the curtain alone, wait, don't be taking your clothes off, oh, jeez, how old are you anyway, twelve? Thirteen? Quit that!" Bull jerked the curtain partly shut after making sure she had pushed the door-lock button down. "Quit that right now!" Bull, backed up onto the far corner of the bed, fighting himself now, the kid with a torn bra in hand which she slung through the slit in the curtain and then she shoved her skirt and panties down at the same time, the sleeper rocking with her vigorous movements. She looked terrified and Bull thought she was about to start crying or screaming when the curtain suddenly whipped back and the first flash went off and then another flash and it took Bull a couple seconds to recognize the huge, black guy behind the camera, Beaufort, in uniform. Bull slowly withdrew his hand from the gun he was reaching for when the third flash went off. The third flash nailed a photo of Bull's half-naked body, his fingers extended toward the trusty 9MM, and Lolita's little tits a blur to one side as she pressed her way past Beaufort out of the sleeper.

"Gotchya!" It was a voice from outside the tractor. An old-guy voice. "Forgot I had keys to my own truck? Dumb-ass!"

Denver reached up to take the camera from Beaufort, the cop keeping his eyes on Bull while he switched hands on his service revolver. Beaufort said: "Thanks for not trying to shoot me while I was taking pictures. I don't shoot back too good left-handed and I hate to just wound a man, you know, make a mess...."

"This is a setup and it's not going to fly."

"Get out, no no, don't touch anything, just get OUT!" Beaufort backed out of the way but Bull froze.

"I don't have any clothes on! Let me..."

Beaufort re-cocked his service revolver. "Out!"

"My jeans?"

"I'll bring you what I decide you can wear after I pilfer around in here a little, see what you got in here. Out now!"

"Oh, man...."

"Just run over to my car and jump in the back. Leave the sheet here. Go!"

Bull clenched his teeth and tried to get around the huge, black police officer without too much body contact, easing past leather and metal accessories dangling from the man's belt, and holding a hand over his privates so his pubic hair wouldn't snag in the handcuffs.

He jumped barefooted down past Denver to the pissy, warm pavement. Denver had the man's nightstick in both hands and before Bull could react, Denver got in a quick jab to the ribs, and another jab to the small of Bull's back when he hesitated at the rear door of the police car. A stab of pain shot all the way up to Bull's shoulders and he was in, bare-ass on the greasy, hard, backseat vinyl. Denver kicked the door shut on him with a hand-tooled, pointy-toed boot.

Caged. Naked. The back windows smeared with prints and body grease. No door handles. Junk under his bare feet on the floor. The cruiser was parked across the front of the Pete, blocking it, and Bull pressed close to the glass to watch his stuff winging out of the tractor. His laptop carry-on case landed on the pavement with an audible thud. He heard Denver holler and Bull watched him climb up in. The suitcase was ejected more gently, and Denver came backing out now with Bull's cooler, setting it down carefully — same with the box of snacks — then coming out with his glasses — at least nobody sat on them — Denver looking through the lenses briefly before placing them in the snack box. Lolita and Clive were nowhere in sight.

Fuckers are keeping my guns?

Fuck!

The AC was on full blast and seat was cold and filthy, and gritty on his bare ass and balls. Bull looked away and dug the heels of his palms into his eyes.

How did this happen?

Always got a gun ready for anything and now this!

It's pussy. Lolita. She got my head fucked up. Pussy. Just like in the Bible. It's pussy does it every time.

Just like in the Old Testament.

The cruiser suddenly heaved to one side as Beaufort slumped in behind the wheel. The big fucker was quick, Christ, Bull hadn't even noticed the door opening.

"Ever spend any time on the inside of a zoo, mister truck-driver? Naked? Right in there with the other animals?"

"No!"

"It's an experience." Beaufort sat facing straight ahead over the wheel, not even checking a mirror. "Tell me. Just how far would you go, no, let me rephrase. What would you do to get out of this situation?"

"Anything."

"Good. Now tell me what's the deal..."

"That's my tractor, not his."

"I know that, I already called McKay — but nobody knows I know, get my drift? I could haul you in, finish my paperwork, and go home to mama. Fuck you."

"Yes sir."

"The reward on those girls is, what, a hundred grand?"

"There's no reward on those girls."

"Don't fuck with me. So, what girls? And what's with the Airstream?"

"I was hired to find that out!"

"No big deal then. Okay. Well, soon as we're on our way downtown the man can drive out of here — we're blocking the way." Beaufort cranked the engine and heaved himself out. "I'll put your gear in the trunk."

"Wait!" Bull's brain was frying. Why was Denver moving his stuff back toward the Airstream? Pierretta Z had wanted to make a deal, too, and what about Dopey in Miami? "Wait!" Christ! What about Janey and the girls? "Wait! Janey knows more about it. My sis..."

"The redhead?" Beaufort was leaning back in, his head up against the cage, his broad, brown nose flaring with each, noisy inhalation. "Why don't you fuck her instead of sucking after little school girls, huh? The judge gonna love it."

"I wasn't trying to.... You set that up."

"Well, you know who you can tell that to now."

The engine in the Pete cranked and then Bull saw her for the first time — over Beaufort's shoulder — the old lady, little eye-glasses glinting in the orange crime-light glow, coming right up behind the man, a finger to her lips, shhhhh!, and before Beaufort could flinch she had his service revolver. Bull could hear the hammer cocking.

"I'm your slave, Ma'am" Bull hollered.

"Let him out!"

Beaufort eased out backwards and without turning to look, opened the back door. Bull was at the passenger side of the big Peterbilt 377 in a heartbeat, ready to dodge his own bullets if he had to, but Denver looked unconcerned.

"You're ugly. Get dressed."

"I need to be told?"

"He was fixin' to fuck both us."

"Where's my gun?" Bull was behind Denver now, in the sleeper, trying to jam a leg down his jeans.

"Your guns stay here in the cab. Don't try nothing. Pee Zee can pot you with one shot."

"Where's my sister?"

"In the motel with Lolita and the little pickaninnies."

"Shit, am I the only one who doesn't know anything?"

"Just you and Officer Beaufort. Hurry up, you're riding in back in the Airstream. I'm going to the motel to get the ladies."

"And Clive?"

"And Clive."

Denver dropped down to the pavement and disappeared. Bull felt around for his guns, which were gone, and finished dressing and lacing up his Reeboks. It was time to get out and talk to the boss.

Beaufort was behind the wheel of his cruiser with Pierretta Z sitting on the passenger side, the door open and the interior lights on. Bull stepped over to her side.

"What do you want me to do?"

"I am changing my plans." Her voice was as tiny as she was, but with a barb of authority. "Get in the trailer and wait for me." She made no attempt to conceal the money she was counting out into the palm of Beaufort's hand. Hundred dollar bills, Christ.

She stopped for a moment, the last of the hundreds in mid-air. She was staring at Beauford. "Why's your radio off? Let me see your book."

"What?" Beaufort shook his head, his thick neck.

"You log any of this in?"

"No, Ma'am."

She was out so quickly Bull couldn't offer her a hand. He saw that Beaufort's revolver was back in his holster, the 35MM camera was lying on the console, and one of the Polaroid pictures of the old lady and the two girls, standing in front of the Airstream with their little bulldog puppy, was on the seat. Bull pointed at the camera. "That camera has Lolita and me, uh..."

The old lady turned back. "The camera, please, Mister Bo-for."

CHAPTER 22
Valdosta GA to Carrollton GA

Bull picked his remaining pair of glasses out of the snack-box, which was on the floor of the Airstream with his other stuff, and wiped them with a hankie before folding them into his shirt pocket. He thought of moving some of his gear to get it out of the way but figured it was better near the door in case he could make a quick exit. Bull looked around — the tiny interior so clean and elegant — then the generator cut off and in the silence, voices outside — Lolita and the old lady? The door opened and Lolita popped in, averting her eyes and turning sideways past Bull, Clive following at the end of his leash. No problem on eye contact with the fucking monkey, however, and Bull could feel the hate, Clive baring his teeth and gums. Lolita jerked him back toward the rear.

Janey and the old lady were next, followed by the little girls, Janey still looking good but running her mouth non-stop. "Oh, so pretty in here. Is this my new home? Where do I sleep?" She caught Bull's eye with a wink. "Is it time to eat yet? Oh, this paneling! I saw the same thing at Wal-Mart!"

Jeez, Janey, don't overdo it.

Pierretta Z scrunched her eyes at Bull, and he shrugged. "She's not playing with a full deck. I mean, she's, well, dumb. Real dumb."

The old lady turned back to the door and punched in the lock button. Her movements were energetic and quick for someone so skinny and old. "Sit!" she said to Janey, pointing at the dinette. To Lolita she yelled: "You stay back there with the girls!"

Bull slid onto the seat beside Janey, and the trailer gave a lurch before the rig began to ease out of the hole. The window curtains at the dinette were drawn but Bull could see the running lights of the truck they were parked next to trickling by through the fabric.

"When I hired him, he didn't tell me he had another load to deliver." Pierretta Z standing and holding on, her purse hanging large and heavy from a thin shoulder.

"Oh."

"Do you need money?"

Bull stifled a smile. "Yes Ma'am."

"Isn't it illegal to transport a retarded woman across state lines?"

"What? Uhhhh...." Bull didn't know how much the old lady already knew. "Janey's my sister."

"I know." A flicker of a smile. I need somebody with a little more intelligence, I think...."

"I'm not dumb like she is."

"So have you figured out what we're doing here?"

"You're on vacation!" Janey said.

"And the little girls?"

"Great-grandchildren! Ooops, I'm sorry. Grandchildren?"

"Janey," Bull said, "they're not the same race for chrissake."

"Oooops!" Janey held a hand to her mouth, her eyes wide.

"Go back there with the monkey."

Janey immediately got up, slid around Bull, then had to grab the edge of a cupboard to keep her balance.

"You didn't have to say it like that," Bull said.

The rig was picking up a little speed, and turning, and through the curtains they could see headlights as they crossed an intersection.

"I meant, go back there with that dumb blond girl and the monkey."

Janey lurched from side-to-side on her way to the back, past the tiny bathroom on one side, to the rear bunk. Bull watched how she carried her purse, and by the way it hung on her he was almost certain Janey's .38 was still in it.

When he looked back to the old lady her eyes locked right into him. "You try to reach for me or trip me up you're dead." She smiled and shoved her octagonal spectacles up in place with the tip of a ringed finger. A diamond. Had to be more than two carats, but Bull wouldn't know.

"First," he said evenly, "I want my guns back."

"Everything in due course."

"Where are we going?"

"Why, are you in a hurry? Do you have a funeral to go to?"

"No...."

"Well I do."

Bull suddenly realized that her accent was French, not Italian. "I hope it's Denver's funeral."

"No. That one's up to you."

§

"This is national," Beaufort said. "Nation wide. And look what you got here. A description of an everyday Airstream, a picture of twin black girls who don' look nothin' like what comes with the Airstream, and an old lady but ..."

The two, young suits were leaning over Beaufort's shoulder at the small monitor. "What's that come-with-the-airstream crap? How can you see anything on this smeared-up shit monitor? Looks like it needs an oil change. No money for glass cleaner? You sneeze on it all the time, or what?"

"Says here there's a set of twins and a gray-hair old lady but what we got was a titted-out babe, a red-head, and two little colored kids ain't twins."

"Colored? Is the word colored cool again?"

Beaufort swiveled his chair around and looked up at them. "You sure you FBI? You bofe dumb as border patrol. You see the number pasted up on the monitor? You recognize that number? Tha's the new homeland fatherland security whistle-blow hotline for fuck-ups don't share inter-agency information. I'm gonna give'em your names. It'll take you a year to clear up your personnel files."

"And your beef is ...?"

"Look here." Beaufort swiveled back and made a point of touching the greasy monitor with a fat finger.

"See this? One of you even punched in the tag number on the Airstream."

"And...?"

"It's the wrong trailer!"

"Twins don't always look exactly the same."

"I took a Polaroid. It's outside in my car. We gonna look at it. You think we all stupid aroun' here. You look at it and then you go and fix this shit off the computer. I'm goin' home and goin' to bed. Tomorrow morning I'm gonna check. Them people told me they been stopped in four different counties. You take it off there and I won't write you up."

"Don't get all excited. We didn't do it."

"That's what perps say. I'm innocent! Well, we up to our armpits in ragheads want to kill us now. We don't need t' be hasslin' citizens just trying to get to their favorite fishin' hole."

§

Abner and Priscilla were sitting at the bar which separated their kitchen from the living-room. They were watching the girls peel potatoes at the sink.

"They'll do anything I tell them," Priscilla said. "Show them, I mean. Kind of pokey, though, but that's because they're so careful. See?"

Abner nodded. "Trouble is, they'll do anything *anybody* tells them." The twins were standing side-by-side, rinsing and peeling, and each turned to look at the other with a smile every time a finished, bright and shiny potato was placed in the colander. Their movements were coordinated and graceful, and their postures perfect even though the sink and counter-tops were a bit of a reach for them.

"They're almost five feet tall already," Priscilla said.

"Still growing, and still dumb as dirt."

"No, they're not stupid, Ab. Still growing? Haitians are small, aren't they?"

"No, they're tall. That's not enough potatoes for everybody."

"We're supposed to feed them?"

"Well, once they swap the girls they can't very well go someplace public to eat."

"Oh, yeah, shit Abner, well, you can just send out for pizza or something then. I'm not cooking for a bunch of porks. They're all criminals, too."

"That include me? You'll cook when I tell you." Priscilla did not answer, and Abner added, "We can send out if they're hungry when they get here."

But when they arrived, the other girls, in a taxi, Janey was with them but no one else. Abner had not intended to let Janey in when he came to the front door but she barged right past. Flowery, swishy, light dress the color of cream, with big red flowers...

"Oh, such a pretty place!"

"Leave your gun at the door."

"My gun?" Oh, I'm sorry, I forgot!" Janey dropped her purse to the floor with a *clunk,* flashed a flirty smile and wink, and kept on going through to the kitchen. "Oh, this food smells so good!" The puffy, starched, white dresses of the girls she brought made crunchy noises as they hugged Priscilla — "Mama, Mama!" —

then Abner, Abner looking to the side without taking his eyes off Janey.

Janey approached the taller girls in the kitchen. "Oh, are these my new ones? You — are — so — pretty!" They were smiling, and looking not the least surprised as Janey reached for the closest one. They each in turn raised their arms and clasped their hands behind Janey's neck as she bent to hug them.

A few minutes later, Janey had to hunt up the two she brought and they were happy to get a hug, too. Their goodbye hug.

"I'll miss you guys!"

"Mmmm - hmmmm."

Abner seemed impatient, but Janey said: "Isn't the taxi driver another witness?"

"It's my taxi."

"Oh! Oh, right! Well, that's the only thing that makes sense about all this!"

"The arrangement was temporary. I wouldn't concern yourself about it."

Janey smiled, winked at Abner again, and headed back outside, picking up her purse on the way. Her long legs and cleated clogs clicked the concrete sidewalk, with the new girls following soundlessly behind her, leggy in their own way; the old, black driver, silver-gray stubble on his chin, shifted his eyes from them to Janey and back. He was out to help with the Haitian girls' only suitcase — black leather with wide straps and silver buckles — while Janey hopped into the front seat.

"Ta!" Janey yelled back at Abner and Priscilla with a wave. Their girls waved back — somewhat sadly, Janey thought.

They were off. Janey turned in her seat to the new ones, sitting side-by-side in the back and looking right at her. Bright eyes wide open, and shy, heart-shaped smiles with their lips tightly closed, their hands folded neatly in their laps.

"Real twins this time, huh? You guys are so pretty! You're beautiful!"

The girls smiled but did not answer.

CHAPTER 23
Mingo County West Virginia

Her two boys were sitting at the kitchen table when Dianna silently poked her head out the bedroom door. They looked fidgety and bored, and they spotted her immediately.

"You cryin', Mama?"

She shut herself back in and turned, the man still dressing, straightening his tie before the mirror over the dresser. He lifted up the silver-framed photo and propped it back on its little, black, cardboard leg. In the photo: a fit-looking man, sleeves rolled up, was standing in bright sunlight next to a semi truck cab. He was smiling, with one leg up on the lowest step.

"I need to give the boys a chore out back so you can get out the front. And I'll decide when it's time to put my husband's picture back up if you don't mind."

"Yeah, well I'm thinkin' maybe it's time to stop all this sneakin'. And me makin' your mortgage payments regular. I'm thinkin' you need to give me that receipt back. Where'd you put it?"

"He'd snuff you in a heartbeat."

"Maybe. If he knew. And what would he do to you? Huh? If he knew? The receipt."

"I earned that money."

"Three hundred an hour? I don't think so."

The man kept running his fingers around the waist-
band of his trousers as he walked to the South window,
trying to shove his shirttails in evenly over the fatty tire
which was his belly — his love handles he called them.
What everybody not worth a shit called them.

Dianna said: "Then don't come by no more. You
said you could afford it. It wasn't my idea, and it's
wrong, and I don't need to be doin' it no more."

"I said, the first time, I'd pay half."

"Double without a rubber."

"Double without a rubber...." He was looking out
over the rocky drop-off through the cedars, down to the
creek, the flow of it silver and narrow down there in the
bright sun, the rocks flashing like diamonds as the water
coursed over them. "The receipt, Dianna."

"No. I earned it. It's mine."

"I'm tired of this bullshit. I want you for myself. See,
I don't need the money back, I mean, I got gas in the
tank, a freezer full of steaks at home, a big, fat-old wife
who loves me 'cause I just bought her a new car, the
mother of my children, one of those Caddy Cateras.
Black. Leather seats.... No, Dianna, I'm thinkin' I need to
buy your place here, set you up..."

"It's my place. And it's Bull's place, too, with the re-
finance...."

"Well, I don't guess you should've let him borrow
money on it then, huh? And when's he ever here?
When can your Bull make the next payment, huh? No....
I'm lookin' out this window and I'm thinkin': this is the
best little piece of West Virginia I seen in a year. Forty
acres with a stream and a brand-new log cabin and a

young cunt goes with it ain't even twenty yet and tight as a pistol barrel and tits so firm and still full of milk from the last kid, well, I'm fantasizin' now, but — you know — you get the picture."

He turned away from the window and snatched at her left wrist and pulled her to him, quick for his fatty girth, the gold watch sliding down to his clenched fist. With his right hand he jerked a tit out of the top of her blouse and gave it a lick and a pull with his teeth.

"Mama!" From the other side of the door.

Dianna tried to turn away but he had both hands on her now. "You guys get out and do the garbage."

"We did the garbage."

"I mean out by the barn." She twisted her head away from him and raised her voice. "Get a sack. Both of you. Pick up all around the barn. Both of you!"

silence....

"Git! I'll be out in a minute to help."

"I'm gettin' horny again," the man whispered.

"No, no, go!" She broke away and pulled the curtain on the East window. "They're outside, both of 'em. Go!"

"Gimme a quickie blowjob."

"No! Besides, you hain't even washed up."

"So?"

"I don't like to taste myself."

"I love you, Dianna."

"Yeah, right. Git!" She eased open the door. "Come on. Now!"

"Let me back in tonight. We need to talk. Think about it. I buy the place. You get a new car. The kids get a man who'll play with 'em, buy 'em steaks instead of that Hamburger helper I seen in the kitchen, be home all the time, show 'em how to fly that model airplane your husband bought 'em but don't never have time...."

"You have a wife."

"I'll be home half the time then."

She turned to find him unbuckling and pulling his pants down, and he caught her and tried to shove her down to her knees on the shiny hardwood floor, his pink knob — short and thick — stiff and swaying while he slapped her long hair out of her face with one hand.

"I been takin' them DHEA tablets lately. They work, let me tell you. Come on. Come on. Suck harder, hey, come on, harder. Can we see some enthusiasm here?!"

CHAPTER 24
A Greyhound Bus Station at Night

With the airstream still chained to the lowboy trai-ler, Bull's back was to the direction of travel as the RV swayed and the tires of the lowboy slapped against the interstate pavement. They were sitting across from each other in the dinette, and the old lady was staring at him through her spectacles. The curtains were still drawn but Bull could see lights from other vehicles through them, and he figured Denver was driving at a legal speed.

Janey called from the back. "I have to pee!"

"We all have to pee," Pierretta Z screeched. She turned back to Bull. "The camera is empty, if you are thinking something stupid. Officer Beaufort has the film, and I can switch his lights back on any time.

Film? Bull's mind was racing. He could use some kind of ruse to get them both standing up, then nail her with a kick. Shit, he could nail her with a fist right now across the table, um, no, not with her right hand hold-Ing a gun In her lap, probably cocked and ready to shoot him in the gut under the table before he could do any-thing. Well, how tired could she be? She looked beat. Not much of a chance she's had any sleep. How long did it take her to figure out where Kate or the terminal was, and then actually go there, and then go to Uncle

Ralph's, plus finding Mom and Dad and going there, too!

She must be twins herself!

Does she have a private plane? Christ!

This is my chance. Right now.

I'd have her big .45 and Denver will be easy.

Beaufort.... What about Beaufort?

Wait. Think.

"So what do you want from me?"

"I need to hide the Airstream and the twins for a time."

"You want to tell me what's going on?"

"You want to know? Your Mister Denver knows too much and now we have to do something about him."

"We?"

"We."

§

The big rig was scrunching on gravel and slowing to a stop but Denver set the parking brakes prematurely, and in the hiss of released air Bull and Pierretta Z nearly lurched out of their seats.

"Fucker drives like a kid," Bull mumbled. "He nearly jerked this thing off the chains. Where are we?"

Denver was already at the Airstream door — round on top and cute as a Hobbit- house door — and he snatched it open. "We're outside a very small town." He grinned through his silver, handlebar moustache, his head of silver hair glowing in the only yard-lamp that wasn't shot or burned out. A Greyhound bus sign adorned a shabby building set way back. "This place has a bathroom, and I have to take a dump."

Pierretta Z said, "I'm making the decisions here."

"Besides, I want to put Lolita and Clyde on a bus home. To Valdosta."

"We know where your stupid little brick house is." Bull said.

"I have to pee, too!" Janey yelled from the back.

"Me, too," Lolita said, "and Clyde's out of diapers, and we forgot to bring the punch to punch the holes for his tail, and..."

"Shut up, all of you!" Pierretta Z slammed the big .45 U.S. government automatic down on the table with the muzzle inches from Bull's chest, the hammer cocked. Bull winced, and the sight of her bony, blue-veined little hand gripping it for a big kick was no comfort. He knew what one of those 45's kicked like and she looked ready to fire and hang onto it.

"Okay, okay, you're the boss!"

Nobody moved except Bull and he moved slowly, turning his head just enough to get a good look at Denver, frozen in the open doorway.

"Ummmm," Bull said. He locked eyes with the old lady and was surprised at the grim ferocity. "What do you want us to do?"

"Im thinking!"

Now he knew she was at the end of her rope. He whispered, "You only need one driver."

"Denver, you said you had to take a dump!"

Bull watched him hesitate, then turn and take off toward the building. "What if he goes for the pay-phone," Bull said.

"To do what?"

"Call Dopey? I mean that guy in Miami. Ahearn."

"Get him."

"He's got my guns."

The old lady's face shipped a momentary look of disgust and disappointment. "Go!"

§

Janey had watched Denver, moving with a kind of bowlegged sailor-walk, head for the tiny Greyhound office. But now, when she pulled the curtain aside again at the rear window to watch her brother, a light rain was streaking the glass. Bull was walking slowly but looking confident. He had been so nerdy when they were both growing up, but now, hell...

"Let me look!" Lolita whispered, but Janey elbowed her back.

"That black girl in there is fly," Janey muttered. "She came out to empty trash or something but she ducked back in when she saw Denver. She's all figged out, too, for a dumb bus station job." Janey watched Bull hesitate at the door. "He loves those jungle bunnies. Hope he can concentrate in there."

§

The girl had just made it around to the other side of the dingy, dark wooden counter when Denver banged open the door. The bell above the door clattered to the floor, and Denver kicked it aside. "Sorry Honey, but the pakies you work for will use a nail instead of a screw every time."

"Packies?"

"Paks. Indians. Afghans. The rag-heads who run all the motels and bus stations in America. Glad to see you ain't one." Denver moved up to the counter and leaned over as the girl adjusted herself on the seat at the keyboard. "Oh, mama, you are a little hottie aren't you."

"May I help you?"

"May you, can you.... I need to use your phone."

"There's a pay-phone outside, sir. We're not allowed...

"There's a dumpster outside, too, if you get my drift. Give me your cell." Denver moved down to the end of the counter so he could go around.

"Please, I'll hand it over the counter."

"No, no, see there's people in that big rig out there, bad people, and they're watching me, so I'll just duck down here where they can't see me, good, oh my how the legs get creaky when you get old, put that phone down on the floor here for me, thank you, but I'm not too old to get it up for a babe like you."

Denver, down on the floor now with a portable desk phone between his legs, didn't see or hear the front door ease open, but he had already worked loose a .32 automatic before hunkering down, and the gun butt was half out of a front pocket and ready to grab. He unbuttoned a shirt pocket and pulled out a slip of paper, then winced at the loud tones when he punched in Ahearn's number.

"Pick up, asshole."

Bull left the door ajar and was sneaking across the room, heading for the hallway with the restrooms sign, when he saw that the girl sitting behind the counter was blinking her eyes frantically. He raised his eyebrows and caught her slight nod toward the floor to her right. Bull returned the nod, and froze.

"Come on, Ahearn, dammit."

Bull slowly dropped to a crouch. The light rain had only dampened his head and shoulders, and he wiped his hands against his pant legs. He could feel his body revving up, his heart pumping, the muscles tensing, his mind rushing through the familiar catalog of his life: no money, kids missing him, sexy young Dianna abandoned at home.... His body was charged with the feeling he often got when it was time to act, much stronger than when he nailed the J.B. Hunt driver who kicked the little puppy — he would have punished that dude if he were twice the size — no, now his blood was rushing with the possibility he could lose.

Bull heard the phone slam down, saw the girl turn to the side and look down, her mouth in shock. Bull figured she was looking at the barrel of a gun, and he could almost see Denver's position, near the floor and just behind the counter beyond some papers held down by one of those glass globes filled with water and a snowman, you turn it over and this pretty snow falls peacefully down.

He could end-run the counter and kick Denver in the head from behind but that would give the man time to twist around and shoot. Or he could grab the paperweight and hurl it over the counter at Denver's head. If he missed he could duck back behind and then.... Then what!?

Denver's voice: "I got to pee and you're coming into the bathroom with me."

Bull dug in for a dash for the paper-weight. Before he launched he could see it, the grab, his belly slamming him to a stop and his upper body arched over as he hurled the heavy glass at Denver's small, silver head. But he didn't count on the girl moving first, rising up out of her chair and kicking back and Denver suddenly shooting — **POP POP POP** — Bull knowing the sound of a .32 auto but not really registering it as his body slammed into the counter with his grab for the glass ball and — **POP POP** — Denver swinging toward him now as the ball crashed into his nose.

Denver went down, the gun still in his hand as Bull leapt over the counter and stomped on the man's head. The auto had a few more rounds in it but Denver was stunned.

"Motherfucker!" A stomp on Denver's gun hand and a kick to the man's head and Bull was looking at the girl, on her knees facing him, spurts of bright red blood pulsing between the fingers she was holding over her chest, her mouth open, eyes wide, staring at Bull, her lips moving but nothing coming out, and Bull dropped down beside her and held her, and lowered her all the way down.

§

Janey said: "Now is it time to call the law?" She was squatting and pissing beside the tractor tandems, with Lolita beside her. Bull ordered Janey back inside the Airstream as soon as she stood up.

"No panties as usual I ..."

"Bullperry!" Janey turned to Lolita who was still squatting and drilling a hole into the ground. "Jeez, Lolita, when was the last time you went to the bath-room?!"

Bull saw two sets of headlights coming down the highway, one from each direction, the headlights dazzling in the cool, rainy mist — sounded and looked like cars — and he hoped the drivers would be paying more attention to passing each other than noting what kind of rig was parked in front of the Greyhound station, so easy to remember with the shiny Airstream on a trailer. Neither vehicle slowed, and they sounded old and shitty, one of them with a tire slapping hard on each revolution. "Janey, you keep a look-out while we drag her father into the truck.

"Clyde hain't peed yet," Lolita said, standing now with her back to Bull and tugging her jeans up over her young ass. Bull turned to the monkey, tethered to a lowboy tie-down ring, standing upright and holding his diaper in one paw. He was glaring at Bull, and Bull thought his little dick looked like a bright-red, pencil eraser.

"It get's bigger," Lolita said.

"You would know."

"You could leave Clyde here with Daddy."

"And you?"

"I want to go with you." She followed Bull into the station, but when she saw Denver lying there she said, "Daddy needs to go to the hospital."

"Get over there and grab his feet. Two things. One, he'd talk, and two he wouldn't want to be left behind. He just killed this nice girl here."

"Daddy would never. You did that."

"That his gun?"

"You shot her with Daddy's gun." Lolita reached for it, the hammer still cocked and ready for the next shot, but Bull beat her to it and jammed it into a back pocket. "Your father killed her for no good reason. Get used to it."

"You should've called the ambulance for her!"

"You see all that blood? You see her eyes? You know what dilated eyes means?"

"Not your call."

"Okay, don't grab his feet. Just hold the front door open when I get there. Check nobody's around first."

While Janey and Lolita helped pack Denver into the cab and onto the sleeper floor, all of them wet now, Denver pulled in a deep breath and moaned. Janey whispered, "You got his gun, right?" She looked at Bull and saw that he was staring into space. "Bull, what are you doing?!"

Bull jerked. "I was — I was thinking about Mom. She always had dry clothes laid out for us if we came in wet, remember?"

CHAPTER 25
Stony Hill Missouri

To Harold, the hardest part was going to be keeping Uncle Axel from getting the law involved. Bull probably wouldn't, or his mother, but Axel, well, Axel would
rather flip burgers than do anything illegal. He had said
so once too many a few months back, at a rare time
when they were all home together, and Harold's mother got pissed.

"You never fudge your log? You never pack a gun
when you're in DC? You never speed, go around scales,
pick up underage riders, change the date on the DOT ..."

"I don't take advantage of them Kate."

"What? Advantage of what?"

"Hitchhiker girls..."

Harold remembered perking up on that one. Axel
picking up girls?

"Better me than some pervert, the way I see it."

"Yes dear brother, and if I'm fool enough to believe
that, is picking them up legal?"

"Do we have to burn Little Harold's ears with this?
Jeez, Kate, you're his mother!"

Axel had always been that way. Now he was giving
everybody until morning before he'd call the law. That's
what he said. By morning. So when Harold finally con-
nected with Ahearn by telephone he made it clear that

settling everything soon was in everyone's best interest. "Especially mine."

"How old are you, kid?"

"Old enough to figure out it was you pretended you were Denver last time."

"What's in it for you? Huh? Convince me. I'm about to lose my ass here."

"Okay, Mister Ahearn, I ..."

"You still want to call me Dopey?"

"Uh, if Mama and Uncle Axel go bankrupt they'll lose the company. They'll move away from here. I got this girlfriend lives down the block. If we get our load back, and our trailer, we stay, and I make some extra bucks."

"Like what kinda bucks?

"I got my eye on a cool Kawasaki 4-wheeler. It's not new but it doesn't have any miles on it. I can take Juanita to school with it."

"Juanita?"

"Not the nude one on the internet."

"Heraldo, there's five thousand Juanita's on the internet suck your dick through a straw. Right through your modem."

Harold winced, and Ahearn's laugh was insulting. "My name's Harold. How do I know I can trust you."

"Okay, let me convince you. If we make a deal and nobody get's caught, you can buy ten fucking Suzukis or whatever. You can go to your Juanita's house and buy her from her mother. Take her home and chain her to a leg of your bed. Feed her dogfood."

"That's not what..."

"Listen. The reason I'm telling you this is so you know I'm not trying to bullshit a kid. You be honest with me and I'll do the same with you. Think. I didn't have to tell you there was that much money in it, did I?"

"Uhhhh...."

"You were going to settle for a motorbike. Listen to me now. There's enough money in it for you to get your mama out of debt. She'll be bringing you breakfast in bed and you won't even have to get off Juanita's face when she sets the tray down. Think about it."

"And once you get what you need from me I'm out of the picture, right?" Little Harold let out one of his best, slow, wet burps. "I have to have something in the hand, otherwise my uncle's going to call the law back in."

"Wait, wait, your uncle? What do you mean, back in?"

"They were already here about your fat-ass moustache man getting blowed away and that old lady tried to kill my mother."

silence....

"But they don't know about the missing load and our rig."

"I had nothing to do with it. That old lady is a criminal and I'm straight."

"Yeah, right."

"Does your Juanita put out? I mean, do you guys make out?"

"Not yet, but...."

"Listen, kid, I was your age once. Okay? Maybe not as smart as you back then, granted, but I was just as horny as you, okay? Seems like all my buddies were get-ting laid, or they said they were, and I didn't even know what a tit felt like. You know what I mean?"

"Well, yeah...." Little Harold straightened up a little, and swung his feet down to the floor. He had called from his bed, lights long out, with his mother asleep and Axel who knows where. On the other side of the window of his room, bugs were flitting about the yard light attached to the outside wall.

"Listen, Harold, when I was your age I would've killed to have a girl just let me feel her tits. I was ob-sessed with what a tit must feel like. I would lie awake all night just trying to picture it. Sliding my hand under a sweater. Under a bra. Feeling it, stroking it, squeezing it. At the time it seemed like something like that would never happen. You know what I mean? Like I would never be so lucky."

"Yeah!"

"Harold? I want you to know something. You're a smart-ass but I like you. I'm going to promise you some-thing. Okay, I know you have your heart set on this girl in school. Juanita? Long, silky-black hair, blah blah, okay, I'm not putting that down. I know where that comes from. I've been there, okay? I'm going to prom-ise you something. Money is power, right? You and me make a deal, we work this out, and besides everybody ending up happy as flies on a pig's ass, I'm going to send over this girl I know, fucks for money but cute as a bug, beautiful — you can't be far from Saint Louis — and she's going to come over and take you behind the build-ing and pull her tits out and she's going to let you do anything you want with them. Lick 'em. Suck 'em. Whatever, okay? That's a promise."

"But Juanita is my ..."

"Truly. I've been there. Okay? It's a time of life you never forget. Listen, Harold. Girls respect a guy with a roll of cash. I'm not saying your special honey would do it for money, but when she sees that the kid down the block is going to own a trucking company one day and is the only kid in school where the extra bulge in the front of his jeans is a roll of bills I want you to be wearing goggles because when a chick rips her blouse off the flying buttons can take an eye out."

"Yessir, but how do I know..."

"You don't have to tell me anything. From now on we deal only with each other. Okay? When we're ready to make a swap we'll do it blind. Blind, okay?"

Harold tried to think about how everything could be done blind. "Blind. Okay. Deal."

"Can you drive a big truck?"

"Well yeah, but I'm not old enough for a license."

"Can you drop and hook trailers?"

"For sure, but can't you drive a truck?"

"Kid, I've been up in the cab of one of those things and it freaks me out. Do you know this dude your mother hired?"

"Bull? Yeah...."

"You two get along okay?

"Oh yes."

"Then we have a deal. This is what I want you to insist on. You tell Bull there's no..."

"I don't know where he is right now."

"Find him. You tell Bull not to let the old lady take the kids away or there's no money in it for any of us."

"Kids? What about our load? Our trailer."

"You're getting that back when you produce the kids. Twins. Little black girls."

"What about the Airstream?"

"Not important. You can stick that Airstream up Pierretta Z's ass."

CHAPTER 26
Moon Over a Georgia Truckstop

Bull kept the wheel cranked until he had the low-boy almost jack-knifed before they touched the black-top, and had to lean forward to see past Pierretta Z to check the road on that side. "If we run down the shoulder we'll leave tread imprints in the dirt. This gravel won't. We can't count on more rain, so..."

The old lady said: "I know what you're doing."

"We're going to have to fuel soon, too, and I'm not sure if Janey's credit card will clear any more big ones, so..."

"I'm not your mother."

"Yeah, but it's your trip."

"And if they're tracing my plastic?"

"You've got cash."

"Almost gone, son. Just drive us the fuck out of here please."

"So where does my payday come in?"

Pierretta raised her banjo voice. "I've got money in the bank!"

Bull idled off the mark and went up through the gears on the blacktop. Away from the yard-lights it was difficult to distinguish between the pavement and the shoulder of the narrow county road, and Bull was squinting. "Forgot to put on my glasses and this fucking road is so..."

"So, so, so.... Where are they."

An oncoming vehicle was approaching, some asshole with bright lights dead on, and Bull gritted his teeth and hoped he was all the way over without printing the shoulder.

"Shirt pocket."

She reached over, fished the glasses out, and unfolded them. As she leaned to place them on his head he could smell her scent, so light and subtle. He himself stank at this point, he was sure.

"You smell good."

"You haven't been around a real lady."

"A real lady? No."

"I was born in a barn."

"A barn...."

"I can let my hair down to the crack of my ass."

Bull slowed for a curve and shifted down one. "Sign back there said Talbot County something."

"They cut it off one time, in jail, and it was ten years to grow back. Hair grows slower when you get old."

"All the years I been driving I don't remember any Talbot County, Georgia. I don't have a clue where we are." He slowed to a crawl at a fork in the highway coming up, no signs, but the road here was dry. The bit of rain they had experienced at the little Greyhound station had been local. Bull leaned out of the window a little, the AC in the cab still on.

"Left. West," she said.

"It's so dark, how the hell...?"

"That glow in the sky. Ahead. Moon glow. We head there and we hit I-85, or I-185."

"You know that for sure?"

"It's as good as I can do."

They were passing a billboard advertizing a local store and "DIESEL". Two miles.

"We need to get fuel on the interstate," Pierretta Z said. "Interstate only."

"The gauge is on E, and both tanks are hooked to-gether. I don't know this tractor or how accurate the gauge is, so..."

"We are all on E, Mister Bull."

§

It was midnight when they came up on US-27, and Bull suddenly knew where they were. South of the junc-tion of I-85 and I-185, and south of the scales. Not far from where the adventure had really begun. If they headed northwest, the fuel stop at LaGrange. But Pier-retta Z said no, and she had Bull pull off the road briefly in a dark area, the horizon lighted not from moon-glow but from an outpost of civilization a mile or more to the west. She said they would be making some changes. Denver, still on the floor, was fully conscious now and Pierretta Z ordered him out. "Bull, help me cover him with his gun. Lolita, bring out the monkey."

"You knew I had his .32 all along?"

Pierretta sighed but the cocked .45 in her tiny hand held steady on Denver's chest.

"You idiots need me," Denver croaked, and after limping down the cab steps he nearly slipped into the ditch in the damp grass, all of them except the twins on that side of the tractor now, while Lolita brought Clyde up on his leash, dropping the loop at her end over the fender indicator.

"He's hungry," she said. "And his diaper's wet."

Clyde and Bull stared at each other, the monkey's eyes glowing like the Devil's own in the light from the amber running lights. The swampy woods beyond the ditch was a chorus of bugs and frogs.

"Hand Mister Denver his gun," Pierretta said.

"It's still loaded."

"Mister Denver, when he hands you that gun you keep it pointed down. You know what I can do."

"I got him covered, too, Janey said, her Smith & Wesson .38 Airweight on both hands.

Denver said, "You guys are going to kill me."

"No, Mister Denver, you're going to shoot your fucking monkey."

While Lolita screamed no, "Not Clyde!", Bull was re-counting the shots he had heard at the Greyhound station and how many could be left. He wiped the .32 automatic on a pant leg and handed it over, muzzle down, feeling a creepy shock at contact with the man's tough, grizzled hand. Vulnerable once again, Bull began to back away. He suddenly could see what was going to happen. Denver would begin to comply, shooting the monkey once maybe and then, raising the automatic in the same motion, fire at Pierretta first and then swing on Janey. It was his only chance.

Headlights appeared from behind and Pierretta ordered everyone closer to the truck, not that there was much room to stand away from it with the deep ditch right there. It was a pickup, with mud tires that sang as it speeded by. One taillight. Typical.

Janey and Pierretta were on both sides of Denver now, Janey holding a steady aim at Denver's head. Bull moved between the lowboy and the tractor out of the line of fire, with Clyde now staring at the gun in Denver's hand.

"Cock it," Pierretta said.

"Clyde is like a child to me," Denver croaked, his voice box bruised. He cocked the gun and aimed it between Clyde's eyes.

"Bullshit, shoot," the old lady twanged, and before anybody could move Clyde was on Denver's leg, clamping his teeth well above the ankle and hanging on. Denver screamed and fired a wild shot at him, splitting Clyde's collar in two. The second shot hit Clyde somewhere — there was fur flying — and the third shot missed again. Bull saw the slide lock back on the .32 — empty — and Denver began slamming it into Clyde's head, the monkey and the man both screaming and then — **CRACK!** — Pierretta's tiny hand bucked up into the air and a balloon of blood blew out of Clyde's middle. The white diaper drifted down into the dark ditch but Clyde was still hanging on to Denver with his teeth — both of them still screaming — **CRACK!** — the top of Clyde's head disappeared with the jaws still clamped on Denver as his gun hand came down on the animal over and over, smushing the empty .32 into what was left of the monkey's brain while the two of them slipped down into the ditch.

Bull moved up to the edge, trying to make out what was happening. "Motherfucker killed that girl ..."

"Get 'im off me! Get 'im off me!"

"... for no fucking reason!" Bull looking down at Denver on his back down there with the monkey, silent now, clamped to his leg and still jerking and flopping though his brain was gone.

"Get 'im off me!"

CRACK! Pierretta right beside Bull now, the discharge from her .45 stinging Bull's ear. **CRACK!** Bull turned, thinking it was Janey's gun this time, shooting the old lady, but Pierretta just stood there, lowering the hammer on her pistol before Janey lowered hers. The fuzzy ringing slowly left Bull's right ear.

From the ditch and the nearby swamp there was nothing but quiet.

§

They pulled into a Pilot truckstop after crossing I-185. Janey agreed she would deal with the fuel desk, manned by a middle-age baldy.

Janey eyed him through the window. "Looks like a child molester," she said, and she bitched about the use of her card again and wanted to know why Bull's wife in Miami, if she was so wealthy, never gave him any money.

"She wants me to stay home."

Janey waved to the driver who had pulled in the fuel lane beside theirs. "Hi, Danny!"

The driver smiled and waved back.

"That's Danny Glover over there," Janey beamed.

Bull looked over and rolled his eyes up. "Janey...."

"The movie actor. You think she'll kill Lolita, too?"

"What? Oh. The old lady?"

"She'll probably kill all of us."

Bull said: "She let me have my guns back."

"Are they on you?"

"Am I wearing my pants?"

"I could've shot her when she was blowing that Denver away."

"And go home penniless?"

"And go to jail. So far we're not guilty of anything."

"Yeah right...."

"Not me, anyway."

They were talking between the tractor and the lowboy trailer, filling the fuel tanks, with Janey manning the slave pump on her side. But they shut up when they saw Pierretta Z lead Lolita to the payphone near the fuel-desk door. Lolita, her hair brushed and no sign of tears now, was nodding her head to something the old lady was telling her as they walked by.

"She sure has some power," Janey whispered.

"Lolita?"

Janey hesitated, and shook her head. "Bullperry, you are so dumb."

§

The man at the fuel desk wanted Janey to produce an I.D. for the plastic, which he was squinting to read. "Photo I.D., or someone here who knows you, or ..."

"Knows me?!"

"...or a tattoo of this name here on your ass."

"You're dumb, Jack. The card cleared, didn't it?"

"Company policy. And I am not dumb. Jack?"

"The name on your shirt says Jack! Right. Well.... Actually you can't be too dumb because I do have my name tattooed on my ass. My brother's name."

"Come on, can we get moving here?" It was the driver who had been fueling in the next lane, the black guy looked like the movie actor. He had a roll of cash in his right fist, which he transferred to his left.

The fuel-desk guy said: "You don't have time to see the name on her ass?"

"Bullshit. She's just fucking with your head, dumbass."

Janey looked at the fat roll, gave Danny Glover a wink, and began to tug her jeans down. Jack said, "No, no, not in here, I was just kidding, I mean..."

"Shut up, man! I got the time! You don't have the time?" Danny widened his stance as Janey grabbed his left arm briefly for balance. She mooned the desk.

"See?"

Jack leaned over and squinted. "Says Perry Schaffner. The card says Janey Schaffner."

"She said it was her brother's name you dumb fuck. Turn around, beautiful Janey, an' let me see."

"Ten dollars."

"Oh, get real."

"Free, if you kiss it."

"That's a deal!" He turned Janey around and squatted. Holding her leg with his free hand, he gave the tattoo a slow, noisy smack.

"Your moustache tickles."

"You want me to move in a little further?"

None of them noticed Bull walking up until he spoke. "Oh, Janey. Janey, you are so dumb."

§

They idled out of the fuel lanes and parked in the back row. Bull suggested they purchase enough bungee cords to re-tarp the Airstream, and when he returned from the truckstop store Pierretta Z announced she had to take a dump — her exact words — and she walked one of the twins to the restrooms with her.

"We all had a talk," Janey said.

Lolita nodded. "It's a deal you can't refuse."

"Oh shut up you little bitch."

"Bullperry!"

"She set me up in Valdosta, Janey, remember?"

"They made me," Lolita said. She was wearing a bright white T-shirt said *FRUIT KOLA* on it. Below her teen-age points *Delicious & Fruity* and *Port-au-Prince.*

Janey said: "Pierretta is taking the twins to the restroom one-at-a-time so people think they're both one person. Remember that fax Beauford had? The photos of the girls? It was these same girls we got now. Oh, and Pierretta has to check her email on that, um, coin-operated computer, whatever, in there."

"And, yeah, well...." Bull was still looking at Lolita. "You miss Clyde?"

"Bullperry!"

"You miss your asshole daddy?"

Janey took a swing at Bull but he ducked. "Okay okay!"

"She's in this for the long-haul, just like you. Isn't that a trucker word? Long-haul?"

"Yeah, yeah."

Coin operated computer.... Bull shivered. The night air was cool but they'd be heating up in a minute. "You guys can help me with the tarp. It's a lot heavier than it looks and we have to get it up and over."

Janey said: "Lolita doesn't want to go back home."

"Whatever."

"She said when all this is over she wants to take my place. With you. In the truck. See the world. You know, when I go home."

"Oh, sure, right. Duh. If we're still alive!"

"The old lady left us here alone. With our guns!"

Janey, Lolita is what, thirteen? Or..." Bull stopped in mid sentence.

Thirteen....

"I'm fourteen," Lolita said.

"Yeah, sure. Like we believe that".

Fourteen....

"The twins have to ride in the trailer until we find them a better hiding place," Janey said. "So I guess I get to meet your Dianna finally!"

"Better hiding place...."

"Until we ransom them off."

"Jeez, Janey, I wish I'd been in on your little talk!"

"You were in the store getting the bungee cords! Duh!"

Fourteen....

Janey smiled and said, "You can always have me! Underage is underage. She might still be twelve! Bull? You there? Hello!"

Thirteen....

CHAPTER 27
Stony Hill Missouri

"Give me that phone!"

Little Harold slapped his mother's hand away. "Mama, stop!" He lowered his voice. "Sorry, Bull. Mama doesn't have a clue to what's ..."

"I'm his boss! I'm his dispatcher!"

"Mom, just listen for a minute please? Bull, Mister Ahearn says to dump the Airstream, deadhead to Miami with the twins, and swap them and the Duplan trailer for our trailer."

Kate screamed, "What about our load?!"

"Mama, I can't hear!"

Kate managed to get past her overweight son to mash the speaker-phone button.

Bull said, "Drop the Airstream? You mean, like hide it?"

"Mister Ahearn said to stick the Airstream up the old lady's ass."

"Oh, sure. I see you don't call him Dopey any more. Harold, I'd have to kill her first, and that means not getting paid."

Kate yelled, "Who the fuck are you working for, Bull?!"

"Mister Ahearn said the ransom money is gone. Somebody intercepted it. There's no ransom, and the best we can do is swap the twins and the trailers."

Kate plunked into a chair. "And our load?"

"Oh, Ahearn said he'll get a Duplan driver to drop it off as a gesture of good faith. It's probably already there. Florida City. He said we should call them and check. He said Denver left all the paperwork."

On the speaker-phone, Bull's sigh sounded pitiful. "And I'm supposed to believe after all this trouble the old lady's going to agree? Right."

"He said tell her the ransom money is gone. He said to tie her to a tree first."

"Right. Tell you what, I'm not doing shit until the McKay load is confirmed in Florida City."

"How do we get you?"

"Janey's cell phone."

Kate yelled, "Janey? Who's Janey?!"

"Take it easy, Kate. Janey's my sister. If it weren't for her you'd be filing for bankruptcy right now."

"And the number is...?"

"Janey! What's your cell-phone number?"

Little Harold plopped his ass onto Kate's desk and mashed a small pile of files to the floor. "Got a pen, Mama?"

On the speaker-phone, they heard a woman yell, like from a distance. "Get your own fucking cell phone, Bullperry! Damn!"

Harold grinned, and his mouth opened with a slow, rumbling, wet burp.

Juanita....

I'm coming to get you soon, Juanita.

CHAPTER 28
Pike County Kentucky

On the next afternoon, heading northeast, Bull insisted they do the last leg to his place in West Virginia — "a tricky drive for an eighteen wheeler" — during daylight hours. So they stopped to spend the night east of Pikeville, Kentucky, near Meta, on a deserted, pipe-storage and maintenance lot cut into the side of a mountain off Highway-119. All of them emerged from the Airstream and the tractor cab at the same time, Lolita first out from under the tarp over the RV. The sun had just dropped behind a ridge but the shadows were eerily lit by the reflected, golden light from high up the western slope opposite the roadway. Bull sucked in a deep breath but the mountain air wasn't all that good, and Pierretta Z had to herd the excited twins back to the near side of the Airstream so they couldn't be seen from passing vehicles.

"Must be shit seeping out of the coal mines," Bull said. "Bad air. I used to haul pipe up here. When I first started driving. Used to scare the shit out of me, too. Coal trucks coming the other way tearing around hairpin curves...."

The women weren't listening, the five of them squatting now in a circle, and the splatter of their piss was the only thing breaking the silence. That and the distant cries from a pair of circling hawks, gleaming in the glory of the sun up there.

Lolita didn't look too happy, but Janey seemed to be as excited as the twins. Even the old lady turned her face up to Bull with a tight-lipped smile.

"I should ditch my forty-five," she said, but I've had it for over fifty years and if there is a god I'll take it with me when I go." She hitched up her panties as she stood, lacy and golden colored they were in the strange light, her legs skinny but knotty with muscle and blue veins.

"See, Janey?" Bull said. "A lady wears panties. And a slip!"

Janey was up and passing out tissues to the twins, both of whom were plopping perfect little, brown, identical spheres onto the gravel. "You girls are so sweet, so pretty," Janey said. "So elegant. Everything you do is so graceful and perfect!" She hesitated. "I wish you could hear me."

Their happy faces did not change, and their brows furrowed simultaneously as each dropped the last segment of her load at the same time. Janey turned on Bull. "Will you stop staring at them? Turn around!"

Lolita found a short length of pipe and used it to prop up a corner of the tarp so the twins could scoot back into the Alrstream if anyone stopped. They seemed to know what they were supposed to do, and when the old lady snapped a finger to the back of the nearest twin's head, they both ran for the opening and disappeared. The old lady said, "There was a time when they could have owned my country."

Bull said, "Yeah, well...."

"Haiti is so beautiful!" Janey said. "You must miss it!"

"Oh, Janey.... You ever watch the news? Jeez. It comes on after Oprah."

"I know when the news comes on!"

The old lady touched a finger to her lips. "Shut up!"

The distant sound of a machine, and strange cries, impossible to tell from which direction with their parking spot cut into the mountain the way it was. Louder, more cries, and a car horn.

"Yahoos," Bull said. The twins were just emerging from hiding and Pierretta motioned them back into the Airstream.

Bull said, "They act like chipmunks, I mean, hardly like they're royalty, you know, ransom material."

Suddenly two pickups came roaring around the bend, neck-and-neck, and there was a *clunk* on the other side of the Airstream.

"Yaaaaaaay - who-o-o-o-o-o-o-o-o-o-o..."

"Nice Doppler effect!" Bull squatted down and looked underneath. "Beer bottle. Dumb fucks...."

Night was falling quickly, but Lolita and the twins began a game of hide and seek, running around the long, empty, steel pipe racks and hiding in the clumps of stunted cedar and scrub-oaks on the perimeter of the lot, the old lady back in the Airstream — changing clothes, she said — and Bull and Janey sitting on empty, rusting, five-gallon hydraulic-oil drums. "No, a campfire is out," Bull said for the second time. "Let the locals think it's just a tired trucker catching up on sleep. In fact we'd be better off if another truck or two pulled in here. I expect one will. It always takes the first one to let the others know it's a cool place to pull over. Then we can build a fire."

"Lolita sure is handling the loss of her father and her pet monkey well," Janey said.

"Tell me about it."

"Yeah...."

"She's a tard. Gotta be."

"Oh, no, I don't think she's retarded, I mean, that she's mentally, what, challenged?"

"The word used to be retarded and it will always be retarded. Even when the world comes to an end the proper word for what we are talking about will be retarded. Jeez, Janey...."

Pierretta Z emerged in a light blue suit with a matching, broad-brimmed hat. Colorful, cork and canvass clogs on her feet, seamed nylons, and a large bag in one hand and a folded towel in the other — to sit on, Bull figured — and the usual purse slung from a shoulder. He jumped up and pulled over another, five-gallon drum for her.

"This gravel is sharp. I don't want the girls to fall and cut themselves." She flicked down her towel and lowered herself onto the drum, and spread out her skirt, knees and ankles together.

Janey hollered at Lolita. "Slow down! Sharp gravel! No doctor for miles! Gangrene! Rocky Mountain spotted fever!"

"Thank you." Pierretta opened the bag. "Food. We forgot the snacks we bought for tonight."

Janey hollered again and the girls came over. In a few minutes they were all munching on potato chips and cookies and a long hunk of summer sausage Janey had cut into six pieces. Bull and Janey both noticed the old lady handing each of the twins a small pill, or capsule. "They get this in the evening," she explained. "At noon a vitamin, and in the morning a Ritalin."

"Oh."

"Do you love them?" Bull said. He looked to Janey, who opened her mouth but didn't say anything.

"They are my grand-nieces. Yes, actually, yes. I love them, but not at first. I'd kill for them now."

"But you kidnapped them for ransom?"

"It's a little more complicated than that, young man."

Without anyone noticing, Lolita had moved off and was lying on her back at the edge of the lot, looking up at the stars. Pierretta said, "The poor girl has never been anywhere. When I was her age I was already gone from my home for two years, and living with a rich man in a house overlooking the ocean."

§

It was Lolita, Pierretta Z, and the twins in the Airstream, and Janey and Bull in the tractor sleeper. Windows rolled down and the engine and AC off. Bull had finished his outdoor tooth-brushing, and had managed to slide into his bunk after undressing without Janey getting a glimpse. By the time she came in and began to strip right next to where he was lying he was stuck on her cell-phone with Little Harold. He ended the call just as she scooted up to the top bunk.

"I saw your pussy."

"So what did he have to say?"

Bull was horny. He was so close to home now, and Dianna was by far his youngest and foxiest wife. He had been picturing her even while Harold was rambling on and on about the changes in plans, and Bull's erection had remained on a war footing through the entire conversation. "I changed my mind about it being wrong for you to sleep with me."

"So what did he say?"

"Since you're my sister, I mean. Still want to?"

"Bull, the last time he called he said the old lady we're traveling with nearly killed your dispatcher, and him, too, and we both saw her blow that Denver away, so, I mean, isn't every extra piece of information we can get, like, important?!"

"Would a blowjob be sex with my sister?"

"After you tell me what your Little Harold said."

"I'll tell you everything after you climb in here with me."

"No, you tell me first."

Bull had to pause, and a shiver ran up his spine. "Look at the hair on my arms," he said finally, sticking an arm out for her to see. "I just had this flashback, like, we were back home when we were kids, and in our beds, and arguing with each other just like now. It was just like twenty years ago."

"Not that long. And you wouldn't fuck me then, either."

"I grew up."

"Suddenly?"

"Suddenly."

Bull watched a long leg swing over, then the other. Her bare heels looked kind of rough but the painted toes were sexy.

The voice from above said: "First you tell me everything Harold said. Then you give me a hundred dollar bill for every time I can make you come."

§

"Bull, wake up!" Janey was looking down at him from the upper bunk. "It's hot in here. The floor is hot from the transmission or something. How do you turn on the AC?"

"Jeez, I was dreaming! Thanks a million! The engine has to be running."

"Can you tell me how to start it?"

Bull switched on a reading light. "I can start it from the bunk here."

"God, Perry, you look gross down there on top of the sheets. Don't you ever trim your bush or your pits?"

"You didn't mind a few minutes ago." Bull snapped open the control panel cover at the head of the bed, and the engine came to life with a steady, faithful, heavy idle. Another switch and the AC in the sleeper came on.

"Want to try again?"

"I'll be seeing my wife tomorrow. Dianna."

"Well, if you would pay her phone bills you could call her and let her know we're coming." Janey swung both legs over, and after not hearing an objection, dropped down and shoved Bull over against the back of the sleeper.

"I'm horny and everything, but what happened before, well, it's thinking about you being my sister messed me up."

"No problem. There's nothing wrong with that. Just relax, little brother." She began to nibble around on him. "Relax! Forget I'm your sister. Pretend I was sent by a devil. Close your eyes maybe. So what were you dreaming? It looked like you were smiling when I woke you up."

"Dreaming? Oh!" Bull, on his back, clasped his hands behind his head and closed his eyes. "I was in this big house — it was my own house somewhere — lots of rooms — like a rooming house with a big kitchen and dining room — I don't usually have dreams I can remember so good — and it wasn't a sex dream per se, not a wet dream — but there were all these ladies — and they all had jobs and stuff, though — and whenever one of them would come home from work they'd look to see how I was, and bring me stuff, and iron my clothes, and make my breakfast...."

"And....?"

"That's it."

"Oh, Bull, that's so sweet!"

"Yeah?"

"And then I had to go wake you up. Okay, keep on thinking about your dream, I think I'm making some progress here, okay, just relax, now, you don't have to do anything, just let me do all the work."

§

They were lying together on Bull's lower bunk, head-to-toe, with a sheet over them and the AC on, Janey smoking a cigarette and trying to blow the smoke out the vent she had opened over her head while Bull played with her toes. He was saying: "Funny, but you know, at first, that guy in Miami, Ahearn, he wanted the Airstream back but he wasn't interested in the twins. Now he doesn't care about the Airstream but he wants the twins in trade. So Little Harold says."

"I'm more worried about Lolita."

"That brat? The two most important people in her life. Her father and her monkey. They're murdered right in front of her and it all shook off the little heifer with the flick of her tail."

"Her tail.... Interesting choice of words, Bullperry."

"Remember when the old lady took her to that payphone at the fuel stop?"

"That old woman's going to kill us, Perry."

"Find out if Lolita told her mother that Denver and Clyde are fertilizer."

"I'm not going to bring that up unless Lolita does."

"I'm picturing the headlines when they find them two by the road. The local newspapers." Bull raised his voice: "Bizarre final act in local ditch! Man-eating monkey blown away with victim! Final curtain descends on depraved human-monkey team!"

"Can we be serious here!?"

"I'm thinking about her gun."

"What?"

"Pierretta's forty-five. She says she's had it fifty years, that old army 45. Can you imagine what a trail that thing has made? All the matching bullets in every crime lab all over the fucking country! Or the world?"

"She must be pretty smart or she'd be dead or in jail by now."

"She's smart all right. She was telling me how the American government could invade the next Islamic country and do it without a sweat, I mean, and actually pacify it afterwards."

"Right."

"No, listen. She's got this idea that would work!"

"Perry.... I'm still horny. Want to go for two-hundred dollars? You can owe me."

"The Americans pick a spot in the middle of Syria or Iran or whatever the next country is going to be, some-where in the middle where it's unpopulated wasteland. We chopper in enough troops and equipment to build and hold a small airstrip, and simply fly in everything. Build it bigger as we go along, with missiles and stuff all around the perimeter, because we're going to make the enemy come to us. We're in the middle of their coun-try! The centerpiece of the camp isn't the airstrip though, but a kickass TV transmitter. Twenty-four-hour-a-day broadcast of regular American programming from back home that shows average Americans dealing with all the day-to-day problems of having more stuff than the average sheep herder can even imagine. Oh yeah, and free TeeVees to anybody who shows up and asks for one — after getting through the metal detectors & bomb-sniffing schnauzers, of course. Listen, here's the beauty of Pierretta's plan. The ragheads living closest to our little airfield in the middle of their country get other stuff besides free TV's. Building materials, free food, and pretty soon they start applying for jobs. As the numbers increase, we teach them the base constitution which includes human rights, religious freedom, all that, while we keep on moving the perimeter farther and farther out. We help them start their own police force but we ban fundamentalists. We give away pretty dresses to all the women who want to join us, and everybody allowed inside has to wear western clothes and be like us, because if they can't do that we don't want them and why would they want us? Whenever a fundamentalist manages to worm his way in we suddenly get mean until they take care of the mullah himself. Pretty soon we suck in the nearest town, and the next one and the next one, like a big, friendly amoeba which everyone who gets swallowed loves! Before you know it, we have the entire country eating out of our hands and loving it, and we didn't have to bomb civilians or accidentally run tanks over little girls to do it. Isn't that great? That old lady has some brains! Don't you think that's the smartest military plan you ever heard?"

Bull raised his head to look at Janey, but she was asleep.

CHAPTER 29
Mingo County West Virginia

"I feel sorry for that Clyde."

"Oh, jeez, Janey...."

They had already crossed into West Virginia and it was a beautiful morning, cool and sunny, with the sun glaring into the windshield only when they happened to round a curve and head east along a valley at the same time.

"Janey, it was just a nasty Monkey."

"He knew he was going to be shot." Janey was riding up front with Pierretta Z back in the sleeper, sitting on the edge of the bunk with the curtain open.

"He was an animal," the old lady said in her little, banjo voice. The voice she used when nothing was going wrong.

Without thinking, Bull took Janey's side. "Humans are animals with clothes on. And we have memories. The only difference between you and that monkey is you can probably remember your mother's face."

Janey tried to stifle a laugh.

"I never fucked my brother," Pierretta said.

Janey's mouth opened and shut. Bull said, "That's a shltty assumption on your part, isn't it?"

"Don't get hostile with me, young man. You need me more than I need you."

"I didn't mean anything. And I do need you for something right now. I need some cash to give to my wife when we get there."

Janey turned in her seat and looked back. "We need you more than you need us? I don't think so!"

Pierretta narrowed her eyes but just for a moment. "Oh, hush." She reached up and touched Bull's elbow just as they were coming out of a sharp curve, with another switchback up ahead and a sheer rock-wall running alongside on the right not two feet from the edge of the road. "You are a good driver," she said. I'm low on cash but I can help with some gold. I can't use my plastic until I find out if I'm being watched."

"Oh, you mean, like nuggets?" Janey was smiling again but Bull was biting a lip.

"Listen," he said. "In a couple more miles we're going to take a fork and it's a lot worse than this." He shifted down a gear, then another, and swung into the oncoming lane to clear the lowboy and the Airstream around the next, rock-faced curve.

"Perry, what if a car is coming around the other way?!"

"I need to concentrate. No more talking. It's worse on the downhill." Two turns later and they came around a corner and barely did miss a big dump truck coming from the other way, and in their own lane a rock had fallen and was sitting there right in the middle. Bull could straddle it but he knew instantly the lowboy was not going to clear. He hit the brakes but not enough to jack-knife the trailer, and just when he thought they might just clear the rock, the rig straightened out with a screech as the stone caught somewhere underneath. The old lady came flying forward and her body knocked the shift-lever out of gear. Janey screamed but at the same time she was already pulling Pierretta back.

Screeeeeeeeeeeeeeeeeeeeeeeeeeeeeeeeeeee!

They came to a grinding stop in the middle of the narrow highway between two sharp turns. "One of you run ahead and wave your arms. The other run back!" The three of them jumped out and Bull dropped down to his hands and knees to look. The rock had lodged just ahead of the step-down, and enough to the side where he might be able to back off of it. Before climbing back into the cab he hollered to the women to keep going. "Make them stop! Lolita, get back inside there!"

Five minutes later they were all back in and on their way. Janey was bitching. "Goddam, Perry, didn't you know it would be like this?"

"Yeah, yeah, but I forgot a lowboy is lower to the ground than a flatbed. Okay?"

Pierretta Z leaned forward between them. "I think you did quite well, Mister Bull. Tell me, where you live, is it really a good place to hide everything? Is it a good place to hide me?"

Bull had to smile, and for the first time he thought he might just be able to trust this dangerous old bag.

"Don't get ideas. I am so old and tired I could die any day. I don't care. The knowledge makes one bold. Everybody should know they can die at any moment because it's true. Do you understand what I'm saying?"

Bull nodded. "Makes sense...."

"We could go together, Mister Bull."

§

The last mile was a private road half way up the mountain. Dirt and gravel, with forest and bramble so thick on both sides there was no view of the valley below. Bull's home was at the end — a dead end — and he saw the car just before his log house came into view.

"Black Cadillac Catera," Janey said. "Way cool! Is that your wife's?"

Bull slowed the rig to a stop and blipped the airhorns. "No. Dianna's got my old Mustang. There's only one way I can park this rig and that's by pulling around behind the house. That is, when nobody's blocking the damn drive." Bull opened his door and swung his legs down to the first step so he could stuff the 9MM into his waistband. "Wait here." He dropped to the ground, leaving the engine idling.

Janey eased open the door on her side. "Wait here," she said to Pierretta, and pulled her purse from the floor after dropping to the ground. She walked up to the Cadillac and looked it over. The hood was still warm, the windows were rolled down, and under a long-sleeved sweater folded on the passenger seat was a .357 Smith & Wesson. "Hmmmm...." Janey hesitated, but decided not to do anything about it before moving on. The log house looked new. Single story with a nice, long, front porch and a gravel drive which she could see circled wide enough for an eighteen wheeler to make it around the building. Here she could see farther, the trees and bushes were cut back and you could look up the steep hill for a few hundred feet. The stream, which she could barely hear, would have to be in the back.

Well, she could sneak a look back there while Bull got everything worked out. Walking to the near side, she peeked into the first window. It was a kitchen window, and the lights were on. Two little boys sitting at the table — sitting on books or something — playing some kind of board game. They weren't moving, though, and looked totally quiet. They looked bored, no, frightened, and Janey backed away before they could see her. She heard Bull's voice from somewhere inside, angry sounding. Then a woman's voice, quiet — too quiet to make out the words — and shouldn't the little boys be jumping up to meet their father? Janey found herself in a crouch now, moving up to a window farther down. She had to step around a large, hinged, wooden cover almost flush with the ground, looked like the outdoor entrance to a basement, and Janey wondered if she could get into the house this way. Or get out later, if she had to. Creepy, that's what this was, and the knowledge that Pierretta was back in the tractor, armed and dangerous, was actually a comforting thought.

Who knows what Bullperry has hid down there.

He wasn't the least concerned when he found all that serial killer stuff on Denver's laptop....

Why am I bent over and sneaking like this?

The old lady's a killer and I'm trusting her for backup?

Lolita and the twins must be wanting out....

Curtains were drawn on the next window, and since the house was built on a slope, the last window at the corner would be just a little high to peek into. There was a hose bib almost directly underneath, though, and

she could step up on that. The gurgling of the stream
was more noticeable now, obviously farther down the
slope, and Janey looked around. She couldn't see the
stream but she had to smile at the little kid project near
her feet, some toy Tonka construction equipment clearing a tiny piece of land, the miniature bulldozer making
a pile of little stones at one end, the dozer with the
name "BULL" written on it with a laundry marker. She
looked back to the window over her head. The hose bib
looked sturdy enough to step up on but to keep her
balance she'd need something along the wall to hang
onto, and the window sill didn't seem like it stuck out
far enough to grip. Well, maybe.... She fiddled with her
purse and positioned her .38 revolver on the top of all
the stuff in there, with the grip up, then set the purse at
her feet. She was just about to step up and grab for the
window sill when she heard a heavy footstep and the
window above her crack open. She dropped back into a
crouch and grabbed her purse.

   silence....

Backing up now, and flat against the wall, Janey
saw a hairy, pink hand, then a long-sleeved arm, French
cuff, gold-initial cuff-link, then a fat, pink, clean shaven
face looking down and from side-to-side. He didn't see
her, and he wasted no time in swinging a leg out of the
window, then another, twisting now and turning, the
toes of a pair of pointy, snake-skin boots clawing at the
round sides of the logs for a grip. Janey continued backing up and considered turning and running for it but
shit, who was this porky asshole, anyway. She drew her
gun and set her purse back onto the stony ground with-

out turning her eyes from the scene at the window. An ass and two legs now, nice light-tan leather belt looped through pressed khakis, the fancy boots still dabbing at the log sides for a toehold, as a bright-white sleeved arm pulled a blue blazer jacket through and let it drop to the ground.

Clothed in white samite, mystic, wonderful...

Goosebumps rose on Janey's arms, and for a few seconds she was in another world. Later, when telling Bull and the rest of them about her side of this story, she would exclaim, "Proof that Bullperry and I have the same mother and father! The same genes!"

It was a line from a Tennyson poem Bull had forced her to memorize, when they were children, after she had lost a bet. "The Passing of Arthur" by Alfred, Lord Tennyson. She even remembered the proper way to spell out his name.

§

"Janey," Bull said. "That poem is about something mystical and beautiful — the Lady of the Lake's arm reaching out above the waters to catch King Arthur's sword — not some scumbag fucking my wife sticking his arm out my bedroom window!"

"Excalibur," Rodney Buckle said.

"Shut up, dead man."

"Above the waters...." Janey repeated.

"Can't you tie me up somewhere else? Or tie me standing up? They's ants all over this tree. Fire ants."

"Rodney, I don't think my brother is in the mood."

"They call me Bucky."

Bull got up from the picnic table and grabbed a stick. The ant mound was on the far side of the tree and Bull dug into it, flicking dirt and ants all over the man's lap.

"You're pissing them off! They'll kill me!"

This picnic area was on the other side of the house, and you couldn't see the Cadillac or the tractor trailer from there. Rodney "Bucky" Buckle began to weep out loud as he watched Bull disappear around the corner.

Pierretta Z, Lolita, and the twins were all hiding in the Airstream, still tarped over but with the air-conditioner running. Bull plunked down at the dinette table, and whispered into the old lady's ear, explaining everything that was going on, or what he thought was going on. "I haven't decided to kill him yet, so if I let him go he can't see any of this. Any of you. Or the Airstream."

"You have to make sure he never comes back."

"Yeah.... But if we bury his ass who might come looking for him. Choppers and stuff...."

"You move his car."

"It's the old lady's car, I mean, my wife's car. He signed it over to her. It's registered in her name."

"Does he need hospital care?"

"Not yet."

"Married?"

"Says he's got a wife and kids."

"Make him call her, tell her he had a little accident and that somebody is going to bring him home."

"Gotchya."

"Don't tell him it will be your wife is going to drive him home until he's off the phone. In her new car."

"Uhhh...."

"Tell her to drive him around the house part way until you can move this rig up so she can get back to the road here. No, better yet, blindfold him until they're clear."

"You're a fast thinker, Miss Pierretta Z."

"With a little more luck I'll be the oldest female criminal on the planet, if not already. The angels look out for us, you know."

"For us?"

"People who are fun to watch."

§

The shadows were growing longer, and the sun was glancing through the trees in sheets of dusty light. Bull had to keep looking up, the tree tops bathed in that late afternoon golden glow. So beautiful. He had the feeling just then, that *knowledge,* that this moment would be remembered more strongly than most others — if he should live so long — and that it would be one of those times an old man would not be able to share because there would be no words adequate to describe it and if there were, no one who would believe.

The twins sounded funny, their deaf-mute squeals of delight as they chased Lolita around the house, Lolita with Bull's older boy on her shoulders and one of the twins holding hands with the other. Pierretta Z coming back into the clearing from her walk. She was wearing another fancy outfit Bull hadn't seen before, a new floppy hat over those glinty little spectacles, but the same purse. She waved a gloved hand and headed around the corner to the front of the house as Bull shifted his bare-ass forward a little more on the bench seat so Dianna, who was under the table, could get her head in better.

Dianna stopped, but just for a second. "This rocky ground hurts my knees!"

Bull was gripping the icy bottle of Corona in front of him with two hands. "Don't stop now!"

"But it does!"

"Next time wear knee pads!"

Bull's body shivered. "There. There. Suck harder. Harder. Don't stop, don't stop, don't stop..."

Ten minutes later he was asking what's for supper, Bull all zipped back up and Dianna with her T-shirt pulled up, the two of them standing in the kitchen and Bull talking with his face muffled between her tits. "You still look like a teenager, Dianna."

"You haven't spent two minutes with the kids yet."

"First things first."

"The freezer is full. Bucky brought a bunch of meat and stuff."

"You mention him one more time and..."

"I love you, Bull."

"Yeah, right."

"And I can keep the car?"

"No you can't keep the car! Every time I see it I'll remember how you got it!"

Janey, who had been leaning in the doorway, said, "She keeps the car, Bullperry, jeez!"

CHAPTER 30
Homer County Florida

The tractor was pulling better than ever and Bull was bragging about it. Frequently. "Maybe all the pieces ain't on the board yet, but in a couple more days this here unit is mine!" The lowboy trailer bounced a lot, though, being lighter with the Airstream left behind at Bull and Dianna's place. Left behind with Pierretta Z and Lolita.

"Ain't? This here?"

"Janey, I know how to talk when I have to. With you I figure I don't have to, okay?"

"Yah yah.... The twins are, like, fighting back there. Can't I let one get up in the top bunk? She won't fall out if I strap her in."

"Wait, you said they're like fighting? Duh."

"There's a belt, comes out from under the mattress or something."

"Yeah? Okay. Cool! Mmm-mmmm! This tractor's mine any day now."

"Maybe. If you listen to me. Slow down! Speed limit, remember?"

Janey moved one of the twins to the top bunk and was back in her seat in a few minutes. "They're all tucked in. I'll pull the curtain to if we have to stop at a scale."

"Curtain to?"

"Fuck you, Bullperry."

"The usual response."

"They look like a pair of little devils when they're naked. Oh, I found out Pierretta's last name."

"I don't want to bring the twins in on Mom and Dad in the middle of the night. We can pull over soon. Can you afford another motel? Otherwise I want my bunk back."

Janey waved a fat, grimy-looking wad of bills in front of Bull's face. "Denver's jeans, front pocket, left side, just like you do."

"Hey, Janey, good one! PZ see you?"

"Shit no. Mostly hundreds, too."

"And you let me think we didn't have any money to leave with Dianna?"

"I'm not Dianna's husband. Anyway, I asked her, I said: 'What does the 'Z' stand for, Miss Pierretta Z?' And she looked at me with that hard-nose look she has and she said, 'It's — French — for — zip!'"

It was late afternoon and they had just switched to I-59 from I-75 in Chattanooga. Without realizing it, Bull had the empty rig back up to near 80 MPH in top gear, the engine turning under 1700 RPM, and the windshield loading up with dead or dying insects.

"Janey...."

"She sure was picky where she wanted that Airstream parked."

"Glad I wasn't born a bug."

"Bullperry, humans can't be reborn as bugs."

"Somebody has to be the bugs."

"But not people, Perry, jeez."

"I don't know.... Did you pick Mom and Dad to be your parents?"

"No, don't be silly, well, maybe I did. Of course I did!"

"You picked **them?!**"

"Bullperry.... I'm surprised you put up with it, unloading the Airstream in the woods behind the house. Good thing you had a winch with a long cable."

"I have everything I need, dear sister. She wanted it out-of-sight and now it's out-of-sight." Bull had to suddenly tap the brakes when a four-wheeler, which had just passed them on the left, cut across in front of them to the exit on the right.

"Dumbass!"

"Dianna was so happy with that little gold bar Pierretta gave her. Your wife is still a kid, though. She said, 'This is so pretty! I'm never going to cash it!'. That's how she said it."

"Heavy for it's size. Stamped weird. Some foreign shit. I figure five oh-zees. That's more money than Dianna's seen in a long time."

"Cash it. A gold bar. Duh. I like her, though."

"Yeah, well.... She's what guys call young stuff."

"Oh?" Janey stomped a platform clog into the floorboard.

"Well? You used to be young stuff."

Janey stomped her foot again. "Why is it that it's okay for men to get old but it's not for women? Huh? Can you answer me that?"

"Janey, you have to ask the same dude who decides who becomes a bug and who becomes a human. You have to ask Him. Or Her."

"Yeah, right."

"Lady Luck. She's the one decides who becomes a man and who becomes a girl."

"Girl...."

"Exactly."

§

In the middle of the night, at the motel, one of the twins snuck out of the bed they were sleeping in and slid in between Bull and Janey. Bull awoke immediately, and hoped Janey wouldn't. The lust that erupted when he pretended to accidentally flop an arm around the unclothed little girl shocked even him, but then the other twin climbed in and Janey bolted awake.

"Bullshit!"

"They're scared, Janey."

Janey reached under the covers and gave Bull's erect penis a yank. "Bullshit! How old are they? Five years underage?"

"More, with the new rules. They keep moving it up."

"Asshole!"

"Janey, I was asleep. I had nothing to do with it. They probably just got scared."

Janey was out of the bed now, naked herself, and she pulled her thirty-eight out and pointed to the head of the nearest girl. "Move!"

The other twin was already back into the other bed and hiding under the covers, and her sister dove in right after her.

Hours later, just before dawn, Bull awoke when Janey slid back into bed beside him. He could hear the commode rumbling in the bathroom. She was pretending to be still angry.

"Asshole." She muttered it quietly, the twins apparently sound asleep, face-to-face but close together in the middle of the other bed. Janey had turned up the AC so that everyone would want to be under the covers.

"Janey...." Bull was whispering. "How do you think Dad is going to resist them."

"Daddy's a man, not a pervert."

"He's still going over to see Ivory and he's living with Mom."

"Ivory's no kid anymore. She wasn't when he met her. Well...."

"Well, there's nowhere else to stash them. They're, like, collateral."

"When we need them delivered to Miami, Dad can be down there in a day."

"Yeah.... But we don't need to let on they're kidnapped."

"They're not kidnapped. Pierretta told me."

"And you believed her."

"They're with her willingly. It's obvious."

"So then why the ransom?"

"Maybe it's not ransom. Maybe they're being sold. Sex slaves. Twin sex slaves. Some rich German...."

"Why does it have to be a German?"

"Just another good guess."

"So you agree that it's a possibility?"

"Like we said, it's obvious they're with Pierretta Z willingly."

"Ummmm.... Anyway, we need to come up with a story before we drop them off with Mom and Dad."

"There's another thing. Let's say it's time to make the swap in Miami, we have everything lined up, Dad brings them in and they start screaming when they see where they're going. I mean, who they're going to."

"Oh. Yeah.... Shit."

"Right. And Dad's not going to go for that. He'll be wanting to keep them by then, anyway. Picture it."

"Shit."

Janey turned her back to Bull and wiggled her ass up against him. "How can you always be so horny?"

"I gave up French fries."

"I eat a lot of seafood."

"This is wrong, you know."

"No, I don't know."

"The law of God is written in our hearts. Bible says so."

"Not in mine. Not this."

"Then it must be okay with God."

"You don't even believe in God, Bull. Jeez. Mmmmmmm, oh, that feels good, so good.... Perry, Bullperry, would you fuck, I mean, would you go to bed with Mama?"

Bull froze, and almost lost his erection. "Janey! That is so gross!"

§

It was just before noon — partly cloudy and not too hot — when they pulled in under the live oaks behind their parents' double-wide. Cooter was first up to greet them as Bull and Janey dropped down on each side of the tractor.

"She had her pups somewhere while you guys were gone," Annie said, her long, gray braids festooned with chrome-plated jingle bells.

"Somewhere, Mama? Not in the house?"

Bull corrected his sister. "Not in the fucking trailer?"

Cooter was on her hind legs, sniffing at the sleeper escape door, her claws sliding down and her long tits swaying from side-to-side. The engine ticked in the heat, and a spring on the lowboy groaned.

"Well, she might've had them in the trailer somewhere," Annie said. "What's Cooter so interested in back there? You sell the Airstream?"

"We had to hide it for awhile."

"Yeah, hide it."

Annie said, "You could've left it in the tobacco barn."

Janey and Bull shouted simultaneously. "The Magic Lincoln!" They all laughed.

"Our goofy childhood," Janey said.

"Teenage-hood."

"The fugly-hood years, Perry."

"Pregnant and ugly?" Annie said.

"Fucked and ugly, Mama. Where's Daddy?"

"He just started his nap. He'll be out. He never did tell me what happened to that car. Not in all these years."

"The Lincoln?" Janey looked at her brother. "Mama, you don't want to know."

CHAPTER 31
Bull & Janey: Now & Back Then

Annie had gone back in, and Janey and Bull still didn't have a story about the twins.

"Fuck it," Bull said. We can't even figure out how to do their ransom when we get to Miami without them."

"For the swap, not their ransom per se," Janey corrected. "And I think we should deal with Daddy alone, and let him deal with Mama."

"Well, you've blackmailed Dad into shit before."

"Harry?"

"How many father's you got?"

"Our father?"

"Janey.... When he first fell in love with Ivory — which was thanks to you, by the way — you made sure he got to meet her."

"Blackmailed? Never."

"Blackmail, Janey. That 51'Ford F-1 he loved so much, that classic pickup he towed home? You made him give it to you so he could get your cooperation on Ivory."

"Oh, that."

"You were such a bitch. Remember how you refused to call them anything but their first names? No mommy and daddy for you."

"Okay, that, yes, but that was then."

They both shut up for a moment. Janey was tired of arguing, and for Bull, looking back on those days, it all made more sense now. But as a twelve-year-old it had seemed like Hell, when he was known only as Perry — or Little Perry — before he had reinvented himself as "Bull". When Janey was, what, fifteen, and their father still had a good job at a boatyard in Miami, 600 miles away.

§

TWENTY YEARS EARLIER

Harry arrived home after dark after only a week this time in Miami. One of the first things he did the next morning was head for the old tobacco barn to check on his masterpiece. "The Magic Lincoln", he would often call it. After a long look, he reached up and carefully rotated each of the four wheels exactly one-half turn. He wanted to make sure that the tires would not get out-of-round from remaining in the same position too long. When he finished, he stepped backwards all the way outside of the open-ended barn and surveyed the whole scene. His pride in the building and the magnificent automobile which hung within, suspended from the roof-beams by chains, warmed his heart. His body shivered for a moment in the crisp, sweet, early-morning air.

Annie came sneaking up from behind and gave him a hug. "I love you, Harry."

"I love you, too, Annie." Harry wished he had said it first.

"I just.... Oh, never mind."

"What?"

"If you would just stay home. Find a job here."

"There aren't any jobs here and nobody pays anything here. Besides, I've only been gone a few days and I'm back for the weekend already. Huh?" Harry tried to sound sufficiently pissed so she would shut up about it.

"That was a nice surprise, Harry, but you'll be leaving Sunday morning. We have one day."

"Beats zero."

"Remember when we first moved here? You were so happy to get out of the city you stayed home and worked on the garden, and your truck, and the reefer. The kids were happy, too. Now I can't handle them anymore. And I miss you. Sometimes I wake up in the middle of the night and I reach over for you and..."

"Yeah? And when I was staying home we ran out of money! Besides, getting this Lincoln out of the barn was the first thing you mentioned when I got back last night. That's all you cared about."

Annie backed away from him. Her eyes brightened. "Well? Look at it! Do you know how much stuff we could put in here if it weren't for this car hanging up in the air in the middle of everything? Is it supposed to be the 'Spirit of St. Louis' in the Smithsonian or something? It's not an airplane, Harry. It belongs on the ground. Outside!"

"I did it for the effect. It's art."

"I have furniture behind the trailer with plastic over it, furniture that belonged to my parents, getting wet and ruined, just so you can have this nigger-car hanging in the barn. This was supposed to be our storeroom,

Harry! I paid for the roofing repairs on it with my own money!"

"Redundant."

"Harry!"

"Funny thing is, I was standing here just now, before you walked up, looking at it and trying to figure out how long it would take to winch it down to the ground, and how long it would take to get it gassed up and running — get it out of here, tow it back to Miami — I figured it's too much of a job to have it ready by tomorrow morning. You know, get it out of your sacred storeroom — this was supposed to be my garage before we decided to buy this property, if you'll recall — and thinking about how lucky I am to have a wife who understands — and here you are bitching and squalling and..."

"Harry!"

Harry faced her. Every time he came home she looked more loveable. Older and more independent, though. He shook his head. "Annie. It's good for both of us for me to be away to work so often. You've become so independent, anyway. We'd be fighting like dogs all the time, like we were starting to do before we sold the house down there." A smile crossed Harry's face. "Besides, when I met you, you were country. If I stayed home, you'd have to go to work again, like at one of those gas stations off I-10. Only you'd need a gun under the counter instead of that mallet you kept behind the bar in Blackhawk."

Annie wiped away a tear. "Maybe we should've moved all the way back to Colorado. I would've been there when Mom got sick. And Dad...."

"I belong down south, Annie."

"Oh, Harry."

They hugged. "I love you so much, Annie. If I didn't have you to come home to...."

"As long as I'm in the background, huh, Harry? The background?"

"You're my home, Annie. I'd hardly call that background!"

"Harry, look. Let's just step back aways and look at a typical Harry Schaffner scene." She broke away and backed off from the building. Harry followed her. "Now," Annie said. "Turn around and look at this."

The barn was small but larger than a garage, the floor was rotten, and the sides were long gone. But the frame and roof beams were solid and the tin roof was only two years old. At just above head height, with its chrome-plated grille and shiny headlights, a huge, midnight-blue, mint-condition, 1979 Lincoln Continental hung silently, observing them.

Harry's heart swelled with pride.

"Harry. Look, okay? Do you think there is another woman — anywhere in the world, Harry — who would put up with something like this?"

"Yeah. I figure, probably, millions of them. You're wrong."

There was a long silence. They watched a hen go by with her brood of biddies, the baby chicks chirping and pecking at the ground as they hopped along. Suddenly, the peace was broken by noises coming from the trailer.

"Kids are waking up," Annie said.

"Daddy's home, you better watch it!"

"Harry doesn't care. I'm a girl!"

"Ohhhh, Janey. I'm going to tell!"

"Sheeeit! You have to get out of bed for that!"

"Syph-mouth!"

Annie and Harry reluctantly started for the trailer. They heard what sounded like Perry and Janey slapping each other, and furniture clunking around.

"They need their father, Harry."

"They have their father." Harry spit. "I love them, Annie, but I have my own life, too. When I was their age I had to live the way my parents wanted. Now I live my own. The kids'll have their way after they're old enough and on their own."

"I understand, Harry."

"I wish you did."

"What about the Lincoln?"

"Annie! It's a '79! It's the last big Lincoln they ever made! The last of the big hogs!"

"Oh, Harry!"

Annie stomped off ahead of him toward the trailer — "the house" as they called it — a private joke about the compromise they had made when they moved into the woods in the Florida panhandle. Harry turned back to get his fill of the Lincoln. It was still hanging there, so patient — so quiet — like it knew its day was coming. Its glory.

"You don't even have a title for it!" Annie turned and screamed. "It's hot!"

Harry moved closer to the Lincoln and looked up at it again. It was almost as if the machine were looking back at him.

Annie doesn't understand....

The Lincoln seemed to agree.

The last of the big hogs. Tilt-wheel. AC. Power windows. Big 460 V-8.... As the early morning sun slid under the tobacco-barn roof through the slatted sides, the Lincoln's gleaming chrome began to glow in burnished gold.

He hadn't met her yet but Harry could see Ivory in it. He could feel her gratitude. He could see her pulling up to him at the curb on palm-lined Biscayne Boulevard in Miami. He recognized her from his dreams. Even when he was a boy he believed.

She sat so tall and elegant behind the wheel, and icy-cool, and ebony black. A ghetto princess shipped in from the jungles of darkest Africa by The Lord Himself, just for Harry.

The driver-side window was whirring down and Harry leaned forward to receive her kiss. Her lips, flushed with pink, parted.

"Do it have a title?" she said.

the title....

"Harry!"

Harry followed Annie's trail — the bent grass, the suction-cup pattern of her cheap-ass jogging shoes in the sand — up to the trailer. Perry was still in bed, reading comics. "KORAK", and "CONAN the Barbarian". He was in his tan, flannel pajamas, backed up against the pillows, and Harry went up and looked over the boy's shoulder. Conan was rescuing a long-haired, blond, jungle princess. The scene was so familiar that it gave Harry a little rush. It was the kind of stuff he loved when he was a boy — the exotic, wild white women who ruled savage tribes in remote, tropical places. The best was when they were captured and enslaved, and then rescued by — The Phantom?

Africa....

"Perry reads that shit and plays with himself under the covers, Harry," Janey said. She was standing in the doorway of Perry's little room in her panties.

"Oh, Janey, that's not true! You skinny bitch!"

"Get dressed, Janey!" Harry said.

"Then why don't you ever turn the page, little baby?"

Harry ruffled Perry's hair, pretending to be unfazed by Janey's brazen flashing. "He's just daydreaming. I used to do it, too."

"You mean, jerk off?"

"Janey!"

"Here's one we saved for you, Pop," Perry said. He was raising up, pulling a comic-book off the shelf over his bed.

"Open it to the story in the middle," Janey said. She was in the room now, and she reached past Harry and snatched the worn, limp book out of Perry's hands.

"The whole thing is just one story, Dummy!" Perry said.

"Her name is Nightshade, Dad. She fights the Avengers sometimes." Janey pushed the open comic under Harry's nose. "Here she is."

The children studied his face while he looked. The comic-book character was a long-legged, black girl wearing a skimpy, leather bikini. A thick, gold choker encircled her neck and a large pistol hung from her wide, leather belt — a gun like The Phantom used to carry. Harry's heart speeded up. He flipped the page. In every frame, Nightshade was dancing and prancing and stretching her devil body as she told Captain America off. In peril of his life, all the mighty hero could say was: "WOW!"

Who drew this?

Whoever it is — he knows....

I'm not the only one!

"It's a hit!" Janey yelled.

Harry jumped.

"Janey, your father said to get dressed!" It was Annie standing in the doorway now.

Janey did not move, and Harry refused to give his fifteen-year-old brat the satisfaction of looking at her bare breasts. Annie walked into the crowded room. Harry wanted to put the book aside but it was too late. There was a long silence while Annie looked.

"Harry?"

"Hmmmm."

The children were watching both of them now.

"Do you have a colored girl down there in Miami?"

"Oh, Annie...." Harry turned and gave Annie a hug, which she did not return. "No."

"Well if you don't," Janey said, "you ought to. Soon! Before it becomes a disease!"

Harry lost it and grabbed Janey by the upper arms and began to shake the shit out of her. "Get dressed!"

Janey did not flinch and tried to keep looking him in the eye as her head flopped around. "I — thought — that — with you — I'd be — safe!"

"She means because she's white," Perry said.

Harry gave Janey a final shove which sent her sprawling backwards out the door and Annie managed to swat her a good one as she flew past.

"I smell breakfast," Perry said. "Burning!"

Annie narrowed her eyes at both of them and stomped back toward the kitchen. Harry closed the comic-book and laid it gently on Perry's bed. "I want to read this later. Okay?"

"Sure, Pop." Perry carefully placed it under some others on the shelf. "Pop? Look. This is the one I like." Perry turned to a page in a book he had been hiding under the covers. A tall, blond, Nordic warrior was leading a group of bare-titted females through a valley infested with dinosaurs and crawling with snakes. All of the females were young, and beautiful, and white. All of them had long legs and tight little asses and perfectly formed breasts with swollen, up-turned nipples — even the ones carrying suckling children. High above, crouching on a rock-ledge, was a gleaming black man, rippling with muscle. No doubt by the look in his eye he was lusting after the women in the harem below.

"Heavy stuff," Harry said. "Where do you get these?"

"A kid in school is a collector. He only sells books he has duplicates of. His father takes him to flea markets and comic book conventions and places like that. He says that at night sometimes his father smokes pot and then he reads the comics himself and nobody is allowed to talk once he starts."

"Oh, yeah? Ha ha! Do they live near us? What's their name?"

"I just told you stuff I promised not to tell, so I can't tell you their name."

"It's okay. Your parents smoke pot."

"Yeah, but I don't tell on you, either. Dad. Look at this page."

Harry sat down on the side of the bed and put an arm around his boy. He tried to remember exactly what his own fantasies were at age twelve, and it didn't seem like he'd progressed nearly as far as his son. Perry had turned the page and was tapping his finger against the right-hand side. A new female was on the scene: taller, tougher, but just as wonderfully formed — standing, legs spread, behind the black warrior on the rock-ledge. She was an Asian Amazon, no less. (There was no doubt that the artists were an improvement over the hacks Harry had found so inspiring in his youth — well, no, there was R. Crumb and Wallace Wood. No, he was older than Perry when he discovered them. And Vaughn Bode. Harry would never forget that tiny Deadbone dude rappelling down from this big earth-mother girl's nipple to her belly-button in "Climbing Abroad".

The lewd, Laotian huntress' fingers and wrists and ankles glittered with circlets of jewels, and she wore a G-string made of... (Harry squinted his eyes).

"Shark teeth, I think," Perry said. Dad? I know that there aren't any girls in the whole world really like this, but, well...."

"Oh, I don't know." Harry thought about that. Himself, he had always maintained the hope. But then, it was best to keep in mind that Perry was fifty percent Annie. "Perry, even if you could find a whole litter of females like this in some faraway land, or maybe in, like, New Orleans, the god squads would lock you up if you took home more than one."

"Yeah.... Dad? Did cave-men really go out and when they saw a girl they liked they just knocked her in the head and dragged her home by the hair?"

"Ha! Naw. I think they probably carried them back. Seriously, Son, the fact is, for most of our history, the foxiest ladies were bought and sold. Or just kidnapped."

"Well, then somebody had to own her first. See what I mean?"

"Or captured as booty." Harry had the feeling Perry was leading him into some kind of trap. "You've been thinking this all out, haven't you. Ha!"

"So how did the original owner get her?"

Harry sighed. "Fathers. Fathers sold their daughters, or traded them for stuff."

"Bullshit, Harry!" Annie was standing in the doorway again. Arms across her chest. "In the old days women had to have a dowry and she used that to pay for a man!"

"That came later, Annie. I was talking about ancient history. You shouldn't have smoked so much rope when you were in school."

"Breakfast's ready, Master!" Annie stomped off.

"Can we sell Janey?"

"Perry!"

"She's not old enough?"

"Too old. I think in Bible lands they sell them at about age twelve. Thirteen max. Yeah."

"You mean, like nowadays?"

"Yeah! The rich guys have harems, like the Saudis, and the poor men fuck what's left. That's been going on since Adam and Eve."

"We have Bible class every day in school here. Yeeech! It's supposed to be against the law, so they give us this other book about the religions of the world, but everybody knows that if you want a good grade, you better know the questions on the Bible."

"Oh, yeah? Well, all this stuff is right there, in the Bible. The right to own slave-girls, I mean."

"Where?"

"They tell you what chapters to read, huh? You want to have some fun in religion class? I did when I was your age!" Harry became animated and he stood up and went to Perry's window and looked out, not really seeing anything. He sat back down next to Perry again. "You got a Bible here?"

Perry clambered out of bed and dug a Bible out of his school books. Harry grabbed at it and began to riffle through the pages, the tip of his tongue licking from side-to-side between pressed lips. "You'll love this, Son. This is what I used to do before religion class. Your grandfather made me go to this parochial school and we had an hour of this shit every day!" Harry reached for a ballpoint pen on Perry's desk and began to underline passages in Genesis. "Now remember, this King James version here substitutes the word servant for the

word slave. In the Hebrew and Greek it says slave —
don't let them bullshit you. If you don't believe me,
check it out. Look it up! Okay. For starters, Chapter Six!
This is where the angels and God's buddies or whatever
come to Earth and fuck all the Earth women they want.
Perry, you need a New Revised Standard version — it's
called the NRS — I'll get you one. Okay! Leviticus, Leviticus. Here it is! Chapter 25! Verses 44 to 46! I'm marking
it for you. This says you can get slaves from foreign
countries!"

"Dad. Dad!" Perry grabbed his father's hand.
"We're not supposed to write in the Bible. It's against
the law!"

"What? Bullshit! This is America! And your parents
paid for this book. I didn't risk my ass overseas for freedom so that..."

"Dad! I heard your freedom speech!"

Harry's nose was still in the Good Book. "Genesis,
Chapter 9! Slavery a common practice and condoned by
God. See? Here are the rules on how you're to treat
them. Wait, wait..."

"You don't care if I get an F in religion?"

"No. But you have to pass all the other stuff. Wait,
here it is! Wait..."

"Dad...."

"And tell them that if you get an F in religion, the
whole school board's going to jail!"

"This is interesting." Janey had returned, dressed,
her wild hair pinned back.

"Chapter Sixteen! Genesis!" Harry quickly moved
down Perry's bed to make room for Janey. "This is

where Abraham's wife Sarah gives him one of her Egyptian slaves to fuck, so he can have a kid by her. Which he did but then he threw them both out in the desert to die and that started the Israeli-Arab war, and they've been killing each other ever since, oh, for about three-thousand, four-thousand years, but that's another story. Anyway, the Egyptian slave girl was younger and better looking than Sarah, anyway."

"An Egyptian slave-girl?" Perry said. "Wow!"

"Oh, Perry," Janey said. "Big deal. Probably didn't even shave her pits."

"Was Sarah shaving her pits?"

"Right on, Perry!" Harry and Perry slapped fives. "The slave-girl's name was Hagar. When I was your age I used to dream about what she must've looked like." He turned to Janey, who had plunked down beside him and was squinting into the open Bible on his lap. "And your age. I used to ask your grandpa about her, figuring he'd know more, but he would always change the subject. Hagar. I used to write her name in all my school books, in secret places. I wrote Hagar on my arm once, too, in ink, and it wouldn't wash off for a long time. I was afraid my parents would see it but it finally wore off."

Harry showed them the spot on his left bicep.

"Sick, Dad," Janey said.

"God outlawed slavery when Jesus came, Dad."

"Wrong, Perry! It's A-OK with The Man. Genesis to Revelation. Even with Saint Paul, who had a problem with sex. Check it out! Besides, Jesus is the same God and God is unchanging. Gotchya! He didn't suddenly get religion from one dip into Mary."

"Boy!" Perry said. "Am I going to have fun Monday! Mister Preston — we have him for religion — he's going to shit! He has this huge Bible on a stand and in the middle it has this dictionary. It's called a concordance. I'm going to look up in there every place in the Bible that tells about slaves!"

"It's not in there," Harry said.

"Dad," Janey said. "If it's in the Bible, it's in the concordance. Every word. By subject. Every passage that has to do with that subject."

"Except slavery. They took that out, and you have to look up the word *servant.* At least in every concordance I've ever seen. You have to get an NRS translation or look up the word *slave* on a university computer or something."

"I'll find it by hand," Perry said. "Fun, fun, fun! I can't stand Mister Preston. He has yellow teeth and he wears these baggy, plaid pants and he wears white socks and big, black shoes. He's always telling us you should take us to church."

"Us? You mean, he tells you and Janey that?"

"Yes, Dad. He says he's coming out to see you one of these days."

"Good! Tell him to bring his fucking Bible! Tell him to bring God's address, too. Or at least a 1-800 number!"

"Funny, Dad," Janey said. "You better be careful — Jesus is supposed to be coming back soon."

"Yeah? He can't. If He did there'd be so many negligence suits slapped on his ass he'd have to hire every lawyer on Earth!"

"Negligence?"

"If we're all God's children, then he's the original deadbeat dad. Not enough food in the world, won't pay our medical insurance, won't divulge medical secrets, leaves lead out in the open to poison us. Ever see a baby born with an *Unleaded Only* decal on its ass? Forget it! Not a word. No cures in this book. Nothing! I can show you pages and pages on how the draperies should look in the temple, though!"

Perry was hunched over a little notebook, scribbling as fast as he could. When Harry realized what he was doing he felt a rush of pride.

"What else?" Perry said.

Harry sighed. "I could go on for hours."

"He could," Annie said. "Breakfast's cold."

"Just one more item for now," Perry pleaded.

"Leprosy. Know what that is?"

Janey said: "It's catchy, and your nose and your ears and your fingers rot off. Stuff like that."

"Okay. If Detroit makes cars where parts are falling off, the government makes the company recall all the defective units so that they aren't dangerous to life and limb. Okay? In the Bible, when Moses asks The Creator what to do about all the people with leprosy, instead of telling him the cure God tells Moses and Aaron to kick all the lepers out of the camp so nobody else can catch it."

"That's a good one!" Perry, bent over, scribbling.

"Breakfast!" Annie said. "Unleaded!" She disappeared down the hall.

Janey got up and followed her. Perry stopped writing and was staring at the ceiling, pen poised over the notebook.

"I love you, Son."

"I love you, too, Pop!"

"So!" Harry made a move to get up.

"Dad? Do you think slavery will ever come back?"

"I hope not."

"Really?"

"Yeah. It's not right. But, well...."

"I know what you mean.... Anyway, I know I wouldn't want to be one."

"Right. In a way it never really died out, though. People with more money can buy you to do things."

Janey stomped back in. "Annie says to tell the males that breakfast gets fed to the dog in one minute!"

"Janey. Please call Annie, Mommy. Okay?"

"Okay, Harry." Janey stomped back out. "Mommy? I told them!"

"She's a bitch, Dad."

They made it to the kitchen table, Perry still in his pajamas. Annie and Janey were sitting there, waiting. Harry sat down.

"You drink coffee now, Janey?"

"Hot and black."

"Cause you're so sweet." Harry tore into his bacon and eggs. "I haven't had a breakfast like this since I left."

"That's what you said last week," Annie said. "Think about it."

"We were talking about white slavery, Mom," Perry said. "It used to be okay. Thanks for not putting grits on my plate!"

Annie looked at Harry and shook her head. Perry gulped down a mouthful of eggs and shoved a corner of grape-jelly toast into his mouth. "Hey, Pop, we have a black kid in school now. The first one for our school ever. The principal said that our school was the last one in the entire south to integrate and we might as well get used to it. I said I was already used to it and he said it's because we're from Miami and don't know any better, and all the other kids laughed."

"Yeah?"

"She's in Janey's class. Janey, stop staring at me like that! Anyway, Janey's the only one who talks to her. Everybody else hates her."

"Well, that's nice, Janey," Harry said. "Good for you!"

"Janey just doesn't know any better, Dad. Anyway, her name's Constance or something like that."

"Connie."

"Constipated Constance. On warm days she comes to school wearing this dumb, wool hat, and on cold days she wears these awful jogging shorts. Yuk! Her legs look like liver!"

"Should I make liver for dinner tonight, Dad?" Janey said. She took a long slurp of coffee while staring at her father over the cup.

"Janey's nice to her because they both smoke reefer during recess and lunch," Perry explained. "Waiting for the next time they bring the dope-dog over, I guess.

And the nigger's nice to Janey 'cause Janey gives her the reefer. Free!"

"Not during recess, dummy! Just at lunch time! And she gives me some, too. Only she says ours is better. You can be proud, Harry. Her father grows it, too."

"He does?" Harry looked at Annie and raised his eyebrows. Annie shrugged.

"Seems like everybody here in the sticks is into weed, Annie. Surprise, surprise. Janey. You didn't tell her we grow it, did you?"

"I lied. I told her we grow ours down in Dade county — not here. Her father wants to trade some seeds."

"That's out, Harry!" Annie said.

"Dad's much too old for her, don't worry about it, Annie," Janey said.

"Damn! I wasn't even thinking about that! Should I be? I was thinking that we all agreed we weren't going to tell anybody. We should've started a whiskey still as soon as we moved here. Nobody would bother us for that. Harry, listen. In last week's paper they listed a bust for felony possession of paraphernalia over in Washington County. It was a roach clip, Harry! A crummy roach clip!"

"It won't stick," Janey said.

"Not the point! Jail, lawyers, bond, all that time and money!"

"Connie's father has a still, too," Janey said.

"Now this is getting interesting!"

"Yeah, but he only sells to other niggers, I think."

"I didn't mean that. I already have the shine lined up for taking back to Miami tomorrow. I'd just like to meet this guy."

"Oh, Harry," Annie sighed.

"Nothing wrong with that, Annie. I need a male friend here."

"They live way off the main road, just like us," Janey said. "It's a neat place. And Connie has this weird sister, too. She's real tall and thin, like a model, only she won't talk to anybody. She just hangs out at home. She always carries this big purse, even being at home and all, and she has a gun in there. She's older than Connie."

"Oh, yeah?" Harry bit his lip. Doesn't she go to school?"

"Maybe she's too old for school. She quit high-school, anyway. No! wait! She graduated!"

"Jeez, Janey," Perry said. "Duhhhh...."

"You've seen her?"

"Jeez, Dad...."

"Well, yeah! I go over there sometimes. After school mostly. The sister always looks real neat and sort of dressed up to go somewhere but she never leaves."

"I told her not to go there, Harry, but Janey ignores me when you're not at home."

"Sometimes I just stay on the bus and get off with her, and her father drives me back here in his truck. He drops me off at the bottom of the hill, though, because he's afraid of Annie."

"Annie, you're a bad one." Harry attempted a smile.

"They have pigs and stuff — the little piglets are so cute. When you pick them up they feel so solid! And Connie's house, well, I guess you'd call it a cabin — it's so neat inside. Inside it looks like — I don't know — but they have neat draperies and like Indian blankets and stuff on the beds — like hippies live there, only everything is so neat and clean and cheerful looking."

"What's the sister's name?"

"The sister? One time it started to rain and we all had to go inside, and the sister fixed me a place on her bed to sit — it's all one big room — so I thought she was being friendly, and I said: 'What's your name?' But she just looked at me."

"That's not what you told me, cum-wad."

"Shut up, cum-for-brains! Anyway, the next time I was over we were sitting around in the back — they have fruit trees there — and I was helping them snap beans, and she sat next to me on the bench, and all of a sudden she reached over and pulled on my hair — no, she was just sort of feeling of it with her fingers, you know. Her fingers are real long. And she was smiling, and she said: 'My name is Ivory.' Just like that!"

A chill shot through Harry. *Ivory....*

"Well, what do the rest of them call her?" Annie said.

"Nothing! And she doesn't have to help with anything if she doesn't want to! Connie has chores all the time and her father always has all this stuff to do."

"Probably too dumb to help," Perry said.

"How would you know! Anyway, ever since then she still won't talk. Sometimes she'll just sort of look at me and smile, you know, but I never see her smile for anybody else. And last Friday I was helping Connie shuck corn — late-corn, they called it, whatever that is — and I saw Ivory in the doorway and I called her name and asked her if she wanted to sit with us and she smiled and came right over to me and sat down with me the whole time. With her purse in her lap."

"Our dog knows her name, too," Perry said.

"That's beautiful, Janey," Harry said.

"Sheeeit, Dad! Janey has you snowed, just like she does everybody else! Except me."

"Harry," Annie said, "would you believe that when our vegetables came in Janey was too busy to help?"

Harry nodded.

"Do you think it's okay for her to go over there? Especially when I specifically told her not to?"

"Well.... It's too late now, Annie. If there were any harm in it, it would've come up by now. Let her go."

"Thanks for the back-up! What about that woman with the gun? What if she goes off the deep end when Janey's there?"

Perry snorted. "Sounds like she's already over her head."

"Well, Annie, maybe we should — maybe we should let Janey make some decisions of her own now that she's older."

"Me, too!" Perry said.

Annie got up from the table and began to shout. "You always take their side! That's why they think I'm such an idiot!"

"That's not the reason," Perry said.

Ivory.... Harry closed his eyes and started his deep breathing exercise.

Ivory....

§

BACK TO THE PRESENT TIME

One of the twins was knocking gently on the tractor window from the inside of the cab.

"Shit, It must be hot in there."

"Bullperry, I told you to leave the motor and the AC on."

"Bullshit. You were so happy to see your dumb Saturn wasn't moved. Maybe that's where Cooter has her puppies."

"We can let the girls out on the other side. They can pee and stuff out here."

"Okay, but then we march 'em in and let the story create itself. Soon as Mom and Dad see we're lying they'll light up a joint and start grinning, and we'll be able to walk right past them with the twin's clothes and stuff."

§

The novel "Harry & Ivory" — prequel to "Lowboy #22" — which features these inglorious characters twenty years earlier, is available as an eBook and in print. There, the dangerous and bad-ass brother and sister team of "Lowboy #22", Bull and Janey, provide an entertaining look into their early teen years as they manage to disrupt the local, bible-belt school while surviving life with their abnormal, drug-loving parents. Their humorous escapades provide the canvass for the endearing title story: their father's obsession with an exotic black woman named Ivory.

CHAPTER 32
Homer County Florida

"Well, this is new!" Annie had gotten up early to make a big breakfast, and found Bull and Janey already at the kitchen table.

"We get up early now, Mama." Janey was wearing a white, terry-cloth robe with one of her new tits sticking out.

"Crack of dawn," Bull said. He in only a pair of briefs.

"We're on a mission, Mama."

"A case," Bull said.

"Son, do you have to sit there in your underwear?"

"Janey's not wearing any!"

"Well, how would we know that!" Annie looked between the two of them, avoiding eye-contact. "Your father said they can stay. I say, not for long."

"They're nice kids, Mom."

"And they do chores without a complaint, Mama, you'll see."

"And they couldn't talk back if they wanted to."

Annie sighed. "I thought they were having trouble sleeping last night, and when I looked in on them they were playing with themselves."

Bull chuckled but Janey remained silent. Annie said, "They were having orgasms, Janey!"

"I didn't even discover my thing until I was a tee-nager!"

"Dear sister, the latest would have to be your 13th birthday, then."

"Well, at least I don't get turned on by little girls."

"I'm more worried about your father," Annie said. She did not look worried, though, as she flew around getting the frying pan out, lining up bread and eggs, and slam-bamming into the refrigerator for milk and bacon.

"Daddy's too moral, Mama. But I can see my little brother has been tempted." She paused and toed him under the table. "It's disgusting, Bullperry!"

"Tempted?! Men are animals, right Janey?"

"Exactly!"

"Animals are born with instincts. Re-naming in-stincts *temptation* is how churches get people to give money."

Janey sighed. "Is Daddy up?"

"He's waiting for them to get out of the bathroom. They're brushing their teeth."

"Did you have to tell them?"

"No.... Actually, no!"

"See?"

"Okay, but listen. They can't hear, right? So how do I tell them to get dressed?"

Bull bit a lip. Just the memory of seeing them run down the hall jammed his brain. Those flat little tum-mies and knobby belly-buttons and the premature, pointy tits with the purple-black nipples....

Janey said, "You lay out what you want them to wear and you take either one by the hand — the other one will follow — and you lead them to the clothes. You want them to bathe, you lead them to the filled bathtub. Same with a sink full of dirty dishes. They're price-less, Mama."

"They have a problem with the shower for some reason," Bull added.

"Okay...." Annie pretended to be pre-occupied with slicing an onion on the old breadboard Harry had made, back when Janey and Bull were little kids, from a com-munion bench he had stolen from his father, which was originally from his grandfather's first church. "Okay, but what if one of them gets sick? No, what if both of them get sick? You said don't let anybody see them together. As twins."

Bull thought, *shit!* and Janey said, "Take one of them in to the clinic. If they need antibiotics get a scrip, and the very next day run back with a story that the scrip went into the garbage disposal by accident and you desperately need a refill."

"We don't have a garbage disposal."

"Quick thinking, sister!"

"Mama, you and Daddy don't even have a doctor!"

"Where do they sit?" Harry was in the opening to the kitchen where a wall and door used to be. Both shi-ny-black, happy-looking, twin girls each holding his hand on either side. The girls in matching, tan, silk pa-jamas with old-fashioned, crocheted loops for button-holes.

Bull burped. "They're a hit, Janey."

Annie looked like she wasn't sure she hated or loved them, and she nearly tripped while shoving two, high, youth-chairs over to the empty side of the table.

"I remember those chairs!" Janey said. "Perry, re-member?"

"Unfortunately."

Harry was wearing PJ's, too. Old, maroon flannels with gray piping, and as the girls dashed over to their chairs he scratched his ass and quickly re-adjusted his balls.

"Daddy, there is no magic hole in time and space when you can re-adjust your equipment and nobody sees it. Bullperry, remember when you first could lift your chair straight up with one hand, by one leg, and you thought it was such a big deal?"

"Remember when you used to flip up-side-down and do a split with no panties on and you thought you were Cleopatra?"

"Clitopatra's barge to Paradise, dear brother."

Annie put a finger to her lips and then shrugged. The twins couldn't hear, of course. "But I can hear!"

"Oh, Mama...." Janey said.

"Something's burning," Bull said.

Annie and Harry looked at each other and smiled.

§

The adults sat at the table while the girls did the dishes. It had taken them only a few seconds to figure out the sink and dish drainer system, and the two garbage pails, one for burnable stuff.

Janey said, "And when they're done there won't be a spot on their clothes!"

Bull was having a muted conversation on a portable phone, his brows knit, raising them when he caught Janey's eye. He ended the conversation, though, with a smile and a shrug, sitting there in his Homer Simpson underwear briefs. "That was Little Harold, and I called him just in time, too!"

"Little who?"

My dispatcher's son. The boss's son, remember? He's thirteen? Or fourteen? He's flying down there. Miami. Been in touch with Ahearn all this time. He's making all the arrangements."

"A - boy - is - making - the - arrangements...."

"I told you about him. Big and porky. Brilliant. Killed a dude while we were gone, or had a shootout back there at the terminal, or at his Uncle's house, or whatever. Dispatcher's son, well, Kate's half owner, too, and... "

"Shit, Bullperry! I see you have all the important details nailed down!"

"Let me finish! Little Harold's going to arrange the ransom details, I mean, the transfer, in Miami. Oh, and he says Pierretta Z is definitely the one who had Kate tortured and who dumped a clip at him in the gun battle, et cetera."

"We're all dead," Janey said. She pulled her robe closed and looked around. The only sound came from the sink, the peculiar giggles the twins liked to make, and the clinking of dishes.

"Little Harold said the crows are still picking at the guts left behind on his Uncle Ralph's lawn."

Annie said, "We saw Stevie Ray Vaughan in concert right before he died.

"Mama, I saw Garth Brooks!"

Bull grunted. "Unfortunately, Garth Fucking Brooks is still alive."

"We saw Jimi Hendrix in concert," Harry said. "We saw Chicago, live, free concert at F.I.U. in Miami."

"And we saw Janis Joplin right before she died!" Annie added. "That was Miami, too! And The Chambers Brothers! Live!"

Bull shook his head. Nobody could out-Woodstock his parents when it came to the concerts they had scored.

The Chambers Brothers....

"Time"....

Proof God still stops by Earth every now and then.

Everybody, when they're in church, should holler "Time" instead of "Amen".

Bull braced himself as he caught the sight of Harry and Annie both sucking in deep breaths to let out a window-rattling yell.

"Time!"

The twins stopped their work and turned around, both of them staring at the adults at the table, their mouths puckered into little round O's.

CHAPTER 33
Little Harold's Excellent Adventure — Part 1

Little Harold was away from home, alone, for the first time. As he trundled down the long aisle with his carry-on bag, it took him a few seconds to find and figure out the letters AB - CDE printed on the overhead storage areas. He had an aisle seat, good, and he found his three rows back from the emergency exit, near the wing. "I'll try to get you aisle seats," Ahearn had told him. "You can watch chicks head to the bathroom." No sooner had he plunked his big body down, however, a mother and daughter were hovering over him, the mother asking him to move so they could get in, the mother barging ahead to score the window seat and the girl, about Harold's age but thin and cute, eased past him to the middle. Harold looked at her as he plunked himself back down but the girl had her Game Boy out already and was punching away at the little keyboard.

bee-bee-beep-bee...

Harold was wearing his only pair of cargo pants, khakis, the pockets loaded with the little equipment items which had temporarily slowed his security check-in. Pants he had neatly pressed himself the night before. Along the length of the plane, stuff was beginning to pour out of the overhead air-ducts — looked like smoke — and Harold was surprised that none of the other passengers seemed to notice. He craned his neck and there, too, people were settling in without a care. The carry-on bag Uncle Ralph had lent him was well within size limits, yet here were jerks boarding in Atlanta with the most outlandish shit. A golf-bag too long for the overhead with fluorescent-green tennis balls in it, a couple of them falling out and bouncing down the aisle as the greasy-looking dude, looked like a TV Eskimo, was trying to grunt it into the compartment. A suave looking old guy and his foxy-youngish moll were taking seats just ahead of Harold (the advantage of the aisle seat again) and as she backed up and bent over to retrieve one of the tennis balls Harold's face got as close to a high-dollar, subtly-scented ass in a tweed skirt as a common man can ever hope. After she moved away and eased gracefully into her seat, the shape and texture of the cloth, and its scent, became a memory Little Harold would take to the grave.

"You're not going!" Kate had told him. "You'll never get back alive."

"Is Atlanta eastern time?" he asked the girl next to him.

bee-bee-beep-twiddle-de-de-bee-beep-beep...

The girl's mother looked at him, made a face, and continued her wiping at the window which was obviously dirty on the outside, Harold thought. Dumbass. The flight attendant was briskly moving down the aisle checking seatbelts and he had to mess with the latch to get more belt lopped through so it would fit him, even though he was not *that* much overweight. Suddenly, her wonderful, pitch-black, smooth and silky hair was right in his face, this goddess in uniform tugging at the belt and snapping him in. She was a real woman, and her breath was sweet and warm. "That's not smoke," she said. "It's just the air-conditioning."

"Huh? Oh."

She was already moving past him but she came back and whispered in his ear. "I saw you looking at it. Nothing to worry about."

Huh. Oh.

How dumb am I going to get!

Engines were whining. Another flight attendant was up near the front, demonstrating the pull-down oxygen mask and stuff. She was kind of small and emaciated looking, butch hair, not like the one who had belted him in, the mama one with the black, French braid and the tits full of milk, that plump warmth brushing up against his shoulder and arm.

clunk-clunk-clunk-clunk... She was heading back — hitting the aisle in long strides — and she patted Harold on the head as she flew by.

They're not supposed to do that.

Touch the passengers....

She likes me.

Harold was in love. What he didn't know was that he would be falling in love several times before the day was over. As for Ahearn's aisle-seat maxim, from that moment on it was watching infirm old men and hump-backed old ladies heading for the restrooms, both flights.

CHAPTER 34
Weighed in The Balance

It was just Janey and Bull now, Janey moving up to the front after a nap in Bull's lower bunk in the sleeper, the top bunk being too rough and unsafe while under-way.

"Where are we now?"

"Florida."

"Thanks, Bullperry. Big help."

"Palm trees, see?"

"Dear brother, like, how far from Miami?"

"Four, five hours."

"That empty trailer sure bounces around a lot back there without the Airstream on it."

"Yeah."

"Don't talk my ear off."

"Wants to come around and jack-knife if you hit the brakes too hard. You slept right through a couple hairy ones."

"Bull, are you okay?"

"I took a pill."

"Like what?"

"A capsule."

Janey peered through the bug-splattered wind-shield. "A capsule.... Give me one. I feel on edge."

"You don't have a prescription."

"So? And you do? From a veterinarian?"

"Those steel pipes I found underneath, all bundled so tight together, must be four five deep? Looked like thin-wall but maybe not. I've been thinking and I figured it out. They're heavy-gauge iron, and that's what makes the unit so heavy."

"Oh, whatever. PeeZee said the trailer was bomb-proofed. She said you could hit a land-mine with it. I asked her about that pipe. I thought they were maybe uranium fuel rods or something. It's home-made bomb-proofing."

"Uranium fuel rods, ha ha, duh."

"Oh? Like why not!? Anyway, they run sideways, between the frame, all the way from the front to the back, the whole length. You know what? You could have asked her yourself why the Airstream was so heavy but you're a man." Janey's cell-phone began play-ing the theme song from *Mission Impossible* and she grabbed for it.

"It's Harold. I'm in Miami."

"Little Harold? Miami?"

Harold turned loose a premium-grade, dewy burp. "This is important," he said. "They want the twins, like now. "

"They? Now? Who's they?"

"Mister Ahearn. He's real nice. This Russian lady picked me up at the airport and before we got to Mister Ahearn's office she was real nice to me. He promised me a Mexican girl but she apologized and now I'm glad. Her name's Lyubochka and she smokes those little ci-gars and she lets me play with her tits and stuff. Mister

Ahearn said I don't have to marry her but I want to! Anyway, when I ..."

"Harold!"

"She's a little older than me but not as old as you. I mean, you're older than Bull, right? He told me about you."

"Bull!"

Bull, who had been trying to listen in, suddenly had to hit the brakes for the weigh station just a few feet up ahead, and when the lowboy trailer started to come around he had to swerve and let off a little on the brakes and it was all he could do to avoid hitting the pipe-barriers on each side of the entrance.

Janey's phone dropped to the floorboards and when she picked it up she accidentally mashed the END key. The CB crackled. "Bet that redhead was blowing him and he didn't see the signs."

"He saw the signs but they don't register that far down."

"Think he got off in time?"

Bull grabbed the mike. They were trailing behind the trucks in front of them now at the required one-hundred feet spacing, the engine purring in a lower gear. Bull was happy no officers over in the coop were coming out to investigate but he couldn't think of anything punishing to say to the smart-asses on the radio.

Janey snatched the mike from his hand. "My driver gets off in Greenwich mean time."

"Oh, baby doll!"

"He's my brother. We have the same mother, but we have the same father, too."

"Janey for chrissake, they have a CB in the control station here!"

A new voice, loud, clear, male, and obviously from the scale house: "Pull out of the line and park in the rear, lowboy. Have the papers authorizing your passenger ready."

The sound of a scuffle, and a female voice from the same radio: "Ignore that order, driver. Pull out of the line and exit. That empty lowboy is obviously not overweight."

The CB crackled. "She swattin' him with a clipboard or somethin'. I can see 'em in the window."

"I copy that. They're husband and wife. I come through here all the time."

"Fuck'em."

"Fuck her!"

"You better not be overweight, motor-mouth."

Bull was moving down the emergency aisle on the left and heading back to the interstate. Each truck he passed, the driver leered at Janey and she stuck her tongue out. The one female driver stuck her tongue out at her.

Bull finally thought of something and grabbed the mike after moving up a gear. "We call ourselves The Aristocrats," he said.

CHAPTER 35
Little Harold's Excellent Adventure — Part 2

It was the next morning and since Lyubochka hadn't put out for him yet — although she came close — Little Harold was near-bursting horny. Ahearn was talking non-stop and Harold kept on swiveling the stool he was sitting on to peer out the 2nd floor windows overlooking the Miami River. So exotic. Triple-engined speedboats and tiny freighters and cranes and palm trees, and guys and babes looked like they were in the movies, and little, dark men giving orders to shiny black men (although Harold could not hear them) and the tallest black man Harold had ever seen — purple black — T-shirt full of holes but sporting an immaculate, Panama hat with a red band with a feather in it, giving orders to all of them.

"Pay attention, kid. This is serious shit."

"I'm horny. I can't concentrate. I need to unload."

"When I was your age I jerked off."

"I could, but you promised me a, um, never mind."

"A Mexican. She didn't show up and Lyubochka being a Russian I thought we'd present you with something you wouldn't forget, but..." Ahearn hesitated, surprised at the boy's willful, steady eye contact. Harold was more impressed with how natty and carefully groomed the middle-aged man was, the deep tan, the perfectly barbered salt-and-pepper hair, the expensive loafers with the black, silk socks.... But the blue dress shirt with the white collar was a disappointment.

Ahearn said, "What?"

"The shirt."

"You, too?"

Harold shifted his considerable body on the stool, which was between Ahearn's cluttered desk and the windows. There were no walls in the office and the rest of the 2nd floor was tools and boat parts and un-opened, wooden crates. At the near corner a small, liv-ing area and at the far end was an elevator looked like the ultimate Erector Set project. Harold was quietly sucking air for a defining burp.

"I told Lyubochka not to go all the way. I need to teach you a lesson."

Harold let the burp rip. "My people are on the way with the Duplan trailer but they stashed the twins and the Airstream."

"Your people...." Ahearn laughed. "And you are going to get them back for me. Jeez, I wish I had your composure and forthrightness when I was your age. I'd be a rich man now."

"Mm - mm - mm - mmmm!" Harold had turned back to the window and was looking down. "Woof," Ha-rold said.

Ahearn got up and took a look himself. "Oh, yeah, she's one of ours ."

"One of ours?"

"Okay, wait. Wait here. The lesson you need to learn is coming up." Ahearn headed for the wooden stairs next to the open elevator. "Don't touch anything. Be right back."

The first thing Harold wanted to do was pilfer through the desk drawers, see if Ahearn kept a gun handy, but he thought better of it and ambled over to the corner with the small, open but clean living quarters, or bunking quarters, with the perfectly made-up twin-size bed and the fridge, stove, sink with an empty dish-drainer, apartment-size gas-stove, and a pink commode at one end with the lid down, so clean, besides he needed to take a leak so he lifted the lid and sat so as not to leave any tell-tale dribble on the floor, and before he could get up he heard two sets of footsteps pounding up the stairs, the black-haired head of the girl coming into view first, the one he had been leering at down at the wharf.

"He's just a boy," she said. This one looked Mexican, like Juanita back home, only tougher. Her platform clogs hit the top step and the wooden floor just as Harold finished jerking up his jeans.

"Okay? Now go back down for a minute. Maybe two minutes. I have something to tell him."

"Okay." The girl tossed her long hair, brushed her bangs aside, and gave Harold a last look before leaving. No smile, no nothing.

"Sit," Ahearn said. "Not back on the commode, kid, jeez." Ahearn plunked down behind his desk and Harold perched back on the stool as the toilet flushed.

"You a virgin?"

"Well, yeah, but..."

"I like you, Harold, but I'm not going to tell you how old I was when I lost mine. Way older than you is all you need to know."

Harold straightened up. "Yes sir."

"Do you think about it a lot? Sex? What it would be like? What a woman feels like? What a real tit feels like? Huh?"

"Well yeah, but..."

"I'm trying to show you that I know where you are coming from and how much you have to learn. I know you're supposed to be way ahead for your age but that doesn't count for everything. We need each other. I know that but you don't. Not yet. You like that little Indian you just saw?"

Indian....

Mayan?

"Yeah, but..."

"Yeah? Is that all? She's gorgeous!"

"Mmm-hmmm."

"If I tell her, she'll do whatever you want."

"Me? I mean...."

"If I tell her to."

"Oh, okay, but..."

"Because I have the power. You know where that power comes from?"

"Um.... Money?"

Ahearn smiled and got up. He reached for Harold and gave him a friendly shove. "Good one, kid. You don't need the lesson. You already know. Just don't ever forget it." Ahearn headed for the stair-case and called down. Just before his head disappeared he turned and looked at the boy. "Go for it, kid. I'll be back in an hour. Look at the clock. An hour."

The large clock on the wall looked old-timey, and Harold could hear it ticking. It was just at 9:30. It said West End Watch Company on the face.

"Come on," the girl said. Harold twitched.

"On your feet," she said. "You shy?"

"Um, yeah."

"Over here. Sit on the bed. Take your shoes off. Look at me. Do you like me?

"Oh, yes!"

"My name's Juanita. Look me over, it's okay."

Juanita....

"Mister Ahearn told me about your Juanita at home. Now when you get back you'll know what to do with her." She smiled and leaned over him and planted a lipstick kiss on his forehead. I'll take my clothes off and then I'll take your clothes off, okay?"

Harold stuttered. "Your English... Your English is perfect."

"I was born here." She took his hand and slid it into her blouse. "Easy! Hey, go easy!"

"I'm sorry. It's just that..."

"Just take it easy. You hurt me you're dead."

"I could never hurt you."

"I know that."

Juanita stripped and lay back and allowed Little Harold to explore. She was everything Little Harold had ever dreamed of.

"I love you," Harold said.

Juanita got up and straddled him. "We're not done yet."

§

Ahearn took south river drive to I-95, Harold and Juanita in the back-seat of Ahearn's immaculate, '66 Mustang convertible, white, black interior, the AC blasting away at Ahearn's muscular, tan but hairy legs even though the top was down. Harold noted that Bull had told him he also owned a '66. What was the big deal with those?

Ahearn yelled, "I told you to change into shorts. "

"Harold yelled back, "I told you I didn't bring any!"

Juanita placed a finger against Harold's lips, and shook her head. They stopped at a light. She pointed down a busy street. "My high school," she said.

"School? How old are you?"

"Fifteen."

Ahearn laughed. "He's not that dumb. I told you. Remember?"

"Yes, Mister Ahearn."

They took off onto the interstate and in a minute they were doing 70, 80, and a few minutes more hitting US-1 and Homestead. Harold ogled the damage on both sides of the highway from Hurricane Andrew years earlier. "I thought this would all be cleaned up by now," he said.

"It'll never be the same, kid." Ahearn slowed way down when they finally entered Florida City, Harold surprised at how country much of the town looked. He could smell the sea, too, sulfurous and humid and heavy, the air, like nothing in his experience but still it all seemed to be the way it should be. Ahearn pulled off onto a side-street and the tires scrunched on the coral gravel at the shoulder. Get out your cell and see if you can get them now."

Harold pulled away from Juanita and flipped his phone, re-dialing Janey's number. Bull answered. They were on the move and Harold could hear the rumble of the big Pete.

"It's Harold."

Ahearn pulled out and headed back to US-1. Harold raised his voice. "Can you hear me? We're in a convertible."

"Loud and clear. You better have a good story."

"They're taking me to see the load. Our trailer and those two new tractors."

"You're mother's ready to kill you."

Harold heard some static, and sounds of a scuffle. "Harold, this is Janey."

"Um, yeah. Well, okay. They're taking me to see the load and our trailer, to show it's all there, in good shape, blah blah. We're going to take a couple pictures."

"Where are you now?"

"I'm not supposed to say." Harold looked at Juanita, who was poking him and pretending to turn a scarf into a blindfold. "They blindfolded me up until now."

"Blindfolded? Are you okay? Who is they?"

"Mister Ahearn and my girlfriend."

"Your girlfriend? Oh, Harold...."

"We love each other."

"Yeah, right. Harold, we're only 50 miles or so from Miami now and we came to swap trailers. That's it. Plus deliver the load."

"I'm delivering the load. Mister Ahearn said to show good faith. Then we're hiding the trailer again until he gets his end of the deal."

"You? Deal? We don't have a deal, young man. They're making a fool out of you!"

"He said for you to park it and wait for instructions."

Ahearn reached back, pointed a finger at the phone, and drew a finger across his throat.

"Call you back later, Em Es Janey."

§

The tractor Ahearn wanted Little Harold to use was parked in the hot sun, windows rolled up, in a vacant field near the Florida City state farmer's market. It was a ratty-looking cab-over, a faded sky-blue, and was sitting in tall grass between two newer conventionals hooked to van trailers. Harold said, "Been sitting here a long time."

"And...?" Ahearn plowed his way around it, checking the tires, grasshoppers jumping onto him. One of them landed on Harold's arm and Juanita picked it off and held it gently while she gave it a kiss.

"That was cool," Harold said. "I love you so much."

Ahearn groaned, and handed Harold a set of keys. Juanita said, "The AC work?"

Ahearn spit. "Might it be more important to see if it cranks?"

Harold dropped to the ground and rolled on his back, gnats swarming around in his eyes, and peered underneath. He pulled his body farther in. "Pre-trip," he explained.

"Pre-trip? Get in and see if she cranks!"

"Pre-trip inspection. Every driver is required by law to..."

"In! I got bugs crawling up my shorts!" Ahearn lowered his voice. "Pre-trip, right. How about no tag, no authority, no log-book, no driver license..."

"Somebody's coming," Mister Ahearn."

"Chicks up front, Juanita darling."

Harold got to his feet and they watched Juanita hustle toward the shirtless dude heading toward them on the road, shaved and sun-fried head, pierced with gang-tats everywhere, wearing shorts with black Doc Martens boots. They met on the grass about a hundred feet away and talked for a few seconds before the thug grabbed Juanita by the shoulders, turned her around, and gave her a rough shove back to where she came from. Harold's heart pounded up but he was relieved to see the dude wasn't following her.

Juanita didn't look the least perturbed. "He says you owe him five hundred."

"Yeah, well tell him now he owes me." Ahearn dug into his shorts, pulled out a wad of green, and peeled off five one-hundred dollar bills into Juanita's hand. "Wait! Harold, get up in there and see if she cranks. Check the fuel."

Harold did not hesitate this time, and hoisted himself up into the cab.

7-speed
An old J B Hunt tractor.
Juanita will love me even more when she's sees I can drive this big truck.

The engine cranked easily and in a minute was idling nicely. Harold rolled down his window. Juanita was still standing there with the bills in her hand, the dude keeping his distance, arms crossed over his bare chest. "AC works!"

"Fuel, Harold!"

"Ummm, both tanks over half."

Ahearn's lips moved as he calculated something, then he waved Juanita away. Harold watched her through the grimy windshield, his heart bursting with the love for her. He was relieved to see that when she handed over the money and the dude grabbed her wrist she snatched loose headed back. She looked up at Harold and blew him a kiss, her full mouth lipstick-red and pure wonderful.

§

Harold said: "Why didn't he just come over and get the money himself?" They were standing in front of a pad-locked, tin warehouse waiting for someone to arrive. It was still hot — no wind — Ahearn running his fingers through his stand-up, perfect, short hair, so natty looking, like a golf pro or a yachtsman or something — Harold wouldn't know. Juanita was a little fidgety and jogging in place, not in Harold's face or anything but close enough, her lug-nut nipples poking at the tight, mint-green tube top, her priceless tits bouncing and driving Harold senseless.

"Everything has a price, boy," Ahearn said. "That young asshole kept his distance because he knows if he gets close to me I can snuff him. He's got a record, and all I'd need is powder burns on his chest."

"You got a gun on you?"

"Am I wearing my pants?"

A long silence ensued, the only sound Juanita's clogs hitting the ground and an occasional car or truck clattering past on the rough, seldom used road. On the way over after picking up the tractor, Ahearn insisted Juanita ride with him in the Mustang, but he went slow enough so that the bobtail truck Harold was driving wouldn't bounce around too much. Harold had heard his uncle Axel say often enough how he hated driving without a trailer, and now Harold knew why. What bothered him, though, was watching Juanita and Ahearn up ahead, the two of them chatting away the entire half-hour, Ahearn sometimes waving his arms, gesticulating, even shaking a fist a few times, Juanita's eyes on the man, nodding frequently, apparently in agreement with everything Ahearn was saying. It didn't take long for Harold to realize Juanita was getting instructions — detailed instructions — but Harold was so besotted with her that he decided to go with whatever plan they came up with. Until he could get her away from here, that is.

CHAPTER 36
Switchback

Bull sat with his laptop open on the wheel, while Janey sat on the other seat with Denver's. Denver's battery was low, as was Bull's which was charging. Janey said, "I'm going to need the cigarette lighter thing."

"So you can read more of Denver's atrocities? Jeez."

They were backed in a slot at the Seminole Truck Plaza, in range of an internet connection and where they could see almost all the action coming and going in the semis-only area plus all the weird stuff coming in from US-27 at the fuel island for passenger cars.

"What if it's not notes for a novel but real stuff? Now that he's dead who's going to feed and water these sex slaves he has caged up?"

"Feed and water? Oh, Janey, you're all heart. Hey! Email from Harold!"

"Got five minutes left." Janey reached for Bull's 12-volt charger cord but Bull slapped her hand away.

"Shut that thing down for a minute! Look, there's pictures!"

Janey scooted over between the seats. "Can you turn your screen a little? Is that the missing load? That the infamous 12-year old? Little Harry?"

"Yup. Harold. Thirteen or fourteen now, I think. Suppose to be a genius his mother says."

The two of them stared at the two images Harold had attached. In the first he was standing proudly between the ratty cab-over and the McKay trailer with two, red, shiny-new 4WD Massey-Ferguson farm tractors chained to it. In the second, the lowboy trailer empty with Harold holding up a sheaf of paperwork, big grin on his porky face. Almost out of the photo, on the far right, was a Mexican looking girl.

"God she's a babe."

"God? Babe? Bullperry, this Harold kid just earned your commission!"

"No, no, read the text. There's way more!"

§

Ahearn had allowed Harold to use his desktop computer to send the email before leaving for the rest of the afternoon. He didn't say when he'd be back and Harold kept that in mind, hoping to get the photos they had taken transferred and the short, email sent off so he could play with Juanita again — he would never get enough — but staying out of Ahearn's in-box was an order. "You'll be chum, and you'll smell like chum. Dead meat you bait sharks with." Juanita sat next to him but when she went to take a pee Harold took a quick look at the programs on the harddrive and saw that Ahearn would be able to check every word he typed. When she was back, she said, "I won't tell what you write."

"You won't have to."

"Tell me about this Bull and Janey."

"Let me finish this first, I'm horny again, I can't concentrate!"

"Looks like you're writing a whole book there."

"Can we, like, make love first?"

"And Mister Ahearn comes back and you haven't sent the email yet?"

"What if he comes back and catches us, you know...."

"Fucking."

"Yeah."

"And?"

"Will he get pissed? Or want to watch? You know...."

"Finish the email." Then we can go to bed and you can tell me about this Bull guy."

Ahearn did not return for a long time. The session in bed with Juanita was wondrous but brief, Little Harold being just a boy, and when he awoke the clock was not visible from the bed but the sun was still bright in the windows facing the river and Juanita was on the phone at the desk. She was naked. Harold faked sleep and watched her through a partly open eye — she kept on glancing his way — and his ears strained to hear. Her voice was deliberately low. His heart pounded up when he recognized the words "West Virginia", "Mingo County", and "Schaffner", Bull's last name. She was spilling everything he had told her. It must be Ahearn she's talking to, he thought, but when she hung up he feigned sleep for a couple more minutes, hoping she'd come over and wake him by dangling her tits in his face. Instead, he heard clunking coming up on the wooden steps and Harold sat up. He yelled at Juanita, "Your clothes!"

Juanita took her time about it, and Ahearn, big grin on his face, plunked down at the desk and hollered, "Get your own fucking clothes on, boy!"

Soon as he could, Harold was standing over him. "So did she tell you everything you needed to know?"

"What? Back off, Harold. You're forgetting I can flip the switch on your little girlfriend any time."

Juanita got between them, and just as Ahearn was about to reach for a tan leg under her short-shorts he pulled back, his eyes locked on Harold.

Juanita said, "That wasn't Mister Ahearn on the phone, Harold."

Ahearn looked puzzled. "Who then, Miss Tijuana?"

"Duplan. He's coming up in a minute."

Ahearn groaned. "Mister Port au Prince, shit, if he had a brain he could have bought the whole country with the money he pilfered. I need to shut down the computer and do other stuff."

Juanita put a finger on Ahearn's mouth. Harold turned toward the staircase in time to witness the fanciest human being he had ever seen — including in comic books — his tall, straight body rising silently and smoothly up to the 2nd floor as if he were on an escalator. He was in full fig: a perfectly pressed, beige linen, Haitian Easter-Sunday suit, pegged cuffs, two-tone, alligator, wingtip shoes, gold watch chain hanging half-way to his knee below the coat, purple tie, and a white gardenia in his lapel. His skin was purple-black and the hair so close cropped it was hard to tell he was balding. In his hand he held the Panama hat with the feather in the band, which Harold had seen earlier when he was looking down at the activity on the small wharf. When the man was in a T-shirt. When Harold had first seen Juanita.

Harold said, "That T-shirt you were wearing yesterday, all those air-vents, is it underneath?"

Ahearn and Juanita didn't laugh, and Little Harold held his ground as the man approached, his face breaking into a broad smile. He ruffled Harold's hair. "No, no, funny Ami boy."

"So what's up," Ahearn said. Harold noticed that Ahearn had gotten to his feet.

"Every thing fall back to Earth, Ahearn." The smile was gone and the man looked from Ahearn to Harold, then a long look at Juanita. "Can I assume you have this clever boy clued." His accent sounded French but more loud, more musical, flipping octaves from one word to the next. "Clued in?"

"Yes, Mister Duplan." Juanita spoke without moving a muscle.

Ahearn said, "Harold, meet Mister Duplan. El Jefe. The boss. So what's happening?"

"Shit happens, Ahearn. Good shit. Bad shit. The good is the location of my finance, my money."

"And the bad shit?"

It will take me a few days to get it. When I return, I will have the ransom money, yes, and by then I expect my girls to be here, my princesses, and how you take care of the nappers is your business. If all goes well, Harold Ami, you will be well rewarded."

"A few days?"

"A week." Duplan looked down at Harold, caught his eye, and winked. "Is that as tall as you will get? Ahearn, go down with me. Everybody seems to have gone home and I need help loading the Mercedes. As you can see, it would be facile to soil my suit."

Harold looked at Ahearn, whose more modest en-semble was just as neat and clean.

"Juanita," Duplan said. "Keep Tiny here busy."

Ahearn and Duplan left, the computer still running. "Shit, Juanita said, he left his cell on the desk. Soon as her head disappeared down the staircase Harold hit his own cell phone and did a redial.

§

They were plunked on bar stools at the beer-chickee watching a brand-new ambulance fuel up, a young couple, the woman pumping and the guy with the hood up checking stuff. Janey said, "They look dreamy."

"Dreamy? They look stoned is what it is. So we have to make a move soon and I don't see how or what, dear sister."

"How do you think Dad is handling the twin situa-tion?"

"Handling? Nice choice of words! Can we get se-rious for a minute?"

"Okay. I don't think we're in trouble yet because Harold is saying this Ahearn dude is changing his mind every hour. I figure he doesn't have a plan, either. Then he says the ransom money for the twins was stolen and now it's located and they'll have it in a week. So if we decide to bring the twins we have plenty of time. Plus he's decided to forget the Airstream again."

Janey ordered another Corona and turned to the two Latinos to her right. Young, muscular, handsome, the one on the near bar-stool wearing a vintage Leonard Skinnard T-shirt. Light-blue, big round graphic in front which included a skull wearing sunglasses, a quart of Jack Daniel's, panties riding up into an ass-crack, et cetera, and a huge revolver. Bull was besotted with the barmaid, also Hispanic looking, so foxy. "The jukebox is busted," he heard her say down at the other end, her long, purple fingernails poking at the register to ring up a drink. The darkening sky was flashing through the lower fringes of the grass roof — heat lightening — and a cool breeze blew up but no rain. The other patrons, mostly drivers, were fairly quiet for a South Florida, outdoor bar scene. Bull noticed suddenly that they were all looking toward him, not the barmaid, and he turned just in time see Janey tugging down the Leonard Skinnard shirt over her tits. In a wad on the bar was the one she came in with. The Latino on the stool next to her was shirtless.

Janey's mouth suddenly opened. "I think I figured it out! I did! Again!"

Bull leaned past her and looked at the shirtless guy. "She get your wallet, too?"

"No, no, man. She liked the shirt and I gave it to her, no big deal." But he felt his jeans for his wallet anyway.

"Bull! Get back to the truck. We need to talk!"

The coral gravel crunched under their feet. Bull looked up at the sky, didn't look like rain, but the breeze was nice and he said so.

"Bull, that Mister Duplan Harold was yakking about, he..."

"Yeah, yeah. What did you promise that poor dude at the bar?"

"Nothing. I didn't even ask for it, I was just telling him how rare and pretty his T-shirt was and he went right ahead and pulled it off! Look! It's even dated! 1979!"

"Chicks," Bull said.

Just as they got to their rig, Janey's cell rang. It was clipped to Bull's jeans pocket but Janey snatched it before he could.

It was Little Harold again. "You said that killer bitch old lady is staying at Bull's place in WVA? Well guess what. I was watching them load Mister Duplan's Mercedes, like suitcases and stuff, and suits on hangers, I mean! I couldn't see everything from up here, but just when he's ready to drive off the old bitch scoots out from somewhere and jumps in on the passenger side."

"What? Wait. Bull talked with Dianna this morning and she was there."

"I saw her plain as day."

"It's starting to get dark, Harold."

Bull snatched the phone away, and Harold repeated the story. "I'll never forget what she looks like and what she did to Mama."

"Listen, Harold, Dianna was even telling me what they did today. Nice stuff. Gardening stuff. She said the old bag gets bossy sometimes but then she apologizes. She's home at my place."

Harold hesitated. "Um, Mister Bull, I don't think so."

CHAPTER 37
On The Road Again

"You think Ahearn knows Harold's been phoning us?"

"He says no."

"We could fly to Charleston," Bull said. Rent a car for Dianna's."

"On my credit card? Leave our guns behind? Pull that heavy Airstream back with a pissy-little rental?"

"Ahearn doesn't want the Airstream anymore, just the twins."

"Which are at Mom and Dad's. In Florida. Besides, now they want the Airstream **and** the kids, remember?"

"I don't remember that."

They were still parked at the Seminole Truck Plaza. Janey was poking around in the sleeper trying to get her clothes organized. "I'll pay for the diesel."

"What?"

She poked her head out and swatted Bull on the head. "The fuel!"

"If we take my truck, the Duplan dude will get to Dianna's before we do."

"It's not your truck yet, Bullperry. Besides, we don't know how he travels, and he doesn't have a real address to work with. Once he gets to West Virginia that black dude will have to pull teeth to get directions to your place."

"Little Harold thinks that girl loves him so he spills all the beans, jeez. Hey. Harold doesn't know how to find my place, either. Okay, maybe you're right this time."

"This time? He loves her, Bull. Don't you remember what that's like at his age?"

"Well, I hope he's good and pissed at her now!"

"Dear brother, you - are - so - dumb!"

§

Little Harold was waiting for Juanita to come back from the deli, but staying behind to probe Ahearn's computer proved fruitless — so many files password protected — and to make it worse, Ahearn returned unexpectedly. Fortunately Harold was away from the desk when he heard Ahearn clunking up the staircase, and Harold was standing at the windows before the man's head appeared. The windows overlooking the river were dark but Miami, 'The Magic City', was lighting up and the scene was dazzling. Harold wished he could turn off the AC and crank open those windows for the sweet and heavy smells of the river and the sounds of the wharf, but it was still hot out there.

He told Ahearn about spotting the old lady, then related his experience with her back in Missouri, the shoot-out, Uncle Ralph pissing off a deputy by handing him a shovel to scoop up the last remains of the moustache guy off his lawn, the rescue of his mother, the shell casings on the floor from the old lady's .45 automatic.

Ahearn kept on saying, "I didn't have anything to do with that."

"Is she Mister Duplan's mother."

Ahearn laughed. "Oh hell no! You color blind?"

"So you know about her. Gotchya!"

Ahearn's face screwed down but then another laugh broke out. "Okay, you're a smart boy, but don't forget you're just a cog in the machinery here."

"Where's Juanita?"

"Which one? Look, kid, you need to remember who you are. I told her to go home, reassure her mother, take a break."

"She's.... She's my girlfriend now."

"Oh, yeah. She's part of your cut is all. Not something you can deposit in the bank. You know something? When you get home to your mama in Missouri you're going to know a lot more than when you left. About everything."

"What's the cut for Bull when he brings the twins back?"

"That's if you can get him to bring the twins back. Plenty. Enough Euros to start his own trucking business. I can even keep him loaded and running. In other words, more than he can imagine, and you be sure to tell him that."

"Euros? What's wrong with dollars?"

Ahearn began to fidget, something Harold had not seen before. "Here in Dade when you convert gold to dollars the feds be up your ass before you can fart."

"Gold?"

Ahearn sighed. Harold sucked in a deep breath, hoping to get the fear out of his voice. "So what is my cut?" Now he stopped breathing entirely.

Say Juanita. Say Juanita.

"You already have it. The McKay trailer and load."

Harold swallowed, and hoped the man didn't notice. "What if I want to keep Juanita, Mister Ahearn."

"You go home in a box. Cash On Delivery."

§

Dianna came out to call the boys before the rain came sweeping in, but so far there was only lightening. Pierretta Z was on the porch, rocking, her thin legs stretched out, feet on a pillow on the railing. "When I was your age, the mountains in Haiti had much forest, and the thunder sounded like this. The echoes soft and deep. This reminds me of that. It's different now. Back home."

Dianna sat in the straight chair next to the rocker, always aware of the power and mystery of her strange guest. The warnings Bull gave her about the danger, though, had all but evaporated. "I'm worried about Lolita. She's just a girl. She's in over her head with Bucky."

"Rodney Bucky Buckle." Pierretta cackled, and spit a zinger out over the railing a good twenty feet. "He has money and little Miss Lolita doesn't have any is all that is."

"Well, I wish she'd come home. He can't have her staying at his house with his wife."

"She'll be back before you want her back."

"Pregnant."

"She's on your pill."

"My pill?"

"American pill we used to call it."

"She told you that? She never said much to me. How many languages can you talk?"

"English, French, a little Portuguese. If you want to succeed, foreigners are important."

"I barely passed English in high-school," Dianna said.

"Yes, yes, but you weren't born sucking a dry tit. Poor. Starving."

"You were starving?"

"They gave the mule more to eat."

§

They stopped at Beckley, West Virginia, Bull having stayed on I-77 too long, not thinking. "Janey said, "Mingo County doesn't look all that far on the map if you're not too tired.

"Yeah, but it can take hours, you'll see, and no way am I driving this rig to Dianna's in the dark. The last leg is tricky."

"I thought it was your place."

"Mine and hers."

"Your wife in Miami, that place yours?"

"I wish. You should see it. A palace. In Miami."

"And the wife in Milwaukee?"

"Um, Janey, could you lay off?"

They scored a motel room with a view, truck parking, so beautiful, so high up it seemed, and they got the cook at the restaurant to make them a big southern breakfast al a carte. Eggs, grits, toast, bacon, and waffles with some local syrup. While they ate, Janey had Denver's laptop charging in the truck, while Bull had a 120 volt unit he could use in the room. As soon as they got back, while Bull was in the shower, Janey went through Bull's files, not finding much interesting. She quit before he was out of the bathroom and retrieved Denver's unit from the truck.

"Your turn, old sister," Bull said. "Lots of thick towels."

"Shhhhh."

"I can't decide whether to switch the AC to heat or not."

"Shhhhh!"

Bull slid into pajama bottoms and took a look. "Janey, that stuff is just the old fart's fantasies. It's not real. Come on, we need to figure out tomorrow. And cleaning guns might be a good idea, too. I haven't done mine for a long time."

"Ya, ya...."

"I'm going out to get the cleaning kit. Take your shower."

"There's a porn channel on the TV."

"Ya ya."

A half hour later they had all three pistols laid out on a clean, white towel.

"This is what I like about revolvers, Bullperry. Nothing to disassemble. You run a brush through a couple times, some patches, you oil stuff, and you're done."

"Well, my .22 Beretta is easy to clean. You're messing up this clean towel."

"It's not my towel!"

Bull still had his 9 millimeter CZ 75 P01 to do. His deadly, Euro police, killing machine. Fourteen-round clip for the export version, a fifteenth round in the chamber. Laser grip-sight. "Did I ever tell you about Little Harold's father?"

"You are wrong about trusting that kid."

"His mother says he's an angel. No drugs, never steals, blah dee blah."

"That was before Ahearn set him up with that Columbian hooker."

"Columbian, ha ha, funny. Anyway, his father shaves his head and has a battery terminal tattooed behind each ear. A red one for positive, and a black one for negative."

"If he's a Ford fan it'll have the red on the right. I think."

"On the left."

"You wipe all your cartridges with an oil rag?"

"You want an automatic to feed every time." Bull looked over to his sister. "Serious shit tomorrow, Janey."

"You scared?"

"No."

Janey said, "We feel sorry for our guns the reason we're cleaning them?"

"Funny."

"Revolvers feed every time, dear brother. Clean, dirty, no check the chamber shit, no jams, no complications.... Yup, they feed flawlessly. Faithfully!"

"Six times. Five times, in your case."

"It's an Airweight!"

"Exactly."

Janey shoved her Smith & Wesson under Bull's nose. "Cops carry these for backup in their boots!"

"It's called dying with your boots on."

"You wait and see, Bullperry. This here gun will be doing duty tomorrow before you can remember where yours is."

"Janey, you're living in a dream world. Can you please shut the fuck up?"

"There is no real world, dear brother."

CHAPTER 38
Locations Unknown

Bull's cell was answering *Not in service at this time* and they were looking for Janey's number. The old lady was crowding Dianna at the refrigerator, both of them peering through the thicket of stickies and notes on magnets, Pierretta pulling her octagonal lensed spectacles down and looking over them. She said, "You can't win a war with record keeping like this."

Dianna noticed Pierretta Z smelled funny, for the first time, up close, and wondered if she took a bath every day. "War?"

"What is it filed under? Jane? Janey? Santa Claus?"

"It's a new sticky. A yellow one. And you can't cover a dead mule with perfume and deodorant."

"Don't get smart with me. You're still a child. You have no idea."

"I've been doing okay."

"We're not talking past here, we're talking future. Can you shoot?"

"My .45 Colt. Revolver. Bull gave it to me."

"Revolver?"

"Long colt revolver, and I'm good at it, too."

"Keep it loaded and keep it handy. Close. When they come, get your gun and hide somewhere. I'm going back to my trailer and putting on boots. My sister..."

Dianna laughed. "With that dress?"

"My twin sister has a pair of hiking boots just like mine, and she'll probably be wearing them, so take a look at my dress. Remember my dress."

"Bull said stay out of any shit you get into."

"Mister Bull will be changing his mind directly."

Soon as Pierretta Z was gone Dianna found the sticky with Janey's number.

§

It took Bull and Janey all morning to get close to Dianna's — the missed turn the afternoon before and the stop in Beckley being out of the way — but Janey was happy. It was her theory that the later they got there, the less perps would be alive to sort out. She had taken Dianna's call while Bull was at the motel desk checking out, and Janey told Dianna not just to hide, but hide herself and the boys from the old lady as well. When she related this to Bull, he said that Pierretta Z was okay.

"We're all from the same seed catalog, Janey, including all the bad-asses in the world. I can see that old lady when she was born. A little baby. A little tyke in her mother's arms, or in new clothes on the first day of school. I can see every person I meet in their baby crib. That gives me confidence. When somebody like Pierretta comes on hard, it's just a front. The person behind it isn't any bigger or badder than I am. We're all fucked when we're born, we just cope in different ways."

"Right. Like torturing Little Harold's mother near to death to find out where the Airstream is? Killing Denver? Denver, well, okay, but..." Janey's voice trailed off.

"You were ugly in your crib."

"So who's the black dude in the Mercedes?"

"Lolita told Dianna it was a Mercedes?"

"Dade County tag."

"And Lolita is where?"

"That Buckle dude has her stashed somewhere. She's running away soon's she can. Back to Dianna's."

"I should've killed him. You think Buckle told him how to find my ranch?"

"Ranch? Oh, Bullperry, too funny. Ranch. Ha ha."

They were pulling to a stop at a country gas station — plenty of room for the long rig — a few men with pickup trucks gathered at one end, skinny guys, suspenders holding their work-pants up, talking over one of the pickup beds. There was a dead eagle in it swarming with flies. Before getting down from the cab, Bull checked with Janey re how much money she had left from pilfering Denver's pockets.

"Plenty. It's damp and it smells like blood and it's mine."

The pickup's doors were wide open and one of the men pulled a long rifle from the rack behind the seat and stood it up on the ground next to him as Bull approached.

Older guys. Red, rheumy eyes. Several stained, fedora hats, and one straw hat looked like a bird nest. Bull got up close and looked right at the illegal kill. "We need a ride," he said. "Cash money."

Silence....

"I got a place up the mountain maybe 15 miles.... I figure my rig will be safe if I leave it here."

"Won't make it all the way? Too long?"

There was no traffic, and the day had been heating up. All you could hear was the flies.

"I can make it in there but I need to sneak in, if you know what I mean. My truck you can hear a mile away."

Another man spit. He said, "I seen you before. You're not from around here."

"My wife is."

The one with the rifle, the youngest, maybe 35-40, said, "You know Bucky? Rodney Buckle?"

Bull's heart jumped but he didn't move. "I see him I'll kill 'im."

Chuckles all around. "Wife name Dianne?"

Another said, "I know the place. Dead-end road?"

"Right. Dianna. Any of these vehicles quiet? Got a muffler?"

"Vehicles?" More chuckles.

"What kinda money we talkin'"

"Sneakin' is double."

Bull said, "A hundred dollars. If you have to wait more than an hour to bring us back, two-hundred."

"That comes to four-hundred then."

"Three hundred. Plus fuel."

"Deal."

A noisy argument ensued about whose truck would be used, who would go, et cetera, when Janey emerged. She had changed into her short, white, pleated tennis skirt. Barefoot. A nipple-popping T-shirt completed the ensemble.

Bull could hear the flies again.

§

Janey made them wait while she went back to the rig to get a towel to sit on for the gritty bench seat up front.

"Scoot over. Chicks in the middle."

"Not this chick. Get in back with everybody else."

"You got a gun in that purse, I can tell."

"I can pull socks on a rooster, too. Now git!"

When Bull climbed up over the tailgate they yelled at him not to step on the eagle and mess up the feathers.

"It's rotting, jeez!"

"They come out easy when they ripe."

"Oh, right." Bull was glad he was wearing his jeans and boots, and a shirt over his tee to conceal his guns. He was glad he had made Janey change, also. "Does everybody have to come along?"

"That a nine?"

"Nine? Oh!" Bull pulled the CZ from his waist-band. When one of them reached for it he refused to hand it over but let them get a good look. The extra clip for the 9MM was in his right shirt pocket. They had no idea just how fucking handy his backup Beretta was.

"Two pockets, that shirt."

Bull wished he had brought a bottle of water. Janey had one up front but maybe negotiating for that would look like a sign of weakness. The truck was quiet for the way it looked, but the springs were hard and it was rough sitting back there after they finally turned off onto Bull's road and began the steeper climb. About a half-mile from the house, the pickup stopped and the driver got out.

"Last place we can turn around."

Bull clambered down to the ground and looked around. "You sure?"

"With luck. We be turned around when you get back."

One of the men in the back began plucking the eagle, the longest feathers first, white and black, laying them side-by-side in a neat pile. "We seen that nigger in the Mercedes," he said. "If he comes back 'fore you we got a surprise for 'im."

"The wife always wanted a Mercedes Benz," another said.

"Maybe we should get the rest of the money up front."

The others all nodded. Janey, who was out now and shaking the dust out of her sit towel, said, "The nigger hain't coming back fucking first."

§

Little Harold had pissed him off, and it took Ahearn a few minutes to regain his composure. "Harold, we're on the same side here." He watched the boy swallowing air. Harold could do it almost imperceptibly, but Ahearn had learned the signs. "Okay. You know where the girls are, right?"

"Girls?"

"The twins."

"Where's Juanita?" Harold began the most perfect, slow release of air lubricated with guttural phlegm of his career, and the burp rolled out long, deep, and thunderous.

"Listen, kid, that old lady you saw, she knows where to look. Duplan said so. Said she'd been there before. Besides, I told Juanita to get her ass over here ASAP."

The air-conditioner at the windows gave a little burp of it's own and the light over Ahearn's desk dimmed for a moment. "Oh, God, not now," Ahearn said.

"I don't believe in God."

"You are so full of shit. I could feel you praying when I first hauled Juanita up the stairs. There was so much energy in here my socks got hot. Admit it."

Harold thought about that. Yup, he had prayed. Big deal. "So when did you tell Juanita to come back?"

"When you went to get the take-out. I phoned her mother."

"Her mother talks to you?"

"She owes me money."

"You want her back here so she can pry out where the twins are."

"And to stop your fucking whining."

Harold's mouth opened but the second burp was stillborn. "Well, if it goes the wrong way when Bull goes to get the Airstream we're both out of our cut the way I see it."

"Duplan is a fuck-up. The fittest will prevail."

"So why care about where the twins are if you think he'll fuck up?"

"A million Euros. In Europe. A German buyer, to be precise."

The lights dimmed again and Ahearn got up from his desk and went to the windows. "Those yachts down there have their own generators."

"You mean you'd sell them?"

"Beats feeding them for the next ten years."

"But..."

"Plus sending the little dummies to a special school. Plus explaining to the authorities, so fucking called. Then there's their shots, their doctor bills, their doctor fucking appointments, their clothes and fucking shopping for their clothes, plus..."

"But..."

"Plus protecting them from predator pimps getting them hooked on drugs and peddling them by the hour to pedophiles."

Little Harold kept on keening his ears for footsteps on the wooden staircase. Juanita's footsteps. "I don't get it. Isn't the German buyer a pedophile?"

"Sure, but this way I get the money. We get the money. Not some street pimp here in Miami."

"All I want is to keep Juanita."

The two of them were side-by-side now, at the windows overlooking the river. Ahearn suddenly reached for Harold and gave him a sideways hug, then held out a hand. "Deal?"

"Deal!"

CHAPTER 39
Mingo County West Virginia

"This road is so beautiful," Janey said, slightly out of breath with the climb and the altitude. You own all this free and clear?"

"There's a mortgage on it."

"Well, if we keep our shit together you can pay it off soon."

"Not so loud." They were trudging around the second from last turn, and Bull lowered his voice even more. "I don't hear any birds."

"I can hear the stream."

Bull stopped and hunkered down. "Janey, streams don't shut up when something's wrong." He pointed. "I saw a flash of white through the trees. The Mercedes I think."

"Your Mustang's white."

A single gunshot rang out from well ahead of them and Janey flinched. Bull moved off the road and crouched behind some huckleberry bushes. Janey came in behind him with her .38 pistol out. She whispered, "That was close."

Bull shook his head while he tried to un-snag the 9MM from his waistband. "Far. Other side of the house, at least."

"Dianna?"

"Sounded like an auto. Like an army forty-five. The old lady, maybe. There's an old path to the side of the house from here. Grown over but I know it."

They were just getting to their feet when they heard another shot, even farther.

"Same gun."

"Or one just like it."

They waited for over a minute. Bull said, "Dianna might be in trouble."

"You think? Jeez, Bull!"

"You called me Bull!"

"Shhhh!"

It took only five minutes to reach the clearing at the house, Bull hitting the path first and cutting vines which had grown across with his Gerber Gator lock-blade. The weather was cooler than at the town where they had hired the pickup truck, and there was a gentle breeze blowing up from the valley. Both of them were crouching at the edge of the clearing — the white, four-door Mercedes parked on the front lawn — when they heard a third shot. Even farther off, but this time a spent bullet whined overhead. "I think they're down by the creek. One of them lower than the other."

"I think there's three," Janey said.

"Seven round mag, those old forty-fives."

"Three people shooting," Janey whispered. "Just a feeling. What's Dianna's?"

".45 long-colt revolver. Sounds completely different. Make a run for the house. I'll cover."

"Me? You run to the house!"

"My gun shoots farther and faster than yours."

Bull was just about to get up and go for it anyway when Janey surprised him and made a dash across the clearing. On the porch she dropped to all fours and made it under the windows to the front door. After waiting for a few seconds, Bull followed suit.

This time, two shots from somewhere down the hill, sounded like directly below the house at the creek, then another from farther to the right. Then silence. Bull entered his house first and headed for the bedroom. The boys and Dianna were nowhere to be seen, and Dianna's revolver was gone.

"She took her gun?"

Bull nodded.

Inside the house, the next three shots sounded muffled and distant. Evenly spaced, as if each shooter was waiting to determine the location of the others by sound. It was eerie. Single shots. No panicking and snapping off round after round.

"Back out the front. They might can see us in the back."

"Might can? Here! The crawl space under the porch."

"Is it buggy?

"Jeez, Janey." Bull pulled a small lattice section away from the side and crawled in first. "Pull it back behind you."

"Bull!" It was Dianna, way back under the floorboards of the house.

"Daddy, Daddy!"

Off in the distance, three more evenly spaced shots were followed by a scream. It sounded like a man.

§

The shadows grew longer and the yard darkened quickly as the sun dipped behind the mountain top to the west of them. Dianna insisted the boys stay farther back under the house while she and Bull and Janey peered out through the lattice-work along the porch posts. Two more shots followed, even farther away, then two more, then nothing. Janey was fidgeting about getting bites from bugs she couldn't see, and Bull was having a problem keeping both women's voices down.

"At least we don't have mosquitoes here."

Dianna kept on saying, "Those two old bats are twins!"

"Could you tell them apart at all?"

"They must be eighty-ninety years old!"

Janey said, "Can you tell them apart?"

"Ours told me to remember what dress she was wearing before the shooting started."

"Pierretta," Bull said. "What's the other one's name?"

"Bull," Janey said. "I don't think they introduced each other first. What was the man like?"

"Shine, tall, thin, wearing a suit. Light colored suit. He took his hat off when he got out and then he got a gun out. Same kind of gun as hers. Then they both aimed at the Airstream holding their guns across the hood. We snuck under here through the storm-cellar door.

Janey said, "How long do we have to hide under here?

"Until one comes back, I think."

"What if all three are dead? We're armed, hell!"

"And they're probably out of ammo."

Janey and Bull decided to get out. Dianna insisted the boys keep hiding, but they wouldn't stay without their mother so it was Bull and Janey, brushing themselves off, saw the old lady emerge from the creek path. Black lace-up boots, hair a mess and her dress torn. A U.S. army Colt .45 in hand down at her side.

"Dianna!" Bull hollered. "What's the dress look like?"

"White. Little red flowers. The other one had a purple something."

The lady kept on coming, but favoring one foot. "Mister Bull, I presume."

"Pierretta Z."

"You must forgive me," she said. "I just killed my sister."

They eyed each other up, Bull's pistol raised higher than hers. "And Duplan?"

"The twins no longer have a father, Mister Bull."

§

They had showers in Dianna's bathroom, Dianna and the boys first, then Bull, then Janey while Dianna was in the kitchen getting some steaks ready for the grill.

Bull felt clean and horny. "Steak?"

"I have money now."

"Oh, yeah, right." Bull tried to be cool, but Rodney Bucky Buckle was back in his mind and he couldn't dig him out. "You cash that gold bar? Where?"

"She gave me a gold coin and the mailman gave me two-hundred for it."

The old lady, who had been stumbling around the house, room to room as if she'd lost her mind, went down to the bathroom with a stack of clean clothes. Bull was about to feel sorry for her until she gave the door a good kick while Janey was still in there.

Imagine," Dianna said. "That old thing beating around in the woods down there running for her life. She must be exhausted!"

"Baby, Miss Pierretta Z just snuffed two people."

"Maybe the sister killed that man."

"They came to get her, remember?" Bull put his arms around his young wife, from behind. She still looked like jail-bait to him and he wanted her. He mumbled, "Janey eat your heart out."

"What?"

"I'm horny."

"You don't get any of this till you go play with your sons. You act like they don't exist!"

"I was just in their room and they switched TV channels the minute the door opened. They ignored me."

"See?"

"See what? Keep an eye out for Pierretta's gun. She said she re-loaded but I think she's lying. I need to check."

"She's okay, she's not going to hurt us, Bull."

Janey emerged from the bathroom, busting out of a set of Dianna's flannel pajamas. She said, "I wonder how long those dudes in the pickup waited for us to come back?"

"Locals?" Dianna said. "Until they heard the shots."

§

Dianna was wrong. First the men had to wrap the eagle feathers they wanted to keep, and when they heard the gun-shots they decided to wait for the black dude in the Mercedes to come high-tailing out of there. For courage, they broke out the bottle of 150-proof Everclear whiskey they had been saving for later. When that was gone and it was getting dark, the engine wouldn't crank. They decided to start the motor by coasting downhill a little way and popping the clutch in 2nd gear. The pickup had already been turned around earlier, with much maneuvering after they had dropped off Bull and Janey. The second attempt to start it did the trick but then an argument ensued over the other half of the 300 bucks they had been promised.

"We can turn back around at the tee and go get it."

"There was a gun-fight up there."

"Sounded like target practice to me."

"A hundred-fifty beats what we had this morning."

"We can get another bottle in town and decide then."

"Oh, yeah."

They were off. Two in the truck bed and two in front. "That Janey babe, I wish she was sittin' here right now."

"With that 'un you'd be sittin' in the middle."

"Maybe, but you'd be busy drivin."

They heard yelling and pounding from the back. "Stop! Stop!"

"Back up!"

"Stop!"

The two men in the back stood, and the two in the cab got out and froze.

"That Everclear does the job."

"This is real, Sherlock."

A skinny old lady down in the ditch, half naked, was trying to get up on all fours. She was covered in blood. Her voice sounded pissed and twangy. "A hand please!"

"Uhhh..." The youngest one jumped down in the ditch but then hesitated, afraid to touch her. "She's all shot up!"

"A hospital please!"

"Uh, ma'am, that 'er be a good fifty mile from here."

"Then call a fucking ambulance!"

§

The next morning, Lolita said, "I seen your big truck in town." Before Dianna could run over and give her a hug, Lolita let her knapsack drop to the floor and plunked down at the place which had been set for Janey. For a moment, even though the kitchen windows were open, Lolita's musky atmosphere overcame the scent of frying bacon.

"You look like you haven't had a bath in a week," Bull said. "Same shorts, same shirt, same pissed-up sandals."

"I ain't had breakfast in a week."

"You mean you didn't cook Bucky breakfast every morning?"

Lolita stared at Bull with half open eyes. Half-open mouth. The tip of her tongue appearing briefly.

Dianna gave Bull's chair a kick. "I'll cut your balls off."

The boys looked up from their plates. "Balls." They giggled. "Balls."

The old lady limped in wearing a pink bathrobe, her gray hair all tricked out and a bejeweled comb in it. Lolita said, "Miss Pierretta!"

She stopped and looked at the girl. "Hi, Honey. Nice to see you."

"Honey? See, Bull? There's some people like me!"

"You tried to set me up. You ever sit naked in the back of a cop car? You think I'm going to forget?"

Dianna was back at the stove, and Lolita lowered her voice. "Next time it won't be a set up."

"There won't be a next time, kid. We're leaving tomorrow. Soon as we can get the rig and winch the Airstream on the trailer.

"I'm coming along."

"In your dreams."

"In **your** dreams."

§

Each time they hit a bump or had to slow down, the old lady would start rolling on the rusty bed of the pickup, and one of the men would put a foot out to stop her. By the time they hit the gas station where Bull's rig was parked, she was unconscious.

"I hain't never seen nobody so wrinkled up and skinny at the same time."

"Payphone's workin'!" the youngest man yelled from the building.

"Looks like that tit's been shot clean through."

"You gotta talk about her tits right in front of 'er?"

"She's out of it. She can't hear nothin'"

"Looks like that hole in her side went clean through, too."

"Still bleedin', though."

"Mash the rag tighter. She might still make it."

"You do it, I hain't touchin' her again. She's gone, man."

"So how come the tit stopped bleedin'."

"That other's hit a vital."

"She just shivered."

"She needs a blanket."

"In this heat? She needs the ambulance."

"Back her up under the tree."

"It ain't my truck."

Just then, the first blo-fly landed on the blood-soaked rag they had placed against the bleeding wound, the exit wound in the back. The rag was white and looked fairly clean, a fragment from the bed sheet they had wrapped the eagle feathers in.

There were more flies by the time the ambulance finally arrived, but by that time all four of them were sitting under the tree sipping Everclear and keeping an eye on their vehicles.

It was suppertime at the local, thirty-bed hospital when the two EMTs radioed in their ETA — five minutes

— and their patient's dwindling vital signs. When they backed up to the ER dock there was nobody in sight. The concrete loading area smelled like piss but the old lady didn't smell that good, either. The younger EMT, blond hair down to his shoulders, no name tag, black T-shirt with Mickey Mouse on the front, said, "You ever watch ER on TV?"

The tall, red-headed one, name tag of NEWSOME, said, "There's more on cable now."

"Yeah, well, notice anything different?"

"You mean like on TV they have doctors and stuff?"

They pulled the gurney out and dropped the wheels as the automatic door began to wheeze open. "And TV hospitals have nurses worth pressing."

"I heard that!" The middle-aged porker in white who yelled at them took one look at the patient and disappeared.

"They got some nice ones here, though. The three-eleven shift."

"And the doctors on call ride in on a mule."

"I seen one of them imported rag-head doctors checking out this guys' heart and lungs with his stethos-cope last week, and the ear-piece end was still hanging around the beardy's neck."

The first of two ER rooms was empty and they properly slid the old lady onto the exam table.

"I'm outta here," Newsome said.

Two, tiny, Filipina nurses showed up, followed by a disheveled, black-bearded man in green scrubs and slippers, looked like a fundamentalist in terrorist pho-tos.

Newsome said, "My, my, so cute, so so cute, my heart's just a flutter."

The nurses giggled and covered their mouths while the patriarchal apparition of a doctor burned a hateful look at the two men. He bent over the patient, held her wrist, and looked at the monitor. "No monitor?" His voice was high-pitched and whiney for such a formidable-looking man. "You hook up please?"

"Your job, doc. We're outta here. Way past Miller Time."

The doctor was looking away as he slid his stethoscope around the old lady's bony chest. "Please, no, put electrodes on first."

"Pashtu? Wahabi? If you're not allowed to touch a female what are you doing here? Hey, let the nurses do it!"

The doctor glanced at the little nurses, standing side-by-side doing nothing. "Worthless. Worthless."

"Spoken by one who'd know."

"I report you, you know."

"Go fuck your mule."

"I report you!"

They were gone, but not before grabbing clean sheets and a pillow case from the shelf and dumping the blood-soaked stuff from their gurney on the floor. Before the automatic door clunked shut behind them, Newsome hollered, "She's bleeding to death, asshole!"

The old lady's eyes fluttered. The doctor leaned over her face but avoided looking at the rest of her. In his high-pitched voice he said, "What - is - your - name?"

Her eyes opened and stared, and her mouth curled down as she took a breath.

"Anastasia!"

The porky white nurse was back and she got down to business, flipping away the bra the EMTs had cut away, and cutting away her panties. She began to give orders to the Filipinas while the doctor looked away, pacing around in his sheep-lined slippers.

"Grand Duchess Anastasia Nikolaievna Romanova", the old lady said, all in one, twangy breath.

The nurse in charge laughed. You know what that means in English? "No ID, no address, no insurance."

A county police cruiser came roaring up in full festival mode, siren burping and lights flashing. It was the 2nd-shift, town police officer, also name of Newsome. Older, red-hair graying. He said, "They lent us one of their wagons. Awesome. Ours is in the shop."

"The important stuff."

"Yah, yah."

"We have gunshot wounds here."

Newsome bent over to take a look, his belly shoving the gurney sideways a little. "Gunshots? I don't see a gunshot. I get called away from my kid's game for this? Doc?"

The doctor turned and shrugged. Newsome rolled his eyes. "Looks like a car wreck to me."

"You have to fill out a report for that, too, you know."

"Wild boar attack?"

The doctor said, "Maybe gun-shot. Two."

"Jeez, the wife's chihuahua-dog weighs more than her. Show me a bullet. You find a bullet, call the county."

CHAPTER 40
West Virginia to Florida

A day and a half later they were nearing LaGrange, Georgia again — there being no more direct route to Harry and Annie's home where the twins were stashed — and I-85 was steaming after a brief rain shower. Janey and Lolita were in the Airstream and the old lady was poring over Bull's map. She looked up when he began slowing.

"Scales up ahead and they're open. Shit, can't they take Sunday off? The fucking Sabbath or whatever?"

"The Sabbath is a Saturday, I believe, Mister Bull."

"They thought the sun was a flaming, horse-drawn chariot, too."

The old lady laughed in her banjo voice.

They were turning into the scale entrance now, Bull dropping the rig back to keep the 100-foot space required behind the truck up ahead. "That's the first time I ever heard you laugh, Pierretta Z."

"And the last."

"Ha ha. Oh, shit. We got the red X. Fuck, and I forgot to do my logbook, since, what, before we went to Dianna's? Now we have to weigh again."

"That child bitch Lolita is a worm in your brain."

"Yah, yah, well if you had balls you'd know what it's like to be a man."

Lolita's okay.

She had a chance to check out Pierretta's pistol. One in the chamber and two rounds in the clip, different brands...

"Oh, I have balls, Mister Bull."

Stopped after pulling onto the scale pad, the green OK-light switched to red. Bull lowered his window so he could hear the intercom.

"Pull over to the inspection area and wait for an officer. Have your paperwork ready."

Bull raised his window and dropped the rig in gear. "Fucked again!"

The old lady touched his arm. "Be cool, young man. Piece of cake, Brits say."

"Right, oh yeah. Sure." Bull pulled into an empty spot between three other rigs and in the mirrors watched a young man in a Smokey Bear hat and a black uniform looked like Nazi SS leave the scale house. Definitely not like any DOT officer Bull had ever seen. As the man approached, cocky walk, another guy, similarly figged, came out with a German Shepherd dog on a leash. Bull opened the door, hating the humid heat pouring in.

"Stay in the vehicle! Hands on the wheel!"

Close up, the cop seemed like a little guy. Mean blue eyes looking up at him. Bull said, "I expected a Nazi accent." He felt a sharp pinch on his right forearm.

"What do you have in the RV. It weighs a ton!"

"A ton, right. That's two-thousand pounds, officer." This time the old lady dug into Bull's arm with her nails and he flinched. In the big spot-mirror on the front fender he could see the distorted figure of the other cop circling the Airstream with the dog.

She whispered into his ear: "Lined with lead. Under the floor. The bottom. Radon protection. The owner is a hypochondriac."

Bull repeated what he was told.

"Doors unlocked? Radon protection?"

"Ground radiation."

"I know what radon is. Mind if I take a look inside?

"Do I have a choice? Hey, there's two people in there."

The officer pivoted on his heel but then turned back. He looked like a high-school punk. With pimples. "Who are they? Any guns?"

"My sister and her daughter. No guns, jeez."

The young cop was gone, but before he could cross over to the side which the RV door was on, the old lady hit the pavement. In the right-hand mirrors, Bull could see Janey and Lolita bouncing out of the Airstream, all three women now hugging, then separating, Janey zeroing in on the first cop and Lolita heading for the German Shepherd, bending over the animal while the handler looked down her loose top. Janey followed the first cop inside.

Bull sighed and slowly eased his door shut to give the air-conditioner a chance, glad that the blackshirts hadn't remembered to make him shut the engine down.

The ladies are good in a pinch.

No script. No plan.

What a team!

The cop with Janey suddenly jumped out of the Air-stream and waved Lolita back in. The two men and the dog ran out in front of the four trucks waiting there and began yelling and waving for the ones on Bull's right to move. The old lady clambered up on the passenger side but Bull hesitated.

"Go, Mister Bull. Go! The truck on your side is on fire!"

§

A tugboat down at the river let out a horn blast, loud enough to rattle the closed, wide-glass jalousies. For Little Harold the scene at Duplan Marine had not lost a bit of it's charm. He decided right then that as soon as he was old enough, Miami would be where he would live for the rest of his life, with Juanita at his side.

Ahearn said, "If I wanted to bullshit you, son, I'd be painting you a fantasy of how this is all going to work out, but I like you and I'm going to be honest."

"Yes sir." Harold liked Ahearn, also, and had begun using the "sir" thing because he could see the man ap-preciated it.

"Trouble is, we're not holding a good hand right now."

"And the deck's missing a few cards."

Ahearn laughed. "No need to work a metaphor to death, Harold."

"My dad is a perp, too, but he looks down on edu-cated people."

"Perp? Too? I'm a perp?"

"Criminal."

"Beats beavering away at some dreary job in a cubicle somewhere. Or teaching school. Okay, let me spell out the reality. Your reality."

"Juanita didn't come back from the store."

"Son, I do not have a radio bracelet on her ankle. She'll be back directly!"

"Yes sir."

Ahearn got up and went to the window where Little Harold was standing. "If Duplan doesn't come back, I'm fucked. If he comes back before the twins get here, I'm fucked if he sees them."

"If they come back."

"That's the whole point, son!" Ahearn put an arm around Harold's meaty shoulders. "It's your job to make sure they get here. Sooner the better. I can't do it, but you can. Bull Schaffner and his whatever sister trust you. They think I'm a self-licking ice-cream cone."

Harold stifled a laugh. He was thinking about Juanita again. His part of the deal. No deal, no Juanita. "What about the Airstream?"

"At first I thought those old, twin, Jismite sisters had money stashed in it but then, how much money could a couple of six-volt old hags steal from a country doesn't have anything?"

"Haiti?"

"Totally fucked now they have democracy. Listen. Harold. I get the twins, you get Juanita, remember? And don't forget they need to come here to swap the Duplan trailer for their new lowboy."

"You said you don't have a collar on her."

"No radio collar. You know better than anybody she'll do exactly what I tell her to do."

"Yes sir."

§

It was well past Janey's turn to sit up front with Bull but the old lady wouldn't budge. She said it was important to her she knew where they were going.

"To our parents' place. Where Janey and I grew up. Where the twins are."

"I know that!"

"Well?"

"I need to learn the roads."

"You won't be staying."

"Nobody knows where they will be tomorrow, Mister Bull. Nobody."

Janey and Lolita were trying to signal Bull from inside the RV to pull over but to no avail. Dianna had just gotten Janey on her cell and had some scary news. Pierretta's twin had turned up in a local hospital and telephoned for money. Dianna tried to explain that she was broke herself unless — unless — I cash that little gold bar Miss Pierretta gave me."

"That would not be enough child. I need blood, I need more surgery, and they won't even medivac me out of here without insurance."

"Medivac?"

"Helicopter. I need you to go look where the Airstream is parked. There is a pipe lying nearby in the weeds. It has a cap on both ends. Inside are some Krugerrands. One end the cap is loose. I need you to bring me some to the hospital right now."

"Krugerrands? How many do I bring?"

"Hide them all in the trunk somewhere. When you get here I'll figure out how many. Can I trust you?"

"No! You tried to kill Pierretta!"

"Honey, I am Pierretta. My sister stole my dress."

"Oh. Um...."

"Listen. I tried to get another pipe out but I only got one end loose before my sister showed up with Mister Duplan. I can explain when you get here."

"They took the Airstream away."

"They, who? Police?"

"No, Bull did. I can explain when I get there. How do I know you're the real Pierretta?"

"Is that gold piece I gave you stamped only on one side. Arabic? Did you cash a Krugerrand with the mailman? My sister wouldn't know any of that."

"Oh shit." Dianna paused. "Oh God." Another, longer pause. "If I can't find the pipe I'll still come to the hospital right away."

"Don't go too fast. No accidents. No attention."

"Oh, Miss Pierretta? That black, fancy looking man I think is dead. I can smell something funny when the wind comes up the hill."

"You don't know anything about him, dear. Remember that. The smell will go away in a week."

"Then after my husband and Janey left with the Airstream these neighbors came back here, and they took the Mercedes."

"You don't know any Mercedes. You never saw it."

"Yes Ma'am."

"Go look for the money."

"Money?"

"Gold is money, child."

In the Airstream, Janey relayed the story to Lolita.

Lolita said: "Uh-huh. When I mentioned Clyde she acted like she didn't know Clyde was a monkey." Lolita turned away and ran toward the back, and that was the first time Janey saw Lolita crying.

CHAPTER 41
Homer County Florida

When they finally arrived at Bull and Janey's parents, Annie suggested that her daughter Janey sleep on the living-room couch since the twins had been using her room. The old lady would be sleeping in the Airstream, so....

"Annie, I mean, Mama, Bull said we could share his room."

"Did not," Bull said.

"In one bed?" Annie said.

"Things are different now."

"I see that. You guys used to want to kill each other!"

"Still do," Bull said.

The four of them, mother and father, daughter and son, were sitting at the kitchen table after dark. Lolita was off somewhere, the twins were in bed, and the old lady had retired to her RV.

"Mama, we have been through some serious shit and we need to make plans for tomorrow, blah blah, and if we don't do everything just right they could lock us up for life!"

"Oh, Janey...."

"Number one, we have the Duplan trailer. Proof we've been dealing with those people. Two, we haven't recovered the McKay trailer, which is still in Miami.

Three, we need to get Little Harold off the hook, bring the twins back. Four, we..."

"On, no," Harry said. The twins stay with us. I'm going to enroll them in school and stuff."

"Daddy, stay out of this," Bull said.

"Harry, you have no idea," Janey said.

"The twins have to go, husband." Annie said.

Harry slammed a fist on the table. "They love it here!"

In the silence that ensued, the night sounds through the open windows briefly enchanted.

Bull said, "Dad, don't you have Ivory? Isn't that enough Africa-in-Florida for you?

"Apparently not," Annie said. She was unwinding her long, gray braids but it took some wild shaking of the head to whip her lion's mane into full battle-mode.

Bull said, "I don't know if I can handle another run right away. We've been back-and-forth, back-and-forth, on the road on the same highways and getting in deeper and deeper. Janey, don't look at me like that."

"We go down there with the Duplan trailer and the twins and the old lady and you pick up Harold and take him and the McKay trailer back to your terminal in Missouri and it's all over."

"Dear sister, we take the Duplan trailer with the Airstream back to Miami."

"No, I'm keeping the Airstream for myself. That's my cut. Daddy, would you hook up water and the septic for me. Electricity? Temporarily, I mean."

Harry rolled his old eyes. "Does it have a title?"

"You? Daddy? A title?"

They all broke out laughing so hard that the old lady could hear it in the Airstream.

§

As Harry eased himself down from his pickup truck, stiff with arthritis, Ivory came gliding out from her front porch. Graceful as ever and not showing her age much — by Harry's calculations she was 42 now — still so tall and slim with not a wrinkle anywhere. She was wearing a long, flowery skirt and cork platform sandals and a burgundy peasant blouse with ribbons at the sleeve. No scarf this time but her hair was in rows of freshly made knots.

Harry gave her a hug and kissed her lips but she did not kiss back. "Still Lady Sad, I see."

"Mmm-hmm."

"You always look perfect, your clothes, your hair, no matter what time I come over."

"Mmm-hmm."

"I don't know how you can make those perfect knots by yourself."

"I have to do ever-thing myself. Mama dead, Daddy dead, Auntie Indigo dead. I ain' got nobody."

"I know that, but you never call me when you need stuff."

"You have your wife. Your family...."

"Baby, we've been over this a million times."

Ivory did not respond, but her lioness eyes were boring right into his brain.

"Remember? You're supposed to say, 'I'm not your fucking baby!'"

"I miss that place we had in Miami."

We had.... Harry thought he saw a flicker of a smile. "Believe me, so do I."

They stood there, Harry at a loss. He wanted to ask her, as he usually did, if she needed anything from town or if anything needed fixing, but with the situation at home now he didn't want to stay long and he was horny. He slid his hands down past her waist. "You still have that nice little meatball ass."

"Because I don' never have a baby."

Harry sighed.

"You be horny, I know," she said.

Harry followed her into her cabin, everything so neat and clean. The difference was that with her father gone, for a year now, the scent of the hog pen was missing. "You don't have as many chickens, seems like."

"Coons been gettin' em. I can't shoot 'em like Daddy could."

Harry watched her unbutton her blouse but she stopped abruptly, and looked him in the eye. "I miss travelin'."

"I know, Baby, but the good news is we can afford to do that again soon."

"Soon?"

"Yep. For real."

She hooked back the pearl buttons on the blouse. "I'll get the map out."

"I remember that first time you showed me your map. Your Florida map. You remember that? Twenty years ago."

"I 'member." She spread out a map of New Mexico, a map Harry had not seen before. It was out of date, from the box of maps Ivory kept in her special cabinet for favorite things. "Santa Fe," she said.

"Santa Fe...."

Auntie Indigo tol' me about it. She said to be there in the Fall. After school start."

Harry pictured it. He and Ivory in his old, faithful pickup again. Motel rooms. Ivory happy. He pictured how he would be able to afford stuff like that again soon.

Ivory said, "I mem'rize the highways. From here."

"Santa Fe!" Harry said. "Okay!"

Ivory laid back on the bed and raised her legs so Harry could pull her panties off.

"I love you, Ivory."

"Mmm-hmm."

§

The next morning, the sky clear and the temperature cool at first, Janey thought she could wheedle some info out of the old lady, but the unfamiliar twin had other plans. Despite the uncommon friendliness both women were displaying, Janey and the old lady both kept their handguns close. They were standing outside the Airstream, both women figged out in crisp, clean clothes — Janey's short, pleated skirt contrasting with the old lady's billowy summer dress.

The old lady made the first move. "We don't need to be carrying purses out here."

"Well, ha ha, you mean two purses in the bush is worth two pistols in the hand?"

The Old Lady lowered her purse onto the little portable table they had used the day before. "Lolita told me you figured out which twin I was."

"Oh, bless the little slut's heart!" Janey placed her purse on the table also. "So what is your name, I mean, if it's not Pierretta Z?"

The old one cracked a brief smile. Looking over her octagonal spectacles, her eyes were dark and glinting. "Pierretta X."

"Oh! You mean, like Malcolm X?"

"Yes! No. No no, child. Malcolm wanted to change the world. I just want to survive."

"In style."

"Yes! Now, let's get down to business. I see how much you adore my RV here, and I think we can make a deal."

Janey thought *Lolita* again but wasn't sure. "That guy in Miami wants it back."

"Mister Ahearn wants my little girls back. Well, they were never his to start with."

Janey watched her eye up a dog-fly which had landed on her slender forearm — the skin so translucent — and a split second after the fly lowered its head to bite Pierretta X smeared it with a slap.

"Good one!"

"If you people would kill them instead of brushing them off there would be none left to breed."

"Right."

"If your brother Mister Bull would just pull up a little, and push the RV off to the side, right in there — she pointed — it would be better concealed."

"Concealed?"

"It's hot."

"Oh. Yeah."

"I'm giving it to you."

"Oh, really?" Janey moved up and gave the old lady a brief hug, and then after a lifetime of waiting and practicing, Janey got to do that back-and-forth kissing either cheek thing. Three times, just like in the movies. She was thrilled.

"It's a trade Janey." Pierretta noticed the sudden look of disappointment on Janey's face. "No, no. No signing a pact with the devil. I'll spell out the details for you. Facile." Pierretta X pulled a lower eyelid down with a finger. "Between you and me. You and me."

"You and I," Janey said.

"Between you and me and that poor dog's empty water bowl over there."

CHAPTER 42
Limbo

Annie was grumping about the old lady being on the telephone so much but what really bothered her was the little, Haitian, black twins, so naughty. They did everything Annie showed them as far as chores were concerned, and were always neat and clean; it was the attention they paid to Harry. Even though they seemed not to know the damage they were doing, it pissed Annie off. The sooner they were gone the better!

She would miss them, though. So loveable.

Harry said, "It's a local number. DeFuniak Springs." Harry was sitting back away from the kitchen table with one twin in his lap and the other behind him holding his eyes closed. "I give up!" Harry said.

"Harry!"

The twins jumped away at the sound of Annie's bark — must have been loud enough to register in their deaf ears — and their pink dresses and frilly-white panties flashed away to the living room.

"Harry, how do you know that's the number she's dialing?"

"She punches the number in — seven digits — and I mean she punches!"

"Who would she know around here? Maybe a hit man?"

"I don't think that one needs one." Harry sighed. "I really don't care. They'll all be outta here day after to-morrow, Janey says. She says there's money in it for us, too. All we have to do is keep our mouths shut. I asked how much and she said thousands."

The microwave dinged while Annie pulled out a tub of vanilla ice-cream from the freezer. "Your favorite, dear husband," Annie said. "Hot cherry pie al a mode. What does Perry say about this?"

"Janey said he's getting crabby and not to discuss money with him."

"Lolita said she's going along to Miami, just for the ride. I guess you don't mind her leaving, she's white."

"Oh, Annie...." Harry twisted in his chair to see what the girls were doing. "I want to take some pictures of them before they're gone. The twins."

Annie slammed the pie down in front of Harry so hard the ice-cream rolled off the plate.

Through the open windows they heard the lawn mower start up. It was time to close the windows, any-way, and turn on some air-conditioners. Harry said, "Lo-lita promised she'd mow the paths around here but I didn't believe her."

"That's Bullperry. Janey insists the grass and weeds be mowed flat where they're putting the Airstream."

Janey flounced into the kitchen, all smiles. "Bugs and roaches could crawl up the tall grass and get into the unit."

"We could spray weed killer first."

"No poison, please!"

"The old lady can piss a tree just like a man," Lolita said. Lolita had come in with Janey and was hugging Janey's arm, the girl so much shorter.

"I can do that," Janey said. "You have to squeeze your pussy just right. It takes some practice."

"Oh, I been practicing," Lolita said. "It's so cool!"

§

The day after was just as hot as the day before, and Janey was sweating. They were securing the chains to the Duplan Marine trailer after off-loading the Airstream.

"I had a long talk with Little Harold. He thinks that when Mister Ahearn sees the twins he won't get too pissed about the Airstream."

"I'm naming my new tractor PEQUOD," Bull said. "Captain Ahab's ship."

"The important stuff."

"And I'm thinking if we run into any inspections on the way down, we should leave Denver's laptop here, at home. It's full of child porn and serial killing and, you know, it's all fiction except for some of the pictures, but, well, I don't want anything to go wrong now."

"That laptop's mine now, anyway," Janey said.

"Yours? Bullshit. You're already getting the Airstream!"

"You already have a good laptop!"

"If the government ever looks at it, you'll have a lot of explaining to do. Behind bars."

Janey laughed. "The government? Do you realize what a bloody trail we left and they don't have a clue?!"

"You hope they don't. I was thinking FBI." Bull and Janey both headed for the truck cab but Bull got there first and grabbed the laptop. "Finders keepers." He pictured when he had first seen it and what had happened since. He watched his sister as she went back to tighten up the last, loose chain on the lowboy, so full of surprises since he had gotten to know her better. Plus the life ahead of him looked so good! New tractor, more money than he had expected (but he planned to bill McKay trucking, anyway, when he dropped off Little Harold and their lowboy at the terminal in Missouri), credit cards would be paid off, his cell-phone soon back in service, and last but not least (he was grinning now) a host of better caliber, mo'money hookers beckoning to him from the horizon.

"Earth to Bullperry!"

He pictured how that could all be blown away if he were ever caught with Denver's laptop. He could let Janey have it but copy the harddrive first. Burn a CD....

That would be incriminating, too.

He remembered that Lolita was coming along. Maybe she would want to ride with him to Missouri after he dropped Janey off back home. Jail-bait. But hey, pedophilia is natural. Where did he see that recently? Oh. Denver wrote that.

Lolita's father....

Fuck 'im.

Janey walked up to Bull, looking down at him from the lowboy. "Earth to Bullperry!"

Bull thrust the laptop up to her. "Yours."

"Thank you, Bull!"

"I love you, Janey!"

§

After dark, they crowded the dinette in the Airstream: Janey, Bull, and their parents Harry and Annie. Harry and Annie were stoned on reefer, Bull was drinking beer, and Janey and the old lady were straight as bullets. Back at the double wide Lolita was helping the twins pack. Pierretta X was standing, wearing another outfit from her endless trove of classy, 40's/50's era dresses. Large, lavender polka dots. Seamed nylon stockings. Patent leather shoes again with the silver buckles.

Bull, ever so cool himself, he thought, said, "So what time can we be up and ready to boogie down to Miami tomorrow?"

"There has been a change of plans, Mister Bull." There was a hint of acid in her banjo voice.

"Yes, boss."

"I will explain."

"Forget it. Your .45 is empty. Take a look. Unloaded. All three rounds."

"No need to get smart with me, young man. I have your CZ with fourteen jacketed hollow-points plus one in the chamber."

Bull straightened up. Where did he leave it? How did she get it? He calculated the distance, he being closest to her at the table, but before he could launch himself she had his 9MM aimed at his chest, her arm close to her body so he couldn't grab for it.

"Shit," Annie said.

Harry said, "Can we change the subject?"

"No," Pierretta said. "This is the way it is. I am not leaving with you tomorrow morning. Miss Janey will be driving me to the airport. I have no desire to have any more dealings with Mister Ahearn in Miami. When I leave I expect an exchange of pistols. This is a very nice, European police gun, Mister Bull, but I've had my army .45 all my life and I expect to be buried with it. I have given Miss Janey a sum of money which she will distribute in a way which she deems to be fair. I would give her more but my sister, may she rest in peace, has stolen nearly everything we have saved together. If I thought Mister Ahearn knew where it was I would be paying him another visit, believe me, but it is obvious she has left him desperate also."

"Bull said, "How can you steal much from a country doesn't have anything? Even if Duplan was finance minister or whatever."

"Shut up, Bullperry."

"We are ..." Pierretta hesitated. "We were international thieves, Mister Bull."

§

Janey's job the next morning was to distract Bull and Harry soon as her Saturn was loaded. The twins' stuff was ready to go and Harry wanted to take it out to the truck, then take some photos of them, but Janey said no, she needed help with Pierretta's things first. All of them noticed the twins were excited, and were signing to each other more than usual.

"Daddy, you need to forget about them. Poor Mama, she..."

"You called me Daddy!"

"Harry, isn't it time you did something to make Mama happy? Feel secure? Anyway, I have an errand for you."

Harry sighed.

"Take Bullperry to town and pick up a box of .45 ACP for the old lady."

"Arm that old bag? She thinks she can take that gun on a plane?"

Bull walked up. "She'll probably take over the fucking DeFuniak Springs airport."

Harry thought about it. "Bull can borrow my pickup. Or Annie's."

"Daddy.... Mama has been wanting that cedar chest for months. You two can put it in the back."

"Po'Boy's Gunshop doesn't have those."

"The country store. I called. They still have the cedar chest and they have the ammo."

§

Bull had his feet up on the old dash, the heat and the bugs blasting through the cab from both windows. "I forgot how stiff the springs are in this thing, Dad. Jeez."

Harry dropped to 2nd gear and they wobbled over the railroad tracks near Highway 90.

"Westville is a left turn, Dad."

Harry quickly corrected his turn and headed east. "I had DeFuniak in my head. The airport."

"Yeah. That Portuguese couple still run it? Who knows what they're up to!"

"No, no, they sold out years ago. I don't know who runs it now."

They slowed down for a pregnant dog crossing the empty blacktop, and Harry had to drop a gear to get back to speed. Bull said, "You notice how Janey's changed?"

"Noooo."

"She got smart or something, I mean, she's not as dumb as I thought."

"She never was as dumb as you thought, Perry. You were just jealous."

"If you say so." Bull began to fidget. Fifty miles per hour and they had a chest to load before they could get back. He noticed that his father was getting antsy, too. "Can we step on it, Dad?"

"We're low on gas. We can score fuel in Westville."

"We can go fast after that?"

"Son, I want to get back home sooner than you do!"

"Tell you what. On the way to Miami I'll take a whole roll of film of the twins." Bull saw his father smile. "All different light conditions." The smile disappeared. "All different positions, I mean."

They both laughed. "You still porking Ivory, Dad?"

"I go see her. I don't think porking is the right word. You think Janey will keep her end by dishing out some cash when she gets back. I want to take Ivory on a long trip. She wants to go to Santa Fe."

"Janey? She's got plenty of her own. She doesn't need to pull a tit on the money. Santa Fe, huh?"

"I can picture it." Harry slowed and turned off the highway, stopping at the gas pumps at Pozo's Mini-Mart. "Ivory is still beautiful, son. Her skin still feels slick and tight as a lizard. When I look at her, so black, and myself, so motley white, I feel like a god. I can see her right now, climbing up out of a motel swimming pool, smiling, cutting her eyes at me, toweling off inside the room, near the sliding glass doors trying to piss me off with guys walking by. I can see her ..."

"Dad. You want me to do the gas?"

"Oh. Yeah. Sure!"

CHAPTER 43
DeFuniak Springs Florida

They didn't haul ass on the way back from the country store, and when they hit the dirt road Harry crawled it. "That chest back there didn't have a scratch on it when we left and Annie's going to be so happy!"

"Happier than Ivory stepping out of motel swimming pools?"

Annie, in fact, was standing out in the yard waiting for them when they pulled in, and Janey's refrigerator-white Saturn was gone.

"Surprise for you, Annie. Look in the back!"

Annie took only a brief look, and as Harry's face fell she waved a hand at Bull getting out of the pickup with the box of ammo. "You might as well take that back," she said. "I have bad news."

Two minutes later, after Bull and Harry lowered the cedar chest to the ground, and after a brief argument about who should drive, Bull yelled at his father to stop. He jumped out and ran back to his mother, who was finally taking a good look at her new chest, lifting the lid and bending over to sniff the scent of the wood. "Mama, what about the guns? She has my new CZ!"

"Oh. I forgot."

Bull followed her to the double-wide. "Can you move faster?"

"She dumped your ammo out. Left you three rounds, she said."

"To Bull's relief, his nine was on the kitchen table, empty clip and the slide locked back. Three, shiny, Remington 115-grain jacketed hollow points gleamed in Annie's rough-old hand. Bull rushed down the hall to his room and came back with more, dumping the box upside-down on the table. "Shit, I forgot my loader!" It took him nearly two minutes to cram 14 rounds into the clip manually, and he was shoving the fifteenth cartridge into the breech just as Harry entered the kitchen.

"Dad, get back in the truck!"

Bull dropped the slide and bumped in the clip. "Dad, can you move a little faster!"

When they got back to Harry's pickup, tailgate up and the engine idling, Lolita was in the back, hunkering down in the hope they wouldn't see her.

§

Annie felt let down, despite the cedar chest surprise. Her daughter had lied to her — not for the first time, of course — plus they now owed more money than ever at the country store, plus her husband looked like the blood was draining out of him when he heard that those devil twins were gone without even a goodbye, plus the prospect of Janey divvying up any money when she got back seemed just as hopeless as all the rest. It was quiet, though, for the first time in days. Quiet like it used to be, the kids gone and just her and the dog. And the puppies.

Shit, I forgot their water.

If Janey plans to live in that RV, there goes Paradise.

No peace with her around all the time.

I'll just have to tell her.

I'll smoke a doobie first, then do the water bowl.

Maybe the puppies can eat solid food now. Leftovers.

Enjoy the peace while I can.

Enjoy the solitude.

Fifteen minutes later Annie was pulling on her long, gray braids hanging down in front, and flipped them back when she refilled Cooter's water bowl from a high spigot at the side of the double-wide. The splashing water against the stainless steel dish sounded like a brook rippling over stones, well, that was the reefer, how nice! The heat didn't feel as oppressive, either.

Why don't more people do marijuana instead of just getting drunk?

The puppies were hidden somewhere under the tobacco barn and she was about to look for them when she saw a glint of light reflecting off the Airstream. Perfect time to take a look in there and poke around. Annie took her time, though, walking over. What a beautiful place they lived in. What a nice life!

Before going in, she stopped and looked at the new scene, this expensive RV parked in the middle of a freshly mowed rectangle, out of place but pretty in the middle of all the weeds and huckleberry bushes surrounding it. The trailer tongue was perched on a concrete block and a favorite stone from her garden. Her most prized stone, in fact. It looked like marble with veins of red and gold. Well, when Harry got around to blocking the wheels off the ground she'd demand it back. She was about to drop down and look to see if they had hooked up a water line to it, or electricity, well, no, not yet, there hadn't been enough time for that, but she looked underneath anyway and saw a pipe hanging down, one end stuck in the dirt, looked like it had snagged the ground when they backed the Airstream in.

Anyone else would have let it go at that, but not Annie Schaffner.

§

They had to take Highway-90 through the middle of DeFuniak Springs, past 331-South, past Consolidated Ace Hardware and some dumpy-looking motels, past Dr. Blackwood's veterinary clinic, all of this at not more than 45 MPH, the speed-limit there, because Harry had long ago decided he didn't need to renew his driver license now that he was an old fart. On the left was the sudden open space and the small town airport, single engine private planes, a couple of new twin-engine aircraft looked like big bucks but neither Harry nor Bull would know, and a World War Two B-26 medium bomber neither of them had seen here before, looked refurbished and had both engines running in place.

"There it is! That's the type of plane I flew in during the cold war!"

"Not now, Dad."

"I had a three-foot long camera between my legs, right there in the nose!"

"Dad...."

They made the left turn off the highway — the double gates in the fence open — but Janey's Saturn was nowhere to be seen. Bull looked around and spotted Lolita hunched up behind the cab. "Dad, stop."

Bull got out. Lolita was barefoot as usual, and in one of her jail-bait outfits: bush-flashing cutoffs and a white, nipple-popping T-shirt. She stood up in the pickup bed while Harry got out to look at the B-26, engines revving up and making an ear-slitting racket.

"I think they're going to fly it!"

"What?" They were stopped near the small, main building but were far enough in to look down the length of the field. A few open hangers dotted the right-hand side of the runway, diminishing in size and quality the farther from the main building. Bull pictured Lolita alone with him on the upcoming trip to the McKay terminal in Missouri.

The B-26 was turning, and the prop wash blew stinging dirt and sand into their eyes. Harry hollered, "I can't believe this! I remember that sound so well! This is so beautiful!"

Bull could barely hear his father, but he had to admit the sight and sound of a fully operational B-26 was exciting. They watched it taxi down alongside the runway and stop way down at the last hangar, which was more like a huge, tin shack. Bull remembered the little hangar had been there as long as he could remember, he always looking at the runway and the mix of parked planes when they passed by on 90. Harry was standing in front of the pickup and Bull was at the side of the bed, looking past Lolita and squinting his eyes. All of them had momentarily forgotten what they were at the airport for. Harry said, "Let's drive down there and see what they're doing!"

The plane's engines suddenly coughed and cut-off, and in the ensuing silence they could her a *clang* as a man in coveralls slapped a bright-aluminum ladder up against the right wing. Harry yelled, "You have to get on the wing first to climb in, through the canopy on top, see?"

"Dad, you don't have to yell now." Bull saw Lolita give his father a good look-over, as if flying in an real bomber upped his Darwin points for procreation. She was still standing in the back as Harry climbed in the cab to crank up and drive down there. The starter turned over once and stalled.

"Ten minute rule!" Harry yelled.

Lolita said, "You can stop a hot engine for one minute and crank it up again, or you can wait for more than ten minutes. Anything in between it won't get off."

Bull stared at her. It was a lesson his father used to repeat over and over again, but how could Lolita know? "You sit on his lap and he tells you stuff?"

"I could sit on your lap and tell **you** stuff."

Harry popped the hood and began wiggling battery terminals just as a woman emerged from the office, looked at them, and went back inside. Bull tore his eyes away to look down the field. The guy in coveralls was on the ladder and a petite, dark-haired woman was hand-ing up stuff. Some boxes and suitcases. They were too far away to tell their age but the man had a droopy,

Mexican bandit moustache. Bull went over to take a look under the hood himself.

"The lug is loose on the starter relay, Dad."

Lolita yelled, "The twins!"

Harry and Bull both looked around as Lolita jumped to the ground. "The twins! I seen 'em! Up the ladder down there!"

Bull turned but there was nobody at the ladder now, but Harry thought he saw a flash of pink drop down through the canopy on top of the plane. *The twins!* The multi-tool he had just opened up so he could tighten the relay lug fell out of his hands. Bull reached down to get it but Harry beat him to it. He dropped it again and Bull snatched at it. "Give me that!"

The lug had just appeared to be loose, and Harry rushed back to the cab to give the starter another try. *click...click...click...*

Lolita took off running down the hot asphalt and Bull grabbed for his 9MM and crammed it down into the waistband under his shirt. Two guys on a scaffold in the first hanger, working on an engine, turned to stare at Lolita as Bull ran after her down the field.

A whistle. "Go for it, old man!"

"Get it while it's hot!"

Bull wasn't gaining on her but he was keeping up.

Old man?

I'm in better shape than both those fuckers.

Lolita slowed momentarily and turned to see if she had some backup, then sped up again. Bull slowed to a walk to catch his breath, then angled over closer to the next building to get out of sight. Nothing inside there but a couple tool carts and rolling ladders. He stopped and watched Lolita hesitate before reaching the last building, and he flicked a wave back to her when she spotted him. She dropped back a little, turning into the grassy area between the hangars.

Well, she's not totally brain dead.

The old lady's probably still in the hangar.

With her old forty-five.

Nobody at the ladder....

Bull angled between the buildings, approaching Lolita through the grass and weeds. When he got up to her she had that same, sour milk and shampoo smell he had noticed first at her father's house in Valdosta. But her eyes were cold now.

Bull pulled his gun. "I'm going in."

"Whatever."

The man and woman Bull had seen first from a distance were sitting at a small, dark, wooden table in the back. It looked like they were counting money, and the woman had a calculator in hand. Both of them handsome, middle age, small. The woman looked up first but neither of them flinched when they saw the pistol in Bull's right hand. He walked up slowly, his eyes adjusting to the dim light in the back.

"What's going on?"

The man shrugged, and nodded toward the woman.

"This is private business," she smiled, pretty face, dark eyes. "Private building." She was wearing a summer dress, light, flowery, her black hair pulled away from her face with barrettes.

Bull scrambled for what to say and do. "Nobody wears dresses anymore."

"I do."

Bull wheeled around but Pierretta X had snuck up on him and her .45 was aimed directly at his eyes.

"Hand your pistol to Lolita, Mister Bull."

Lolita, eyes on him, held out her hand as a male voice yelled from the waiting aircraft, "Ready to go!"

"We should have killed you with the monkey," Bull said. "Don't drop it."

The old lady spoke, her banjo voice as high but steady as ever. "It's a de-cocker, dear. No safety. Double action. You don't have to cock it. Just pull the trigger if you have to."

Bull turned to the pair at the table who were just sitting there, watching. The woman smiled and said, "We don't know you but be cool. Just be cool."

Bull turned toward the airfield and watched the old lady clamber up the ladder, handbag hanging heavy over one shoulder. She tested her shoes on the wing before heading for the open canopy. When Bull turned back, Lolita had his weapon aimed at the middle of his chest. She was almost close enough for him to rush her.

The man at the table was back out there, removing the ladder, and the canopy on the B-26 closed. With a whine of the 24-volt starter, the near engine of the old bomber coughed, spit smoke, and roared to life. As soon as the RPMs settled down, the other engine cranked with the same, characteristic display which Harry loved so much. He said so. "I love it," he yelled. I love it!" He had walked all the way over but didn't see Bull's situation until too late. "Oh!"

His shirt billowed in the feathered prop-wash whooshing into the building and the pretty woman at the table leaned over it and covered the stack of bills with her arms.

As soon as the plane began taxiing toward the end of the runway, Lolita turned Bull's pistol around and handed it to him butt first.

He snatched it away and both of them ran outside where his father was standing. The man with the ladder passed by them, no eye contact, as if nothing untoward were happening.

Down near the main building, several people had come out to watch the unusual aircraft take off. Now they could see Bull raising his weapon, aiming it with both hands at the receding B-26. "I can stop that thing in its tracks!"

Harry yelled, "With the twins inside?"

Lolita said, "Tracks?"

CHAPTER 44
Travel Plans

Bull left Lolita with his father and went back into the building. The strange couple was counting money again. Didn't seem like a whole lot, a few fifties and hundreds but mostly twenties in two little stacks, like they were divvying up equal shares. He noticed that the woman's blouse had shoulder pads.

"Any of that mine?"

The man raised his eyebrows and the woman said, "We don't make much. It's a small, family business." The man whistled and a little girl and boy came running out from a door in back. Clean, well-dressed, happy, foreign-looking kids, with nothing Wal-Mart shopper about them. Bull's shoulders slumped, the kids waved like bye-bye, and for the first time Bull saw a smile under the man's moustache and a twinkle in his eye.

God what an act!

And I thought I was cool!

Lolita and Harry were playing around in the hot sun, slapping hands, Harry pulling at the strings and threads hanging from her denim cut-offs.

"The ten minutes is up," Lolita said.

Bull grabbed her by the neck and gave her a good shake. Where's Janey?!

"How should I know. I was at home, remember?"

He shoved her toward the pickup.

He pictured her and Ivory and his father lying together on the same bed.

Ivory would never go for that....

Bet Lolita would. She's so fucking dumb.

"All this shit we went through didn't pay me a dime," Bull grumped.

Me, neither," Harry said.

Lolita smiled. "I got paid."

§

When they returned, Annie's pickup was where it belonged but she was nowhere in sight. Harry yelled for her.

"I'll be in in a minute!" Somewhere off in the direction of the Airstream.

"You see Janey?"

"She was here for a minute and rushed off. No hello, goodbye, nothing!"

Lolita was at the door of the double-wide just before Bull, and he grabbed her by the neck again and slung her back so hard she went flying by Harry.

"No need to be that way, Bullperry."

"Dad, she held a gun on me. My gun!"

"I'm sorry," Lolita said.

Harry said, "You have your gun back, don't you?"

Bull sighed, and whipped open the door. On the kitchen table was an envelope with his father's name on it. Janey's distinctive block letters written with her purple laundry marker.

DADDY

Bull snatched the envelope and pulled his waist-band open to stick it under his shirt but the CZ 75 P01 slid down his leg and dumped onto the floor.

"Tee hee," Lolita said.

Bull lunged at her but his father blocked him and nailed the envelope at the same time. "She said she wants to ride with you all the way to Missouri and you want to turn that down? I wouldn't, son."

Son....

"Yeah, Dad, I'll bet Mama would be pleased to hear that."

Pleased....

Nobody ever gets the nuance of my choice of words.

"I'll be nice to you from now on," Lolita said. "I'll be loyal. And we can make it legal, like, you can make up a phony rider pass and stuff for me and print it out for the trip."

"And stuff?"

"Something that says I'm eighteen, you know."

"Make it legal," Harry added.

"Yah, yah, okay, yah!" Bull stormed down the hall to his room. "Legal. Right! Of course! Legal!"

§

Through a window over the kitchen table Harry spotted Annie grabbing a rake and heading away from the double-wide again. Good. The envelope was sealed, and it said Daddy, not Mama and Daddy, hmmm, he slit it open and took a look. After a deep breath he trotted down to the bathroom and for the first time in years wished it had a door. A thousand dollars in hundreds plus a few tens and twenties.

Not enough to take Ivory to New Mexico.

He tried to calculate just how much the gasoline alone would cost round trip.

Not in lavish style, but....

Harry pictured the tall, black beauty once again sitting beside him on a road trip, sitting so tall and erect the way she did. Sitting straight up in the morning, in bed, seconds after being sound asleep. Her tits still firm, her skin smooth as a lizard.

His body more beastly-white and wrinkled than ever as he pressed her down with it, the devil under him, the prey pinned.

After he hid the envelope, deciding to wait and see if Annie knew about it, Harry went back to the kitchen in a fog, the opalescence of his vision pierced by Ivory stepping up out of a motel swimming pool, her glistening body turning heads while mothers snatched their children out of the way.

Annie had just come in with the egg basket, red-and-white checkered cloth over the top, her cliché egg-gathering mode. She pulled out her chair at the table, and the strange expression on her face scared Harry for a moment. Like she knew about the money.

"You fall down in there?"

Her arms and the palms of her hands were brown with dirt and the sleeves of her shirt looked like she had been crawling through the hen house. Annie smiled and winked, and with a flourish she whipped off the cloth and dumped the basket up-side-down on the table.

Gold coins spilled out in a pile, some brighter than others, some rolling off onto the floor. Harry bent to pick
some of them up. Krugerrands. Every one of them, it
looked like. An ounce of gold each.

"Annie!"

"We're rich! There's more!"

"Jeez, Annie!"

"Can you imagine, husband? Now we can travel to
all those places we always wanted!"

CHAPTER 45
Little Harold and Juanita

Luckily for Little Harold, especially since the bad news had arrived about the escape of the twins, the UPS truck delivered Harold's package to Duplan Marine while Ahearn and Juanita were both out. It was the pistol he had sent to himself, a trick Bull had told him about one day back at the truck terminal. "When I have to fly somewhere, I UPS my guns to where I'm going."

When Ahearn came trotting back up the staircase, Harold had the packing materials stuffed down in the trash can and his trusty, 9-shot .22 magnum revolver stuffed under the mattress of the bunk. This time it was loaded with all nine cartridges.

Ahearn looked more tired than angry. "You win some, you lose some."

Harold decided a burp at this point would be inappropriate. "That sounds like a good way to look at it."

"Yeah?" Ahearn flipped on his desktop computer but switched it back off before it could boot. "Let's see how well you take losing."

"I did the best I could. That old lady outsmarted everybody."

"I'm talking about how you are going to take losing."

Harold slumped. He was on the stool between Ahearn's desk and the windows, the sky still somewhat bright with summer's longer days although lights were beginning to turn on here and there along the Miami River.

"You mean, like, Juanita?"

"That was the deal."

Harold swallowed. "Mister Ahearn, I mean, you have other stuff going, right? Other work? Other deals?"

Ahearn leaned back in his swivel chair and placed his hands behind his head. "Sure, kid, but not like this one. Anyway, you have another Juanita."

"Huh?"

"At home."

"Yeah, but..." Harold felt a stab of pain in his gut when he realized that Ahearn might never let him see his true love again. His Miami Juanita.. "May I see her? Please? May I talk to her?"

"Sure. She'll be up here in a few minutes."

Harold straightened up. "Really?"

"I told her we would be hungry. To bring up some chow."

"Thank you, Mister Ahearn."

Ahearn switched the computer back on. "What's your return flight? Flight number. Airline."

Harold's heart leapt. *How many days had he been here? What day was today?* He went to the bunk and was pulling out his carry-on from underneath just as Juanita trudged up the staircase. She was balancing three Styrofoam trays and some coffee cups.

Harold dropped the carry-on and went to help her but Ahearn barked for him to go back and get his ticket folder.

"Ummmm..." Harold didn't want to say out loud the news he hated to think about. The flight which signaled that it was all over. "Day after tomorrow. Delta. Number fifteen-twelve. Ten-fifteen to Atlanta. Um, I have over two hours in Atlanta to make my connection."

"Two hours? Hey, that airport's got lots of Juanitas. Extra ones. Some of 'em even take credit cards."

They ate in silence, Ahearn at his desk with the keyboard shoved out of the way, Harold on his stool with his tray in his lap, and Juanita cross-legged on the floor. Tan legs. Bobby-socks with kittens printed on them. Harold had to tear his eyes away from her with each new bite of food even though she was avoiding his gaze. Between mouthfuls, Ahearn was telling Harold how to stay in touch with him in case he needed a driver or somebody to move a truck for him in the future. "Plenty of people here but I trust you, Harold."

Juanita got up and pushed her half-eaten meal into the trash can, and Harold's eyes followed her over to the little living area. She pulled out a plastic bag from the cupboard and began to gather what few things she had there.

"You can't stay with me one more night?" Harold half expected Ahearn to answer before Juanita could, but both remained silent, with Ahearn hunching over his food.

§

At the crack of dawn, Little Harold snuck down the staircase with his carry-on. He was hoping Ahearn would not be down there this early, and Harold had left a note for him on his desk. Inside the bag was his pistol but he had no intention of taking a plane back to Missouri.

The Duplan Marine gate was locked but days before Ahearn had showed him a way to come and go, and outside on the street were several workers waiting to get into the business next door. "RIVER REPAIRS" the sign said. Harold walked up to them, the group suddenly growing in numbers as a van dropped off a few more. Hispanics, blacks, and one or two whatevers. "You guys repair rivers?"

"Oh, yes, look at the sign, little man."

"The owner is a drop-out, too, just like us." *Laughter.* "A white drop out."

"I need a ride to Florida City."

"We just came from there!" One of the Hispanics stuck two fingers against his teeth and let out a piercing whistle. The van had turned around at the end of the commercial section and it slowed to a stop on the way back to pick Harold up.

"Thanks, you guys! Hey, don't tell Mister Ahearn where I'm going, okay? If he asks?"

"Ahearn?"

Harold pointed to the Duplan Marine warehouse.

"We don' mess with him."

Harold smiled, and did a thumb up as he turned loose a prize-winning burp which built in majesty as it rose above the street traffic and river noise.

The driver was so short she had wooden blocks fastened to the brake and accelerator pedals. Her red shorts were tight and her weapons-grade, black legs looked like they might split the seams. On her head was a sombrero with little, fuzzy, Easter-basket chicks, blue and pink, pinned to the hat-band.

"I need to get to the Farmer's Market. Florida City?"

"Well I declare."

"How much, I mean, to take me there?"

"Well, that's on my route, so...."

"So how much?" The van took a sharp turn into a McDonald's.

"You run in there and bring me two bacon, egg, and cheese biscuits and a small coffee. You got enough money for that?"

"Yes, ma'am."

"Don' be lookin' at your bag like you sayin' good-bye. I ain't movin' out of this here seat 'til I have to pee."

§

"He didn't get on the flight," Kate said.

"Missed the connection in Atlanta?"

"He never left Miami."

It was the morning after Little Harold should have arrived back in Missouri, and Kate had called Bull's parents and gotten Janey. "Well, I've been away for a couple days and I don't know what's been going on. Here's Bull."

Bull picked up the phone and before Kate could speak he informed her that finding the uninsured load was the important part and returning the new McKay lowboy was secondary but after he figured out how to accomplish that she owed him. "Be glad I'm not charging by the hour!"

"I'm not calling about that! I'm worried about Little Harold!"

"Oh. Um.... He wasn't part of the deal."

"Give me that!" Janey snatched away the phone. "You're Harold's mother. Do you realize how sending him down there almost messed up the case?"

"I didn't send him! He..."

Bull grabbed the phone back. "I wouldn't worry too much about him, Kate. He has a new girlfriend in Miami and she probably has his head up her ass."

"He's only thirteen!"

"In Iran the legal age is nine."

"For marriage!" Janey yelled. "Jeez, Bullperry!"

"You need to get back here to the terminal so we can transfer you the title to the Pete. How soon can we expect the lowboy back?"

"I don't know where it is yet, exactly."

Silence....

"He's only thirteen, Bull."

Just as that was over, Harry came in and plunked down at the kitchen table across from Bull. Janey announced that she was ready for brunch.

Bull and his father both said, simultaneously, "Brunch?"

"I feel brunchy. Hubby's check went in, my credit card is flush, and I'm hungry."

"Brunch?" Bull laughed but his father kept silent this time. He was grateful that his daughter had not told Annie about the thousand in cash, not that it mattered much anymore. Annie was grateful to Harry about his not telling either child about the Krugerrand stash under the RV Janey was going to turn into a second home. Bull was energized with fantasies about Lolita riding along with him, but he doubted she would be much help when it came down to swapping the Duplan lowboy for the McKay unit.

Janey said, "So what is your plan for swapping trailers down there? You think Ahearn's going to even talk to you now? And by-the-way, you still owe me money."

Bull sighed.

"I guess I'll just have to go down there and steal it."

Lolita slid out of her chair and got down on all fours. She poked a hand under the edge of the refrigerator and came up with a gold coin with a little dust bunny stuck to it. She looked up at them all at the table. "Finders keepers?"

"Now where did that come from?!" Annie said.

Lolita held the coin up under Bull's nose and flipped a leg over onto his lap. "It wouldn't be stealing," she said, "if you say I can have it."

§

Miller Time at the old homestead, but now everything had changed.

Bull said, "This feels so good!" He sucked in another hit from the doobie which was passing around, and handed it to his mother. They were sitting in lawn chairs between the Airstream and the strange, old, cab-over rig which had arrived two hours earlier, with the McKay lowboy.

Harry said, "Where does this reefer come from, Harold?"

"It was in Ahearn's tractor. There's a whole bag of it under the mattress." Harold reached over and sucked in a hit himself. "Now I gotta return it. And haul the Duplan trailer back."

"You don't need to do that," Bull said.

"Yes I do, and before I go home. Ahearn trusts me."

"After you stole his tractor? You'll get a bullet for a thank-you. Besides, that unit's not legal. You'll get pulled over."

"I made it up here okay. I know what I'm doing."

"Thirteen years old and he knows what he's doing," Harry said.

"I'll be fourteen next month."

"And no driver license."

"My dad never gets caught doing anything, and he's a criminal. It's in my blood. He never went to jail for not paying my child support, either." Harold burped. It was an uncharacteristic, weak one. "And Bull never gets caught doing anything, right?"

Janey came out with a cooler bag full of Corona beer. She handed one to Harold. "To El Maestro!" They all smiled, and Harry handed him a bottle opener.

"He's only thirteen," Annie said.

"Send him back to the house!" Harry said, winking.

Everyone yelled except Harold. "It's not a house! It's a fucking trailer!"

CHAPTER 46
Stony Hill Missouri

Ten days before school started and a week before his fourteenth birthday, Little Harold had it made. His birthday present was ready at the Kawasaki dealer and he had permission to pick it up ahead of time, this morning. If all went well the lettering on both sides of the gas tank would be exactly as he had specified, and on top of that, Uncle Axel was home and would get to see it — as well as his mother, of course — and Harold's only regret was that Bull was away on a run. That fact prompted another pleasant thought: as the newly designated and official McKay Trucking yard-boy, Harold was now drawing a salary. A salary! The other kids at school had allowances. He - had - a - fucking - salary!

There was no sign of activity yet through the floorboards of his loft above the office, and Harold punched the alarm clock before it could ring. Through the window over the terminal entrance the sky was beginning to brighten and it looked clear.

"There is a god," Harold muttered, as he rummaged around for his red-tag Levi's. With a sudden grimace, he renounced what he had just said.

I'm sorry, Miss Luck. Lady Luck.
I'm sorry for that praying I did in Miami, too.
I wanted her so bad.

Harold did not believe in God, which Bull had told him was silly; that god was dreamed up by primitive people who were afraid of lightening. Bull believed in luck. Lady Luck. Her whims and the roll of the dice. Harold was trying now to picture Lady Luck as Bull had described her one perfect evening while he poked around the new tractor he had been promised. The tractor he and Janey had taken their murderous adventure with. "She's a redhead, son, and redheads can get a hair up their ass in a heartbeat. She's a beauty, too. Green eyes. Freckles. Listen carefully, Harold. This is important. If you don't love freckles on a pretty woman you'll never amount to shit in this life. That's a rule. She's a killer dresser, too. Neat stuff. No Wal-Mart. No size Xtra-Large. Even her T-shirts fit."

Harold had wanted to interrupt but Bull held up a hand.

"Take her shoes. No stiletto heels. High heels, yes. Those thick, cockroach-stomper heels strippers wear in clubs. A woman who wobbles around on stilettos would be better off wearing army boots. Lady Luck is tall and lean, too, but not skinny, you know what I mean? And when she gets near you, you can't hear her coming. She likes men to grovel, but only before her. Are you listening?"

"Yes, but how do you know what she looks like?"

Harold remembered this like it was yesterday, the long silence which had ensued.

"I saw her once."

This time Harold hesitated. "Do you pray to her, Bull?"

"Everybody prays to something, Harold. Even when they know it's bullshit."

§

More luck. Axel, Kate, and Benny, Kate's favorite of the drivers, were all outside near Axel's bright-green Kenworth T-600 when Harold came blasting in with his new, fire-engine red, Kawasaki ATV.

"Well, well," Axel said. "The four-wheeler from Hell."

Benny walked up and took a good look. "They don't make that model anymore, do they?"

"No miles. Unclaimed order. A deal, too. Three thousand."

"Three thousand big ones," Kate said. "That's birthday and Christmas, young man. Hey, what's this Juanita business?"

Harold dismounted so they could all look at the large, gold lettering on both sides of the fuel tank.

"JUANITA"

"The dealer did that for free," Harold said. "His birthday present to me."

Axel got closer even though you could read the large letters a mile away. "Juanita?"

Harold's mother said, "Is that the little Cuban hooker they set you up with in Miami?"

"Mexican. No, American." Harold's voice choked up. "She's not a hooker."

Benny ruffled Harold's hair and dragged him over toward hood of Axel's tractor. He handed Kate the tiny, high-res digital camera he always carried, and placed

Harold on one side of the lettering on Axel's truck, then stood on the other end. "Take a picture, Katey."

"Katey?" Axel said. "You're a fucking employee!"

"Axel!" Kate yelled.

"Dear sister, I fail to see…. Hey. Is there something wrong with the name Jezebel?"

Kate snapped a photo and Little Harold turned loose a burp. It wasn't one of his best again, and not nearly as cool as Benny suddenly bursting into song. "If ever the devil was born, without a pair of horns, it was you, Jeh-hez-uh-bell, it was you-u-u-u…."

§

It was illegal to drive ATVs on the public roads in and around Stony Hill but the law was rarely enforced. The reason Little Harold was moving so cautiously down the shoulder was to prevent dust from settling on the shiny red paint. He also wasn't sure about gripping the gas-tank too tightly with his thighs and taking a chance on wearing down the new lettering. Something else was bothering him as well and he was in no hurry to confront it.

She'll think I had it named for her!

She's not even my girlfriend yet!

How dorky is that?!

Nevertheless, Harold hoped she would be outside when he arrived, and he had already decided not to knock on the door if she wasn't. He hadn't done that before and now was not the time. If she was outside he'd troll past, hoping she would spot him and wave, and then he would turn around as if stopping by was just an afterthought.

He tried to picture her the last time he had ridden by on his bicycle. Just a couple weeks ago? It seemed like a year with all the things that had happened.

One more block to go.

The yards in her neighborhood looked brighter and greener than he remembered, but there was a problem.

I can't picture her!

I forgot what she looks like!

He had to swing around a few parked cars after he crossed the small intersection, and now her house was only three down. Harold dropped a gear and got onto the pavement. His wish came true and Juanita was outside, at the side draping laundry over the chain-link fence. She didn't look up as he went by and he almost didn't recognize her. The Juanita of his dreams was a smallish, 9th grade school girl.

Harold sucked in a breath and turned around. He was more terrified than with any of the things he had had to confront in Miami, mostly because of the prominent gold lettering on the Kawasaki. He swung into the yard through the open gate.

"Remember me? I used to ride my bicycle by here sometimes." He cut the engine but kept his knees pressed to the sides of the gas tank as she walked up. The memories and his fantasies about her tried to come back.

"I remember. We start the same school next week. The new school."

Harold felt his ears beginning to flush. She was wearing a tube top and although he had forgotten how small she was it had been those pokey nipples and her pretty face and that long, pitch-black hair and those dark eyes and bright-toothed smile which had started it all. From a distance. Love at first sight.

Her lipstick was the same, thick, vampire-red that Juanita in Miami used.

Harold swallowed and he was going to ask her if she wanted a ride but his voice choked up. All he could get out was, "You make me choke up. I mean, I'm nervous because I like you."

"Me? You don't even know me."

"I like the way you look. And..."

A short, dark-skinned woman called from the front doorway. "Juanita!"

"Just a minute, Mama."

"...and your smile. When you waved when I'd ride by. I just knew."

Juanita pressed her lips together and looked down. She was wearing white socks and sandals, and little kittens were woven into the socks.

"Thank you, Lady Luck," Harold said.

"What?"

"Well, some people say 'Thank you Jesus!'"

"Ha ha. We do that. Mama does all the time."

"Juanita, come here!"

Juanita turned away and Harold blurted out, "You want to go for a ride? See the school? See how to get there from here?"

She stopped.

"I'll bring you right back. Just to the school."

Silence hung heavy in the warm and humid air.

"Mama, may I go for a ride? Just to the school and back?"

"No!"

"Mama, please?"

"Too dangerous! No helmet. Et cet terra!" Juanita's mother, scowling, stepped down from the front porch and stopped half-way to her daughter. "You the McKay boy? McKay Trucking?"

"Yes, Ma'am."

She looked over to Juanita, then back to Harold. "You and your mother own that company?"

"Yes, Ma'am."

She looked to Juanita, who was bobbing up and down on her toes, hands clasped together in supplication.

"Okay, but you behave. You bring her right back."

EPILOGUE

Bull Schaffner's story is huge. The conclusion of LOWBOY #22 leaves a few loose ends, or clues, for the sequel. Several are mentioned below and the reader will likely remember others.

What happens when the owner of the mysterious Airstream, Pierretta Z, gets out of the hospital? What happened to the twins? What does Janey find when she tracks down the "items of interest" in Denver's laptop? When Little Harold returns the Duplan lowboy and Ahearn's semi tractor to Miami, does he meet up again with the Miami Juanita? What happens with the innocent Juanita at home? What happens to Ivory when Harry takes her to Santa Fe and the Mexican border calls?

THE END

...to be continued!

Bleep-Free Press
http://bleepfreepress.com

Novels by John Aalborg:
Harry & Ivory
Children of The Lambs
Gulf Coast Stories
Lowboy #22

More About the Author

In addition to his monthly trucking column, radio plays, novels, and internationally published cover stories, John Aalborg has an exciting history of working jobs rich in personal experience: three years living large off the German black market, culminating in his being deported back to the USA (but without his rare, 1947 Mercedes roadster). Six years as a licensed locksmith in the "Magic City" of Miami, where many of his less than ethical assignments were for law enforcement; five years as an EMT for a backwoods, Florida panhandle hospital and ambulance crew; many more years driving long-haul for interstate trucking companies; and winter respites from the road working the graveyard shift at fuel-stops on exits off I-10, where he packed a gun and took care of his own law enforcement.

From an obscure hidey-hole in the deep south, Aalborg takes his readers into worlds the average person would love to get a window into, but from the safe side of bullet-proof glass.